Praise for The Road to Testament

"*The Road to Testament* is, like the autl
ern charm. It's a tale of new South meet
with all the right ingredients: colorful ch
tic tension, a small-town scandal, even a
There's no one more qualified to pen a southern novel than Eva Marie Everson."
—Dan Walsh, bestselling author of *The Unfinished Gift*, *The Discovery*, and *The Dance*

"No one writes southern fiction like Eva Marie Everson. I loved this book, her voice, her humor, and her poignant look at life through the eyes of Ashlynne Rothschild. *The Road to Testament* is about discovering what is really important in life and finding the courage to live it out."
—Rachel Hauck, best-selling author of *The Wedding Dress* and *Once Upon A Prince*

"Eva Marie Everson's emotionally evocative novels are so well written that we see, touch, taste, and hear the story. It's no wonder she has such a faithful following."
—Gina Holmes, award-winning author of *Crossing Oceans* and *Wings of Glass*

"This is one book for which I can honestly say I enjoyed every single page. In *The Road to Testament*, Eva Marie Everson has skillfully woven together all the elements of a great read: suspense, humor, faith, morality, romance. For my own personal library, this one's a keeper!"
—AnnTatlock, award-winning author of *Sweet Mercy* and *Promises to Keep*

"A fun and slightly sassy read about a fashionista from Florida who finds herself in small-town North Carolina with the challenge to 'get to know people.' Determined to prove she is worthy to 'inherit'

the head editor spot of her grandparents' and parents' magazine, Ashlynne Rothschild accepts the condition to live in Testament, North Carolina, for six months. Once on site, the sparring between the mysterious Will and the proud and private Ashlynne sizzles as they both learn to look deeper and dare to reveal their pasts. A bit of Southern history sprinkled throughout adds to the enjoyment."
—Elizabeth Musser, author of *The Swan House*, *The Sweetest Thing*, The Secrets of the Cross trilogy

Other books by Eva Marie Everson

The Cedar Key Novels

Chasing Sunsets
Waiting for Sunrise
Slow Moon Rising

Unconditional
Things Left Unspoken
This Fine Life
The Potluck Club series
Reflections of God's Holy Land (non-fiction)

The Road to Testament

Eva Marie Everson

The Road to Testament

ISBN-13: 978-1-4267-5798-3

Published by Abingdon Press, P.O. Box 801, Nashville, TN 37202
www.abingdonpress.com

Published in association with Wheelhouse Literary Agency

Library of Congress Cataloging-in-Publication Data

Everson, Eva Marie.
The road to testament / Eva Marie Everson.
pages cm
ISBN 978-1-4267-5798-3 (soft back : alk. paper)
1. Heiresses—Fiction. 2. Women journalists—Fiction. 3. Small cities—Fiction. I. Title.
PS3605.V47R63 2014
813'.6—dc23

2013035253

Printed in the United States of America

1 2 3 4 5 6 7 8 9 10 / 19 18 17 16 15 14

To Sharon and Bob
Extraordinary friends.

"Love you, Cuzes!"

Acknowledgments

I am inspired by locations—as a writer, as a photographer, and as a human being walking this planet. I see more of God's handiwork—His artistry, His brushstrokes, and His inspiration—in landscapes. And so it was the first time I went to Rutherford County, North Carolina, some years back. But more than the quaint towns that reminded me of what I'd found precious about growing up in small-town America back in the 1960s; and more than the rolling hills, the lush valleys, the rambling brooks, and the shimmering lakes; and more than the time-worn trails winding through it all under brilliant blue skies; and more than the nights when the moon is so large you swear you could touch it and the stars are so bright you almost don't need a night light; more than all that the people spoke to me, to my heart. This is Southern hospitality walking and talking, I said.

I discovered something even more special (if you can believe it). I discovered family. Whether by blood or only by love, we're not sure (her mother and my father had the same not-so-common last name), but Sharon Decker and I are family nonetheless. For me, trips to Rutherfordton, N.C., and Rutherford County became a must-do. Somewhere along the way, I met Sharon's friend, Jean Gordon, a reporter for the county's newspaper. I watched her work; I listened as she interacted with those around her with smooth assuredness, and a story began to form.

What if . . . a big fish in a little pond came to a place like Rutherford County to become a little fish in a little pond? And what if . . . and what if . . . And so, *The Road to Testament* was born.

So, first and foremost, thank you to Bob and Sharon Decker, who inspired Bobbie and Shelton (sorry, guys . . . best I could do!) and the Decker Ranch for inspiring the "unmarked grave" story line. Thank you, too, for the use of "the Cottage" while I wrote and researched the book and the killer hike up Chimney Rock (and, Sharon, the shopping trip to Bubba O'Leary's!). Thank you Jean Gordon (from *The Daily Courier*) for allowing me to trail you as you worked. Also, thank you to Matthew Clark, editor of *The Daily Courier*, for allowing me to hang out in the office, trail Jean in and out of the office, and take lots of notes during your meetings. (Just a note here: a *lot* more goes on in Rutherford County than I portrayed as happening in Testament!)

Thank you to the folks in Rutherford County, especially those at Spindazzle and The Spinning Bean, where I bought lots of fun things, drank wonderful coffee, ate delicious food, and observed everything y'all were doing and saying—whether you knew it or not.

Thank you to my agent, Jonathan Clements, of Wheelhouse Literary Agency, who believes in me even when I don't.

Thank you to Ramona Richards, who is not only my editor but also my friend. Thank you for seeing the gift inside this story and helping me shape it. Love you, girl!

Thank you to all those at Abingdon Press who made this book—this little idea born out of a location—a reality.

Thank you to Word Weavers International, Inc., and especially to Word Weavers Orlando for the excellent critiques, guidance, and advice.

Thank you to my husband who allows me to fly off hither and yon to be inspired and to write.

And, it goes without saying but I'll say it anyway, *Ani Modah Le'Elohim*—I thank you, God.

1

Line 4 on my office phone flashed red, letting me know my grandmother, who also happened to be my employer, wanted to speak to me.

"Ashlynne Rothschild," I said, supporting the handset between my ear and shoulder. "Hey, Gram."

"Ashlynne, do you have a minute to come to my office?"

I looked at the piles of work strewed across my desk. For the last hour, my fingers had flown across my computer keyboard in a futile effort to meet a deadline for *Parks & Avenues*, our family's well-heeled local magazine. "Ah . . ."

"I told your father," she said with a tone of confidence, "that we should just wait until this evening over dinner to talk, but he seems to think you need to come to my office now. Come save me, hon."

All right then. Obviously, our meeting was more than a business matter; it was a *family* business matter. "Sure, Gram. Give me ten minutes and I'll be right there." My mouth lifted in a half-grin. "You know, to save you." Though I knew if anyone needed saving, it would be Dad. Constance Rothschild steered this ship, not the other way around.

"Thank you," she whispered before disconnecting the call. I tossed the handset back to its cradle and returned my attention to the computer's monitor. On my desk, a cup of spice tea grew tepid in my Winter Park Arts Festival mug. I took a slow sip, enjoying the flavors and the scent. Looking over the last line I'd written for the cover article I was nearly behind on, I mumbled under my breath: " . . . no more than a footpath leading to . . ."

Fingers poised over the keys, I flexed then typed the conclusion of the sentence.

I hit Control-Save with dramatic flair, as if playing the final notes of a Sergei Rachmaninoff composition. I stood, took a last sip of tea, and left what often felt like a too-small office, but that was—in reality—plenty big.

Courtney Howard-Smith, my young assistant and research guru, worked at her desk, her customary headset firmly in place. I never knew if she listened to music as a muse, if she was doing some sort of research, or just goofing off. In truth, I never asked and she never volunteered. She got her work done and, as the ink still dried on her Rollins diploma, she did it well. She was, like me, a research hound. If I didn't have time to dig, she not only took the assignment, but she often found things I feared I may have missed.

For me, her attention to the most minute of details trumped the issue that Courtney Howard-Smith lived a life completely devoid of revering anyone older than herself by even so much as ten minutes. Or, in my case, ten years. And counting.

I tapped her desk several times with my index finger. She stopped typing, pulled the headset from her head, and laid it to rest around her neck and throat. "Hey there."

"Hey yourself," I said, doing my best to make some sort of personal connection. I smiled, but got nothing short of unblinking eyes in return. "I've got a meeting with my grandmother and, apparently, my father."

"Okay," she said, clearly not impressed. As usual.

I paused to regroup. Once again, when it came to Courtney, there was no connection. I should be used to it by now. Not just with Courtney but with most people. Even though I knew being used to it wouldn't make the pill any easier to swallow. "Do me a favor. Have you seen the photo layout for the new retirement center article?"

"I haven't. No."

"Can you get that for me? I'm not sure why it hasn't been sent yet, and I'm nearly done with the article."

Courtney picked up a pen, jotted a note on a pad of purple paper, and said, "No problem. I'll get to that as soon as I can." She smiled as if the notion to do so had just hit her, then let the smile go.

Unnerving.

I tapped her desk again. My way of saying "good job and goodbye," not that I'm sure it registered. Although I wished it would.

I headed for Gram's office, all the way on the other side of the once one-room warehouse, now sectioned by low cubicle walls. Everything about the room was bright. Cluttered but efficient. Faces of employees focused on computer monitors. Rapidly pecked keys, the musical medley I'd grown up with, echoed around me. This—the desks, the faces, the sound of work—had been a part of my childhood. I'd known, even then, I'd one day be a part of it all. And, all of my life—or so it seemed—I'd dreamed of one day occupying the office with my father's name on the door. And then, one day . . . Gram's.

Yet I knew only a few of the employees by name. And most of those were last names. With the exception of Courtney, they all called me "Miss Rothschild," which suited me just fine. I'd learned a long time ago that the more I protected myself from the intimacies of the personal lives of others, the better off my life would be.

My grandmother's office sat beyond the maze of desks and cubes. I walked purposefully to the glass door etched with CONSTANCE L. ROTHSCHILD across the center, the entrance to a sanctuary barred from view by sheets of glass and white blinds. I tapped, then opened the door without waiting for a response.

Gram sat on the far side of the L-shaped room, beyond a retro bookcase—blond wood, long and low—and behind her sprawling desk, whose size made her diminutive frame seem even more petite. At seventy-eight, she remained in excellent health. She wore her silvery-gray hair in soft curls around her face, brushed back from her forehead, and wore very little makeup. She didn't need to. She was and always had been a natural beauty. An earthiness shone in the sparkling of her blue eyes and the God-given blush of her cheeks.

Her smile welcomed me as I stepped in. "Come in, beautiful child. Come in."

I closed the door behind me. To my left, my father sat on the olive-green sofa in the 1960s-inspired sitting area, one ankle resting casually over a knee, foot bobbing up and down. He talked on his iPhone, "Uh-huh, uh-huh . . . ," then looked over and sent a wink my way.

I smiled at him. He was, like his father—my "Papa"—had been, extraordinarily handsome. "A catch," Gram called him when she teased my mother. "When I gave you my son," she says, "I gave you quite the catch."

And he'd *received* quite the catch, truth be told, and I considered myself *most* fortunate to be their only child.

I didn't know whether to sit with him or amble over to my grandmother. Gram made her way to us, so I lowered myself into one of the boxy, gold-colored chairs and crossed my legs in one movement, a process learned from my mother. Not by instruction, but by observation.

"All right then . . . ," Dad continued. I could tell he was ready to close the conversation. Though I didn't recognize the voice on the other end, the caller clearly wasn't finished speaking.

Gram stood next to me, ran her fingertips along the wide collar of the Kay Unger eyelet suit I wore. "Very pretty," she said.

I smiled at her. In spite of her financial influence and position, Gram rarely wore anything ostentatious. To the office, she typically donned khaki slacks, casual tops, and oversized sweaters. Even in summer. Never at formal gatherings, of course. On those occasions, she slipped into gowns by Veni Infantino or Alberto Makali. Me? I dressed every day as though our mayor might just happen to drop in to say hello. And don't think it hasn't happened. That's just my life.

"Rick," Gram said, "tell Shelton we'll call him again later."

Dad gave his mother a look of appreciation. "Uh . . . yeah. Listen, my daughter just walked in, and both she and Mother are staring at me, so . . ." The voice from the other end rattled off a few more lines. Dad laughed good-naturedly. "All right then. We'll talk about it later . . . thank you again . . . no, seriously. Thank you. Good-bye, sir."

He ended the call, dropped both feet to the floor, hung his head between his shoulders, and rested his elbows on his knees as though he had just run a marathon. "My word that man can talk."

"Talk the ears right off a mule," Gram said. One of her famous sayings she'd picked up while, as she puts it, "living Southern in the earlier years of my marriage." She smiled. "But he is a good egg and a better friend."

Gram sat directly across from me in the matching chair. A maple coffee table stretched between us, its surface scattered with issues of the magazine. Dad leaned back, resting an arm along the sleek line of the sofa. The track lights shining overhead brought a twinkle to eyes the color of a robin's egg. "How ya doing, Kitten?" he asked.

"I'm doing just fine, Dad," I said, suspicion now rising inside me. If the looks they were giving each other—not to mention me—were any indication, something was most definitely up. I looked from him to my grandmother and back again. "What's going on here?"

Gram clapped her hands together. "My darling, your beloved grandmother has decided to retire. Officially and *fully* retire. I see afternoons of nothing but reading and mahjong in my future."

The air rushed out of my lungs. "Gram . . ." As much as I'd known it would one day happen, I couldn't imagine *Parks & Avenues* or my life without her on a daily basis.

Her face glowed, appearing ten years younger simply having made the announcement. I looked to my father. He swallowed hard, his Adam's apple bobbing up and down in his slender neck. "Dad?"

"It's her decision," he said, leaning over and resting his elbows on his knees. "Don't you think she's earned it?"

I looked around the room. The paneled walls Gram had chosen to complement her '60s-themed décor boasted with award plaques. Framed photographs of Gram with celebrities—local, national, and international—showed her growing older with grace. Not a superstar in New York or Hollywood could compare to her. Joining the plaques and photographs were framed covers of her favorite editions of the magazine.

The only thing hanging that wasn't directly work-related was the massive print over my father's head. A color drawing of a glamorous, curvaceous woman from 1960, gloved hand resting under her chin, hair held back by a Holly Golightly scarf, eyes shielded by Jackie O sunglasses. She leaned back, tilting the full width of the print, from lower right to upper left. The Eiffel Tower stood in abstract white contrast behind her.

Few people knew my grandfather had the print of my grandmother made after one of their trips abroad. "I don't like to brag," she said to me the day I realized the identity of the captivating woman. I was all of thirteen at the time. "But I was quite a beauty, wasn't I?" she asked with a giggle.

Yes. And she still was.

"Wow," I finally said, when nothing else came to mind. "So . . . what does this mean? Exactly." Because I could guess . . . and if I were right, all the work, all the laying of the foundation of my career, would finally allow me to reach the first part of my goal.

Dad cleared his throat. "Well now, that's why you're here."

I had thought as much.

"With Mother leaving the magazine, I'll move up to Editorial Director . . ."

My heart hammered in my chest. Oh. My. Goodness. *Finally.*

The promotion I'd worked my little fingers to the bone and my stiletto heels to nubs for. I would take Dad's position as Editor-in-Chief of one of the most prestigious local-color magazines in the entire state of Florida. Perhaps even in the United States.

I sat straight, ready to hear the rest of what my father had to say. But when he said nothing, I looked first at Gram, then back to him. "I assume you are about to tell me I'll take your position?" I tried not to gloat.

Dad's elbows continued to rest on his knees. He cracked his knuckles, an irritating habit both Mother and I typically chastised him for. For now, I chose to stay silent on the subject. "That depends," he said.

"On?"

Gram shifted in her seat. "On how you do."

"Do what?"

"Not do what, dear. Do where."

"Where?"

"So glad you asked. Testament."

"Testament?"

"North Carolina, darling. You'll love it. Start packing."

2

My eyes widened. “What . . . in the world . . . are you talking about?”

Dad looked to his mother.

“I suppose,” she said, “I should explain some things to you.”

I didn’t respond. One thing I’d learned from Gram was the importance and power of listening.

“When Richard and I started in the business, we worked in the most charming little town up in North Carolina.”

“Testament . . . ,” I supplied, guessing, but I knew I couldn’t be wrong.

“That’s right. Shelton Decker and your grandfather served in the army together. They became fast friends. Both wanted to go into journalism when their time in the armed forces was done. They went from Basic to the end of their four years together. All the way. And, when they were done, they married their sweethearts . . .”

“You being one of them.”

“Yes. And Barbara—we called her Bobbie—Shelton’s wife, being the other.” Gram’s gaze seemed to drift far away to another time and place. “We went to Testament, North Carolina. It had been Shel’s birthplace, you know.”

No. I didn’t know. The only thing I really knew about the early years of Gram’s life with my grandfather was that they’d started a small magazine together with friends in North Carolina. And that eventually, the Deckers had wanted to start a newspaper, which came on the heels of my grandfather wanting to return to where his and Gram's parents lived. Here. In Winter Park. Florida. My *home.*

"Oh it was a lovely, lovely place, Ashlynne. All the charm the South has to offer. Simple people. *Good* people. God-fearing, hardworking."

"Simple people . . ."

Gram slid back in her chair, crossed her legs. "You know what I mean. I'm not saying they aren't educated. They are. What I mean is . . . well, you won't find them dashing off to some of the affairs we have around here." She ran a finger along the jawline of her heart-shaped face. "Although they certainly have their social circles."

"Gram," I said, inhaling before I continued. "What does this have to do with me?"

Gram looked at Dad, who cracked his knuckles again.

"Dad, please," I said, giving him my best don't-I-look-like-Mom look.

"Sorry, Kitten. I know it bothers you, but it's a nervous habit."

"Gram, he's *your* son. Can't you stop him from doing that?" And, furthermore, why was he so nervous?

"Why should I?" she asked with a raised brow. "Your grandfather did the same thing. It's like having him in the room with me again." She smiled at her son, who sighed in relief.

"Let's get back to the subject, shall we, Mother?"

"Yes. Well . . ." Gram looked at me with wide eyes. "My darling, you are the heartbeat of my life. You know that."

"I do. And you are mine. You know that."

Gram's expression turned poignant. "You see? *That,* sweet Ashlynne, is the saddest thing you could have said to me. At thirty-two, you seem determined to make the magazine your life, but you never connect with any of your coworkers. You have only one close friend. You have acquaintances but not friends. You hardly date. By now I'd hoped to be a great-grandmother." She closed her eyes slowly before reopening them. "I suppose I cannot control that. Your rise to position here, however, I can." She folded her fingers together in a "here's the church, here's the steeple" fashion. "What you have in business sense you never seemed to have gained in people sense."

I felt my brow furrow. "What does that mean? You think I don't know people? Believe me, Gram. I *know* people." And what I knew typically wasn't all that wonderful.

"It means that you need some time away from all that Winter Park has afforded you. You are a recognized fish in the Winter Park pond. But I—and your father—feel it's time you know what it's like to be, as the old saying goes, a little fish in a little pond." She looked at Dad. Sighed. "You will one day—the good Lord willing—sit behind the very desk that is in this office. I want you to have the same marvelous beginning I had."

Oh. Dear. Lord.

"Dad?" I cast him what I hoped was a pleading gaze.

"Ashlynne," his voice confirmed, "if you want my current position and—as Gram says—hers one day, you'll spend six months in Testament. You'll live with Shelton and Barbara—Bobbie—in their guest cottage. And work for his newspaper."

"And," Gram said, her voice raised in excitement, "help him restart the defunct magazine we began nearly sixty years ago." She lifted her eyes toward the ceiling. They shone in memory. "*Hunting Grounds & Garden Parties.*"

"*Hunting* and . . . *what* did you say?"

Her chin dropped and her eyes were like corrective fingers aimed toward me. "This is exactly what we're talking about, young lady. You need to learn that life is not all about parks and avenues. And I *don't* mean the magazine."

I knew that already. Instinctively, I knew she spoke of the lifestyle. I also knew my grandparents' spunk coursed through every vein and artery in my body. What I lacked in understanding the everyday person, I had in tenacity. "Let me see if I understand you. I spend six months in Testament helping restore a magazine and working for a newspaper. Then I return to Winter Park as Editor-in-Chief." I spoke the words not as a question, but as confirmation.

"If you do well there . . . ," Dad answered before Gram could speak.

I blinked. I did nothing if not "well." "Dad. Do well? What does that mean exactly?"

"If you don't know, my darling grandchild, I suspect you will learn while you are there."

So this would be the way of it. Gram had issued some challenges to me in my career and I'd accomplished each of them with absolute perfection. She knew me probably better than I knew myself and, in the knowing, was betting I'd rise to her *dare* as well.

I stood, drawing my five-feet-ten-inch frame to its full height. Almost six in my Ferragamos. Shoulders squared. Back arched. I took several steps around the coffee table, extended a hand toward my grandmother, and cocked a brow. "You're on," I said.

"This isn't a challenge," my father said.

My grandmother had not taken my hand yet, but I left it jutted out as I glanced across my shoulder. "Oh. Yes. It. Is. And, I might add, one I'm fully up for." I looked at Gram. "Are you going to shake on it, Mrs. Rothschild, or are you going to leave me here looking foolish?" I winked at her.

She stood, took my hand in her cool one. Squeezed lovingly. "You'll make me proud," she said. Her grasp changed to something more serious. She looked up into my eyes. "But Ashlynne, make no mistake. If you embarrass me in any way, upon your return you'll find yourself working as a copy editor. Or worse. In the mailroom."

I leaned over and kissed her cheek. It wasn't exactly professional and I didn't care. "You won't be ashamed of me, Gram. I promise."

I went to my best friend—my only friend, if you listened to my grandmother—Leigh's on Friday evening. She'd hosted a small gathering of friends—mostly hers—to wish me a fond farewell. Everyone else had gone home and, at nearly midnight, only the two of us remained.

We leaned against opposite sides of the living room window in her Orlando high-rise condo. I looked out, across, and down. From our vantage point, I could see Lake Eola's nightly fountain show—multicolored water spewing into the thick Florida air.

"My father's behind this," I said to her after several moments of silent contemplation.

"What makes you say that?" she asked, tucking a curly wisp of hair behind an ear.

I shrugged. "I just know him. He's always said I need to be more of a *people person*. Yet, the *one time* I tried—and miserably failed, if you remember—"

"I remember." Leigh knew my most secret secret. I could think of no need to rehash it beyond this.

"After that, who would *want* to be a people person?"

"*I* think you're a people person," she said in my defense.

An old sadness washed over me. "No, I'm not." I swallowed, knowing full well I need say nothing more. "I don't *get* most people. How can I? I've never shopped where most of them shop. Never eaten in their fast-food restaurants. Never wondered how I was going to pay rent or put food on the table. None of that."

"It's not your fault, Ashlynne, any more than it's mine. We're not to blame that we were born in the families we were born in. The proverbial silver spoon and all." Then she made a face to let me know she didn't want the end of our evening to go all heavy.

I smiled weakly. "That's why I love you. You get me."

"I do my best."

We were silent for a moment before I raised a finger and said, "But, you know what, Leigh? If my going will make Dad happy . . . if it will prove to him that I've got what it takes in spite of *not* having scads of friends or a date every Friday night, then so be it. Six months will go by like six days. And I can walk with a pebble in my shoe for six days."

"And God will rest on the seventh," she muttered as she looked out the window. "I'm going to be honest. I've never even *heard* of Testament, North Carolina."

"I've heard Gram talk about her years in the 'real South' as she calls it, but I surely never heard of *Hunting Tea Parties*—or whatever she called it—until the other day." I smiled at Leigh. "Of course, after my meeting with Dad and Gram, I Googled it."

"The town or the magazine?"

"The town *and* the newspaper."

"And?"

"*The Testament Tribune* is a daily paper that serves a county of about a hundred."

Leigh's eyes sparkled. "A hundred?"

I pretended to sneer at her. "A hundred thousand, you goon."

She giggled. "I know."

"I know you know."

"What did you find out about the town?"

"Very much a hometown look to it. Dates back to the 1700s." I looked out over the lake again. "Rolling hills and the Blue Ridge Mountains."

"We surely don't have a hill or a mountain anywhere around here," she joked.

"Mount Dora."

"Ha. Elevation what?"

I grinned. "One hundred feet."

"How about Testament? How many people live there?"

I glanced up at the ceiling with its sparkle-strewn paint. "Around five thousand."

"You're kidding . . ."

"No."

"I'd venture there are five thousand people living in our building."

I shook my head. "Roughly seven hundred."

Leigh crossed her arms over a black Michael Kors ribbed-knit turtleneck. "And just how do you know this?"

I laughed. "I live here too, remember. Besides, I wrote a piece about it five months ago." I pointed at her playfully. "Which only goes to show that you do *not* pay attention to what your best friend is doing at all times."

"So, is that it? That's all you found out?" She gave her best I-don't-believe-it-for-a-second look.

"Looks charming. Chimney Rock is nearby."

"Chimney Rock? I think we vacationed there when I was a kid once."

"Oh yeah?"

"Lots of steps to climb, if I remember correctly." She smiled sadly. "Lawson thought it was some sort of a race."

I blinked. Lawson, her twin brother. Gone too soon. "He always did," I whispered.

She pouted. "Hey," she said around a swallow. "I'm going to miss you." Leigh reached to pull me into a hug.

"I'll miss you too." I pulled away, looked over my shoulder. "I'm going to use your little girls' room and then make my way up to my apartment."

Leigh placed her hands on her hips. "And keep your nose out of my medicine cabinet," she said.

I gave her a wicked laugh. She knew well my habit of opening the medicine cabinets and peeking behind shower curtains of every bathroom I walked into. I knew the secrets of hundreds of Winter Park's and Orlando's most socially elite, not to mention which shampoo they used. "Oh, Leigh, don't be silly. I'd already snooped through your medicine cabinet before you even pulled the hors d'oeuvres out of the oven."

On Saturday, during my quiet time, I decided the minimum nine-hour drive from Orlando to Testament was more than I wanted to do at one clip. By eleven that morning I had enough clothes and toiletries packed to get me through the first few weeks. After that, when the weather cooled, I'd drive back to Orlando and switch out. I loaded my silver Jaguar XKR-S, leaving no room to spare. Even the passenger seat was occupied. I drove out of the parking garage, said good-bye to the guard, and drove first to Gram's before a final stop at my parents'.

Gram was notably upset, which to some degree made me happy. She'd miss me, I knew, as much as I'd miss her. "But I thought we were having dinner at your parents' tonight."

"You three can still get together, Gram. I've decided to drive as far as Savannah, get a room in one of those charming bed-and-breakfasts downtown, and maybe even mosey around a little in the morning before I head out. That'll put me arriving in Testament at roughly the same time as if I'd driven straight through."

She patted my hand. "You're right, of course. Even at your young age, you shouldn't push too hard. I'd worry the whole time you were driving."

"I knew you'd understand."

Gram took my hand and drew me from her foyer to her favorite sitting room, an area of the house where the late morning's sunlight spilled through unadorned windows and onto chintz-covered, overstuffed furniture. We sat side by side on a loveseat flanked by baskets of yarn and crochet needles, magazines, and correspondence she "needed to get to." She pushed a basket with the point of her shoe and said, "See how full this is? All these letters need responding to." She patted my hand as she so often did. "Now you know why I must retire, my Ashlynne. I have many letters to write."

I couldn't help but smile at her. Gram was the only woman I knew who planned to retire to write letters. Read. Travel. Get caught up on sleep. Yes. But letters?

"I see that you do," I said, mainly for something to say.

"Before you go"—Gram's face turned serious—"I want you to listen to me. Your father believes you need help in the people department. He wants you to find something in common with all those who will work under you."

"I know."

"So then, I want you to hear this one thing I say to you. If you want to *have* friends, *be* a friend. Listen to what others have to say about themselves, about their world, just as you do when you conduct interviews for the magazine."

I nodded.

"Do not simply nod at me and think you have appeased me. Repeat back, please."

I swallowed, knowing the price behind the words. All too well. "To have friends, be a friend."

"And?"

"Listen to what others have to say about themselves. Their world."

"And don't prejudge, Ashlynne. You are about to enter a different world in Testament, North Carolina. Open your arms to it, dear child. You might be amazed at what it has to offer you." She took my hand in hers, kissed it once. "Put that awful event from seventh grade behind you." She studied me as I blinked back tears. "Don't think I don't know it's always there at the forefront of your mind whenever this type of conversation comes up. It's that one awful era of your life that has kept you in shackles. Time to let it go. Be who *Ashlynne* was meant to be."

I felt the old ache grip my heart. I had opened my arms to something different once . . . and once had been enough. Still, I smiled weakly and said, "I will, Gram."

"Promise me?"

"I promise."

One thing Gram knew for sure, I'd never promise anything I didn't intend to fully carry out.

After a half-hour visit, I kissed her powdery cheek one more time, then slipped out the ornate front doors, through the wide portico, and to my waiting car. She stood in the doorway, blew me a kiss. "Remember what I said."

I waved a final time. "I will."

"And you'll love Bobbie and Shel," she called out. "I promise you will."

I doubted I'd *love* them. That would take more of a promise than I was willing to make. Still, I could *get along* with anyone for six months.

Yet, even as I bolstered my confidence to succeed, the familiar fear snaked through me. I shook it off.

I wasn't in middle school, after all.

3

My next stop was my childhood home, a sprawling example of luxury in the exclusive Windsong area. I passed through security with a wave of my hand to the guard, then continued through the winding streets until I reached the iron gate that safeguarded my parents' home. I pushed a remote in my car programmed to the keypad. The gate opened like a mother welcoming her child home—graceful and wide. I proceeded onto the circular driveway, turned the gearshift to park, and pushed the ignition button to stop the motor.

Mom met me at the door beneath the semicircular, Spanish-inspired portico. The arch above framed her perfectly. She was stunning, even in her late fifties and dressed down.

As always, my admiration for her soared, knowing that while I have my father's angular features and his business sense, I *aspire* to be like Mom. She is exquisite not only on the outside but on the inside as well.

"What are you doing here so early?" she called to me with a smile. She wore a pair of slim ankle pants with a baby-pink cardigan set, which showed off the rose in her cheeks.

"I've decided to head on out." I slammed the driver's door shut, raised my hands, and said, "Can you believe he's doing this to me?"

Mom extended her arms and I rushed into them, leaning over to accommodate her petite frame. She laughed good-naturedly. "Oh, child of mine, child of mine." She stepped back. "Just as your heavenly Father knows what is best for you, so does your dad. You *have* to trust him."

"Mom," I said in exasperation. "I trust the Lord. But sometimes I'm . . ." I started to laugh, in spite of my frustration or maybe because of it. "I'm just in awe of what he asks me to do."

"God or your dad?"

"Both."

She pulled me by my arm to the inside grandeur of my childhood home. "Let's have some lunch before you leave, and tell me what has inspired your new plan to leave so early."

I looked around the wide expanse of the entry hall as the soft soles of my Sam Edelman moccasins shuffled across the marble. "Where's Dad?"

"He's upstairs working out. Go on into the kitchen and I'll let him know you're here." She was halfway up the stairs when she turned and said, "I'm so disappointed you'll not be here tonight, but I think I understand already."

My mother had always been able to read my mind. She and Gram understood me as few could.

As I prepared a sandwich and a glass of cold milk in the kitchen, Mom entered. "He'll be down in a few. He's upset, naturally, that you're leaving today. That man . . . sometimes . . ."

I laughed. "Want to split a sandwich with me?"

"You bet." Mom grabbed a glass from a cabinet and placed it on the marble countertop next to mine. I filled it with milk before returning the gallon jug to the refrigerator. "I'll get the SunChips," she said. "Or would you prefer Baked Lay's?"

"Baked Lay's."

We busied ourselves in food preparation while I continued to explain my plan for the day. "I don't want to drive nine or ten hours straight," I said. "I'll be tired when I get there and I shouldn't start my new business venture tired."

"I agree."

"He can be upset all he wants, Mom, but truth is, he should realize this is a mature and rational decision on my part."

"Hear, hear."

Mom and I turned toward the door where Dad stood. He wore a pair of shorts, a perspiration-soaked tee, and a towel around his neck. His silver-white hair, cut short, was spiked with sweat. Without a word, Mom reached into the refrigerator and brought out a water bottle for him. "You'll need this," she said.

"Did I hear you say something about leaving early?" Dad asked, twisting the top.

"You heard me," I said. "I'm quite positive you were eavesdropping on your way in."

Dad winked. "You're right, of course." He took a long swig of water. "On both counts."

"You were eavesdropping and I am right in that I shouldn't start off tired?"

"Absolutely. Where will you spend the night?"

"Savannah."

"I'll call ahead for you. There's a charming B & B there on Hull Street. Vivian, you remember the one, don't you?"

Mom nodded. "Charming, indeed. Our room had the most magnificent carved French oak armoire. And the most comfortable bed I've *ever* slept in." She looked to my father. "Make sure you reserve that room if you can."

"I'll make the reservations. Knowing you," he said, now looking at me, "you have not thought that far ahead. I'll text you with the information."

He had me there. I'd *not* thought that far ahead. "Thanks, Dad. I'd give you a hug but you're all . . . yucky."

He took another swallow of water. "Eat your sandwich, child, and be on your way," he said with dramatic flair. "For in a moment, I must shower."

My heart soared and dropped simultaneously. I loved my parents so much. And I wanted to make them proud. I did. But at the same time, I knew my new adventure was something more. I had something to prove. To them *and* to myself.

And prove it, I would.

On Sunday, as I entered the quaint town of Testament, I followed Gram's handwritten directions, holding them in one hand and steering slowly with the other. "Don't bother with your GPS," she'd told me. "It'll get you *to* Testament, but it won't get you to the Decker Ranch."

The weather was only slightly cooler than Central Florida had been two days earlier. I'd hoped for different. With the mountains rising around me and my ears popping every time I swallowed, I figured the temperature would have the decency to drop by ten degrees. At least.

Even with my Jag's tinted windows and the air conditioner running as high as it could, I felt the sun burning my skin. I rubbed my hand over my left arm, wishing for sunscreen.

"I'd take off my blouse if I thought I could get away with it," I said aloud. "Oh great," I continued. "I've been in Testament thirty seconds and I'm already talking to myself." I rolled my car to a stop at a red light, taking the opportunity to observe the town around me.

Brick storefront facades ran tall and short on both sides of the road, offering old-world appeal. Many of the stores had been renovated, converted to shops and restaurants. Wrought-iron and wood benches separated by large pots of multihued flowers stretched between the doorways. The few people who meandered the sidewalks wore walking shorts, T-shirts, and colorful flip-flops. They tended to stay close to the shade afforded by scalloped awnings. Two children, who walked ahead of adults I assumed to be their parents, wrapped their cherub lips around ice cream stacked high in sugar cones. I ran my tongue over my bottom lip, wondering where they had purchased such delight. I contemplated rolling down the window and asking.

A glance at the traffic signal showed the light had yet to turn green. I lowered my window to see if I might find an ice-cream shop. Just as I did, the driver's door of a parked and battered pickup flew open. I cocked a brow at the cowboy wannabe who jumped out, scuffed boots landing firmly on the asphalt. In spite of the heat, he wore jeans I'd bet hadn't seen the inside of a washing machine in weeks, a crisp short-sleeved denim shirt, and—I'm not kidding—a cowboy hat wrapped with a sweat ring. He caught me staring—or perhaps it was the other way around. His eyes pierced through to mine—screaming as if he knew I were some intruder stepping on his hallowed ground.

Or as if he knew me . . . and we were archenemies.

I powered my window up. The light turned green. Feeling awkward for reasons I couldn't understand, I pushed the gas a little too hard. My car jerked, but I managed to gain control before I'd caused an accident. A peek at my side mirror confirmed my fear. Mr. Cowboy had taken it all in. He pulled on the rim of his hat and turned away.

My heart cramped. I wanted to do this, even if only for six months, for myself as well as Gram. And the job. But already the first person I made eye contact with had left me feeling . . . I couldn't do this. Could I?

I blew out a pent-up breath and pressed my lips together. Yes, I could.

I could. I would.

Six months wasn't forever.

Minutes later, I drove down a street flanked by antebellum houses with wide wraparound porches and thick columns; their lawns verdant and deep. These soon gave way to flat stretches of land.

I continued, following Gram's directions, taking a deep curve in the road that became Highway 108. My foot searched and found the brake. I was both lost and mesmerized by the mountains looming before me, by the seemingly endless land sprawled beside me. An occasional clearing revealed a house, a barn, or a silo. Wire fencing separated cow-dotted property from the two-lane road.

I drove another ten minutes and, having passed not *one* other automobile, felt certain I'd made a wrong turn somewhere. I was about to pull onto the shoulder and call the number I'd been given for the Deckers when I spotted a mailbox shaped like an old-fashioned Royal typewriter. What appeared to be a sheet of paper jutted from the platen and, upon that, large black keys with D-E-C-K-E-R centered upon it.

I'd found it. My new home. There'd be no turning back now, saying I couldn't find it.

Heaven help me.

I made a hard left off the asphalt road into the rutted narrow driveway, which disappeared under a canopy of skinny-trunked, green leafy trees. My car rocked back and forth as it tilted upward, upward, past deep ravines on both sides. I crossed a man-made stone bridge built over a lazy stream flowing atop glossy river rocks. Just as I despaired my car would simply topple backward and I'd be found upside down in the little creek, the landscape cleared. A sloping yard led to a white-brick house on one side and a shimmering blue swimming pool and pool house on the other.

I followed the driveway to the back of the U-shaped house, stopping beside a classic Jeep, an Acura, and a rather decrepit-looking Dodge truck.

"Wow," I said. I felt a brow arch. A two-story unpainted cottage stood farther up the hill and at the end of the drive. Adirondack chairs, a settee, and footrests had been arranged on one side and oversized planters spilling over with flowers on the other. The entire setting was both grand and primitive. "Wow," I said again.

One of several doors along the back of the main house opened. An older man stepped out. A light gust caught the mop of white waves atop his head, ruffling them like curtains in a breeze. He waved as though he'd known me all my life.

I powered down my window.

"Good afternoon," he said jovially. "If you're Ashlynne Rothschild, you've found us."

"I am," I called back, just as a woman peered over his shoulder.

"Are you Ashlynne?" she shouted.

I sat riveted by all that was around me—the lush beauty of the landscape, the expanse of the main house, the cottage.

The Deckers.

They seemed a nice enough couple. And they were friends of my grandparents. "I am," I repeated.

"Well come on in, hon. It's hot as blazes out here, and I've got some sweet iced tea for you inside the house."

"And she's cooked enough food to feed the army of Moses," the man added.

"Is it okay to park here?" I asked.

"Absolutely. I'll lead you up to the cottage direc'ly and we'll get your car unloaded." He stepped back into the house, allowing the screen door to slam behind him.

I powered the window up again, turned off the car, and unbuckled my seat belt.

"Well then," I said. "I guess I found it."

4

The Deckers' home was unlike anything I'd expected. I'd pictured an older clapboard house with steps practically groaning with age and leading to a wraparound porch. I expected old rocking chairs and a squeaking swing hanging from the porch ceiling by rusting silver chains.

Then there was the inside. No sparse furnishing purchased secondhand at a flea market as I'd anticipated. No sinking sofas and scuffed end tables with shade-less lamps. Instead, Bobbie Decker had blended antique furniture with newer, traditional pieces to form a home of warmth and invitation. Though I suspected many of the accent pieces to have been recently purchased, each held country charm, adding to the loveliness. She'd graced the living room with an antique settee and several velvet-covered wingback chairs. A low-sitting marble-topped coffee table looked cozy, stacked with *Southern Living* magazines, pieces of Oriental pottery, and a collection of "flickering" vanilla-scented flameless candles. Bookshelves flanked every wall, each shelf laden with titles, old and new.

They gave me a tour of the front of the house, which included a formal dining room already set with antique china, ornate silver, and delicate crystal. Inside the living room, I pulled a fraying hardback copy of a novel titled *The Digressions of Polly* by an author I'd never heard of—Helen Rowland. "Some of these are quite collectible," I said. Then, flipping the pages to the copyright page, I added, "Published in 1905."

Shelton Decker beamed beside his wife. He slid his hands into his pants pockets and rocked onto the balls of his feet. "Bobbie's been collecting them things for about twenty years now, hadn't it been, honey?"

Bobbie—an elegant woman with short salt-and-pepper hair, striking blue eyes, and a smile that made them dance—gave her husband a playful nudge. "Something like that."

I opened the book to the beginning of the second chapter and read out loud. "'Would it hurt you very much,' said Polly, digging the point of her patent leather slipper into the wet sand and beaming up beneath a wealth of a shade hat, 'if I were to read you something which I consider a vital blow to masculine egotism?'" I chuckled. "How delightful is this? *Masculine egotism*?"

"Please," Bobbie said, laying a somewhat gnarled hand over the page. "Feel free to take it up to the cottage and continue reading at your leisure."

I slipped the book back into its place on the shelf. "I'm not sure I'm going to have time, according to my grandmother." I looked again at the Deckers, took a breath, and spoke the words I'd rehearsed since hitting the North Carolina border, hoping I could pull them off as friendly and open. "Please allow me to say how excited I am about working for you," I said, knowing full well the only reason I was excited was the pot of gold that lay at the end of the rainbow. "And learning about the daily newspaper business, which I'm certain is completely different from what we do at *Parks & Avenues*." Which reminded me . . . "And, of course, helping you to revive the magazine my grandparents once started with you."

Bobbie's shoulders slumped. "*That* magazine," she said to her husband. "I see no reason whatsoever to start that again."

Shelton's face grew firm. "We've already discussed that," he said. "And we don't need to involve this young lady."

"I'm sorry," I said, heat rushing to my cheeks. "Did I *misunderstand* something?"

"No, darlin'. You didn't." Bobbie looped her arm within mine. "I say we go into the kitchen and start getting the food to the table. You don't mind helping with that, do you?"

"Now, Bobbie," Shelton said from behind us, "Ashlynne just got here and already you're treating her like family."

"She's Connie and Richard's granddaughter. She *is* family." Bobbie Decker patted my arm. Just like Gram. And just like that, I missed having her with me. Or so easily accessible.

"I—I don't mind," I said. My stomach rumbled as Gram's words about making friends came back to me. *Get to know them . . .* "You must be a marvelous cook. It all smells so wonderful." Which wasn't a lie or any slight attempt at "making friends." The kitchen was blanketed with delight. And, if the way Bobbie Decker had greeted me earlier hadn't been enough of a welcome, the aromas coming from her kitchen certainly were. I looked down at my hostess, who stood a good five inches shorter than me.

"Bobbie's a good cook," Shelton said. "Always has been. 'Course your grandmother was something of a fine cook, too."

I smiled over my shoulder. "She still is. When she has time. Maybe retirement will give her a more of a chance."

"City living," Shelton said, with a shake of his head. "I never understood what took them away from Testament. Had-a been me, I'd-a brought my folks up here rather than the other way around."

I started to answer that life in Winter Park had been good to our family but stopped short at the sound of a car door slamming.

"Oh good," Bobbie said. "William's here. Just in time to get the ice in the glasses."

We stood in the center of the large kitchen. Through the wide window over the sink, I spied the same truck I'd seen earlier in town, the same boots, the same dusty jeans . . . the same *cowboy*. "Who is William?"

"Our grandson," Shelton offered. "Loves having Sunday dinner with us after church. 'Course today we're eating a little later than usual."

I could think of not one word to say.

The back door opened with a moan. Scuffed, pointed-toe boots met the hardwood floor before the rest of—what had Bobbie called him? William?—entered.

His grandmother crossed the room and lifted her face for a kiss. He pulled the hat from his head, revealing sweat-slicked dark hair and amber-flecked brown eyes filled with love. "Hey, Gram," he said, using the same endearment I used for my grandmother.

Shelton left me standing alone in the center of the room and joined his family at the back kitchen door. The two men grinned at each other as the younger said, "Told you I'd make it on time, Big Guy."

The older laughed heartily as he slapped his grandson on the back. "Did you remember the ice cream like your grandmother asked you to?"

A brown paper package I'd not noticed shot up from William's right hand. He caught it in midair as though it were a baseball. "Yes, sir."

Shelton laughed again.

"Give me that before you drop it and I end up with a floor to clean," Bobbie said, though not a hint of admonishment tinged her voice.

"Come on over here," Shelton said, as William placed his hat on a nearby butcher-block table. "I want you to meet Richard and Connie's granddaughter we told you about."

William—who appeared to be a few years older than me but only by a few if I'm any judge of age on a man's face—crossed in two long strides to where I stood, hand extended. "Will Decker," he said. His cordiality didn't meet his eyes.

I slipped my hand into his, which remained chilled from the ice cream. "Ashlynne Rothschild," I said. "I believe I saw you in town earlier."

"You did."

My nerves prickled and I cleared my throat. "I'm here to work at the paper for the next few months."

He blinked slowly. "I know."

Bobbie Decker's voice rose above tension I felt but didn't understand. "Let's get the food into serving dishes and onto the table." She cast a smile my way and a frown toward her grandson. "I see you didn't follow my instructions of keeping your church clothes on," she said, as though Cowboy Willie's attire had just dawned on her.

His face went soft. "No, ma'am, 'fraid not. Besides . . ." A twinkle returned to his eyes. "You know me better than that."

"Darlin'," Bobbie said to me, "there's a little powder room right there if you want to wash your hands." She looked at her grandson. "You, sir, can use the kitchen sink."

I thanked my hostess and walked into the little room to the left of the back door.

The first thing I noticed was that it didn't have a medicine cabinet.

We covered the table with bowls and platters filled with food. Will put ice in the glasses. Shelton poured sweet tea from a decorative pitcher splattered with green and red apples.

When we sat at the table, I waited for grace to be said before placing my linen napkin in my lap, though I noticed it was the first thing Will did. *Never, ever place your napkin in your lap until grace is said,* Gram had always insisted, *so that you show respect to God.*

Bobbie Decker peered down the length of the table at her husband and said, "Shelton, give God our gratitude, will you?"

Shelton raised thanks to God for my safe arrival, for the blessing of abundance on their table, their work, their world. After he said, "Amen," the word echoed around the table. Bobbie Decker slipped her napkin to her lap and I did the same. Shelton didn't bother, which made me smile, thinking that *at least* Will had done so, even if not at the proper time.

I quickly became the focus of the conversation, Bobbie and Shelton asking questions, first about my grandmother, then about my father and mother.

Again remembering Gram's words, I said, "Enough about me. What I want to know is more about all of you." Will scowled from across the table, then shoved a forkful of roast beef between thin lips.

"What would you like to know?" Bobbie asked. She faced the picture window overlooking the front of the house. Beyond the slope of lawn toward the highway, the foothills of the Blue Ridge Mountains rose majestically, welcoming the sun as it dipped toward them.

"Well," I said, looking around the room, my eyes stopping to gaze upon the hutch behind her, "I noticed you have several Lladro pieces. Do you collect those as well as books?"

Will shot a glance to his grandfather. "Looks like Gram's got someone new to talk pretty things with." His faux-grin sent deep creases toward high cheekbones.

Shelton chuckled.

"You two stop that," Bobbie said. "At least she recognizes quality." She smiled at me. "Never mind them. They've been like this since William was old enough to be a nuisance."

"Oh? And when was that?" I raised my brow in challenge to the man across the table who clearly didn't like me, though I couldn't come up with a single reason why. The tension had begun from the minute he placed his boots on the downtown asphalt and it hadn't let up over the meal.

Will became still. Then, "Tell me something, Miss Rothschild . . ."

"Please," I said with a canned smile, reminding myself that today—day one—was no time to let Gram down. "Feel *free* to call me Ashlynne."

"Miss Rothschild," he repeated. To my right, Shelton discreetly cleared his throat, but Will ignored him. "Tell me something . . ."

"William—" Bobbie interjected. "I must insist that you remember Ashlynne is our guest."

And here I'd thought I was family . . .

Gain your composure, Ashlynne.

I placed my hand on the table between her and me. "No, no. I'm fine." Whether I was or was not had yet to be determined, but I didn't want Will's *grandmother* fighting even a fragment of this strange battle of wits I'd found myself in. Turning back to William, I said, "Yes, Mr. Decker?"

His enjoyment of the moment became apparent when the amber in his eyes flickered. "Is this your first time in our fair state?"

I pushed my shoulders back, placed my hands in my lap, and fingered the edge of my linen napkin. "It is."

"And, what do you think? So far?" He picked up his tea glass as though reaching for a rare gem, brought it to his lips, and took a long swallow.

I marveled at how much the man across from me managed to rub me the wrong way while, at the same time, managing to be quite charming. And how, in some smooth way, he'd managed to take the conversation from Bobbie Decker's collection of *Lladro* to my opinion of North Carolina.

I glanced out the window. To the vista of tall trees, a running brook, and the blue-hued mountains rolling across the bluer sky beyond. "It's breathtaking."

"I imagine you spent a great deal of time looking us up . . . say, on Google."

I gritted my teeth before smiling again and saying, "I did. My best friend and I even watched *The Andy Griffith Show* on Netflix. You know, to make sure I could understand the dialect." I drew out the last three words and immediately wished I hadn't.

Shelton broke out in laughter so hearty it seemed to shake the room. I cut my eyes toward Bobbie, to the mirth in her eyes. "Finally," she said. "Someone with as much moxie as you, William Decker. She takes it *and* she dishes it out."

"I meant no disrespect," I said to her.

"Oh, honey, you'll have to do more than that to rile me up."

But William Decker was not amused. He swiped at his mouth with his napkin, rested his elbow on the table, leaning toward me. "I can assure you, Miss Rothschild, that you won't find an Otis or an Ernest T. or even a Gomer or a Goober anywhere around Testament."

I placed my forearms along the edge of the linen-draped table, also allowing myself to lean forward. "What about an Aunt Bee or a Barney?"

Will leaned back at my question, picked up his fork and pretended to play with his green beans. "Bee, maybe." His eyes met mine without so much as an upward tilt of his chin. "But not a Barney. I suggest you remember that."

"I'll do that," I said. And I silently thanked God that most of my time in Testament would be spent at the newspaper or working on the magazine and *not* around this table—lovely though it was—with Will Decker.

After Sunday dinner's "face-off" came to an impasse, and bowls of ice cream had been scraped clean, Bobbie insisted William escort me "to the cottage and help unload the car."

"Oh no," I said, as kindly but as insistently as possible. "I can do it."

"Nonsense," Shelton said, rising from his chair and reaching for the bowl of half-eaten mashed potatoes. "William, grab the cottage keys by the door." He looked at me. "There's a code you'll enter into a keypad first. That will allow you to turn the deadbolt key. Fifty-five-seventeen," he said. "Don't forget it, now."

I repeated the number.

"William will show you," he said, as though my repeating the number wasn't enough.

Minutes later I slid into the stifling heat of my Jag. I started the engine with a push of my finger and rolled down the windows before turning the air as high as it would go. I felt my escort's presence more than saw it. When I turned, he stood next to my side of the car. He leaned over and placed his hands on his knees. The brim of his hat shielded any emotion I might read in his eyes. "Nice car," he said.

"Thank you."

"Daddy buy it for you?"

"No, sir," I said, confusion rising in my chest. What was wrong with him that he seemed to have it out for me without even knowing me? Just like before . . . just like back in . . .

Will jerked his head toward the cottage. "I'll meet you up there," he said. After a pat to the window frame, he stood, turned, and started up the hill.

I backed the car up, turned the selector to drive, and rolled the car behind Will as he lumbered in the middle of the narrow dirt road. Purposely I was sure, so I couldn't go around him. Two large dogs—one a black Lab, the other a golden retriever—shot out of nowhere. I pressed my foot against the brake. Will slapped his left thigh, and the dogs fell into step with him.

When I had parked in the shade of several tall pines and gotten out of the car, both dogs came toward me. I pressed myself against the closed door. "Do they bite?"

"Only Floridians." He opened the storm door, shoved the key into the deadbolt, and punched in the code. The door to my new home swung open.

The dogs' tails wagged happily. They panted in greeting. I patted their heads. "Hey there," I whispered. "I come in peace."

Will looked over his shoulder. "Hunh!" he said, with a hint of a smile. "Must not really be a Floridian."

I pushed past the dogs. "Oh I'm a Floridian all right," I hollered toward him.

He chuckled as he walked back to my car. "Pop that trunk so I can get your things."

We unloaded my car in silence, with me so unnerved by his presence I found myself unable to drink in the charm of "the cottage." After dropping my luggage on the living room floor, William tipped his hat at me for the second time. "See you in the morning, I guess."

"What?"

He was halfway out, one hand on the storm door's handle, the other ready to pull the front door closed behind him. He glanced over his shoulder.

"What?" I asked again. "Do you . . . do you *work* at the paper?"

Oh, dear Lord. Please let him say, "No."

"Work there?" he answered with a wink. "Yeah, I work there." He pushed the storm door open and turned. "Didn't Big Guy tell you? I'm your new boss."

With that, he shut the door.

5

I made three calls before unpacking.

The first to my grandmother. I had arrived, I told her, I had met Shelton and Bobbie Decker and, yes, I loved them already. This was a stretch, of course, but it made Gram happy.

The second call went to my parents. I shared the same details with Mom, adding a few about the décor of Bobbie Decker's home when she asked, "What about where *you're* staying? I know how important it is for you to get the lay of the land wherever you go. Are you comfortable with your temporary home?"

"I haven't really had time to look around, although I'd hardly call it a cottage." My eyes swept over the large room I'd entered earlier with Will and my luggage. "Right now I'm standing in a combination living room and kitchen. There's a countertop separating the two, a couple of stools for eating, plus a small round table with four chairs in the living room side," I said. "Bobbie's touch is all over it as well. Lots of golds and reds and burnt oranges." A large tapestry with *Welcome to the Cottage* dominated one wall. The other showcased matted and framed pieces of old handwork—embroidered images of birds perched on dogwood branches. "It's actually quite nice." Nothing like my apartment, but neither did it resemble the Darling shack I'd seen in an episode of *Andy Griffith*—that had certainly birthed some disconcerting mental pictures of where I'd live for six months.

"That's good to know. I'm embarrassed to admit I had a vision of you in my mind . . . ," she trailed off, then added, "You, of all people, in a one-room shanty like the Ingalls place on *Little House*."

I couldn't help but laugh. "I'll be honest," I said. "I had something close to the same vision. But it's nice here." By now I had walked to an adjoining room. "There's a small bedroom with a single bed and some antique pieces just off the living room and"—I continued to explore—"over here is a bathroom. *Oh*."

"What?"

"There's a stacked washer and dryer and . . . over the sink, the coolest mirror I've ever seen."

"We should be FaceTiming."

No way. If I did, if I saw Mom or Dad "face-to-face," I'd lose it.

"Take a picture. And make sure your reflection is in the shot. I miss you already."

"I really, really like this," I said, more to myself than to Mom. Then to her, "I will." I leaned toward the mirror framed by color-painted blocks, each block displaying words burned into the wood. Across the top, the phrase LIVE LIFE TO THE FULLEST had been burned into a scene of green trees and brown hills. I glanced at my reflection, shocked at how tired I appeared. If I sent a photo to her *now*, she'd be frightened by my appearance. "But it may be later, okay?"

"That's fine. But soon. Here's your father," Mom said. "He's all but dancing on his tiptoes to speak to you."

He wasn't the only one anxious.

"How's it going, Precious?"

Uh-huh. "Dad? Did you know about the Deckers' grandson?" The pause was so long, I was forced to repeat, "Dad."

"I take it you mean William."

I walked back into the kitchen and opened the refrigerator, which had been stocked with everything Bobbie Decker could have possibly thought I might like to eat. "Yes, I mean William Decker."

"So you met him."

I closed the refrigerator, swung around, and leaned against it. "Yes, I met him. Dad. He told me . . . just a few minutes ago . . . he told me he was my new *boss*?"

"Well, yes. Yes, I guess technically that's true."

"Technically?"

Dad cleared his throat, so I knew he was sweating through this one. Big-time. I could practically hear him cracking his knuckles, see him looking around to see if Mom had caught him. "Of course Shelton is the overall boss, but my understanding is that he spends less and less time at the paper these days. Will is the senior reporter there. Your grandmother's arrangement includes that you work with him. Shelton is planning to hand him the paper lock, stock, and barrel soon enough and since William knows the ins and out of the—"

"Daddy-dear?" I asked sweetly. "When were you planning on telling me?"

"Is there a problem, Princess? Because, quite frankly, I have no doubt at all that you'll do all right working with him. William Decker is a fine young man. Quite smart. Knows the business. And your grandmother says, and I quote, 'Like his grandfather, he's not so bad on the eyes, either' . . ."

Which sounded exactly like something Gram would say. A fleeting thought of Gram trying to play matchmaker came and went. But surely not. That wasn't Gram's style. If she were planning to set me up on some six-month romantic adventure, she would have come right out and said so. "I'm sure he knows the business, Dad, but don't you think you should have told me? I thought I was coming here to work for Bobbie and Shelton."

"You are. Technically."

"There's that word again, Dad. From now on, you and I need to discuss all the *technicalities*."

"Is there a problem, Miss Ashlynne?" My father's voice now held a surprising hint of mischief.

I pushed myself away from the refrigerator and walked into the living room, averting my luggage and heading straight for the sofa. I sat. "He's pompous. Rude. He obviously doesn't want me here."

"What makes you think that?"

Tears I didn't want to feel stung my eyes. I blinked them back, telling myself I would *not* go there. I would not think about or discuss the look he'd given me on Main Street, the one that reminded me so much of the looks I'd been given that awful day in . . . "Believe me, Dad. He doesn't want me here."

"Then your challenge is to work above and beyond what William Decker wants. Or, what you presume he doesn't want. And remember, Pet, the senior Deckers *do* want you there."

I pressed a hand against my now aching forehead. As much as I hated it, my father was right. If I was going to prove myself to him and Gram—that I could work well with *all kinds* of people—Will Decker was as good a place to start as any. Not since junior high had I been struck down by anyone and I wasn't about to lose my life goal to the likes of some cowboy wannabe. "All right, Dad. I'll stay in the sandbox. I won't pick up my toys and stomp back home. And I'll play nice with the playground bully."

And when playtime was over, Will Decker would be singing a whole new tune.

Dad chuckled. "That's my girl."

"Good-bye, Dad." I sighed. "You know I love you."

"Love you too, Kitten."

I stretched out on the soft, brown couch dotted with burnt orange throw pillows. The armrests were rounded and thickly padded, perfect for laying my head upon.

I placed the third call.

"Ash?"

"Hey, Leigh." I sighed heavily into the phone.

"Oh-mah-goodness. It's a dump, isn't it? You're stuck in the Darlings' cabin out in the woods." Sweet Leigh. I'd made her watch the shows on Netflix with me.

"No, *Charlene*." I giggled with all the energy of a tired old turtle at the end of the race. "It's quite nice, actually."

"Seriously?"

I closed my eyes, unable to remember when I'd ever felt this tired. "It's not Winter Park, but I wasn't expecting it to be. Actually, in many ways, Main Street reminds me of Park Avenue. Same cute little shops established in old storefronts. Sidewalks with awnings. The houses here are different, but just as expansive. Less Spanish architecture and more Victorian. Sprawling, you know, with wrap-around porches."

"The Decker house is like that?"

"Well, no." I opened my eyes and stared at the ceiling. "It's brick. Newer, I think. It wasn't what I expected. Nor is the cottage."

"Tell me about it."

"Well, for one, there's a rock garden out the front door. And wooden Adirondack chairs where I can already see myself sitting. Early morning, sipping on tea, reading under the pines—which are taller, Leigh, than anything I've ever seen. It's like they go all the way up to the sky and beyond. There are hills and mountains and green valleys. After the drive up, I know why they call these the Blue Ridge Mountains."

"That's it. I'm coming up during my vacation. I was thinking Paris again, but from the sound of your voice, *Testament* I have to see."

"Seriously. Every year you and I have sported off to some foreign location. Why haven't we explored our own country? I couldn't believe the beauty in the landscape as I drove up the coast of Georgia. My stay in Savannah wasn't nearly long enough. We should go there sometime. Oh, and South Carolina and then *North* Carolina . . . the lush hills, the valleys . . ."

"You're starting to get all wordy on me. You know, the way you do when an article is about to be written?"

"Maybe. When I get back and take over Dad's job, I might start a whole new section of the magazine. Encourage Winter Park residents to stay in *our* country instead of spending all our money elsewhere."

"I like it." We remained silent for a moment. "There's something else, isn't there? I can't quite put my finger on it, but it's there in your voice."

Leigh James knew me well.

"Yeah, there's something else. Not something, actually. Some*one*. But, honestly, girl. I'm so tired and I need to unpack. I'll tell you all about him tomorrow."

"Him?"

"Call you after work. Promise."

"Don't leave me hanging . . ."

I chuckled. "Tomorrow. I promise."

I ended the call with another sigh, then strained to sit up and peered over my shoulder. My Louis Vuitton luggage stood in the center of the room like abandoned children at a train station. "Time to explore the rest of the place," I said.

I stood and headed for the staircase between the bedroom and the bath. At the halfway landing, I opened an outside door to find a wide porch overlooking sloping acreage. At the farthest end, the windows of an old barn and a newer farmhouse seemed to peer back at me. Rustling in nearby shrubs caught my attention and I gasped. But two wagging tails told me my new furry friends remained content to hang out at the cottage.

Or, perhaps, the cottage was *their* home and I, the unexpected guest.

Well, it wouldn't be the first time I ended up somewhere I didn't belong.

I waggled my fingers at them, but after a glance at me, they kept going.

I sighed, stepped back inside and continued the climb, to another large sitting area flanked by floor-to-ceiling bookshelves. A claw-foot mahogany desk faced a narrow floor-to-ceiling window centered on the far wall. The focal point, a four-poster rice bed draped with a crocheted coverlet, appeared to be authentically antique. Beyond, a second bathroom. This one with a medicine cabinet.

I reached toward it.

"Hello!" I heard Bobbie call from downstairs. "Yoo-hoo!"

I bounded down the stairs as though I'd been caught trespassing. "Hi," I said as I reached the landing.

Bobbie stood next to my luggage. "Oh," she said, peering at it. "I thought you'd be unpacked by now. Do you need help?"

I felt warmth color my cheeks, hoping it had been okay that I'd ventured upstairs. "No. I took some time to make a few calls." I pointed upward. "Any reason I can't use the room upstairs?"

Bobbie appeared shocked at my request. "Darlin', the whole house is yours for the next six months." She walked over to the refrigerator and opened it. "I've put some things in here for you until you have time to run to the store, but if you need anything else, let me know."

"That was kind of you."

"And over here," she said, moving to the counter, "is the Keurig coffeemaker." She pointed to a bamboo basket. "The little cups of coffee and tea are in this basket, but if you don't like the selection, you let me know."

"I'm sure it's fine. I'm happy to order more or buy them . . ."

"We'll cross that bridge when we get to it," she said, coming out from behind the counter. "Now, do you want some help getting your luggage upstairs? Shame on that William for not taking them up for you."

"Ah . . . no. And, really, I think he was ready to go home or . . . something." I swallowed. Squeezed my hands into tight fists. "So, William works for the paper?"

Bobbie crossed her arms. "More than just working. With Shel spending less time there, he's taking on more than his fair share. And he's doing a fine job keeping things running, chasing down stories, getting them written, and then editing the work of our sports reporter, Alma."

"Alma?"

"She's a firecracker." Bobbie stepped over to the door and placed her hand on the doorknob. "You'll get along fine with her, I'm sure." She lowered her voice a notch. "Not the all-around best writer, you see, but she knows her football from her soccer."

I slipped my hands behind me, linking my fingers and straightening my back and wondering if Bobbie knew the real reason why Gram had sent me here. And then figuring probably so. "My job, for now, will be to do . . . what?"

Bobbie looked at me quizzically. "I would have thought your father and Shelton had gone over all that."

"Well, they did, but I don't, in all honesty, remember anything about working *with* your grandson. I have to admit, I'm not used to working with another reporter and I thought I'd do more with the magazine."

The older woman grinned. "You will, from what I understand." She waved a hand. "I try not to get as involved as I used to. William will help you with whatever you need to do on that." She touched my arm. "Oh, I'm sure the two of you will get along famously. He'll probably start you off doing some work on the paper until you get used to the way of things around here."

"The way of things?"

"We're a small community, Ashlynne, but don't let that fool you. We're hoppin'."

"I'm sure you are, but . . ."

She turned the knob, stopping me from speaking further. "I'll let you get unpacked. And I bet you could use some rest. Now, Shelton and I don't usually eat another meal after one like what we had down at the house, and we turn in early most Sunday nights. But if you need anything, our phone number is on a piece of paper under a magnet on the refrigerator."

I looked toward the kitchen. "I'm sure I'll be fine. But—"

"You're going to have a good time here, Ashlynne. I know you will." She jerked the door open and stepped out to where the dogs waited for her. "Oh, you little darlins," she said to them. "Y'all need to come on down to the house and get out of the awful afternoon heat." She closed the door behind her without another word, leaving me to only blink in response.

6

After a satisfying night of sleep, I woke with one question on my mind: what time did work begin at a small town newspaper? A quick look at my iPhone told me daylight had more than broken. It was nearly 7:30.

For my first day on the job, I chose a pair of Vince Camuto houndstooth ankle pants, a white ruched, three-quarter-sleeved dress tee, and my favorite pair of Salvatore Ferragamo peep-toe pumps. I slipped a couple of bangles onto both wrists and selected white pearl earrings and a necklace of black and white pearls. A look in the mirror brought a smile. I looked completely approachable; indeed, like the kind of person another person might have for a friend. Maybe even . . . what was her name? Alma? The sportswriter. Yes. Bobbie said "Alma." I knew absolutely nothing about sports in general, but if I asked her to teach me, maybe I'd make a new friend. I could tell Dad all about our time together and he'd see how well I was doing at the newly required goal in my professional life: becoming approachable to *every*one.

I made a cup of tea and, while it brewed, I threw my phone into my purse. I kicked myself that on my first morning in Testament I'd not managed to wake up in time for quiet reading and prayer. The coffeemaker sighed, letting me know it was ready. I added milk and a packet of raw sugar—God bless Bobbie Decker—and scooted out the door.

River rock crunched beneath my shoes. My heels sank between them, causing me to wobble to my car. When I had managed to reach the Jag, I slid in, started it, and slammed the door, nearly in one movement. The clock registered 8:30.

I wasn't sure what time I should be at work, but I felt fairly confident I was late. I sighed with the realization that I also didn't know where to go. No doubt Will Decker had avoided *that* piece of information on purpose.

I entered the name of the paper in my GPS and waited for the satellites hovering out there somewhere to locate the address.

And me.

My car rolled down the hilly driveway, past the Deckers' home and along the same path it had taken the day before, until I reached the highway. The GPS continued to search. Instinct told me to turn right, toward Testament, and so I did, driving past the same stretches of land from the day before. A glance in my rearview mirror and my eyes widened. The hills of the Blue Ridge Mountains filled the narrow reflection.

I came to a stop sign just as the automated voice said, "Turn right, then turn left."

"Thank you for joining me this morning," I mumbled.

The way was familiar, even after only one trip from Testament to the Deckers'. I drove past service stations, drugstores, a new grocery store on the right, and a dilapidated car repair shop on the left.

"Turn left, then keep right for three miles."

I passed through the sleepy town of Testament, noting the looming courthouse in the middle of town where well-dressed men and women climbed narrow marble steps to massive front doors. Heading to work, to pay their fines and taxes, to serve on a jury, I supposed.

I continued along until I heard the automated voice say, "In one hundred feet, turn right. Destination on right."

The Testament Tribune offices were located in a small building with cream-colored siding and two glass doors centered on its face.

On either side of the doors stood newspaper receptacles with *The Testament Tribune* scrolled across their fronts with one *T* used for the three words. I parked in front, in one of six spaces, all of them empty but mine.

Parking outside in the North Carolina elements was a far cry from the parking garage on Park Avenue. The "Reserved for A. Rothschild" painted on the cement wall above parking space No. 22. The short elevator ride down to the atrium just outside the offices of *Parks & Avenues.*

I squeezed my eyes shut. I missed home.

Then, regaining my resolve, I got out of the car, picked up my cup of tea, my purse, and the black Burberry briefcase I'd left overnight on the floorboard behind the driver's seat. Inside it was a slimline laptop, two legal pads, one TOPS reporter's notebook, several pens, and a framed photograph I'd brought from my Winter Park office—Leigh and me at Disney. No one could say I wasn't prepared for my new job. And, between the briefcase, my purse, the cup of tea, and my sporty outfit, I figured I made an impressive image walking toward the door . . .

. . . which Will Decker swung out of as I neared it. "Where have you been?" he stormed. "Do you know what time we get started around here on Mondays?"

My shoulders squared as my chin grew rigid. "I didn't even know where *around here* was until five minutes ago," I shot back. "Do you know that *no one*—and that includes you, Mr. New Boss—even bothered to tell me where the newspaper office was located?" I sighed in exasperation.

"Well, now you know," he said, turning on his booted heel and pulling the door open for me. "After you, Your Highness."

I managed to squelch the desire to roll my eyes. I would not let him get to me on my first day of work. At least not any more than he already had. I would not. I would succeed.

I would.

I stepped into the building's cool interior with Will following. In the small front room, what appeared to be fairly updated wallpaper graced the top half of the walls. On the lower portion, 1980s faux-wood paneling mimicked wainscoting and extended to the floor. Thick-framed nature prints and myriad award plaques dominated the main wall in front of me. And two wingback chairs sandwiched an octagon-shaped end table I could swear my grandmother had in her home back when I was a child. Or maybe one like it.

"To your left," Will said from behind me, the words enveloped by a sigh.

I walked through a doorway and into a long, boring hall. Stepping aside, I said, "I'll follow you since I *don't* know where I'm going."

Will breezed past me, the lingering scent of Hugo Boss after-shave floating behind him. I gave a half-smile at the irony. If I knew Will Decker even a little already—and I'd wager I did—he'd deduced that I knew one thing above all else—fashion and fragrance. Choosing Hugo *Boss* to wear on our first day working together was his dig at making sure I remembered who was who in this small-town operation.

"I'm sure our little newspaper is nothing compared to where you've worked previously, but a daily newspaper is about news, not about dolled-up offices." He threw the words over his shoulder and kept going past several rooms I hardly had time to look into. He reached a door near the end of the hallway and finally turned toward me, extending his hand as though escorting a patron to a seat at the opera. "After you."

The room yelled *storage room* instead of *office*. Assorted metal filing cabinets jammed between mismatched desks. Dinosaur PCs, new laptops, and stacks upon stacks of newspapers, memos, pictures in frames, and whatnots. The desk to my right and against the back wall had obviously been claimed. Will's cowboy hat rested atop a wire mesh in-and-out box beside a *Chicago Star* coffee mug and a partially used legal pad.

Will pointed to the desk directly across from his. "You may as well take this one," he said. "No one uses it."

"Really?" I asked. "Then what's the stuff all over it?"

"Spillover," he said. He transferred as much as he could to his chair. "We'll get you settled in here, I'll introduce you around, and then we have an assignment to get to."

I winced as the pile leaned, then looked at the ceiling and blinked several times. The surrounding clutter left me claustrophobic. My office back home may be small, but it was uncluttered. I could *work* in it and keep my thoughts straight.

I took a deep breath, looked straight ahead, and placed my purse on the scarred wooden desk, the briefcase in an old slat-back swivel office chair, and my cup of half-consumed tea on the desk.

A woman entered from the other end of the room and called over the four desks between us. "Is this her? Are you Ashlynne? Because if you are, girl, I'm Alma."

Like the Deckers' home and cottage, Alma was not what I'd expected. For one, I'd pictured late twenties, petite, and with an athletic build. Long blonde hair pulled back into a ponytail. And, of course, she would be wearing sporty shorts and a tee that read *Testament Tigers*. Or something like that.

Instead, Alma was a tall, thickly built—and I'd venture not a toned muscle in sight—African American with soft black curls tousled around a pretty face. She wore simple slacks and a polyester short-sleeved top with a horizontal stripe. Basically stylish, but not a good look for a woman of her size. Not that I would tell her so.

Certainly not on our first meeting.

In easy strides, Alma crossed the room with her hand extended. I met her halfway and slipped my hand into hers. I plastered a smile on my face, more determined than ever. "Yes, I'm Ashlynne."

"And she was late," Will said behind me. "On a *Monday*."

Alma leaned in, bringing her red-painted lips close to my ear. "That boy giving you a hard time already? 'Cause I can take him down."

I suppressed a giggle. "He's not a problem," I lied.

A young man with shaggy brown hair and a full beard lumbered in. He wore jeans that appeared a size too big and a wrinkled polo shirt. "Hey," he drawled. "I'm Garrison." He didn't bother to shake my hand.

"Garrison is our layout guy," William said. "And an amazing graphic artist."

"Nice to meet you, Garrison," I said, just as static-laced chatter came from over my right shoulder. A police scanner I hadn't previously noticed sat atop one of the four-drawer metal filing cabinets beside Will. He smiled and glanced over at Garrison. "Can you believe that? Some woman called the PD because she can't find an electrical outlet in her new home."

"Can you tell who it was?"

"The woman who moved up from South Florida . . . what's her name?"

"Migdalia something or another . . . ," Alma supplied. "I hate to say this, being a Christian and all, but have you actually had a conversation with that woman? She's dumber than dirt."

I stood in the middle of the room, the conversation spinning around me. "And she called because she can't find an electrical outlet?" I asked. "Is she mentally well? I mean, what kind of person can't find an electrical outlet?"

"Some of these houses around here are pretty old," William said. "That means some of the rooms don't have electrical outlets."

"Isn't there a law that says there has to be an outlet?" I asked.

"Maybe that's why she called the police," Garrison said with a grin.

An unexpected chuckle rose out of me, followed by a momentary but silent hallelujah. Not three minutes in the office, and though outside my comfort zone, already I felt like part of the group. *I was doing it!*

"All right, everyone," William called out. "Let's get to work." He centered his attention on me. "We've lost time. I'll have to give you the grand tour later. You ready to ride?"

"Am I shadowing you, or something?"

"Yes, ma'am, you are."

"Ah . . ." I dashed over to my desk and pulled my reporter's notebook and a pen from my briefcase. "Will I need these?"

"Yes, ma'am, you will." He reached for his hat, slid it onto his head, and tipped the brim low over his eyes. "Let's rock and roll."

I retrieved my purse and said "Nice to meet you" to Alma and Garrison. Seconds later, I clomped behind Will as fast as my pumps allowed. We left by the same way we'd come in. He opened the outside glass door for me, looking down as he did so. "You wearing shoes like that every day you come to work?"

I paused long enough to hold out one foot. "I guess. Why?"

He released the door. "They're pretty, but not practical. Not for this job." He turned right, ambling toward the side of the building. "By the way, personnel parks over here."

"I didn't know," I said, my recent feeling of belonging fizzling away like the air in an untied balloon.

"Now you do."

I stopped short as Will unlocked the passenger side of his mud-slung truck and opened the door. "Your chariot," he said.

"We're riding in . . . *this?*"

His eyes narrowed. "It's not a Jag, I know, but it gets me where I need to go. Come on, I don't have all day to argue with you."

And just *what* was wrong with a Jag?

I hoisted myself up onto the bench seat, using my left pump to knock litter aside on the floorboard. The door shut behind me with a squeak and a groan. I started to place my purse on the floorboard, then thought better of it, choosing to place it beside me instead. As Will walked around the back of the truck, I pulled the seat belt, then stopped with it suspended in front of me. The driver's door opened.

"Do you mind telling me what's all over the seat belt?"

The truck rocked under his weight as he got in and pulled the door to. "What do you mean?" He jammed a key into the ignition and turned it without looking my way. The radio blared something twangy with words about a "beat-up old guitar" as the truck rumbled to life. Will flipped the volume dial until the agony faded to sweet silence.

"There's something . . . gooey . . . all over the seat belt. Is it tar? Gum? Peanut butter? I can't tell."

Will revved the engine. "No one has ever complained before, so . . . I have no idea." He jerked the gearshift into reverse. "You need to buckle up."

"Question," I said, putting my purse in my lap and using it as a shield between me and the soiled seat belt. "When was the last time a *female* sat in this seat?"

"Hmmm . . . ," he said, twisting the steering wheel to drive us out of the parking lot. "I'd have to say the last person to sit in that seat was Buck Johnson's wife, Minnie."

"Minnie . . . and is she a friend of yours?"

"Not really."

"And, by chance, have you ever asked Mrs. Johnson if she liked having goo all over her nice clothes when she sat here?"

Will rolled the car to a stop at the parking lot exit, looking first to his left, and then to his right. We made eye contact until his lowered, resting on the glove-leather B. Makowsky purse I'd have to scrub clean with alcohol as soon as I got back to the cottage.

He snickered. "First of all," he said, pulling onto the street, "Minnie Johnson never owned anything nicer than a new pair of coveralls or maybe a cotton dress she sewed for church on Sunday."

"So I take it that's a 'no.' You have *not* asked her."

"Nope."

"Figures," I mumbled.

"Because, second of all, when I bought the truck from *Mr.* Johnson, Miss Minnie had already passed six months earlier. Give or take."

"Oh. I'm sorry to hear that."

He shook his head as though he couldn't believe what he'd just heard. "Why? Did you know Miss Minnie?"

"Well, no but . . ." I wiggled a little, feeling uncomfortable with the knowledge that the woman who'd once occupied my seat was no longer alive. Using my thumb, I indicated the gun rack and shotgun hanging behind our shoulders. "Is this necessary or is it a part of your good ole boy persona?"

Will momentarily glanced over his right shoulder. "Around here you never know when you might need it."

I shook my head and looked out the window. "So when do you think I'll start on the magazine?"

"Soon enough."

"Because that's really why I'm here."

When he didn't comment, I looked his way to catch him cutting a sideward glance my way. "Is it now?"

In answer, I returned my gaze outward. I wasn't sure what he knew—that I was really here more to lay claim to *my* grandmother's magazine than the one *our* grandmothers had started together way back when—so I opted for silence. We passed rows of commonplace businesses. Fast-food restaurants. New car businesses. Auto repair shops. An appealing nail salon.

Note to self: *Make nail appointment for next week.*

"Would you be kind enough to tell me where we are going?"

"To the home of Sarah Flannery. She's a college grad getting ready to go into the Peace Corps."

"And?"

William eyed me momentarily. "And . . . that's it. She's going into the Peace Corps. Got your phone with you?"

I dug into my purse and pulled it out, showing it to him.

"It's pink," he said.

"The *case* is pink."

"With little sparkly things on it."

I laid the phone on top of my purse. "Did you ask me to take my phone out so you could criticize it?"

"No. Do you have Internet access?"

"Of course."

"Of course . . . all right. Do us both a favor, since I've been too busy getting ready for your sweet self to come up here to have a chance to do this myself, and Google the Peace Corps. Let's see what you can find out before we get there."

What I could find out? *Well, just wait, Will Decker,* I thought. *You are about to see a research hound in action.*

7

Sarah Flannery—all five-feet-two of her—sat on the plaid sofa in her parents' family room. She wore a pair of khaki shorts, a Peace Corps T-shirt, and a pair of sneakers that looked barely big enough to fit a sixth grader. Her face was fresh-scrubbed, her light-brown hair was pulled back in a tight ponytail, and her brown eyes were vibrant with anticipation. The fragrance of a pine-scented candle filled the room.

After I had been introduced to her parents—Darrin and Jean—William and I were led to where the star of the hour waited patiently, smiling. I couldn't help but see the world of opportunity dancing around her. She was practically giddy.

William had brought a digital camera in from the truck. While I stood by with seemingly no role in the interview, he took several shots. One of Sarah sitting alone on the sofa. One standing in front of the fireplace with her parents. One of her sitting on top of her suitcase with her elbows pressed against her knees and her chin resting on fists. With a final click of the camera, William stood, ran his hand along a leg of his jeans, and said, "Where's your brother today?"

Sarah stood. "Football."

William winked at her, which brought a blush to her flawless cheeks. "Like I didn't know that." He turned to me. "Start taking notes."

Finally, something to do.

Jean Flannery, who'd been smiling with delight as Will snapped photographs, said, "Please, have a seat," and indicated a nearby chair, which matched the sofa.

I did. I took my notebook and pen from my purse, poised and ready to write.

Sarah returned to the sofa, sitting on one end while William sat on the other. He started off with, "So, Sarah . . . why the Peace Corps?"

She flashed her pretty smile again. "Lots of reasons," she said. "Mainly, I wanted to join their Master's International program. I can finish my education, get help with student loans, that sort of thing."

"Do you know where you're going?"

She nodded. "I do. Senegal."

"Tell me a little about what you'll do there," William continued.

Sarah laughed as her parents found their way to a matching love seat on the opposite side of the L-shaped room. "Well, for one thing, I'm going to be living as primitively as Wilma Flintstone."

I smiled at the way she pronounced "thing" and "Wilma." *Thang. Wil-mah.*

"We're still pretty stunned," Sarah's father commented. "This is the girl who likes to get her toes done at least every other week."

Sarah rolled her eyes. "Daddy . . ."

I cleared my throat. "The people in Senegal speak French. Are you prepared for that?" I glanced at Will, who looked at me as if I'd grown a second head. "*What?* Well, they do."

"She's right," Sarah interjected. "I've taken French in high school and minored in it in college. Still, we'll have several months of training in cultural language."

"What other training do you receive?" William asked quickly, letting me know my job was to *take* the notes, not *ask* the questions.

Sarah continued speaking about the level of training she'd receive—language, technical training, cross-cultural training—and that she'd work in the area of youth and community development. When William was finished with her portion of the interview, he turned to her parents and asked, "How long will your daughter be gone?"

"A little over two years," Jean answered, tears springing to her eyes.

Darrin chuckled. "We'll survive, Mama."

"I don't know," she mumbled.

The words jarred me. Our focus had been on Sarah. And rightfully so. But what about those she would leave behind? The *life* she would leave behind.

I realized then how different Sarah and I were. Not just in the where or how we'd grown up, or in the enough-to-be-content versus the silver-spoon-in-her-mouth. Sarah Flannery had willingly decided to leave all she knew for what she didn't know and for a good, long time. Her parents worried. Mine had pushed me out of a secure nest I never wanted to leave. And not up to higher branches in the tree—which would have been fine with me—but to a world I knew I wasn't prepared to be in, much less stay in.

"Two years," I said to William after we'd climbed back into the truck. "I thought being gone from Winter Park for six months was a long time." The easy feeling of six months had changed to a difficult one hundred and eighty days, give or take a day.

William studied me for a moment before saying, "How'd you know that? About the official language in Senegal being French?"

I placed my purse back in my lap before pulling the seat belt over and clicking it into place. "I like studying things," I said. "Geography. Music. Literature. I've always been a voracious reader. And, for your information, I love anything classic. Classic movies. Classic books."

His brow rose. "Favorite classic book," he said, more as a challenge than a question.

"I have a collection of Guy de Maupassant short stories I adore turning to on long rainy days."

He turned the key in the ignition. "Hmmm," he said. "I like *anything* by Dickens."

I hadn't seen that coming. "I would have expected L'Amour," I said, making certain a hint of laughter rang through my voice.

He snickered, but said nothing more.

For the next five minutes, we rode in content silence until I said, "Tell me more about the paper."

He squirmed. Sighed deeply. "Today is Monday. Monday is the only day we don't release a paper."

"So you *rest* on Sunday?"

"You got it." Will pulled his hat off and put it back on again. "Mondays are busy, which is why your being late this morning ticked me off."

"I told you . . . I didn't know where to go. What time to be there. I guess everyone thought everyone else had told me." I left off the part about oversleeping.

"I come in early on Mondays. Seven-thirty. No later than. With us not putting out a Monday issue, I come in, work on obits, church news, the community calendar, and check the police beat."

I swallowed a smile. One thing we never did in Winter Park was contact the "police beat" for our *Parks & Avenues* issues. "The police beat?"

"Who got arrested and why." He sent an unusual smile my way. "That's always interesting."

I supposed that, when you lived in a town small enough for everyone to know everyone else, "who got arrested" could be quite the morsel of gossip, but I didn't say so. Instead, I looked out the window at the home-style cutesiness, even on the outskirts of town. "I can't imagine anyone doing anything illegal around here."

"Our sheriff doesn't stay *real* busy, Thelma-Lou, but he does carry a gun."

"Ha-ha." I felt myself relax.

He grinned at me. "And with more than one bullet."

All right then. Maybe William Decker wasn't so bad. And maybe I was starting to figure out how to get along with him. "Okay, so you come in early on Mondays."

"Right. We work six days a week, but only forty hours."

"Six?"

"Monday through Saturday. If you have to work late one night, you come in late the next day. Unless, of course, you have a story to cover. Anyway, it's up to us to set our hours and it's up to us to make sure they don't go over forty."

Something dawned on me. "Do we clock in? Because if we do, I didn't." I didn't at the magazine, but most of our employees did.

We were getting close to the office; everything around me became familiar. "Like I said, it's up to you to keep up with your hours."

"The honor system. Interesting." My stomach growled.

William looked at me and chuckled. "You hungry?"

"Well . . . ," I said. "I didn't exactly have breakfast." I looked at my watch. Lunch, if I were on Winter Park time, was in an hour.

The newspaper came into view, but Will drove past it. I pointed toward the building. "Ah . . ."

"I could use a little something to eat, too."

"So we're goofing off." And on a Monday. That would never fly in Winter Park.

He grinned. "Trust me. You'll put in your fair share of work around here. Besides, we have to eat."

We rolled to a stop at a storefront, *Testament Drug Company* painted in white across the window. I sighed as William turned off the truck. "Let me guess. Peanuts and a coke?"

He frowned at me. "You really *did* watch *The Andy Griffith Show.*"

"Yes, but I didn't hear about this . . . ritual . . . this *passage* . . . from Andy."

William jerked the handle of his door and jumped out of the seat. "Oh, yeah?"

I got out as well, not waiting for him to come to my side. We started toward the glass door of the business. "Aren't you going to lock it?" I asked, pointing back to the truck.

"For what?" Will opened the door to the drugstore for me.

"Well," I said, "for one, from someone who might come along and think, 'Oh, that's Will Decker's truck. And he carries a pretty nice camera inside. And I need a camera.'"

"Maybe y'all have that issue in Winter Park, but here in Testament, we don't worry about that kind of thing. Testament is the one town, lady, where you can still sleep with your windows raised."

Blended scents of vanilla, coffee beans, and grilled chicken pulled my attention from the conversation to the room we'd just entered. The front of the store was clearly a gift shop, the back a pharmacy. But to the left was a doorway into another world. Another time. An old-fashioned café, joined at the hip to the community drugstore. I had the same feeling of "happy" that washed over me whenever I went to *The Briarpatch* café on Park Avenue.

"This way," Will said. "I'd wager you like crisp salads . . . grilled sandwiches . . . homemade soups."

I breathed in the heavenly aroma. "You'd wager correctly, sir." We made our way past patrons seated on every single chrome-and-vinyl stool along the bar, and toward the collection of wooden tables, each flanked by four chairs. Many were already occupied. The intensity of friendly conversations was nearly deafening.

Will easily made his way to a vacant table. Along the way, he stopped to say hello to people who seemed positively thrilled to see him. Especially those of the female persuasion. None of whom he chose to introduce me to.

"You have a fan club," I said as he held a chair out for me. "Thank you."

Will pulled the hat from his head and tossed it onto the seat of an unused chair. His fingers raked through his hair, pushing it away from his face.

I couldn't stop myself from noticing the five o'clock shadow sprouting along his jawline. My breath caught in my throat. I'd never been one of those girls who ogle boys nor a young woman who swoons at the sight of a good-looking man. I'd always been too focused on my life at the magazine to much care about a love life. But something about his look, so early in the day, made me unusually uncomfortable.

I shook the notion from my mind as Will eased his tall frame into the chair.

Within seconds, a young woman with long copper-colored hair pulled into a low ponytail approached the table carrying two menus. One she placed before me without so much as a nod, and the other she handed to Will with a smile. "Well, hey there, William . . ." Somehow, coming from her, his two-syllable name drew out to four.

"Hey there, Brianna," he returned with a wink.

"Having your usual?"

I blinked. Swallowed the almost choking desire to stand, walk out, and walk back to the newspaper. If I could find it. I understood—to some degree—the young woman's flirtatiousness with William. Even I had to admit that on a scale of one to ten, he hit a nine and a half. But what was I, invisible? And just how was I to achieve my short-term goal of understanding the inner workings of everyday people when a small-town café server didn't even acknowledge me?

I took a deep breath. "Hi," I said.

The young woman turned her head toward me, and her eyes registered surprise as though she really had not seen me at all. "Oh, I'm sorry." She pinked, leaving me to wonder if she might be embarrassed at my having caught her flirting with a patron. "I—I didn't—William doesn't usually—"

Will cleared his throat. He rested his hand on one knee and slanted his eyes playfully toward the young woman. "I don't usually come in with anyone." He glanced my way. "Brianna, this is Ashlynne Rothschild. She's from Winter Park, Florida, and she's going to be working with us down at the paper for the next few months."

The young woman—who I'd say was no more than twenty-five—gave a smile I couldn't read as genuine or not.

"Actually," I interjected, "I'll be working to resurrect the old magazine."

"What old magazine?" Brianna asked William.

"An old magazine our grandparents started together way back when," Will answered before I had a chance.

"*Hunting Tea Parties,*" I said without thinking.

Both Will and Brianna looked at me as though my spaceship had just landed.

"What?" Brianna asked, the word sounding more like "whuuuuut?"

Will shook his head. "*Hunting Grounds & Garden Parties,*" he said to me. Then to Brianna, "It's a look at all aspects of Southern living."

She brightened. "Y'all gonna talk about football?"

"Football?" I said. Wasn't it bad enough I had been sent here to resurrect a dead magazine that featured articles—and probably ads—on killing large-eyed, innocent animals? Me? A journalist accustomed only to writing about society parties, museum displays, art festivals, and grand-scale lifestyles? I now had to write about *football,* which I knew nothing about.

"Might," William supplied the answer before my mind cleared enough to answer.

Brianna beamed. "I can't wait for the season to start. Practically right around the corner. You and Rob going?"

William's one dimple sank into his cheek as he said, "As always."

I had died and gone to my own nightmare. Or maybe I still slept in my bed at the cottage and today hadn't really started yet. Whichever, I was in the middle of a bad, bad dream.

Gram said to *listen* to what others were saying if I wanted to get to know them, but so far, this was all Greek. Or maybe Latin. I'd not done as well in Latin as I had in French, and I was positively failing at my goal of understanding those not like me. If I wanted Dad's corner office, I had to . . . "Actually," I said so quickly I almost choked. Brianna and William looked at me. "I'm not all that up on the hunting aspects of things, but"—I swallowed—"back in Winter Park I work for a glossy local magazine down there and . . . we—we do a lot of society articles and . . . galas"—I took a breath—"and openings."

"What kind of openings?" Brianna asked.

"We—we had—" I had to think. *Think.* "Oh! Park Avenue recently had a new cosmetics store open up and George O came and . . ."

Brianna's blank look told me I'd completely lost her. I looked to Will, who again shook his head.

Friendly, Ashlynne. *Friendly.* "George O," I supplied, "is a well-known makeup artist. Anyway, he came and I interviewed him." I stopped then. Stopped long enough to study Brianna. Had she been with me in Winter Park that day, George would have scooped her out of the crowd of onlookers and shoppers. Her skin was flawless, her eyes large, her brows naturally arched, and her lips full. "You know," I smiled, "Georgie would have *loved* you."

"Oh, boy . . . ," Will mumbled. "Brianna, honey? Can we order something?"

She pointed to the menu. "We have some specials today if you'd like to hear about them."

"I would love to hear about them." My voice shook. I took a slow breath and let it go just as slowly.

Brianna dished on the specials, and I settled on the Vegetable Panini, a seasonal fruit cup, and unsweet iced tea. Without glancing at his menu, Will cleared his throat and said, "And you know what I'll have."

Brianna smiled at him. "I'll have that right up for you." After a smile to me, she sashayed toward the kitchen doors.

I turned back to my lunch companion. His eyes were hooded, as though he were studying me. "Tell me something," he said.

I placed both hands in my lap and squeezed them together. "All right."

"What's got you so on edge?"

"I'm not on edge."

He chewed on his bottom lip for a second before saying, "I make it my business to study people, Ashlynne Rothschild. And you, ma'am, are on edge."

I glanced around, my eyes darting from the framed photos of days gone by, to the reproductions of old tin advertisements, and then back to William. "I just want to get along. If I'm going to live here for six months I may as well try to fit in."

"That's gonna happen," he mumbled.

"What?"

"Here you go," Brianna said as she returned, seemingly out of nowhere. She placed our drinks before us. "And your meals will be out in a jiff."

"Thank you," I said.

"Um . . . ," she said, "would you mind, maybe . . . I mean . . . would it be all right with you if we talk some time about makeup and things like that? I mean, I know you're probably very busy, but I have a feeling you know a *lot* about things like . . . that." She took a much-needed breath. "And . . . I mean, I know it's probably a lot to ask, but I've always been real interested but . . . I mean, I just usually wear Cover Girl and Maybelline, you know?"

"Brianna," Will said, "Miss Rothschild has probably never heard of Cover Girl and Maybelline."

I shot him as mean a look as I thought I could get away with and stay in some semblance of control. "What is *wrong* with you? Of course I've heard of Cover Girl and Maybelline." I'd never used it, seeing as my mother had insisted my first makeover be at the Clinique counter at Bloomies, but I'd certainly heard of it. Then, feeling almost victorious, I turned to Brianna with a smile. "I'd like that very much. I'm working all week, but maybe Sunday? After church?"

Brianna nodded. "That'd be great." She smiled at me again. "I'll have your panini here in a minute."

After she left, I asked Will, "How old is she?"

"Twenty-four? I'm not sure, to tell you the truth."

My mind raced over what I thought would be the perfect products for her. The best look.

"Want to know how old I am?" he asked.

"Not really."

"Thirty-six last Monday."

"Thirty-six?" I wondered then, fleetingly, if the question had been asked because he and Brianna were . . . what was the word Andy had used with Barney? *Sweet* on each other. "Is Brianna someone special?"

Will's jaw set and his eyes turned steely. "No more than any other girl."

"Oh."

"No." He raised a finger in admonishment. "Not what you're thinking."

"I wasn't thinking anything . . ."

"Oh, yes you were."

William clasped his hands together and looked toward the floor. "Believe me, she's not smitten with me. She's just a sweet girl. And even if she were, I don't have time for women in my life. I've got far too much to do. No time for . . ." He looked at me again. "Women."

"Like what? What do you have to do?"

"Like the paper, for one. Big Guy plans to hand it over soon."

Yes. Our grandparents, being the same age, would be taking full retirement into consideration. Even from careers they'd birthed, nurtured, and loved for decades. "I understand," I all but whispered.

"Taking care of my grandparents for another," Will said as though I'd not spoken. "Big Guy can't keep up that property by himself and he's not altogether on top of the men who work the ranch."

Even as independent as Gram could be, she needed Dad from time to time. "What about your parents? Where are they?"

Will took a gulp of what I presumed to be sweet tea. "My parents went to work on the mission field a few years ago."

"Really?" I sat back. Brianna returned with our plates of food.

Will looked up. "Thank you, Bri."

"You're welcome, Will."

I exchanged smiles with her before she darted off to another table.

William closed his eyes and bowed his head, pronouncing a blessing over the food.

"Thank you," I said after repeating the "amen."

"So . . . your parents?"

William popped a French fry into his mouth. "Yeah," he said around it. "It was something they always wanted to do but wanted to make sure they got me through school and thoroughly educated first."

I bit into my sandwich. The flavors of fresh asparagus, greens, and raspberry glaze almost made me dizzy with delight. "You went to college?" I said after I'd swallowed.

William's eyes narrowed. "Yes, I went to college. What do you think? We're all hillbilly hicks barely getting by on a sixth-grade education?" He brought the glass back to lips that had drawn tight.

I'd once again said the wrong thing. Seemed to me conversations with William Decker ran either hot or cold, and I wasn't the one controlling the thermostat.

I laid my sandwich carefully on my plate as Will bit into his hamburger. "No. Of course not." Leaning forward I asked, "You know, you're not the only one who has learned to observe people."

"Meaning?" he asked around his food.

"Meaning that for some reason you think the worst of me. From the moment I got here you've had some sort of grudge against me, which—quite frankly—makes no sense at all seeing as you don't even know me." And made him more like a pack of seventh-grade girls than he realized.

Will swallowed hard. Used his tongue to work a piece of food from his teeth. Took a sip of tea. Then said, "Oh, I know you, all right."

"How can you say that?"

"Because," he answered. "I know your *type*."

8

We ate the remainder of our meal in silence, and with me completely confused. I had come to Testament to work. To prove to my father and grandmother that I could be the kind of businesswoman who identified with others. With everyone. Anyone. So far, I'd done wonderfully well with the senior Deckers, with Alma and Garrison, with the Flannerys and with Brianna. But I'd failed with the one person I would spend the most time with during my stay in North Carolina. The one who, I knew from my own experiences, could hold the success of my climb up at *Parks & Avenues* in his hand.

But why? Why one minute was the man difficult, the next something close to friendly, and the next, a bear again? As a woman—not to mention as a reporter who loved the act and art of investigative research (something I had far too few chances to do at the magazine)—I set my even newer short-term goal to find out why.

The ride back to the paper was as icy as the last half of lunch. Will kept to himself until we reached the newspaper door, at which point he said, "We've got a story meeting at four. I'm going to get the piece about Sarah knocked out and the pictures sent to Garrison as soon as we get inside."

"Do you need my notes?" I asked, hoping for some sort of truce, albeit a professional one.

"Only if the recorder on my iPhone failed me."

I stopped inside the front room. "You were *recording* the interview?"

"Always."

I followed behind him, stomping as we went along. "Then *why* was I taking notes?"

William stopped, turned, and stared at me. "Didn't I just make that clear? In case my phone didn't work."

Ugh.

"By the way," he added. "I'm going to give you my e-mail address. Shoot me the links you found on the Peace Corps."

"I can do that," I mumbled.

We made our way back to the large room with the mismatched desks. Garrison sat at his corner desk, slowly gliding the computer's mouse over a pad.

Talk about antiquated.

Alma sat at her desk, talking on the phone.

I pointed to my desk as Will moved all the stuff he'd placed in his office chair earlier, dropping it to the floor. "I'll shoot those links to you and then . . . ah . . . I'll get my desk organized," I said.

"Sounds good." Will handed me a business card from his desk. "My e-mail's at the bottom." He sat. While his laptop booted up, he pulled out his phone, stuck in tiny earbuds, and slid his fingers over his face.

All right then.

After I'd sent the links, and while the newspaper business buzzed around me—keys clicking, phones ringing, voices chattering on the phone—I kept just as busy, going through drawers, flipping through old newspapers and files that had been stored there. Every so often I'd hold up a collection of items, ask if they were to be kept or thrown away. Will always answered "Keep" until, finally, he sighed, got up, and left the room. A minute later he returned with a bin and said, "Put everything you think you don't want in your desk in here. I'll go through it later with Big Guy and Gram. See what *they* want to keep. What *they* want to throw away."

I felt as though I had been scolded. I forced myself to recover. "Where *are* your grandparents?"

William returned to his desk chair. "I imagine Big Guy is in his *other* office and Gram—I don't know where she is. She'll be here for the meeting."

"His other office?"

"Coffee shop," he said. "Right down the road."

"Not so unlike Winter Park," I said. "We have marvelous coffee shops on Park Avenue and—"

Will pointed to his computer. "I'm sure you do. But I have to finish this piece." He returned the buds to his ears.

"Sorry." I returned to my task of sorting, straightening, and shifting.

Across the room, Alma stood, stretched, and looked my way. "There you are," she said, as though our earlier entry had gotten past her completely.

"Here I am." I smiled.

"Want a cup of coffee? I can show you where the break room is . . ."

I looked at Will, whose fingers continued to fly across the keyboard. I'd never seen a man type quite that fast. "Will?"

One hand flew up in dismissal. "By all means." Then he looked at Alma. "Can you show her around in general?"

"Be happy to."

I walked toward Alma, feeling somewhat like I'd found an oasis in the desert. "Thank you," I said when I reached her.

"For what, honey?"

"For . . . coffee."

She looked at her watch as we walked out of the office and into the hall. "We've got one hour till story time. If I'm going to survive *that,* I've got to have a cup of coffee *now.*"

We entered a room to the left. From what I'd seen, in my opinion, the room won "best decorated." Natural light flooded in from a three-pane window. Mosaic tile between the countertop backsplash and the overhead cabinets added a splash of color. The appliances—refrigerator, dishwasher, microwave, and coffeemaker—were stainless steel. Clearly, not a dime in expense had been spared. A rich, dark wood table and four chairs accented the left side of the room. A pink silk orchid graced the table as a centerpiece, along with a collection of white porcelain salt and pepper shakers and matching sugar bowl.

"This room is remarkable," I said, planting my hands on my hips. I inhaled. Everything smelled of red apples and coffee beans.

"Isn't it, though? Miss Bobbie has such a way with decorating."

"*Miss* Bobbie? You call her *'Miss'*?"

Alma ambled over to the other side of the room where she pulled two mugs from one of the cabinets. "Honey, we're not talking slavery here. But we're still in the South . . ."

I joined her, taking the proffered cup. "So? This is the South. So what? Does that mean you still have to call a white woman 'Miss' because she's your boss and you're, you know, black?"

Alma burst out laughing then steadied herself enough to pour my coffee and hers. "No. I call her 'Miss' because she's older than me. Not because she's white, not because I'm black, and not because she's my boss. That's just the way it is here, Ashlynne. We call our elders 'Miss' or 'Mister.' You know, according to gender."

"So you call Mr. Decker . . . ?"

"Mister Shelton." Alma opened a drawer and pulled two spoons from a flatware tray. "Do you want creamer?"

"Yes, please."

"Regular, half-and-half, or flavored?"

"Half-and-half."

We walked over to the table and placed our mugs on top. Alma went to the refrigerator, brought back the half-and-half, and we sat together. "So, what do you call William?" I asked, pulling the oversized sugar bowl toward me, hoping to find packets of raw sugar.

There were, along with packets of regular, and packets of Stevia.

Alma snickered. "Pain in the rump," she said under her breath.

My eyes grew wide as my hands rested on the table. Could I trust Alma to confide information about Will Decker so early in our relationship, which was nothing more—at this point—than that we shared a large, congested office?

My face must have formed the questions my mouth couldn't, because Alma answered, "Girl, I can only tell you what I've heard and that would be gossip. And I don't go for inner-office gossip. It can only mess things up for *every*body."

"That's true," I admitted. "But just so I'm clear, this . . . *way* . . . he has. Nice one minute. Mean the next. It's not just with me?"

"Mean? Well now, I wouldn't call Will mean. He's never been anything but *polite* to me. He's just moody is all." She prepared her coffee and took a long sip, closing her eyes as it slid down her throat. "Now, Alma," she spoke to herself, "that's good coffee."

I smiled. "Why do you think he's so moody?"

"All I know is," she said, leaning in, "he went to work in Chicago after he graduated college and then, after a few years, he came back here. I don't know if it's because his grandfather needed him—and believe you me, he did—and he's bitter about it or because things just didn't work out in Illinois. All I know is," she repeated, "he's moody, but he's a good man overall."

I ignored the last part. "Chicago. There's a *Chicago Star* mug on his desk."

"And I don't know if he worked there, bought it from their gift shop, or stole it from someone's kitchen. What I just told you is all I know." She took another swallow of coffee and I did the same. "So, he's been mean to you?"

"Not mean exactly. I just can't read him. I'm trying. Really I am. My grandmother sent me here for a purpose and I want to honor her by being on my best behavior."

"Your grandmother?"

I had said too much. Probably. "Yeah . . . old friend of Shelton and Bobbie's." *Mister* Shelton. *Miss* Bobbie. "It's . . . nothing."

"If it means anything as far as what *I* think, you seem to be doing fine. At least you're getting that nasty desk cleaned up."

"Yeah," I said. But I hadn't come to Testament to clean up a desk. Or to be bullied by William Decker. I'd come to resurrect the old magazine.

No. I'd come to *win* my father's job.

I wrapped my hands around the warmth of the mug. "I guess we'd better get back to work before the story . . . *what* did you call it?"

Alma laughed. "I call it 'story time,' just because I like to keep things cheerful around here. The newspaper business can be kind of hard-nosed. Especially when we're hitting deadlines."

"Of course," I said. "I've worked at a magazine for years. It's the same way." Just not every *day*.

Alma stood and so did I. "You can take your coffee back to your desk if you want. As you may have noticed, one of the rooms Miss Bobbie has resigned herself to *never* decorate is the main office for us reporters."

That much I couldn't argue with. "Can you show me where the restroom is, please?"

"Oh. I'm supposed to be showing you around anyway, aren't I?"

"That's okay. I'll go to the restroom and meander for a few minutes on my own. I'm sure I'll be fine."

We stepped into the hallway. Alma pointed to our left. "Second door on the right is the little girls' room."

I handed her my coffee. "Would you mind terribly putting this on my desk?"

"Not at all."

I ventured into a room that had undoubtedly also seen Bobbie's touch. *Miss* Bobbie. All right then. I'd have to work hard to remember that.

An oak-and-marble sink stood in front of me. I opened the lower cabinet door and peered inside to find cleaning supplies, feminine hygiene products, and extra rolls of toilet paper. I straightened, testing the overhead mirror to determine if it was, in fact, a medicine cabinet.

Bingo.

Inside was an assortment of pain relievers, a tube of toothpaste, and several hotel-sized bottles of mouthwash.

Nice.

After a few minutes in the bathroom, I wandered to the back of the building where a large room seemed to stretch for miles. Dozens of wooden cubbies filled the space, each bursting with newspapers dating back several weeks. To the far back stood the remnants of what had been an old printing press, no longer used since the miracle of pdf files. Old metal filing cabinets in need of a good dusting crowded the cubbies, their drawers labeled by yellowing slips of paper scrawled with faded ink. One drawer in particular drew my attention from across the room; its label typed boldly in black: **HUNTING GROUNDS & GARDEN PARTIES**. I glanced over my shoulder, wondering if I was somewhere I shouldn't be. As if Will would walk in any moment and yell at me for not sitting at my desk doing nothing. Or for snooping.

But *this* magazine—or the remnant of it left inside the cabinet—was my ticket up. *This* was why I was in Testament in the first place.

Feeling secure in my mission, I stepped toward the cabinet and gingerly, almost reverently, opened the drawer. The smell of dust and old print wafted around me, tickling my nose. Again, I looked over my shoulder, then back into the deep drawer, where a thick stack of the defunct magazine issues had been stored.

I pulled out the top issue—dated May 1956—and pushed the drawer closed. I laid the magazine on top of the cabinet and studied the cover photograph: an old hunting dog sitting in front of a linen-draped round table adorned with an eggshell china tea set.

My lips crept upward in a smile. I turned back the cover, flipped past the table of contents and a few ad pages to the editorial section, where I found the names of my grandparents and the Deckers.

I ran my fingertips over my grandfather's name and title—*Richard W. Rothschild*, publisher. *Papa*. I closed my eyes for a moment, drawing his scent from memory. His larger-than-life presence. No man could fill his shoes in my heart . . . not even Dad.

I looked at the magazine page again. Gram had been his sole journalist, although I saw under her name a short list of contributors. Bobbie Decker served as the only photographer and Shelton as the copy editor.

Humble beginnings.

"Those were the days," someone said from behind me. I spun around so quickly I knocked the magazine to the floor.

"Oh," I said. Heat rushed to my cheeks as I bent to retrieve the magazine sprawled near Bobbie Decker's feet. "I'm sorry. I guess you could say I was snooping."

"Snoop all you want," she said. "There's not a thing back here that's a secret."

Returning the magazine to the drawer, I said, "I've never seen these before. Any of them." I brushed dust from my palms.

"Really? Connie didn't keep some of the issues for herself?"

I closed the drawer with a click. "If she has, I haven't seen them. Gram is often pretty closedmouthed about the past."

Bobbie's eyes lit up. "Always was." She stepped around me, reopened the drawer, and picked up the magazine I'd just put back along with a short stack of others. "Would you like to take a few of these back to the cottage to look over? We did good work, even if we didn't have a clue as to what we were doing."

I took the magazines from her. "Really? You don't mind?"

"Might help you in the project Shel and Connie set you up to do." She linked her arm with mine. "Have you met the gals in advertising?"

I shook my head. "No, I haven't."

Bobbie led me toward a door I'd not noticed before, on the opposite wall from where I'd entered the room. "I'll introduce you. I'd have thought William would have done all that by now."

My back involuntarily straightened. "He's been busy."

"He's a good boy," she said. "He's just . . . he's had a hard time of late."

A hard time? Really . . . "I didn't know . . . *don't* know . . . he hasn't said."

She patted my hand. "He wouldn't. And don't say I said anything or I'll end up in the doghouse."

We stopped at the door of a brightly painted room with walls dominated by corkboard and dry-erase bulletin boards. The strong odor of paint and the painter's tape outlining the sole window told me someone had been working recently. "You've been redecorating," I whispered to Bobbie.

Miss Bobbie.

"I'm trying. And one of these days I'll get to the office you're in. Good Lord willing."

Three women, two older, one younger, sat behind metal and faux-wood desks, their eyes fixed on their computer screens. "Well, hey, Miss Bobbie," one of the older ones called out.

"Hey there, yourself," she said. Then, pulling me farther into the room, "Yvonne, Dianne, and Carrie, I want you to meet the granddaughter of one of my oldest and dearest friends." Bobbie repeated the pat on my hand. "This is Ashlynne Rothschild. She's going to be working with us for a few months, shadowing William and bringing our old magazine out of mothballs."

The younger women coughed out a laugh. "That's not a bad gig," which brought follow-up laughter from the other two.

"The magazine?" one said. "The old *Hunting Grounds*?"

"I'm afraid so," Bobbie said. "Seems Shelton wants a project and he's picked this one." Bobbie squeezed my hand, leaving me to wonder if the magazine was the project or me.

"My mother used to love that magazine," the woman—whose desktop nameplate read Carrie Birchfield—said.

"Your mother used to send us story ideas," Bobbie added. "Never wanted to write them, of course, but she was full of ideas."

"What was your name again?" the youngest—Dianne—asked me.

"Ashlynne. Ashlynne Rothschild," I added with a smile.

The smile was not returned. "And you're going to work with William, you say?"

"I—uh—only temporarily. Until I get the lay of the land, I guess you could say."

The three women shot messages to each other with their eyes. Messages I'd learned long ago to read without understanding the code.

"Now, girls," Bobbie said. "We'll have none of that."

"Oh, Miss Bobbie," Yvonne said, "we're just being who we are. You know us."

"I know you, and you just be who you are on your own time. While you're here, there will be no funny business."

Carrie gave a half-grin, as though she were in on the greatest secret to hit Testament, North Carolina.

Bobbie squeezed my hand again. "Y'all make Ashlynne feel welcomed, now, ya hear?" She patted my hand again and I wondered if the action was more to calm her or me. "You'll do fine, Ashlynne. Don't let these girls scare you. They think they've got a club up in here or something."

I looked down at Bobbie and tried my best not to cry as an old memory settled around me. I was twelve, standing in front of a classroom filled with ordinary middle-school kids. They were halfway through the Monday in their second week of seventh grade, but I had just started my first day.

For nearly two months I had begged my parents to let me leave St. Andrew's Academy, to attend a public school—even if for only a year—like normal kids. Real kids. *Not* children born with special privileges just because their parents had done well in business and in life. My best argument had been that while St. Andrew's was known for academics, the public school system had a variety of sports none of the private schools offered.

Like I played sports.

Mom had been all for it, but Dad sorely against it. And Dad's vote trumped Mom's and mine put together so, for all he knew, he'd won the battle.

But not the war.

The first day of school, I refused to get out of bed and go to St. Andrew's. On the second day, Dad found me kneeling over the toilet bowl, throwing up from an exaggerated level of drama I'd worked myself into. That was when Gram and Papa stepped in, saying, "Let her try, Richard. Might do her a world of good."

Dad never could say no to Gram or to Papa.

If I'd known then what I learned a short time later, I would have gotten up that first morning of school, dressed in my St. Andrew's uniform, and been the dutiful child—new notebooks and book bag in hand. And stayed out of the lion's den.

I looked at the faces of the three women from advertising.

The lion's den. Exactly where I found myself again.

9

Their faces said it all—nothing had changed.

Old feelings returned. I didn't belong here. Would never belong here, not even for six months.

Miss Bobbie insisted they explain to me their individual roles at the paper. Although they talked for several minutes, each describing their part of the newspaper business, I knew they saw me as an intruder to their world. To their community. Someone who would never fit in, even though I paid careful attention to every word they said because I knew, in the end, advertising was just as important to the newspaper as it would be to the magazine I had come to resurrect.

No, I didn't belong here. The only place I belonged was Winter Park.

The bigger problem—bigger than these women staring at me, telling me that I had intruded into their world—was that Dad and Gram didn't believe I fully belonged back home either. They didn't understand—not fully—that Winter Park, and the magazine specifically, held safety for me. And that my friends, few though they may be, were true friends. They understood. Everything.

I blew out a pent-up breath and looked around, making every attempt to regain my composure. My control. On a small portion of one wall, a *Saturday Evening Post* calendar displaying Norman

Rockwell art hung beside three dry-erase boards. Each board held the name of one of the three women; underneath that, a list of businesses. Stretched over the boards, a banner read: NEW BUSINESSES. Just as in the magazine publishing world, *new* business was as important as old for drumming up ads. We had our loyal clients, of course. But we were always looking to expand the horizon.

"Our paychecks depend highly on commission," Yvonne told me, "so we spend precious little time lollygagging."

Lollygagging. The way she said the word clenched my heart. Is that what she thought I did? "I understand," I said. "It's that way for me too. Back home."

"Oh, really?" Carrie asked, and again I could feel the disbelief in her voice.

"Mmhmm. As soon as I walk into my office, I'm faced with loads to do. Articles to write. Interviews to go out on. Fires to put out. No time for *lollygagging.*" And, in my case, friendship-building. Which was why Dad and Gram thought me incapable of connecting with our employees. And, right now, I couldn't say I blamed them.

"Oh, well then I guess you know," Carrie said.

For several moments, we were at a standoff, none of us really knowing what else to say. The three ad girls looked at one another. Bobbie and I looked back. I blinked a few times. "Miss Bobbie," Dianne finally said, "Testament High is having a swing band dance on the night of their first game and placed an ad for it today. I told them we'd give them a good rate."

"Good, good," Bobbie replied. Then to me, "We always give the schools a good rate. It's only right. And, of course, what would a small-town newspaper be without school news. Especially high school." Looking back at Dianne, she said, "When does school begin this year?"

"Wednesday."

"And first game?"

"Next Friday."

Bobbie looked at me again. "We'll make sure William takes you to the first game. We'll want a story, of course, but it's also the thing to do on Friday nights during the season."

But . . . "I thought Alma was the sportswriter." And, because the ad girls had been so quick earlier to respond to my forced relationship with Will, I watched for any reaction about him taking me to the game. "Isn't she?"

"Honey, if you've got a chance to go out with Will Decker, don't *sneeze* at it," Yvonne said as she laughed.

Heat rushed to my cheeks. "I'm not going *out* with *anyone*."

The three laughed all the harder, sharing their secret joke. I looked at Bobbie again, a silent pleading.

"Girls," she said, and the laughter stopped. She turned her attention to me. "Alma will do the *game* story, of course. We'll need someone to cover the dance. You like to dance, don't you, Ashlynne? I'm sure you do. Your grandmother was a marvelous dancer."

I wondered if dancing may have been how Gram connected to these people so long ago. And, if so, then this was a perfect alley for me to go down in my quest upward. "Yes," I said. "I like to dance." In fact, I was *very* good at it. Years of classes had seen to it.

"Good. Then it's settled. I'll tell William." She looked at the wall clock. "Dear me, it's five till four. We've got the meeting to get to."

"Good-bye, Miss Bobbie," the three said in harmony.

She waved. "Carry on, girls. Make us some money."

They laughed as she turned me toward the door. I glanced over my shoulder. "Nice to meet you," I said. "And maybe I'll see you all at the dance."

"You too," they echoed, but I knew they didn't mean it.

I drove home around 6:00 p.m. in near-comatose condition, except for a lump in my throat I'd been unable to swallow for the past two hours.

Emotional exhaustion had clamped down on every muscle in my body. Ever fiber of my being. My brain refused to think and I was grateful the traffic in Testament was practically nonexistent. I turned my Jag into the Decker driveway, stunned I remembered the way.

The car rocked side to side as though it had already memorized the incline leading to the cottage. I pulled up alongside the unpainted, tin-roofed structure and turned off the car. Too tired to get out, I laid my head back and closed my eyes. I would nap, I decided, for fifteen minutes. Even in the late afternoon heat. I didn't care. If I died, I died. Should I live, then I'd go inside, shower, try to muster up the energy to chew something and call it "dinner," and then fall into bed.

I jumped at a dog's bark and swung my head to the window. My furry friends welcomed me home, tails wagging, tongues falling out the sides of their mouths. Or perhaps they were preventing my attempt at dying in my Jag at the end of my first workday in Testament, North Carolina.

I pulled my purse and briefcase from the passenger's seat and opened the door. "Hello," I said, swinging my feet to the pebble-covered ground. "Are you my welcoming committee?"

They panted in response.

I trudged toward the door with my new faithful companions at my feet. "You know," I said, "I haven't been told your names. We're practically strangers." Yet, they welcomed me. The irony . . . the irony.

The panting continued.

"Are you thirsty?" I asked. "I bet you're thirsty."

One of the dogs yelped in answer.

I opened the cottage door, swinging it wide enough for the three of us to enter. I placed my purse and briefcase on the counter and continued with my one-sided conversation. "Let me find a bowl big enough in here somewhere," I said, now fumbling through the cabinets, "and I'll get you some water."

The dogs continued to pant as they paced in wide circles.

My search turned up empty until I spied an oversized ceramic bowl on top of the refrigerator. "Here we go. Probably meant for decoration only, but it'll do, don't you think?"

I ran water from the tap into the bowl. The dogs bumped into my legs in eager anticipation. I placed the bowl on the floor and watched as they lapped in unison. When they were done, they gave me grateful stares before meandering back to the door. I opened it, giving both a swift pat on the head, then watched them depart down the hill toward the Deckers' home. "Sorry you have to drink and run," I called out as though, if they heard me, they'd get the joke.

I closed the storm door, followed by the heavy inner door, then walked to the sofa, fell across it, and burst into tears.

Could I only get *dogs* to accept me? Okay, there'd been Alma. She seemed to be nonjudgmental. And Bobbie and Shelton. And Garrison. And Brianna and the Flannerys.

But Will Decker left giant question marks. And the three women from advertising! Contending with people like them . . . how would I survive six months in Testament? How could I return to Winter Park to be rewarded with a new job—the job I'd worked for since graduating college? And, if today was just Day One, what would the other approximately one hundred and eighty be like?

I wasn't sure I even wanted to guess.

I woke the next morning, still lying on the sofa. I hadn't eaten, I hadn't showered, and I hadn't changed my clothes. I eased up, propping on my elbows halfway, then straightened and stood. I stretched, first reaching my fingers toward the ceiling and then to the floor.

Feeling less stiff, I walked into the kitchen to prepare tea, glancing at the stove's digital clock. 6:24.

Good, I thought. At least today I had a little time to get ready before facing *The Testament Tribune*. While the Keurig coffeemaker did its thing, I did mine, stripping out of my clothes on my way to the upstairs shower. I tossed them on the bed on my way to the bathroom. I let the hot water pelt against my body, feeling the sting and, at the same time, the release of tight muscles. I washed my hair, breathing in the wild ginger scent. When I'd conditioned and rinsed thoroughly, I soaked a natural sea sponge with water and added a lavender-and-vanilla body gel polish. I took my time, washing away yesterday's pain. Its questions. Especially as they dealt with Will Decker.

He's had a hard time of it . . . Bobbie Decker's words slipped around the shower curtain and into the tub, playing with my emotions. What had she meant? What kind of a hard time? As I stepped under the water a final time, I remembered Alma's words as well.

He went to work in Chicago after he graduated college and then, after a few years, he came back here. I don't know if it's because his grandfather needed him to and he's bitter about that, or because things just didn't work out.

By the time I wrapped myself in a thick body towel, I had determined to find out just what this *hard time of it* was and when he'd come back from Chicago. And why. But more than that. I wanted to know, as far deep as the cowboy's roots seemed to be in Testament, why he ever left in the first place.

One of my favorite clothing designers is Kate Spade. Her style simply fits me. So, for my second day on the job, I chose one of her silk flare dresses—black with white polka dots—and a pair of sassy black flats. I drank my tea, poured a bowl of cornflakes (something I'd not had since childhood, but it was the only cereal in the pantry), and walked into the small first-floor bedroom where I'd previously noticed a bookshelf stacked with books.

My eyes were drawn to a book lying flat on one of the middle shelves.

The cover of *Live Life to the Fullest,* a thin gift-style book, was identical to the tiles of the mirror in the downstairs bathroom. Placing my tea on the nearby bedside table, I flipped through its glossy pages. The left pages displayed a photograph of each of the tiles. The right, Scripture verses and short sayings.

I took the book, my tea, and myself out to the rock garden. I draped one of the Adirondack chairs with one of the sofa throws from the living room. For a moment, I drank in my surroundings. Red-tipped bushes grew high enough to block my view of the Decker home, the road leading to the highway, and the mountains beyond. But I knew they were out there and the thought brought sweet comfort. Above me, the morning breeze tickled the leaves of several hearty maples. Squirrels darted along their branches and wrens sang messages back and forth among them. Periodically, a leaf spiraled to the ground in anticipation of an early fall.

After taking a sip of tea and placing the mug on the small table next to my chair, I opened the first page.

Take long walks, the picture instructed.

The words on the right page read:

> You've let me walk fast and safe,
> without even twisting an ankle.
>
> —Psalm 18:36

> Therefore we were buried together with him through baptism into his death, so that just as Christ was raised from the dead through the glory of the Father, we too can walk in newness of life.
>
> —Romans 6:4

And then, alone at the bottom right of the page, the words WALK IN LOVE appeared in block letters.

I took in a deep breath, allowing the words to inspire me as to my personal walk with God, then contemplated more the picture to the left.

Take long walks.

It had been awhile since I'd taken a long walk. Or any walk, other than the treadmill at the gym. If ever a place was picturesque enough to do so, it was here in Testament. When I got to the office, I'd ask Will about the best places for such an adventure.

Hopefully, his answer wouldn't include a dangerously high cliff.

Will met me halfway down the hall leading to our office, hat in hand and obviously in a hurry. "There you are," he said.

I looked at my watch. "I'm on time today," I declared. "In fact I'm three minutes early."

"We've got a story." He looked me up and down. "Do you not have *anything* less . . . snazzy to wear?"

I returned the glare. "Don't *you* own anything but denim and cotton?" Even as I said the words, I gave myself a mental kick. *How is it that Will Decker brings out all the worst in me?*

"Seriously. You'll need something less dressy for this one."

"This one? I thought I'd start working on the magazine today. I played with some ideas on the way over—" I stopped talking as Will shook his head.

"Not now. Not today. I'm going to need you and"—he clasped his hand under my elbow and turned me around—"you're not dressed right."

I held my hands up in surrender. "I didn't know. You could have called." By now we were halfway out the door, dashing to his truck. "And I parked in the right place today, I'll have you notice."

"Good girl." He opened the passenger door for me and I hopped in, once again catching a whiff of his cologne. HiM by Hanae Mori. Wow.

"We'll drive out to my grandparents' first so you can change," Will said after he'd joined me in the truck's cab.

"Why do I need to change?" I pulled the seat belt over, ready to place my Rebecca Minkoff hobo purse between me and it. But the belt had been scrubbed clean. I started to say something, but Will spoke instead.

"Great-granny, girl. Believe me. You wouldn't want that . . . what is that? Kate Spade?"

I nearly fell to the floorboard. "*You* know Kate Spade?"

His eyes flashed. "You're not the only fashionista I've known."

"I see." *Chicago,* I thought. *I bet this has something to do with Chicago . . .*

"So, you have something you can change into?"

"Why don't you first tell me where we're going and then I'll know if I have anything appropriate."

"A man out on the highway—Robert Matthews is his name—owns about twenty-five acres he's been clearing away for two years now."

"Okay."

"Built himself a nice log cabin, planted some vegetables, a few muscadine grape vines, prettiest roses you've ever seen . . ."

Sounded nice, but so far I wasn't hearing a *story*. "Okay."

He shot another look my way—one I'd already grown accustomed to and learned how to read—just as the front passenger wheel hit a pothole, jarring me up from the bench seat and back down again.

"Thanks," I said.

"Wasn't done on purpose, I can assure you."

"So, where's the story here? Muscadine grapes and roses and . . . what?"

"Recently," Will shot back, "Rob decided to start clearing out an area that's close to the old Revolutionary War road."

"The old . . . as in *the* Revolutionary War?"

"Was there more than one?"

"Well, no. But . . ."

"You like history?" he asked.

"I do. I'm always interested in learning new things. I told you that."

"No, you didn't."

"Yes, I—never mind. So, the guy, Robert Matthews, started clearing . . ." I waved my hand in a "get on with it" motion.

"Yeah, so Rob's clearing out this tract of heavily wooded area and he starts noticing these stones sticking up out of the ground. First one, then another, and another until he comes up on one that looks more like a tombstone. Short, flat, and with a jutting topside. He squats down, takes in the long view, and that's when he realizes, these stones had been placed at the tops of graves."

"Unmarked?"

"Unmarked."

"Where are they from? I mean . . . whose *could* they be?"

"That's what we're going to look into. See if we can't figure it out. Of course, we'll want to get the historical society in on it, which by the way is a group you'll want to get to know when you start working on the magazine."

Whenever *that* was.

Will swung the truck into his grandparents' driveway, floored the accelerator, and bounced the truck along until we reached the cottage. Once he had stopped, he grinned at me again. "Kind of makes your teeth rattle, doesn't it?"

I jerked the door handle in response. "So, what you're telling me is that I need something for walking in the woods?"

"Got anything like that?"

Probably not. "I'll see what I can find," I said. "Just give me a few minutes."

Will looked at his watch. "Garrison is meeting us there with one of his fancy cameras at 9:00. It's 8:45 now. I'll give you five minutes."

"Piece of cake."

Pants, I wasn't worried about. I had brought one pair of jeans with me. Straight-leg. Too expensive to be traipsing out in the woods while wearing, but they were my only choice. My biggest problem was going to be footwear.

I quickly changed into the jeans, adding a simple pink tee, then scanned my boxes of shoes until I found as casual a pair of flats as I owned. They weren't overly sturdy, but at least I could keep my feet on the ground, more or less.

As one last act before returning to the truck, I swept my long hair into a thick ponytail.

I ran back to the truck and jumped in. Will looked at me as if my choice of jeans-tee-flats ensemble had been completely wrong. "Those are the only jeans you have?"

"As a matter of fact, they are. The only ones *with* me, at least. I didn't realize I'd need to bring my *entire* wardrobe." Which, of course, was an impossibility. Pressing my hands into my thighs and running them to my knees, I added, "And what's wrong with these? They're jeans. They're denim."

"They're *purple*."

"They most certainly are not. They're *elderberry*."

He shook his head and chuckled. "Lady, you won't do." Will pulled the gearshift to drive, drove around the cottage, and back down the driveway.

I didn't know whether to be amused or wounded, but the day was young and I had a fresh determination to make this work. I figured a change of subject would do us good. "How far is Robert Matthews' house?"

"Just up the road a piece. It won't take us two minutes to get there."

I looked at my watch. "Do you think Garrison is already there?"

"He's there. He just sent me a text."

"What did it say?"

He answered by handing me his phone where the text was still displayed. *You won't believe this*, it read. Excitement rushed over me. I felt like I was on a treasure hunt. An adventure. The thing that felt most like my wheelhouse, but something I hardly got to even dig into for *Parks & Avenues*. "I feel a little like Indiana Jones," I said. "We don't usually go in search of unmarked graves, or *any* graves, for the magazine."

Will chuckled good-naturedly. "I would imagine not. Not *that* magazine, anyway."

"What does *that* mean?"

"It means this kind of story would be perfect for the magazine *here*." He turned the truck onto a driveway much like that of his grandparents'. "Here we go," he said with a wink, which sent an odd flurry of chills along the backs of my legs. "You ready?"

10

Will parked his truck alongside a fairly beat-up Jeep Cherokee, which he told me belonged to Garrison. I opened the door and hopped down to thick, green grass, pulling my purse over my shoulder at the same time. I stepped to the front of both cars and looked up at the structure before me. "*This* is your idea of a log *cabin*?"

Will joined me. "Impressive, isn't it?" He looked at me, cocking his head. "Let me make a suggestion. Put that purse back in the car. You don't need it."

"It has my notebook." I widened my eyes. "Or do you have your phone again?"

"Grab the notebook, ditch the pocketbook."

I complied, but not before sending my eyes skyward, which made him chuckle. After rejoining him, I looked up at the house stretching high into the blue sky and asked, "How big would you say the house is?"

We started walking the path leading to the house.

"Right around four thousand."

"And you know because . . . ?"

"Because Rob is a good friend and he told me."

"Does he live here with his wife? Children?"

"No wife. No children." Will stopped walking and pressed a few numbers on his cell. I looked around. Will had been correct when he'd said Robert Matthews could grow pretty roses. Those framing both sides of the walkway to the front steps were exquisite.

"What are we doing?" I asked, anxious to see the graves.

"I'm trying to reach—*Garrison*? Will. Where are you guys?"

I heard Garrison's muffled voice, followed by Will's, "All right. All right. Be back there in a minute." Will pointed to the right corner of the house. "Over here."

"Where are they?"

"He said if we walk several hundred yards directly behind the large ditch pipes and the Bobcat, we'll find them. Probably hear them before we see them, these woods are so thick."

My heart skipped. "A bobcat?"

Will eyed me quizzically. Then, as understanding registered, he said, "Not the *cat,* bobcat. The *tractor,* Bobcat."

Even with the explanation, I had no idea what he meant. But a few seconds later, after we rounded the corner of the house, I spied something that looked like small farm equipment with the name BOBCAT painted across its side. Two long metal pipes stretched out on the ground beside it. Though the day was still young, the August heat beat down on me, forcing a question: "Are there . . . will there be . . . snakes of any kind?"

"We have a few rattlers around here, but with all the noise we'll be making, I kinda doubt they'll join us. Just watch where you step."

"Wouldn't now be a good time to have that gun?" I asked, sincere as I'd ever been.

Will just snickered and shook his head.

We made it from the clearing around Robert Matthews' cabin to a white tractor caked with dried red mud. On the ground, several dead branches lay haphazardly where thick brambles and brush ran about knee-high. "Careful now," Will said, just as his hand cupped my elbow.

I looked at him, swallowing hard, wondering if he felt the same anxiousness as I. But his eyes were focused straight ahead, as though planning the path we'd take in advance. I looked back to my feet, carefully stepping over fallen tree trunks and broken limbs. Will's hand grew tighter on my elbow. "I—uh. I think I can walk okay . . . without . . ."

"Oh, sure," he said, releasing me, but his eyes stared straight ahead. "We're going to have to weave our way back over there." His chin rose. "There they are," he said. "See them?"

I saw two men, but they were both far enough away that I couldn't swear either of them was Garrison. But, to be affable, I said, "Yes," at the same time as I swatted at a mosquito. Or some such insect.

About that time, Garrison yelled, "Hey, Will! Over here!"

"Coming!" Will shouted back. He pulled at several low-lying branches, snapping them in his hand. He tossed them aside, sending them several feet off the path.

The trees towered over us, blocking out most of the sunlight, which at least brought relief from the moist heat. As they grew denser, the way became less obvious. "There sure are a lot of different kinds of trees out here," I said, even though my thoughts were more on things like spiders. Ticks. Dead people. And while the trees were an obvious and safe subject—walking through them was an entirely different story. Still, Will Decker seemed to have no trouble at all.

"Let's see what's going on back here," William said after a few seconds, as though he'd finally heard me, "and I'll tell you more about the trees later."

Will had been—for the most part since 8:30 that morning—friendly. Still, his simple words left me all the more confused—did he not want to talk to me? Or did he not want to talk about the trees? I hadn't mentioned the trees for a lesson, but if telling me more about them meant building a relationship that would or could make my next six months easier, I supposed I could live with it.

We neared where Garrison stood alongside a man I presumed to be Robert Matthews. He was tall, slender, deeply tanned, and sporting a five o'clock shadow before 10:00 in the morning. Dark hair tousled around his head as though he'd just gotten out of bed. In spite of the heat, he wore a long-sleeved white tee stained by red mud and dirt, jeans, and hiking boots. "Will," he said. He approached us with his hand out.

Will shook his hand and released it before turning to me. "Rob, Ashlynne Rothschild. She's from Florida, working here at the paper for a few months."

Rob Matthews smiled, sending crinkles around almond-colored eyes. His hand shot out as naturally as if we were old friends seeing each other as we always did. Out in the woods. Surrounded by swaying trees. Overgrown shrub. And, somewhere close by—did I mention?—dead people.

I slipped my hand into his and felt the dryness, the calluses along the base of his fingers. A workingman's hands. "Nice to meet you," I said, pulling back as quickly as I could without seeming rude. I waved away pesky creatures buzzing around my face.

Robert nodded once. His eyes sparkled and his mouth broke apart in a picture-perfect smile. "You, too." He returned his attention to Will. "Man, you've got to see this," he said, clapping his friend on the shoulder and turning him around. "I've been trying to get some of this thinned out back here. I'm not sure what I'm going to do with it once I get it all cleared, but it needed to be done."

Garrison and I followed behind. I flipped open my notebook, clicked my pen, and started taking notes, straining to hear as Rob continued.

"Right here," he said, pointing to the ground, "is where I noticed the first stone."

We stopped, gathering in a circle around a lump of granite in the ground.

"I didn't think a whole lot of it," Rob continued, "until I took a few more steps . . ." He pointed to our left. Sure enough, another stone marked the spot. "And then," he said, drawing us along with his words, "I came up on this."

A larger flat piece of granite rose out of the ground at the base of a thick pine. "That's when I realized what all this was." Rob squatted and we did too. He pointed and we followed the line of vision his finger provided.

"Oh, my goodness," I said. "You can actually *see* the outlines of graves."

"Some have sunk about four to six inches, I'm thinking. Others deeper than that." He looked over at me. "Be careful where you step, now."

"Okay," I mouthed.

Will looked up at Garrison. "Did you get some shots?"

Garrison held up a Canon with an impressive lens. "Got 'em, Boss."

The backs of my thighs burned. I stood and, as if on cue, so did the men.

"How many would you say there are?" I asked, keeping my voice at a whisper. Somehow where we stood now seemed sacred. Like a church. Hallowed ground.

"I've counted close to fifty. Maybe sixty." He looked over his shoulder to a ridge in the landscape. "I haven't even gotten over there yet." Then to Will, "Like I was telling Garrison earlier, I found this last night. I would have called then, but figured by the time I got to the house and y'all got here, it'd be around dark-thirty."

Dark-thirty?

He sent a shy smile my way. "I wouldn't want to be out here with all these graves after dark, would you?"

"No," I said. "I sure wouldn't." Creepy enough in the middle of the day. Interesting, but creepy.

Garrison meandered to the ridge. "Will, come check this out over here."

I followed close behind the paper's layout guy, too enthralled by what we were witnessing to care if Will and Rob came or not. But soon enough, I heard the twigs and pinecones crackle beneath their feet.

"Whew," I said, waving my hand in front of my face.

Garrison turned. "What is it?"

I frowned. "I walked into a spider's web I think." I *hoped*. I turned to look at Will. "You don't believe in ghosts, do you?"

One side of Rob's mouth slipped upward. "Why? You think one just touched you?"

Will laughed. "Don't tease with her, Rob. She's a city girl."

Rob brought his hands to his hips. "Never grew up playing in the woods?"

He had *that* right. I gave a playful shake of my head.

Garrison cleared his throat, I suspected to get us back to the task at hand. "Right here . . ." He pointed to the ground. "Rob just told me this was the main road back in the mid- to late 1800s, all the way up to the early 1900s."

I took a step forward and peered to my left. Then to my right. It was obvious; the path below was a well-worn path. Rob came up beside me, his shoulder close to mine. "If you listen, bet you can hear carriages carrying pretty ladies and high-fashioned gents up and down this road. Heading to social calls. To church." He shoved his hands into his pockets, flexed his elbows out as he came up on the balls of his feet.

"Before the Civil War?"

"Before. After. That was *the* road used until somewhere around the 1920s. It was also a trade route. And if you look"—he hopped onto the path, landing with both feet, keeping his hands inside his pockets—"you can still see the ruts." He poked at the ground with his foot.

"Did you get a shot of that?" I asked Garrison.

He grinned so wide his beard seemed to grow. "No, ma'am. But I can." He stepped onto the path, walked a few paces to the left, then turned and said, "Stand right there, Rob."

Will stepped up to the other side of me. I turned my head slowly, knowing full well he was staring at me. "What?" I whispered.

"Since when do you ask Garrison to do anything?"

"Since I saw a good photo op," I answered, keeping my voice low. "Am I right or am I right?"

"You're right," he whispered back. "But don't make a habit of it."

"Well, you're the one who wanted to bring me along . . ." Okay. I got it. I could ask about trees, but I could not suggest a shot.

One hundred and seventy-nine more days . . .

"There's more," Garrison said, interrupting me. He pointed toward the higher ridge. "Over that lump of dirt there, there's a ditch. Rob says this was part of the road from the Revolutionary War."

"That's the one you told me about," I said, wanting to see more. I took a step onto the muddy incline leading to the other road. The slick sole of my shoe made contact with the mud; my backside soon followed. I felt my spine fold like an accordion, heard it crack. "Oww!"

"You hurt?" Will stepped next to me, his question sounding more like an admonishment than concern.

But Rob dashed toward me, reaching for my outstretched hand. "Hey, are you okay?" He pulled me up easily, righting me.

I held one hand up, showing that I'd managed to hold on to my notebook. With the other, I brushed my hand against the back of my jeans and felt the dampness. I grimaced, knowing they were smeared with the same red mud staining Rob's shirt and his Bobcat. "I'm fine." I dared to look into his eyes, afraid I'd find amusement. That there'd be laughter at the klutzy city girl who couldn't walk in the woods without falling down. But his face only wore concern. "I'm fine," I repeated. "Thank you."

Will walked past me, shaking his head. "Wrong kind of shoes."

"I know."

We crossed the path to the ridge and peered over. Deep in a ravine stretched another road—or, what had once been one—now obscured with scrawny trees growing from its soil. Along the borders, sturdier pines and oaks stood like brave soldiers.

"That was a road used during the Revolutionary War?" I asked, nearly breathless.

"You bet," Rob said next to me. "The Overmountain Men used it to get to the Battle of King's Mountain, which was a major victory for the Patriots."

"Yes, I know," I said. I turned to look at the lay of the land behind us. "Could it be that these are the graves of Patriot soldiers?"

"Or Loyalists," Rob said. He smiled at me again, as though he were genuinely happy to have me there. "You know about the Overmountain Men. You like history?"

The same question Will Decker had asked me earlier, but this one came with a smile. And, if I knew tones of voices, an invitation.

"I like learning about new things," I said.

"You don't say. Well, how about—"

"Rob," Will interrupted, "let's see if we can't run to the hardware store, get some irrigation flags, and start numbering these graves. From here I can see about six rows, maybe running ten graves in length."

"Far more than that," Rob said, leaving my side to join Will. "You're not counting that area over there." Their voices faded as they walked away from where Garrison and I remained. Whatever Robert Matthews had been about to ask me had been forgotten.

"Hey, Garrison," I said. "Can you get a good shot of the road below from up here?"

"Absolutely."

I looked back to see how far Will and Rob had gotten out of earshot. "Would you do that for me?" Then, as an afterthought, I said, "Please?"

"Yes, ma'am," he answered. "I'm right on it."

I felt a smile rise from my toes. *These* were words I was accustomed to. They weren't from Will Decker, but they'd do.

For now.

11

See what you can find out about Native Americans in the area," Will said as we rambled back to the newspaper office. "Look up Overmountain Men. See if there's any record *anywhere* of even so much as a skirmish near Rob's place."

I took notes as fast as my pen would jot. While I mentally wondered if today should not have been the day for me to work on the magazine, *this* brought too much excitement to ignore. "What about Civil War battles?"

"No."

My skin prickled, knowing good and well if *he* had thought of it, I'd be writing it down. "And why not?"

"Because none of the Civil War battles were fought around here. *No* where around here."

Oh. Well, that made sense.

"Then what about slaves?"

Will didn't answer right away. Although his hat's brim shadowed his eyes, I could still see his eyes remained focused on the road.

"Will?"

"Slaves?"

"Yeah. North Carolina had slave owners, right? Ergo, slaves? Could those graves belong to slaves?"

"Maybe," he said. "Could be."

The air in the truck's cab changed, as if a wall had been built, brick by brick.

Frustration grew inside me as easily as I had allowed my own defenses to drop. How was I supposed to prove myself to my family, by proving myself to William, if he constantly shut me and my ideas down? "What's wrong?"

He returned to his silence, forcing me into it. I stared at him as long as I dared, then turned to the front of the truck. When we pulled into the newspaper parking lot, Will turned off the truck and said, "I'll call the historical society. See what I can find out."

I had a sudden vision of the grave discovery and its historical implications as the cover story of the magazine's first edition. "When do you think I'll have all the information to write the piece?" I asked, trying to keep an innocent tone in my voice.

"You?" He opened his door. I opened mine.

"Yeah," I said over the truck's hood. "It would be a great cover story for *Hunting Teas*."

Will snickered as he shook his head. "You might want to learn the name of the magazine before you think about writing for it. Besides, before it makes a great story for the magazine, it will make a great story for the paper." He continued toward the door. "Besides, this requires someone who knows how to write about Testament and North Carolina. *Our* history."

I followed right behind him, determined—for once—not to shrink in the face of rejection. "Will Decker! I *know* how to write. I've been writing full-time since I got out of college and joined the illustrious staff of *Parks & Avenues*." Not to mention my work on my alma mater's newsletter.

"And I'm sure you're quite good at it." He swung the door open, stepping back to allow me to enter. "When it comes to *your* people and *your* history."

"Let me ask you a question. What did you *think* I was going to do here for six months?" I tried to keep my voice low. "Run behind you with a notebook and a pen? Bring you your coffee? Hang that hat you can't seem to go without on a hat rack?"

"I never asked you to bring me coffee. Or hang up my hat." He jerked it off his head as though to prove his point.

"I'm sure you will before the day is over." We were halfway down the hall, both unable to keep our voices from rising. And mine, in spite of Gram's constant voice inside my head reminding me that if I were not careful, I'd find myself in the mailroom. Or worse. "The coffee," I said, trying to regain control. "Not the hat."

"William."

The baritone voice stopped us. We both turned to where Shelton Decker peered around one of the office doors.

"Hey, Big Guy," Will said, though he stayed perfectly still. "You decided to come in a little early today."

"Mr. Decker," I said.

"Can I see you in my office?" he asked.

"Yes, sir." William started toward him. His back muscles flexed.

"You, too," Shelton said, looking at me.

I felt like I'd been called up to the principal's office, not that I ever had been. But I'd heard about it. Read about it. Seen it in the movies and on TV. "Yes, sir," I said, repeating Will's words.

We stepped into a small office, sparsely furnished, and barely decorated. Another room Bobbie hadn't gotten to, apparently. Or, perhaps, wasn't *allowed* to put her touch to.

Shelton Decker closed the door behind us, walked around to his desk and sat. Will and I, on the other hand, hadn't moved since we'd stepped into the room. "Sit. Sit," he told us, indicating two chairs on the opposite side of his desk.

We did, both choosing the same chair. I adjusted, taking the other.

"Now then," he said, pushing a few pieces of paper aside. He picked up a pen and clicked it several times. "What seems to be the problem?"

"Nothing, Big Guy. There's no problem."

"Didn't sound like it from in here." He brought his attention to me. "Ashlynne? Want to tell me what's going on?"

I sighed. Chewed on the inside of my lip a second or two. Sighed again and tried to weigh out my choices. Option one: tell him the truth. Ask Shelton Decker to *make* Will Decker let me play the way I wanted. With a few choice words, I'd have the story we were on for the magazine, rather than Will for the paper. And wouldn't *that* make for a grand first edition of the newly reprised publication.

Option two: take the same road his grandson had chosen. Say nothing and hope the gesture would encourage Will to *let* me play.

"Nothing," I said. "We're just trying to decide the best way to write this piece we've been out getting the initial story on."

"And what piece is that?"

I looked at Will. He placed his hat at the end of his lap near his knee. "Big Guy, Rob Matthews found some unmarked graves over on his land last night."

"Unmarked?"

"There are stones," I said. "But nothing saying who is buried in the graves."

"You don't say? Hunh." Then to Will, "How many are we looking at here, son?"

"I'm venturing about a hundred."

Shelton Decker tapped the pen several times on a legal pad. "What's your strategy?"

It was Will's turn to sigh. "I've asked Ashlynne to do a little research for me. Look up Native Americans in our area. But I'm leaning toward another thought."

"Which is?"

"Ferguson ran through this area just before the Battle of King's Mountain. I know that much from every local history class and Boy Scout field trip."

My eyes slid from Will to Shelton Decker and back to Will.

"Right, right," Shelton said. "Go on."

"What I want Ashlynne to find out," he said, smiling at me, albeit forced, "is whether or not any skirmishes before King's Mountain took place near here."

I cleared my throat. "I also wondered about slaves. Could Rob Matthew's land be a place where slaves had been buried?"

Shelton's brow shot up. "Could be." He tapped on the pad a few more times. "Will, call the historical society."

"I had already planned on it."

"And the courthouse. See what's there. But here's what I want you two to do. I want you *both* to research it and I want you *both* to write it up. One for the magazine and one for the newspaper. Let's let the two publications play off each other a little. And, for heaven's sake, let's make sure we don't rush here."

I sucked in my breath in anticipation as Will exhaled in exasperation.

"And call Rob. Tell him not to go spouting off, you hear?"

"Yes, sir."

"We've got to be careful. If we say too much too fast, we'll have every ghostbuster and soothsayer out there descending on his property. Not to mention any number of rights activists."

I hadn't thought of that.

"Yes, sir," Will said. "Is that all?"

"For now."

We both stood. Will stepped back so I could walk to the door ahead of him. When I reached it, I looked over my shoulder at Shelton Decker and smiled. "Thank you, Mr. Decker," I said.

He nodded. "See you at the story meeting, children."

"See you, Big Guy."

I turned to leave, but Shelton Decker's voice stopped me. "Ashlynne?"

Both Will and I looked back.

"Yes?" I swallowed. "Sir?"

"You seem to have a little something on your 'get-along.'"

I ran my hand along my backside. "Yes, sir," I said with a frown. "Mud." I looked at Will. "I need better shoes, apparently."

William gave the faintest grin as we started back out the door and for that briefest of seconds, I felt his approval.

"And William?"

We looked back again. "Yes, sir."

"Leave the door open, will ya?"

I sat at my desk, opened my purse, and pulled several items from inside, including the notepad and my cell phone. The latter showed I had several missed calls. "That's weird."

"What?" Will asked from his desk.

"I've missed several calls, but I never heard my phone ring."

"Oh, yeah," he said. He booted his computer and flipped through a few pages of a legal pad. "That happens up here sometimes."

"Leigh . . ." I looked at Will, pointing the face of my phone at him. "My best friend. She's called seven times and left a bunch of text messages."

Will didn't respond.

"Do you mind if I call her back?"

He glanced at me. "Yeah, yeah. But keep it short, okay? We've got this story and several others to do before the story meeting today."

"Sure," I said. Did that mean I would actually write one of them? Or was he going to give me time to work on resurrecting the magazine?

I hurried to the break room, passing Alma on the way. She looked busy, but I said hello, she said hello back. I poured a cup of coffee for myself and dialed Leigh's number, but it didn't ring. After I finished preparing my coffee, I walked into the growing heat outside and dialed again. This time, no problem.

"What is going on up there?" Leigh asked by way of answering.

"My phone . . . it didn't ring. I don't know why."

"You *promised* to call me last night. Remember? As soon as you got home? I waited and waited and finally fell asleep. When I woke up this morning and you still hadn't called—"

"Oh, Leigh. I'm so sorry. Really. I was so tired last night. I collapsed as soon as I got back to the cottage."

"I almost called your father. *That's* how worried I was."

"Ohhhh. Noooo. I'm glad you didn't."

"So? What's going on? You said something about a *him* when we talked on Sunday."

Sunday. That had been two days ago. Had it only been *two* days? "William Decker. He's the grandson of the people I came up here to work with." I swallowed. "For."

"Oh?"

"Yeah. I don't think he *wants* me here. But I only feel that way sometimes." I looked past the low-lying stores and various businesses to the landscape beyond—the rolling hills and eventual mountains. "What I mean is, sometimes I think he doesn't want me here and other times I think he's okay with it."

"Did he come right out and tell you that? That he doesn't want you there?"

"No. Never. I don't think that's his style. And, like I said, sometimes he actually acts pretty decent. But even that's like . . . it's like he says or does something nice and then he realizes he's said or done something nice and he kind of takes it back. And it's like . . . like he's holding something against me. Me personally. But until Sunday I'd never met him."

"Is he good-looking?"

I laughed. "Leigh." Seriously . . .

"Is he?"

"Yeah . . . yeah, I guess so." I took a sip of coffee. "Okay, he is actually. But that has nothing to do with it."

"Oh, Ash. You haven't dated in so long, you've forgotten one of the first rules of attraction."

Okay. I would bite. "Which is?"

"That when a guy likes you, he acts like he doesn't."

I shook my head. "Yeah. *If he's in fifth grade.*"

Leigh chuckled. "Hey, kiddo. I know you. How are you doing with that? The not-being-fully-accepted part?"

I closed my eyes against the struggle. "I'm doing all right. Besides, he's only one person."

An important "one person," but still only one.

"You still think you can make it six months?"

"Do I have a choice? I want Dad's position. If I have to deal with Dr. Jekyll and Mr. Hyde for six months, then so be it." The sun dipped behind a cloud, turning the mountains to French-blue. "Look, I've got to get back inside. We're on a big story and I think it might help me figure a cover story for the first issue of *Grounds & Parties*. I'll keep you posted, okay?"

"Okay." She sounded disappointed that our conversation was coming to such a quick end. "But can you call me later? I miss you."

"I will," I answered. "You know I miss you too."

And I did. More than as a best friend; more like a sister.

I spent the rest of the morning researching, not even breaking for lunch. At 2:00, Will informed me that we had another story. According to a tip from Alma, Sean Flannery, brother of Sarah, whom we'd interviewed the day before, had made some fairly magnificent plays on the practice field. "Word is," William said as we headed to his truck, "several colleges are going to be looking at him early on. Alma's covering one side of it, but wants me—*us*—to cover another angle."

He opened the truck door for me and I climbed in.

Something I found myself getting uncommonly used to.

"And that's a good thing, right?" I asked as the truck door slammed. And if it were, could I use a story like this one, too, for the magazine? I knew we would look at *hunting* and I knew something with *teas* would be involved. But should I also consider football?

Will ran around the back of the truck. He opened the driver's door. "*And that's a good thing*?" he asked, hoisting himself up and in. "Listen. In a small Southern town there are three things you pay attention to. For clarity, I'll call them 'The Three Fs.'"

"The Three Fs."

"That's right."

"And they are?"

"The first is faith. Here in Testament, *everybody* goes to church. You can be Baptist. You can be Methodist. Presbyterian. Catholic, Jewish, or Pentecostal. You can even be a snake handler. Doesn't matter. But you go to church on Sunday, Wednesday-night supper if your church offers it, and prayer meeting. No matter what night of the week they hold it."

I hoped he was kidding about the snake-handling part. "Where do you go?"

"To church?"

"Yeah."

"Cabbot's Creek Baptist."

I wondered if he wore his hat in the house of God. "And the second F?"

"The second is family. Only *God* comes before family and, by the way, *friends*—when they're good friends—*are* family."

"Should I assume then that you and Rob Matthews are like family?"

"You bet. All the way back to diapers."

I tried to picture that but feared I'd break into laughter. I took a deep breath and said, "The third?"

"The third is *football*."

Aha.

"You do *not*," he finished, "want to miss a home game."

I pulled my seat belt around me with a smile, happy to know I may be on to something when it came to living in Testament, and more than I imagined I could be in two short days. "Faith. Family. Football. Got it." I swallowed the smile.

He pointed at me. "Don't make fun."

"I'm not." And I wasn't.

"Mmhmm."

"I wasn't—I . . . um." I ran my tongue between my lips and felt the seat belt. "Hey."

He looked at me. "Hey."

I pulled at the seat belt, let it slide back across me. "Thank you for cleaning it up."

His smile grew lopsided at first, full within a second. "Just took a little Goof Off."

I had no idea what that meant, but I smiled back anyway. "Still. Thanks."

I'd just finished off a light dinner of pita chips and hummus when my cell phone rang. "Leigh," I said out loud. "Dollars to donuts."

But it wasn't Leigh and I didn't recognize the number lighting up the caller ID. "Hello?"

"Ashlynne?"

The male voice sounded familiar, but not one I fully recognized. "It is. Who is this?"

A light chuckle came from the other end. "You met me today. Rob. Robert Matthews."

I smiled, remembering the kind man with mischievous eyes, who owned a spooky piece of property and an impressive house. "Oh, yeah. Hi." I sat on the living room sofa. "How are you?"

"I'm good. I'm not calling too late, am I?"

I flipped the Juicy Couture bracelet watch dangling from my wrist so that its face pointed upward—only eight o'clock. "Uh, no."

"Some people like to go to bed early, you know."

Not anyone I knew. But I said, "Last night I fell asleep before I even ate dinner." I smiled as I spoke. *Like this, Gram? Is this how it's done?* "Is everything okay?"

"Yeah. I . . . uh . . . I got a call from Will. He says his grandpa said I shouldn't say anything to anybody for the time being. Is that right?"

"Yes, it is." I crossed my legs. "Mr. Decker wants to make sure you're not overrun by the crazies."

"Like ghost hunters and things like that, Will said."

"Yes."

"Hey . . . uh . . . did the mud come out of your jeans?"

"I don't know yet. I've got them soaking in the downstairs bathroom sink. I probably should have come right back and changed, but . . ." Where was this going? "But it didn't look as bad as I thought it would."

He laughed nervously. "You're probably wondering why I'm calling."

He had that right. "It's crossed my mind."

"Well . . . uh . . . I just wanted to see if . . . would you like to go out? Say Friday night?"

I paused long enough to allow the words to replay themselves. Was he asking me out? Like, on a date? "I'm sorry, what?" Leigh had been correct when she'd said it'd been a long time. More than six months to be exact, and even that had been a benefit dinner with a friend. Not even a close friend. Just someone I felt safe to call and say, "Would you like to go with me to a benefit dinner," and know he'd say "yes." For no other reason than for the free meal.

"Would you—"

"—like on a date?"

"Yeah. I mean, if there's someone you're serious with in your hometown . . ."

"No." I laughed again. "No, there's no one. And yes, I'd be pleased to go out with you on Friday night." I remembered then what Will had said about Friday nights and football. "Will we go to a football game?"

"Football starts *next* Friday," he said, now a little more animated. "I was thinking dinner. There's a great place not too far from here. A restaurant on Lake Lure. You'll like it, I think."

It sounded lovely. "I'm sure I will. What time?"

"Pick you up around seven?"

"That would be wonderful. I'm sure you know where I live."

"Yes, ma'am."

Ma'am? But before I could make a comment, a thought occurred to me. "How did you get my number, by the way?"

He chuckled. "I called Will."

A funny sort of melancholy fell over me. "And he gave you my number?"

"Hope that's okay."

"It's fine." Giving away phone numbers without asking permission was not something anyone I knew would do. But, in an effort to get along . . . "I'll . . . um . . . see you on Friday evening about seven."

We ended our conversation and I stared at the phone for several long moments. I had a date. A man I'd just met had called and asked me out. Had actually called someone else to get my number so he could do so.

But why? Did he find me pretty, perhaps? Or smart? Or did he simply feel sorry for me that I'd fallen on his property . . .

He *had* asked about my jeans.

Or maybe he felt sorry for the new girl.

And, if he did, was feeling "sorry for" built on the same intention as out-and-out rejection?

12

Will's truck was not in the parking lot on Wednesday. Nor was he in the office when I walked in carrying my purse and briefcase in one hand and a potted plant I'd picked up from a street vendor in the other.

"Is William already out on assignment?" I asked, setting the plant on the nearest corner of my desk.

"He's putting in a half day off," Alma told me from her desk. "Called in a little while ago."

"Is he sick?" I opened a bottom drawer I'd previously emptied and dropped my purse and briefcase into it.

"Oh, no. He's just taking some time off because of overtime."

My brow furrowed. "Overtime?"

"Yeah," she said, standing. "We're not supposed to work more than forty hours a week. Didn't they tell you that when you got here?"

"Yeah, I just didn't realize . . ."

She sashayed across the room to my side. "Where'd you get that?" she asked, pointing to the plant.

I smiled. "Street vendor. Saw it on my way in and thought it would brighten things up in here a little."

"Or kill the poor thing," she said. "I know if I were a plant, in here is *not* where I'd want to be."

"I'm hoping the fluorescent lighting will be good for it. If not, I'll take it home." I looked at William's desk. Oddly, I missed his being there. Of course, now I would be able to get preliminary work done on the magazine, but somehow, having him close by . . . "William told me about the forty hours a week, but nothing about how we take time off."

"Oh," she said with a toss of her curls, "we don't just *not* come in. You'll need to let Will know. See, Mister Shelton doesn't want any of us putting in more than forty hours a week. He says working more than that is no way to have a family, a friend, *or* a life. William knows he'll put in hours on Saturday—so will you, by the way—and that means something has to get cut during the week."

I slid the plant closer to the top corner of the desk. "So should I have not come in this morning?"

She held up her hands as though in surrender. "I have no idea. Not my job, girl, to keep up with you when I can barely keep up with Alma." Her words held no sting. She smiled too wide for that and her eyes sparkled. She touched the sleeve of the Burberry blouse I wore with a simple pair of Diane von Furstenberg black slacks. "You sure do have some pretty clothes," she said. "And my bet is they're not cheap."

No, they weren't. Not that I would say that. Even *I* knew better. So I said nothing, because if I did, would that mean I had to say she had pretty clothes too? When clearly, she needed my expertise in the worst way . . . as badly as I needed hers. "Say, Alma," I said, pulling out my chair and sitting. "I'll bet there are some nice places around here to walk."

"You mean, like, hike?"

"Yes."

"All over. Yes, ma'am. You can start right there at the Deckers' place. They've got all kinds of trails in the woods around their home. Then there's Rails to Trails. That comes through here. And, of course, you've got all the hiking trails at Chimney Rock."

"Is that close to Testament?"

"Very."

I looked at my feet, shod in an unadorned pair of Dolce Vita black pumps. "I really, *really* need the right kind of shoes," I said, looking back at her. "Where should I go for something like that?"

"In Testament?"

"Yes."

"Nowhere." She pulled Will's chair out from under his desk and sat in it. I crossed my legs, but I noticed that Alma kept both feet on the floor. So like her personality and so unlike mine. She was solid. Somehow, even with all life had afforded me, I was like a bird with one leg pulled up, easily toppled over in the right breeze. Which may be precisely why Gram and Dad had sent me here in the first place.

"Now, if I were you," Alma continued, "I'd go over to Chimney Rock, to a place called Bubba O'Leary's. They've got what you need. In fact, they've got everything from shoes to clothes to penny candy to Old Mule barbecue sauce."

I grabbed a pen from the middle drawer of my desk, along with a sticky-note pad. "And it's not far from here?"

"Not at all."

"Do you know the address?"

"Not off the top of my head, but it's right there in the middle of downtown, where Chimney Rock Park is." She chuckled as she stood. "Look it up, girl. You can find it on your computer, I'm sure." She started toward her desk, then turned. "Want coffee? 'Cause I'm going that way."

"Do we have any tea in the break room?"

"Tea? In a newspaper office? Not that I know of."

"Coffee then," I said, making myself a mental note to bring some with me the next day.

Alma left the room, and me, in silence. I booted my laptop, signed in to my new *Testament Tribune* account, and found, on the top of a short stack of e-mails, one from WillDecker2@TheTestamentTribune.net. It came with an attachment.

I opened the e-mail, wondering at the "2" in his name.

> Hey there.
> I'm taking the morning off, but I need you to open these attachments. They're the forms we have folks fill out for upcoming wedding announcements, nuptials, engagements, registries, and things that make girls get all tingly.

I frowned at the insinuation, but continued reading.

> Go back to last week's Thursday edition and look at how I've written these things up in the past. I'm sure you'll do fine at the assignment since you're such a good writer. Meanwhile, if you need me, call. My cell number is below my signature.
> See you around 1:00.
>
> W.
> Oh, yeah. I gave Rob your phone number last night. Hope that's okay.

Alma returned with two mugs of coffee. One she placed on her desk, the other she brought to mine. "Just the way you like it."

"Thank you." I peered at it. Indeed, it appeared "just the way I liked it" and it smelled heavenly. Alma walked back to her desk as I clicked the Reply tab on Will's e-mail.

> Hey back at you.
> Got it. So glad you're ready to admit I'm a good writer, even though you haven't read a word I've written, I'm sure. (Insert smiley face here.)
> And, yes. He called. Funny that you have *my* cell number but I didn't have yours until two seconds ago. How is that, exactly?
> Ashlynne Rothschild

I reread the e-mail before hitting Enter, a lifesaving trick I'd learned years ago. When I got to my name, I deleted it, replacing it with A.R., thinking the initials made me look and sound friendlier. More like a colleague ready to enter the trenches versus Constance Rothschild's granddaughter, who—let's be honest—got her job because of *who* she was, not *what* she could do. Oh, I'd had to prove myself, all right, and I knew I'd have to do the same again. Here. In Testament.

But even still, I didn't like the initials. They were too friendly and not professional *enough*. So, I returned to the previous "Ashlynne Rothschild" and hit Send.

I opened the first attachment. There were two forms used by the paper for weddings from the past weekend. Both of those came with photos scanned into the form. The second attachment contained a form for new engagements, which included where the couple would be registered.

This particular couple, the form noted, had registered at a local store called The Village Hut.

I printed the forms, then walked to the back room to get the previous Thursday's copy of the paper, my mind already forming the wedding and anniversary society column in *Teas and Guns*. When I returned, Alma said, "So, what'd you think of our star football player yesterday?"

"Well," I said, crossing my arms, leaving the newspaper in my hand hanging at my side. "I'm not really one who knows a lot about football. But from what I could see, he's pretty good."

"Pretty good?" Alma shook her head. "Girl, that boy is a running back heading straight for the Heisman trophy."

I smiled weakly. "I don't know what that means, Alma."

Alma threw up her hands. "You don't know—girl, please." She placed a hand over her chest. "My heart cannot take this kind of blasphemy."

I laughed at her hyperbole. "Oh, Alma. We just . . . where I went to school, we didn't have a football team, so I never got into the sport. My dad loved it, but my mother only tolerated it. Most Sunday afternoons during the season she and I went shopping or to the movies with Gram while Dad and Papa stayed home and watched the game."

"Mmm—mmm—mmm." Alma shook her head slowly. "So you really had no idea what you were looking at yesterday, did you?"

"No. Sorry."

"Don't apologize." She crossed her arms over an ample middle. "Did you ask Will Decker for clarity if you had any questions?"

My whole being frowned. "Absolutely not." For one, I'd never give him that kind of ammunition, seeing as one of the Fs was *football*. But, even more so . . . "To be honest, I sort of had my mind on the story we were working on from yesterday morning."

"I see. Well, if you have *any* questions whatsoever, you come talk to Alma," she said, pointing to herself with a coral-polished fingernail.

I smiled. "I will." I headed back to my desk.

"You going to the scrimmage game on Friday night?"

I turned. "Scrimmage?"

"That's football talk, I guess you could say. It means 'practice.' Are you going to the *practice* game on Friday?"

"I didn't know there was one." When Rob had called, he said something about going out to dinner, but nothing about a game. But, according to Will, *football* ranked above *food* in Testament, so . . . "I've got a dinner date, actually."

Alma gave me an all-knowing look. "Well, now. Look at you, Miss Fancy Pants and Swanky Blouses. Here not even a week and you've got yourself a date."

My cheeks grew hot. "I wonder why Rob didn't say something about the game," I said to the floor. Then, to Alma, "What'd you call it? Skirmage?"

"Oh, Lawd. Lawd. *Scrimmage*."

I nodded. "Got it. Scrimmage." I sent another smile her way, already figuring that if I chose the game over dinner—which I preferred—I would win brownie points with the folks I'd been sent to live with for six months. "Thanks, Alma." I waved the newspaper at her. "I'd better get this done before William gets here."

"Mmhmm."

I stood next to my car in the parking lot and called Rob's number—the one he'd called from the night before—during my lunch break. The call went straight to voice mail. "Hey, Rob," I said. "It's Ashlynne

Rothschild. Hey, um . . ." I sighed. Not loud enough to sound as though I were exasperated, but more to myself. "I hate voice mail. I always end up rambling. So, let me try to get to the point . . ." The phone beeped, telling me my time had run out. I held my cell phone out, looked at it as though it were a new contraption, then brought it back to my ear. An automated voice informed me that my recording time was up, but I could press "1" for more options.

Which I did.

"One" allowed me to either send with normal delivery by pressing "star" or to note as urgent by pressing "pound."

Well, my message was *hardly* urgent. I pressed the "star" key.

I hung up and called again. When the voice mail recording began, I giggled like a schoolgirl and said, "Me again. Not much of a recording time you have there. Usually, when I call my friends or my family, I get about two and a half minutes. Three tops. But for some reason, I got cut o—" The phone beeped again.

"For crying out loud," I said as I pressed "star."

I hung up. Started again.

"Rob? Ashlynne. For the third time. I'm so sorry . . . I wanted to ask you a question about Friday night. I understand there's going to be a . . ." What was the word Alma used? Oh, heaven help me. "A um . . . well, a practice game and—" *Ugh.*

Again I repeated the steps. I happened to be a magna cum laude graduate of one of the top colleges in the country. I'd won awards in school and in my work. How could a simple voice mail possibly get the best of me?

I drew in a breath and called Rob for what I determined to be the final time. At least for today.

"Rob. Ashlynne. Call me," I said, then ended the pain of my humiliation.

I left the office for lunch a few minutes before noon. I didn't know much about where I was going on my own, but I figured if I could drive in the city of Orlando, I could certainly find my way around Testament.

Within minutes I was on Main Street, driving down the same road I'd driven up on Sunday. Diagonally parked cars in front of old brick buildings, the large pots brimming over with colorful flowers, and the occasional wrought-iron bench charmed me once again. I inched along, looking for a place to eat and a place to park, until I caught sight of Will's truck on the opposite side of the street. I whipped my head around to see if he was in it. Or about to hop out of it as he'd done before.

He wasn't, on both accounts.

A white Toyota slid out of the space in front of me. I stopped, waited, and pulled in. I got out of my car, pushed the key fob to lock it just as one of the storefront doors from the opposite side of the street opened. Will Decker strolled out. I opened my mouth to say hello, but he seemed to be in a hurry so I clamped my lips together.

He jogged across the street to where his truck waited. Instinctively, I felt he wouldn't want me to see him. I hurried to the door directly in front of me, taking no notice of the type of establishment I entered. A handwritten note on a pink index card read: PUSH HARD, so I pressed my thumb down on the handle and jerked the door forward . . .

. . . and walked right into an intimately charming nail salon with lavender painted walls, pink frilly wreaths, and porcelain face wall-hangings. A round antique oak table flanked the entryway. An arrangement of silk flowers dominated its center. Beneath that, flyers from local businesses had been fanned.

Well, hello.

A pretty blonde, who sat at her station working on an older woman's fingernails, looked up at me. "Can I help you?"

"Uh . . ." I pointed to the sidewalk and street beyond the door. "I just happened to park here. I'm new in town and I'd like to make an appointment for Friday, if possible?"

Another woman—slightly older and carrying a stack of pink and lavender towels—entered the room from the back.

"Erin, can you help this lady? She wants to make an appointment for Friday."

Erin dropped the towels onto an unused workstation with a smile. "Have you been here before?"

"No. I'm new here to Testament." I followed Erin to the glass-and-oak display case, which held a variety of polishes and lotions. A cash register and an opened appointment book nearly covered the top.

"Friday?"

"Yes." Alma had said I would need to take time off to balance the forty-hour workweek. I picked Friday morning, already apprehensive of Will saying, "No, that doesn't work for me." After all, it would be a *Friday.* The day before the weekend. I'd not worked a full week in a newspaper office, but I could bet he'd say that Fridays were not to be missed. While I didn't want to cause a problem—or any more than I already had—I wanted my nails done the morning of my date with Rob.

"How about ten o'clock?"

"That's perfect," I said with a smile. Gram had instructed me that to connect to people, make deliberate eye contact and hold the gaze. "The simple gesture," she said to me on my first day at the magazine, "says you care. That you're interested in them, more than anything else, as a person first."

I sought out the woman's eyes.

Erin's locked with mine. "Is everything okay?"

"Yes, why?"

Her expression became suspicious. "Do I have something in my eyes?" She stuck her fingers to the inside corners of her eyes as though clearing away the "sleep."

"Oh. No." Would I *ever* get this right? I pointed to the appointment book. "Ten o'clock?"

"Yes, if that works for you."

"It's perfect."

"Your name?"

"Ashlynne. A-S-H-L-Y-N-N-E. Ashlynne Rothschild."

Erin picked up a pencil and wrote my name in the tiny box. "And you're new here?"

"Yes, I am."

"So you don't have a preference for technicians?"

"No. But can you put me down for a mani *and* a pedi?"

Erin smiled, brought her eyes to mine and held them there. "Yes, ma'am, I sure will."

I smiled at the elongation of the last word, spoken as though she'd said "wheel," and at the fact she called *me* "ma'am."

"See you Friday, then," I said, then thanked the blonde on my way out to the sidewalk, the warm sunshine, and the large primary-colored building across the way. The one William Decker had walked out of a few minutes earlier.

I read the sign and bit my bottom lip. What had he been doing . . . *there*?

13

I shot across the street, darting between the cars that eased along Main Street, and into *Testament Children's Museum.* Everything about the exterior—from the primary paint colors to the storefront window displays of framed elementary art—shouted the joy and innocence of childhood.

What was a man like William Decker doing here? He'd not been married *nor* did he have children. That much I felt fairly certain about. An even greater mystery was why I cared. But I did. I had felt unable to figure the man out since I'd arrived—his hot-to-cold-to-hot attitude toward me. Hopefully, knowing more about him would provide the insight I needed to successfully complete my six-month trial period and prove myself.

Or, was I already serving a sentence?

Walking in and simply asking questions like the journalist I had trained to be could be tricky. I was the stranger in town. William's family had practically laid the cornerstone of the town.

Or so I imagined.

Any wrong move would cost me; that much was for sure. I had to play it safe. Play it . . . how did people used to say it? Play it cool?

I went inside where open spaces were filled with various displays—science, art, geography, a reading corner—and the joyous laughter and chatter of about a dozen children met me. Blue walls had been stamped with child-sized handprints, each in a different primary color. "Wow," I said, turning to take it all in. I'd not been around a lot of children, but I'd reported on the special events for children at the Winter Park Arts Festival, on the grand opening of upscale children's stores along Park Avenue, and on unique classes held for the children of our fair city.

I'd even been a child once.

But . . . this was a special, special place. *Come . . . Dream . . . Create,* it all but shouted.

A woman dressed in khaki slacks, a white tee, and a blue bib apron approached. She appeared to be no more than twenty. Twenty-one tops. "May I help you?" she asked, though it sounded more like "May I halp ya?"

I put on my best smile and said, "I'm new in town and just happened to be passing by." I gave the room a wide sweep with my eyes. "I'm wondering if you can tell me a little more about what you do here."

"Well," she said, elevating her voice so as to be heard above the rise in clatter. "First off, my name is Kate. And you are . . . ?"

"Ashlynne," I said, extending my hand. "Ashlynne Rothschild."

"Welcome to Testament Children's Museum," she said, as though she'd rehearsed the words to perfection. She took a few steps to a table, picked up a brochure, and handed it to me. "We're a nonprofit organization dedicated to bringing joy and fun to the education of young children. We want them to become excited about learning at *this* stage of life so that, when they become older, they will carry that thrill all the way to college."

Definitely rehearsed. "So then, these children . . ." I looked past Kate to where girls and boys interacted with the displays. "Is being here a part of their school day?" Because, hadn't school *just* started? And weren't field trips rare during the first weeks?

"Most of the kids here today," she said, nodding toward them, "are homeschooled. The public and private school kids won't start making field trips until a couple of weeks from now."

"Oh, I see." Again I looked at the children, doing my best to come up with a way to ask why Will Decker had been inside the building earlier. Why would an adult male, with no children of his own, or nieces or nephews that I knew of come inside the museum?

Unless, of course, he had been working on a story.

No . . . he'd taken the morning off. At least, that's what Alma had said.

"Where are their parents right now?" I asked, mainly for something to ask.

Kate laughed lightly. "They're in the back. We have some classes to help homeschool parents with their sometimes overwhelming task of teaching."

Great answer. If only it helped with my real question. "And you're nonprofit?"

"Oh, yes, ma'am."

That word again. *Ma'am.* I bit my lip, thinking. "Oh!" *Eureka.* "Are you a volunteer or are you employed here?"

"No, ma'am. I volunteer a couple of mornings a week when I don't have classes over at the community college. Everyone except the program director is a volunteer."

I turned ever so slightly toward the sidewalk and street. "I . . . uh . . . I noticed a man in a cowboy hat walking out earlier . . ."

The girl pinked. She actually *pinked.* "That's Will Decker."

"Is *he* a volunteer?"

"Oh, yes. He's one of those who doesn't mind actually sitting down with the kids. He comes in once a week to read over there at the reading corner." She pointed to the area with brightly colored carpet, yellow and red cubbies filled with primary readers, and posters advertising the importance of reading. "You should see him," she continued, looking back at me. "He does all the character voices. The kids just love him."

Cowboy Willy? I could hardly imagine. "Really," I said, more as a statement than a question.

"Mmhmm. He's also one of our best financial contributors. And, of course, his granddaddy and grandmama, too. This was Miss Bobbie's brainchild some years back, but it didn't get off the ground until about four years ago."

"How about that . . . ," I said, though my words were not referring so much to Bobbie Decker's great idea as to her grandson reading to children on his time off. Well, I would have never guessed *that* one.

"May I ask?" she said, three words that filled me with dread. "Would *you* like to volunteer?"

Working—whether for pay or as a volunteer—with children had never been something I'd thought to do. But, what I could imagine was doing a story on the museum after the magazine came out. Perhaps holding a type of fund-raiser and covering it. Maybe even making it part of the first issue. I raised a finger as though I were pointing to the lightbulb going off over my head. "I know that the Deckers own the newspaper . . ."

"Oh, yes, ma'am."

"Have they ever done a story on the museum?"

I received a beautiful—albeit "What planet did you come from?"—smile. "Of course." The smile returned, weaker than before. "Like I said, this was Miss Bobbie's idea to start with."

I shook my head lightly. "Of course. I—I'm actually working at the newspaper, you see. Helping to restart an old magazine the Deckers had with my grandparents."

"Does that mean you don't want to volunteer?"

"Oh, no. It just means that I thought a piece on the museum would be wonderful for the magazine."

Kate stared at me. She didn't blink, she didn't speak, she just stared. From the back of the room, the voices of the children seemed to elevate, even as I felt myself drawn into a tunnel of familiar yet uncomfortable feelings. My skin tingled. My head swam. How did people *do* this? How do they connect so easily? How had Gram and Dad and Mom always made it appear so effortless? And why couldn't I *get* it?

I swallowed. "I'd love to volunteer," I said around the knot in my throat, knowing good and well I'd just as soon have a molar pulled. Not that I ever had, but Gram told me once about getting a crown on a back tooth and how awful the whole process had been.

Kate's smile once again spread across her face. "Well then, let me get you a form to fill out."

"Thank you," I said.

"You're welcome, Miss Ashlynne."

Miss Ashlynne.

I'd been beat by a twenty-year-old, twenty-one if she were a day. I'd come in planning to wheedle *Miss Kate* out of information on Will, and I was leaving with yet another job to do. A volunteer job no less, one that would put me directly in the path of people with whom I would have little to nothing in common.

I swallowed again. Blew out a pent-up breath.

Oh, boy.

After my lunch hour—and a meal I didn't get to eat—Will and I left the office, heading to the local schools to get principals' reports as to the first day back in the new school year. What they were hoping for throughout the year. What changes their schools had made since the previous year in hopes of improving.

"Speaking of school," I said as we rambled along in the old truck, "I went to an adorable nail salon on Main Street today—you know, to get an appointment for Friday morning? Oh, and by the way, I'm not coming in on Friday morning now that I know I'm supposed to take time off to make up for Saturday work—thank you very much for telling me—anyway, I left the salon and I saw a place you may have heard of. Testament Children's Museum?"

Will slowed the truck to stop at a red light. His head turned toward me, slowly, as if he were trying to gain the courage to look. I bit my tongue to keep from laughing, until he said, "Take a breath, girl."

"I'm breathing."

"You must have iron lungs to have said all that without so much as a gasp."

"I most assuredly do not have iron lungs."

"That was a joke."

"So have you ever heard of it? Green light, by the way."

Will continued forward. "Heard of what? The nail salon? Yeah. Tips to Toes. A girl I graduated from high school with owns it."

"*Not* Tips to Toes. I'm talking about the children's museum."

"Yeah, I've heard of it. Of course I have. I live here, remember. I do some volunteer work there."

Well, he'd beat me to it. "Really?"

"Yeah, really." He gave me another slow look. "That didn't occur to you when you saw me coming out of there earlier?" Then he chuckled. "Nice shade of crimson you got going there in your cheeks."

I crossed my arms and stared straight ahead. "Very funny." Then, looking at him, "You saw me?"

"On my way out the door. Saw you waiting for the Toyota to pull out."

"Why didn't you say anything?"

"Nothing to say."

"Then let's start with why you have my cell number but I didn't have yours?" A question that, of course, had nothing to do with my intended conversation, which was how I could possibly get out of the whole volunteer thing.

"That's easy. Big Guy gave it to me."

"When?"

"When I asked him for it. First day. When you were late."

Not *that* again. "Why didn't he give me yours then?"

"Did you ask him for it?"

"No."

"Well, then. That's why. What is it the Good Book says? *Ask and you shall receive.*"

"I don't think that line of Scripture is talking about cell phone numbers."

"Truth is truth."

True. "I hardly pegged you for a guy who'd volunteer his morning off at a children's museum." *And can you possibly tell me how I might get out of my own volunteerism without coming across looking like a jerk?*

We pulled into the first school on our list, Testament Elementary. "I'm sure there's a lot about me you haven't pegged."

"I can't argue with that. And I'm sure there's a lot about *me* that *you* haven't pegged."

Will shut the engine off. "I don't have to peg you."

"What does *that* mean?"

He stared at the steering wheel before saying, "Like I told you before, I know your type." He opened the driver's door.

I opened mine, then stepped onto the gravel parking lot of the one-story, rambling brick building with outside covered hallways. "Is that why you've been so snippy with me since I arrived here? Because you think you know my type?"

"I don't *think* I know your type. I *do* know your type." He walked in long strides toward the front doors of the school.

I hurried to keep up. "And what type is that?"

He stopped. Glared at me. "Seriously?"

"Yeah," I said, not afraid to return the stare. "Seriously."

"All right. You're the kind of girl who grew up with the proverbial silver spoon in her mouth. You went to private school. Your mama and daddy paid for ballet classes starting about the age of three until you either got bored with it or went off to college. They paid for piano lessons, too—same thing. You got your nails done the first time at the ripe old age of twelve. Your father bought you the car of your dreams *before* your sixteenth birthday and made sure you had a stretch limo to get you to prom. You never made below an A in school. You were a cheerleader, homecoming queen, and the girl all boys wanted to date and all girls wanted to be best friends with. How am I doing?"

By now my eyes burned with tears, but I refused Will Decker the pleasure of watching them fall. Nor would I let him know just how far off he was when it came to dates and friends. "Wonderfully," I lied. "Do you have anything else to add?"

"You worked fairly hard in college, but truth be told, you had a job lined up for you when you got out, no matter how well or poorly you did."

I pointed my finger at him. "Now that's not true."

"Which part?"

"The part about me having a job."

"You didn't have a job lined up for you?"

I crossed my arms. "Of course I did. But if you think for one minute my grandmother would have given me a leg up for *any* reason other than hard work, then you don't know my grandmother."

Our eyes locked, mine still swimming with tears. I became uncomfortably aware of his breathing. His nostrils flared until, finally, he blinked. Slowly. Breaking whatever spell held us together. "My apologies to your grandmother," he said. He tipped the brim of his hat and continued on toward the school building.

"Wait!" I called, running to catch up.

He didn't stop, but asked, "What now?"

"Don't I get to tell you what I think I know about you?"

"Nope."

"Why not?"

"Because I don't want to know what you think. I am who I am, no matter your opinion of me."

He opened one of the two glass doors and allowed me to walk by him. "We're not done," I mumbled at him.

"Oh, yes we are," he said.

Oh, no we're not, I thought, but chose to say nothing in reply.

I didn't hear from Rob until later that evening.

"I'm sorry," he said after the basic openings were out of the way. "I've been on a job all day. But I got your message earlier." He chuckled. "Messages, I should say."

"Sorry about that. It kept beeping on me."

"I don't know why that happens sometimes. But it does. At any rate . . . are you calling to cancel because of the scrimmage game?"

Scrimmage. That was the word. I mentally repeated it several times. "Oh. No. Not at all." I walked into the kitchen, opened the refrigerator, and pulled out a bottle of water. "But I was of the understanding that in small Southern towns, on a Friday night during football season, *everyone* goes to the games." I twisted the cap and took a long sip, walking back into the living room where my laptop awaited me on the love seat.

"Well, I mean . . . if you *want* to go. I wouldn't mind going. We could grab something to eat around here, go to the game. I just thought Lake Lure might be more your speed."

"Oh my goodness . . . that's so sweet of you. I mean, seriously, seriously sweet. Because I'll be honest, if that's okay with you."

"I wouldn't want you to be anything but."

Completely different from his friend, Will. Will didn't want my thoughts on anything, honest or not, it seemed. "Well . . . okay, then. Here's the deal: I don't know a lot about football." I sat on the sofa and took another sip of water.

"I know."

The water bottle came from my lips so fast, I splattered myself with water. "You know? Did William say something?"

"No. But any girl who can't remember *scrimmage* from *practice game* doesn't know football."

I brushed the moisture from my chin and blouse. "Oh. I told on myself," I said with a laugh. "Okay. So I don't know a lot about football. But you can teach me, right?"

"I'd be happy to," he said, his voice husky and almost seductive.

I shook any thoughts of how adorable I'd found him to be from my mind. "So then . . . what time should I expect you on Friday with these new plans?"

"Six too early?"

"What time does the game start?"

"Seven-thirty."

"Six sounds perfect."

"I'll see you at six, then."

Was he ending the conversation so soon? "Uh, Rob?"

"Yes, ma'am?"

I smiled. Glanced over at my laptop. "I was just looking at the Chimney Rock website. There are trails there, did you know that?"

"Oh, yes, ma'am. I know that."

"Have you ever walked them?"

"Only a few thousand times. I worked there when we were in high school."

"We?"

"Will and me. I don't have too many memories that don't include Will Decker. At least not from back in those days."

"Did Will work there, too?"

"Aww, no. 'Fraid not. He's always worked at the paper. It was sort of a family thing, I guess you could say."

I certainly knew about family business and working within it. "I see."

"What do you want to know about the trails?"

"I've been thinking about taking up walking trails."

"You mean hiking?"

"If that's what it's called. I suppose I'll need the right clothes, of course . . ."

"You need to get you some good hiking boots."

I jumped up, hurried over to the counter where a pad of paper and a pen were stored in a decorative basket. I jotted down hiking boots. "What else?"

"Good socks." He paused. "Have you ever heard of a place called Bubba O'Leary's?"

"Just today actually."

"Tell you what let's do," he said. "How about Saturday we go shopping in Chimney Rock and then we'll go out to dinner that evening at one of the restaurants along Lake Lure."

"You'll show me what I need for hiking?"

"Sure will." He paused. "And, if you like, I'll take you hiking sometime on the Chimney Rock trails."

I straightened. "I'd love that. But, I think I have to work on Saturday."

"Will usually puts in some time on Saturday mornings. Find out what your hours are for Saturday and we'll make a plan come Friday night. Deal?"

I grew uncharacteristically giddy. "Deal."

14

In a matter of only a few days, I had taken to rising early, getting showered, dressed, and outside to sit in one of the rock garden chairs. Cup of hot tea in one hand. The book I'd found in the downstairs bedroom in the other.

The first day's entry had encouraged me to "take long walks." I hadn't yet explored the "Decker Ranch," as it was playfully called, but I at least had a plan to hike along the trails of Chimney Rock. Wednesday's entry correlated with the mirror tile that read: EAT GOOD FOOD. After my conversation with Rob the night before, I made a decision to get to know Southern cooking better, starting this weekend.

I'd always eaten *well*. Nutritionally well. Mom had always been a no-junk stickler and I'd followed behind her along the path to healthy living. I occasionally splurged on something decadent, but rarely enough that I never counted a single calorie. Southern cooking, from what I could tell so far, was far from *healthy*. "If they can slap lard in it," Gram had told me the night before during a phone conversation I had with her after Rob's call, "they will."

Lard.

Eww.

"Not the best for your heart," she admitted to me, "but fantastic on the palate."

Well, all right. I was ready to find out.

Thursday's entry read BELIEVE, and the scriptural entries were from Genesis 15:6—*Abram trusted the LORD, and the LORD recognized Abram's high moral character*—and John 11:40—*Jesus replied, "Didn't I tell you that if you believe, you will see God's glory?"*

The block letters at the bottom of the page read: TRUST HIM COMPLETELY.

I looked at the picture, which was the same as one of the blocks in the mirror, depicting a drawn hand with a heart in the center of its palm. I placed my left hand in front of me, stretched my fingers, and tried to imagine a heart in the center.

I had to admit, the concept of the heart and the palm had me confused. What did the two of them, together, have to do with *belief*? I laid my head against the high back of the chair and closed my eyes, allowing myself to listen to the birds as they sang overhead, the gentle breeze rustling the leaves and sending the wind chimes into motion. An occasional truck worked its gears along the highway, disturbing nature just enough to annoy me. To keep me from concentrating enough to figure out what a heart in the palm of my hand had to do with believing.

Odd. For the first time in my life, progress pressed down on serenity and I didn't like it. As accustomed as I'd been in my life to city sounds, and as much as they had never annoyed me before, now they did. Here, in the still quiet of these mountains and hills and lush valleys, the jarring interruption seemed wrong. Sitting here, I yearned for the silence. The stillness. And more of it. I frowned, looked at my watch, and sighed.

Like it or not, the time had come to leave my early-morning sanctuary and go to work.

While Will worked outside the office on a couple of stories, I stayed in to work on a report for the Deckers outlining the first steps necessary to relaunch the magazine. I also continued my research on the land around Rob's place. The first job took all of a half hour. But the second . . .

Within minutes I found myself immersed in a different world. Another time. Wondering what it must have been like for the earliest settlers to this part of the nation. My need for knowledge and love of research kicked in, transporting me to wagons filled with wide-eyed men, women, and children. British Redcoats demanding taxes from a people who wanted only a fresh start without tyranny. But with the wide expanse and promise of the Blue Ridge Mountains and her lush valleys also came opposition from Native Americans who wanted pretty much the same as those who would be the new Americans—to be left alone and in peace.

As if that were not enough, there were those within the settlements who were loyal to the Crown. To all they'd known and believed in from their previous life.

Loyalists.

Then, just when no one really knew whom they could trust, the British army allied themselves with the Cherokee . . .

"They were after the same thing," I told Will as soon as he dropped into his chair, shortly before noon.

"Who was after what same thing?" He tossed his hat onto the wire in/out file.

"The Cherokee and the British." I felt my eyes grow wide. "The people who settled here in the mid-1700s were up against more than just getting the land ready for farming, building houses and towns. They were dealing with the British *and* the Cherokee, and the British and the Cherokee were basically on the same team."

He smiled. "Nice to see you doing your homework."

I gave my computer's screen a quick glance. "What I've found so far is pretty interesting stuff." I pulled a pencil from where I'd jammed it behind my ear and laid it on the desk. "I'm also thinking the magazine could use a history column. Bring the younger people up to speed on what it cost the original settlers to establish themselves here. And maybe we can use the museum to help with that, too."

Will booted up his computer without comment.

"Don't you think?"

"Hmmm?"

I wasn't accustomed to speaking and then repeating myself. "Were you even listening?"

He ran his index finger over the mouse. "Anything on who might be buried out there at Rob's place?"

Frustration wrapped itself around me like a vise, but I refused to let it squeeze hard enough to choke out my progress in Testament. "Not yet," I said, keeping my voice firm. "But don't you think knowing there were settlers here as well as Redcoats and Native Americans opens up a wide possibility?" When he didn't answer, I changed tack with a new question. "Did you contact the historical society?"

"I did. They're looking into it as well."

I returned to the webpage I'd been studying before Will came in. "So . . . ," I said after a few moments, "will you be at the scrimmage game on Friday?"

He looked at me. "Of course."

"Oh, good. Maybe we'll see you there."

His eyes narrowed. "I thought Rob was taking you to Lake Lure."

"He was. But I didn't want him to miss the game. You *did* stress the importance of football to Testament, after all." I took a breath. "Besides that, Mr. Decker, I *am* trying hard to fit in."

"Humph . . ." He looked at his computer screen and typed a few keystrokes.

"What does that mean?"

"What does what mean?"

"Humph."

He seemed to ponder his answer before speaking. "I guess I didn't see you as the kind of girl who'd want to go to a scrimmage game on a Friday night."

I shimmied in my seat like I was the smartest cookie in the jar. "Well then, I guess you don't really know *my type* after all."

His eyes—completely unreadable—found mine. "I guess not."

I decided to leave the conversation, and William, alone. I returned to my notes on the county's earliest settlers and conflicts while Will's fingers flew over his computer's keyboard. After a few moments he said, "You know, of course, that for all our lives Rob and I have always attended the scrimmage games—and all the home games, for that matter—together. So, in a lot of ways, I guess you're pushing me out of the picture in my best friend's life."

"No," I said, probably too quickly. "No, I'm not . . . Rob and I aren't an *item* or anything. I mean, it's just a first date." I shook my head. "I wouldn't even call it a date. I'd call it 'just getting to know you.'"

Will's fingers remained poised over the keyboard, his eyes fixed on the screen. His brow furrowed. "I think Rob is seeing it as more than that."

"What do you mean? We've had two phone calls and a brief meeting over some freaky graves."

He cut his eyes at me and gave a faux smile. "He thinks you're pretty."

I bit my lip. The deepest part of me wanted to giggle. The teenage girl who'd not had many boyfriends along the way, in spite of her "pretty looks" and her family's money, went to war with the adult Ashlynne, who'd learned not to care so much. This mattered. As much as I didn't want to act like it did . . . it did. And so I smiled, in spite of the lip-biting. A smile I felt all the way to my toes. "He does?"

"Mmm." Will's eyes returned to the screen. "And sweet."

"I am sweet. *Not* to hear you tell it, of course. But I can be."

He shook his head. "All I know is, it's going to be awfully lonesome sitting up there in the stands by myself." He shrugged. "Of course, Big Guy and Gram will be with me, but it's hardly the same."

The absolute last thing I wanted was to sit with William Decker on Friday night while I was supposed to be on a date with Rob Matthews. Still . . . they'd probably been attending football games and softball games and everything in between together since they were young. And yet *still* . . . Oh, Gram!

"But, it does my heart good," Will continued, interrupting my guilt trip, "knowing that you love football the way you do." Again, he cut his eyes toward me. "You know, enough to give up dinner at beautiful Lake Lure for a simple high school scrimmage game."

"Well, yes. Of course . . ."

He swung around to face me. "Tell me something. Just so I know, because honestly, the last thing in the world I want to do is mess up your first date with Rob. He *is* my best friend, after all. But more than that, he's really a great guy."

My breath caught in my throat. "What do you want to know?"

"Rob and I always, *always* sit on the sixty-yard line. You loving football, I'm sure you know it's the best for viewing the whole game."

"The sixty-yard line. Yeah, yeah. I know," I said, keeping my voice as nonchalant as possible. "That's where I always sit, too." I swallowed. "When I go to a game."

"Oh, good. Well, then, how about if Gram and Big Guy and I sit on the fifty? Close enough that we can say hey and be friendly and all. But, you know, not so close as to intrude."

I raised my brow. From the fifty to the sixty. That was what? Thirty feet? Close enough, as Will said, to say hello, but not so close as to ruin my first date in Testament. In all honesty, my first date in *forever.* "That sounds perfectly fair." I smiled. "Thank you. I like that idea very much. That's kind of you."

"And you'll tell Rob, of course."

"Tell him what?"

"That since *you* always like sitting on the sixty-yard line and so does *he*, I'm happy to give that to you. I am *more* than happy to take the fifty."

I squared my shoulders and tilted my chin. "I will do just that, Will Decker." I reached across the narrow aisle separating our desks for a handshake. "And again, I thank you."

His uncalloused, warm hand pressed against mine. "My pleasure."

On Thursday afternoon, about a half hour before "story time," as Alma called it, I received an e-mail, forwarded from Will.Decker2, originating from someone named MBrown@TestamentNursingHome.

"What is this?" I shot the question across the aisle between our desks. I kept my voice low enough so as not to disturb Alma and Garrison, who worked on the other side of the room in their respective corners.

"The nursing home news. Comes in once a week, on Thursdays, so we can print it in the Saturday edition. You'll have tomorrow to work on it, but it really doesn't take much. Maria Brown is the admin over there. She does a pretty fine job of wordsmithing."

"The *nursing home news*? They have *news*?"

He grinned at me. "You just may be surprised."

I clicked on the attachment as I said, "I'm sure I will be." As the document opened, I added, "By the way, why are you Will-*two*?"

"Because my father is Will-one."

"He still has an e-mail account here at the paper? Even though he's out of the country?"

"Yes, ma'am." Will's fingertips continued across the keyboard.

"What did he do when he was here? Your father."

"Same thing I'm doing now." His typing ceased and his eyes cut toward me. "But without the constant interruptions."

I frowned, then looked at the document of nursing home news. First on the agenda: longtime resident Helen Baugh would turn ninety the following week. (The good Lord willing, Maria Brown added parenthetically.) The family was planning a celebration to be held at the "homestead," which would be enjoyed by fellow residents, family, and friends and—according to Ms. Brown—*The Testament Tribune* would cover it. On Saturday. From 2:00 to 4:00. Community also invited.

"We're covering Helen Baugh's birthday party?"

"You bet." Will opened a drawer and pulled out a piece of paper, which he made notations on. "Should be interesting. Ninety is quite the milestone, don't you think?"

"Yeah, sure. So, we're working Saturday *afternoon*?"

"That's right." He looked at me. "Why? Do you already have a date?"

No, but I'd hoped . . . "I'm just trying to get my calendar straight. Is there some way you could let me know in advance? I mean, some sort of calendar by which we *all* know what our schedules are?" I couldn't imagine *Parks & Avenues* being run without the schedule Gram had her assistant send to all personnel.

Will sighed. Rubbed his forehead with thick fingertips as though he had a monster of a headache. "I keep it all right here," he said, pointing to where his fingers had just pushed and pulled.

I crossed my arms. "Well, since you and I don't share a brain—thank goodness—how am I to know what is expected of me on any given day?"

He stared at me. Nodded. Then said, "You've got a point. I'll work on that."

I returned my attention to the document and read about four paragraphs of information before giggling. I looked up to catch Will smiling at me. "What?"

I fought to sober myself. " 'On Monday,' " I read from the document, " 'during Bingo Hour, Mr. Lucas Snyder and Mr. Brian Weatherman both called out "Bingo" at the same time, which resulted in a near-fisticuffs over who would win the week's prize of an extra slice of chocolate cake on Sunday.' "

Will chuckled. "Who won?"

I read, " 'It was decided by the Bingo Angels that Mr. Snyder and Mr. Weatherman would have to *split* the slice of cake.' " I tried every trick I knew to keep my giggles suppressed, like the ones from when Leigh and I would get the adolescent silly-giggles during church services. Mom had instructed us to think on sad things. Like children going to bed without food. Or puppies left out in the rain. "If you can't control yourselves," she'd said, "excuse yourselves." Now, sitting across from a puzzled William Decker, I caught my breath and said, "What's a"—I looked back at the screen—"Bingo Angel?" I swallowed twice more. Hard.

"They're men and women in the community—usually retired, although some are homemakers who never worked outside the home—who volunteer their time at the nursing home. There is a statewide group of them. Each year one Bingo Angel is named Volunteer of the Year. They go on to state competition—if you can call it that. Our local Angel Volunteer of the Year will ride on a float in the Harvest Day Parade in a couple of months."

"The Harvest Day Parade?"

"Actually, it's a festival." He smiled, but the smile faded quickly and a shadow ran across his face. "I'm sure we'll"—he wagged his finger between the two of us—"cover it. And, I'm equally as sure you'll be miserable throughout the whole week."

A harvest festival. I wondered if art would be involved, like at the Winter Park Arts Festival. "But I *could* enjoy it." And by then, the magazine would be in full swing . . .

Will turned back to his desk. "Doubt it."

I continued reading the nursing home news until I reached the end of it. "So, Will Number 2, is there a form for the nursing home news?"

"I just shot you the document you'll need to drop Maria's words into. Be sure to edit."

"All right."

I opened my e-mail. Sure enough, an e-mail with an attachment from Will.Decker2 stood at the top. A thought ran through my mind and I giggled again.

Even Mom's tactics weren't working, though I don't know why, other than that happiness had somehow managed to swell inside me. And happy giggles naturally ensued.

"What is it now?" he asked, though not with the same amusement as before.

"Just a play on words that came to me," I said, still laughing.

Will stopped what he was doing and watched as I tried to compose myself. "And I suppose there will be no rest for the weary until you share."

I waved my hand in front of my face, in some lame attempt to regain self-control. "I was just thinking that . . . if your father is Will *one* . . . but he's no longer *in* Testament . . . and you're Will *two* and you're *still* in Testament . . . well then."

His brow rose as he waited.

"I guess that makes you the last *Will* in *Testament*." When he didn't respond, I added, "Just a little play on words."

He didn't "get" it. Or perhaps he did and he wasn't willing to meet me halfway with the joke. This wouldn't be the first time I'd tried and failed at reaching those I wanted to connect with. Obviously, it may not even be the last.

But, I thought, *I bet Mom would laugh.*

And Dad.

And Leigh.

I frowned as I turned back to my computer, then bit my lip to stifle another laugh.

. . . *and Gram.*

15

I sent a text to William on Friday morning reminding him I'd be in later than usual. That I was going to get my nails done.

Of course u r, his return text read.

With a roll of my eyes, I put down my phone, picked up my hot tea and my new morning read, and headed outside. Heavy air met me, reminding me of Winter Park, where humidity lay like a wet blanket nearly all year long.

"Bad for the hair," Leigh always said, "but great for the face." And then she always patted my cheeks.

How I missed her.

I sat in what had become my favorite place to sit and read. Behind me, the sun made its slow ascent, casting shades of gold and ash across the lawn and the river rocks. A sliver of glitter in my flip-flops caught one of the rays and shot back a brilliant reflection. Overhead, birds had already begun their morning song. The notion that we were becoming friends fluttered across my mind, and I smiled.

As I crossed my legs and took a leisurely sip of tea, I caught a glimpse of my two furry friends from between the red-tipped bushes. They sauntered up the path. Over the past few days we'd formed a morning ritual whereby I drank tea and read; they sat and watched. Our actions, when done together, worked out beautifully.

I'd also learned their names.

"Good morning, Buddy," I said as the black dog reached me. I placed the mug between my thighs, extended my hand; he eased his head under it. His tail swished back and forth before looking back to see how close his constant companion had come to stealing my attention. "Come on, Sis," I said, using the nickname Bobbie gave Kelsey. "Come on, old girl."

Kelsey easily pushed Buddy out of the way for her love pat. Buddy's dark eyes stared at me for a moment. Unfazed by my shift in attention, he walked over to sniff a decorative garden stone with "DREAM" carved into it.

I continued to rub Kelsey's head, scratching behind her ears. I laid my head back against the glossy slats of the chair and closed my eyes. "Ah, Sis," I said. "Do you know what I'd be doing right now if I were back in Winter Park?" I opened my eyes. Sis now sat, her long tail wrapped around one hip and leg. Her pink tongue dropped between sharp teeth, and her mouth formed a smile. "I'd be rushing off to work, that's what." Buddy rejoined us and I shifted my hand to his head. "You see," I continued, "back home, when I get up—I get up very early—I do my reading inside my apartment. I have a settee that once belonged to my grandmother—ah, you probably don't want to hear about *that.* But I don't get to go outside and sit under the trees and feel the breeze on my skin when I do my reading."

Both dogs stared at me, looking at me as intently as Gram and Mom when I bared my soul to them. "What I'm trying to say," I continued, "is how special this is becoming and how much I will miss it when I leave."

The dogs blinked in unison.

"Well, then." I raised the book with my free hand. "I guess I'd better get to reading so I can shower and go get my nails done." Kelsey panted deeply, as though, being a girl, she understood.

I propped my mug on the armrest farthest from the dogs and opened the book to: SING AND DANCE. The artwork on the corresponding mirror tile was of a woman with her mouth open and of a ballet shoe with wide pink ribbons.

"*Sing to God,*" I read to Buddy and Kelsey. "*Sing praise to him; dwell on all his wondrous works.*" I looked at the dogs, both curled near my feet. "That's from First Chronicles, chapter sixteen, verse nine."

Buddy groaned as he rested his head on his front paws.

"I take it you've heard me sing," I said.

Kelsey followed her companion's motions. Her eyes rose to meet mine as though to say, "Uh . . . yeah."

"I'll keep reading then," I said. "*There's a season for everything and a time for every matter under the heavens . . . a time for mourning and a time for dancing.*"

I thought of the upcoming swing band dance. Bobbie had indicated I'd go with Will, but I had begun to think better of the idea. Perhaps Rob would consent to be my on-the-job escort. By then it would be obvious I knew absolutely *nothing* about football. Faking it wouldn't even be an option. No doubt Will Decker would call me out. He'd probably put some sort of sign on my desk: HERE SITS THE DUMBEST FOOTBALL FAN IN ALL OF NORTH CAROLINA.

Well, the joke would be on him. I was *not* the dumbest in all of North Carolina. I was the dumbest in all of the *world.* But what I knew about dancing . . .

. . . well . . . that was another matter entirely. I'd been trained at one of the best schools of dance Central Florida had to offer, after all, and I excelled at everything from the Lindy Hop to the Cha Cha Slide.

I called Mom on my way to Tips to Toes, as I did most mornings on my way to work. "Mom," I said, "I've got a little dilemma."

Mom's smile could be heard across the miles. "I can't imagine."

"Seriously. I realized this morning that I don't have a 'Connie' up here." Connie, the woman who'd cleaned my parents' home every other day for as long as I could remember, had been coming to my apartment every other Friday since I'd moved in. She took out my dry cleaning, brought it back, did my wash, dusted, swept, mopped, and gave the bathrooms and kitchen a once-over. "I've hardly been at the cottage long enough to make a mess, but I'm running out of towels and I'm sure my bathroom could use a scrub."

"Have you asked Bobbie who helps with her house?"

"No . . ." Somehow I couldn't imagine Bobbie allowing anyone to clean her house but her.

"I suggest you start there. And, sweetheart?"

"Yes, ma'am?"

"Yes, *ma'am*? That didn't take long to start, did it?"

I couldn't help but smile. "All right. All right. What did you want to say?"

"I was merely going to suggest that you might want to learn how to do your own laundry."

The smile faded. "Good-bye, Mom. Tell Dad I love him."

"We love you, too. And Dad says let's set up a FaceTime call soon."

"Absolutely. I miss you both."

I arrived for my mani and pedi fifteen minutes early, hoping to get ahead of schedule. But every station in Tips to Toes had already been occupied, including one in the front corner. Who knew so many Testament women got their nails done on Fridays?

Behind the angled desk-type station sat a girl so young, I found myself surprised she was old enough to have a license to do nails. Much less that she was *doing* nails.

Will's school friend, who I now knew was named Natalie, met me with a wide smile and a welcome. "We have some real comfortable chairs over there," she said pointing toward the back of the room. "With some magazines and coffee, if you'd like a cup."

"Thank you," I said. I went to the back of the salon, picked a magazine I knew I'd only glance through, and sat.

"Would you like a cup of coffee?" Natalie called to me from the workstation she'd returned to, her voice rising over a song about exes in Texas, which played overhead.

"I'm good, thank you."

"Something cold? We've got some co-colas back there."

Co-colas? Testament really was a Mayberry. I hadn't heard cokes referred to as co-colas since watching Goober offer one to Andy. "Ah . . . no. Really. I'm good." I thought to smile and did so. "But, thank you so much."

"All right. Well, let me know . . ."

I smiled again in answer, opened the cover of the magazine, and studied the first ad, which was for Cover Girl mascara. Which reminded me . . . Sunday. After church. I was to go see . . .

I'd no sooner thought of Brianna than she walked in from the back of the salon carrying a stack of towels. "Here's the towels, Miss Natalie," she said, placing them on a low glass-topped table.

"Brianna?" I said.

Brianna turned her face toward me and blushed. "Oh. Ashlynne."

She straightened as I stood. "Hey," I said. "What are you doing here? Do you work here, too?"

"Yeah . . . I . . . uh . . ." Brianna pushed her hands along the tops of her thighs. "The salon is one of my accounts, I guess you could say."

"Accounts? I thought you worked at the restaurant."

"I do. Yeah." Brianna glanced around, as though she were a spy about to give out covert information. Her voice lowered, "I have a cleaning service *and* I work at the restaurant."

"You have a cleaning service?"

Was this providence or what?

A flash of embarrassment raced across her face, but was quickly replaced by a sparkle of steel in her eyes. "Yes. I do. And I'm not ashamed of it neither."

I realized I had offended her. "Oh, no," I said. "I'm actually *happy* to hear this. I need . . . someone . . . to help me at the cottage."

"Really? How often?"

Her excitement bothered me on the most superficial level imaginable, even for me. If she came to work for me, even periodically, would the whole "make friends while you are there" order fall away? Or could we—in spite of our age difference—enjoy each other's company, drawing from the other what we needed, in spite of our stations in life? And so I asked, "Every other week?"

"I don't work on Tuesdays over at the restaurant and I don't have any clients that day either. How about on Tuesdays?"

I mentally counted the number of towels left in the linen closet. I might be able to make it. *Or* maybe I could figure out the washer and dryer. "Tuesday would be great."

Brianna looked at her watch. "Well, I gotta get going. I'm due over across the street in a little while." She smiled at me. "We're still on for Sunday after church?"

"Of course. Why don't you come over to the cottage around 2:00? Do you know where the Deckers live?"

"I do, but . . ." Again her cheeks flushed with color. "Well, my little girl goes down about that time and . . . do you think it would be okay for you to come to my house?"

"You have a little girl?"

Pride replaced the blush. "I do. Her name is Maris. She's five and she's, well, she is just my heart."

"I'm sure she is . . ." My mind furiously did the math. Will had said he thought Brianna was about twenty-four. Which meant she would have been about nineteen when she gave birth. Eighteen, perhaps, when she got pregnant. At eighteen I experienced my first year of higher learning, gratefully surrounded by girls like me with the same expectations and dreams. And knowing I had at least four full years before any sort of real responsibility other than my GPA fell on my shoulders. Brianna, on the other hand, faced a new and tiny life, totally dependent on her.

How could I possibly connect? Understand it?

"Ashlynne?" Natalie called, interrupting us. "I'm ready for you."

"Be right there." I looked at Brianna again, determined once again not to step backward. I could do this, if only for a few months. "Can I get your address from Will?"

"Oh, yeah," she said. Her happy countenance returned in full. "Everyone knows where I live."

Well, of course. Small town. Everyone growing up together, for the most part. Family and friends, one in the same. "I'll see you on Sunday then."

I joined Natalie at her workstation. "We'll do your fingernails first," she said. "That okay?"

"Perfect."

"Want to pick your polish while I run to the back real quick?"

"Yes," I said. I chose Spicy Red, then sat to wait. When Natalie joined me, I jumped right in with the question at the forefront of my mind. "Can you tell me how old Brianna is?"

Natalie looked toward the rear of the room from where Brianna had just emerged. "I don't know," she said, looking back at me. "Twenty-four I think." She went to work on my nails by removing the polish.

Which was what Will had said. "And she has a five-year-old little girl?"

"That child is the sweetest thing you've ever seen."

No doubt. But twenty-four? With a five-year-old? I couldn't imagine the enormous responsibility, much less the loss of what Brianna might have achieved if she'd waited before having a child. I wondered then if she was married, but thought it best not to ask. "I'm sure she is," I said with a smile. "And I guess I'll meet her on Sunday."

"Jeanine," someone said from across the room.

The young nail tech popped her head up. "Yes, ma'am?"

"What in the world is your little sister doing in the back on a school day?"

I turned my head toward Jeanine, as though I were a part of the conversation. "Playin' hooky. She says she's got a hurt leg," the woman drawled. "But I can tell ya right now, I ain't seen a limp out of her all day."

I nearly bit through my tongue to keep from laughing.

"Get your nails done?" Will asked after I entered our office. The police scanner squawked across the room, Alma and Garrison were in their corners hammering away at their respective jobs, and a woman I'd never seen before sat at one of the two middle-of-the-room desks where no one ever sat.

I looked from Will to her and back to Will again, hoping the *Who is this?* question I had in my mind came across in my eyes.

"Oh." Will stood. "Hey, Janie?"

Janie—a petite doe-eyed brunette—looked up from her work. "Yeah?"

"This is Ashlynne. Ashlynne, Janie."

I took the two steps necessary to reach her desk and extended my hand. She looked at it as though it were a dead fish, then gave me a loose shake. I frowned. I never liked shaking the hands of women who didn't know how. We weren't at a tea and I wasn't the queen. We were in a business setting, for crying out loud. *Shake.*

"Nice to meet you," I said.

"Yeah, you too . . ." She looked at Will. "I need to get back to work so I'm not late. Sorry."

"No worries," Will said to her, apparently unaware that I'd been dismissed, something that would have never happened at the offices of *Parks & Avenues*. To me he said, "Sit. Sit. We've got a busy day and it's half over."

And with only a few words, I felt back "in the groove," as Dad often says. "Get in the groove, Kitten." or "Are you in the groove yet, Princess?"

I waggled the "Spicy Red" fingers of one hand at Will as I dropped my purse into the empty drawer with the other.

"Lovely," he said. "Toes too?"

I sat in my chair, pointed a Jimmy Choo–sandaled foot toward him. "Of course."

"Nice shoes," he said, more to them than me. "You wearing those tonight?"

I hadn't really thought about what I would wear to the game. What *did* people from small Southern towns wear to football games? "I haven't thought that far."

He leaned over, resting his elbows on his knees. "You'll want to wear purple and silver, of course."

"Purple and silver?"

"School colors."

I mentally ran over the items in my closet, knowing surely there would be an issue when it came to what I'd wear tonight. A new problem for me. "Anything else I need to know?"

Will seemed to think for a moment. "Can't think of anything." He returned to his work.

I smiled. Maybe Will Decker wasn't so bad after all. "Hey, Will?"

He looked at me.

"Did you know Brianna has a little girl?"

"Sure."

"And she works two jobs?"

"A lot of folks around here work two jobs. Times are hard, in case you didn't know." The friendliness in his voice had left, replaced by hard words spoken too loud.

"Yes, I know." My dander elevated.

"Not *everyone* can afford Karan and Wang and Jimmy Choo, Miss Bloomies."

My shoulders squared as heat rose from my belly. "I *know* that. Why do you assume I *don't* know that?" *And furthermore . . .* "And how is it *you* know Karan and Wang, because you *certainly* didn't learn it from living in *Testament*."

"What's wrong with living in *Testament*?"

"Nothing," I shouted, standing to full attention, every fiber of my being now on fire.

All sound ceased, with the exception of the occasional squelch of the scanner. All typing stopped. I didn't dare look around to see who might be watching, what their expressions might hold. I folded my arms and stared down on William Decker, who appeared both amused and unhappy, strangely at the same time.

A visual standoff.

But when he didn't say anything in return, I inched down until I felt myself reach the chair. My own deep breaths reverberated within me. I felt both vindicated and defeated. Yet not once did I break contact with Will's eyes, nor did he with mine. Steel had met steel. Determination; determination. His jaw flinched, he blinked, and turned toward his computer screen.

Only then did I look around. Two of the three girls from advertising stood in the open doorway near Garrison's desk, both with their lips pulled tight. Garrison seemed confused. Alma, disappointed.

In me?

Of course *in* me.

Me.

16

Rob showed up two minutes early dressed in a pair of jeans, a gray tee, and a plaid long-sleeved oxford. He wore the oxford untucked, unbuttoned, and with the sleeves rolled three-quarters of the way up. His hair and his five o'clock shadow remained as they'd been when I first met him, letting me know this wasn't his "I just woke up" look, but rather his "I'm cool" look.

I liked it.

Will Decker could learn a lot from Rob Matthews.

"Hey there," he said, his voice shy, as though we'd not spoken every night since we'd met.

I stepped back from the door. "Want to come in for a minute? I just need to get my purse from upstairs." He seemed taken aback by my invitation. I smiled. "I won't bite."

Even in the early shadows of evening, I could see him blush. "I know," he said, shoving his hands into his jean pockets. He looked over his shoulder. "I just don't want to do anything that might look bad on Miss Bobbie and Mr. Shelton."

I didn't understand at first, then realization hit. Old-fashioned chivalry. *Well, hello . . . you and I have yet to meet.* "Ah. How about if we leave the front door completely open and you stand where they can see you?" If they were looking at all.

He pressed his lips together before acquiescing. "All right." Rob Matthews stepped over the threshold of my temporary home.

I was halfway up the stairs when he said, "Um . . . Ashlynne?"

I looked back at him, my hand on the narrow railing. "Yes?"

"Are you wearing . . . *that*?"

My eyes rushed past what little bit of purple and silver I had been able to find—a purple Halogen pencil skirt, which I topped with a lavender-and-silver sweater set. "Yes, why?"

I took two steps down. "Is a skirt not a good idea?"

"Oh, no . . . ," he said and his eyes twinkled. "You look . . . great. In that skirt. It's just that . . . purple and silver are the opposing team's colors."

I took the three steps back to the first floor. Anger stirred deep inside. "I thought purple and silver were *our* team's colors." As if I'd not been through enough today thanks to William Decker, he'd purposefully steered me wrong with the school's colors?

Yes, of course he had. A prank best served by a junior high girl.

"Ah. No. We're red and white." He grinned a little. "What made you think we were purple and silver?"

I raked my teeth over my bottom lip to keep from exploding. "I guess I misunderstood." As if . . . "I'll change and be right back down." I hurried up the stairs, got to the landing and turned again. "Just curious. Do you think the sixty-yard line or the fifty-yard line is the best seat in the house?"

Rob's laughter was nearly contagious, but I wasn't in a kidding mood. "Well, that would *have* to be the fifty."

"And the sixty? What is that? The worst?"

He crossed his arms. "No, ma'am. There *isn't* a sixty-yard line." His hand—fingers together—made a line in the air. "See, here's the fifty and then it goes forty/forty . . ." His hand worked back and forth in demonstration. "Thirty/thirty, twenty/twenty, ten/ten, then you've got your goal lines and your end zones. See? Like that." His head cocked to one side. "I know you said you don't know a lot about football, but have you never *been* to a football game?"

I didn't answer. "I'll be right back," I said. "Dressed in the best red and white I can find."

He laughed again. "You do that. I'll wait outside in one of these chairs out here."

As I went the rest of the way upstairs I heard him say, "Well, hey Buddy. Sis . . ."

Lucky me. I had a pair of red Topshop shorts, to which I added a white Lafayette 148 New York sleeveless sweater. I pulled my hair up in a ponytail, found a charming pair of red-and-white earrings with a matching bangle, slipped my feet into a pair of backless white sneakers, and flew down the stairs and out the door. Rob stood as soon as he heard me. He turned and his mouth gaped. "Wow," he said. "Ashlynne, if you don't mind my saying so, you look *gorgeous*."

I grinned. Just the effect I had hoped for. "Thank you." *Just wait,* I thought, *till Will Decker sees me*. Then I wondered where the thought had come from. And why.

"No one, but *no one* is going to be watching the game tonight." His eyes twinkled and he looked at his watch. "We'd best get going. We may be late as it is."

"We'll make a grand entrance then," I said.

He escorted me toward his car. "How about we get something calorie-laden and nonnutritious at the game? Afterward, we can get something substantial."

"I can't believe you drive a Prius."

He opened the passenger door for me. I was met with the sweet scent of berry and leather. "I'm earth-conscious."

Unlike William Decker, whose old truck probably emitted enough toxins to kill a small rain forest. When Rob settled into the driver's seat, he turned to me and asked, "So, how about the food idea? Something at the game, then we'll go out later?"

I nodded. I had no idea there were restaurants (or cafés perhaps?) at football stadiums. Or even what they served. "Sounds marvelous."

"Good."

As we drove toward the high school, Rob filled me in on small portions of his life, intermittently asking about mine. I told him about Gram. My parents. What my apartment was like back in Winter Park. "I'd like to see Winter Park some time," he said. "It sounds like something out of a Dickens novel."

"You read Dickens?"

He blushed again, something I found endearing. "In high school. We had to, you know."

We. Him and Will, going back to diapers. "I can't imagine Will reading *anything* in high school."

"Will? Nah. Will's been a voracious reader since we were kids. If he couldn't find anything new to read at the library, he'd bury himself in the encyclopedias."

I strained my brain to get the picture. Difficult, at best. And better to shift the subject back to Rob. "Maybe you can come to Winter Park to see me . . . after I go home, I mean." Which would be after Christmas.

Christmas. The holiday seemed both eons away and just around the corner. How much of it, in Winter Park, would I be expected to miss? Or would Gram and Dad's edict mean I had to spend it here?

A glimpse of what the *Country & Christmas Tea* cover might look like came to mind.

I turned to Rob, to ask him about what the holidays were like in Testament. But before I could, he blinked, all the while keeping his gaze straight ahead, then turned his face to mine ever so slowly. "I'd like visiting you in Winter Park," he said. "I'd like that very much."

I heard the low bass and rat-a-tat of drums long before I saw the lights from the stadium. I clapped like a child. "This is exciting," I said.

"You can hear the music . . ."

"Yes. I like music."

"I'm surprised you never went to a game when you were in school." Rob turned into the high school parking lot, easing through a sea of parked cars, trucks, and occasional pedestrians.

"We didn't have football at my school. We had basketball. And tennis and track. And we had soccer. I guess soccer is a lot like football."

Rob cut the car off. "That's what they say. You know, of course, that in the true South, football is like a religion."

I smiled. "I've heard. *Faith . . . family . . . football.*" I held up three fingers, one at a time.

Rob laughed as he opened his door. "Hold on. I'll come around."

My back straightened. I liked this. Rob Matthews was a real gentleman. A Southern gent, Gram would call him. My door opened and Rob extended his hand to help me out. "Thank you, sir," I said, doing my best to sound ladylike without being pretentious.

Rob opened the trunk to his car, pulled out what looked like two briefcases, both red and white.

"What's that?" I asked.

"Seat cushions," he answered, slamming the trunk shut. "These fold out and form like little chairs. They keep your back from aching and your backside from going numb." He blushed again.

I giggled.

"There's even a cup holder," he added.

Oh. Well. "How convenient," I said.

When we got to the ticket booth, Rob pulled a ten-dollar bill from his wallet and then a laminated card. "What's that?" I asked, thinking that I had started sounding like a parrot.

"My season's pass." His eyes found mine and, for the briefest of moments, I studied the coffee-colored warmth. "If you'd like, I can buy you one."

"Oh, no . . . ," I said. "I wouldn't expect that." Besides . . . how long was a season, anyway?

"Here ya go, Rob," the older woman on the other side of the booth said.

"How you doin', Mrs. Givens?"

"Fair to middlin'."

"Can't complain?"

"Well, I could, but what would be the point?" She chuckled.

"Yes, ma'am. What about Mr. Givens? How's he these days?"

"Not good," the woman answered with a sad shake of her head. "His arthritis just gives him fits."

"I'm sorry to hear that." Rob shoved the wallet into his back pocket.

"He's had it for such a long time, poor man."

"Yes, ma'am."

"His mama had it bad, too, you know."

"I didn't know, but you give Mr. Givens my best and tell him I'll be praying for him."

"You're a good boy, Robert. Always were. Your mama most assuredly raised you right." She pulled her attention from him to me. "Who've ya got with ya there?"

Rob grinned with what looked like pride. "I'd like for you to meet Ashlynne Rothschild. She's working for the Deckers for a few months."

I gave Mrs. Givens my best pleased-to-meet-you smile, but without taking her eyes from me she continued speaking to Rob. "Well, if you ask me, her shorts are a smidgen too short, but her colors are right and I suppose that's what's important."

I frowned as Rob handed me a program. "Here ya go," he said. Then to Mrs. Givens, "We do appreciate loyalty to the old red and white, don't we, Mrs. Givens?"

"Yes sirree bob."

Rob gave another sweet smile toward the woman. He, no doubt, had been born a diplomat. Whatever I had managed to lack, he had in full. "Thank you, now," he said.

"Y'all enjoy the game now."

"We will." He looked at me as we stepped away from the booth. "Come on through the gate here," he said, pointing to a fairly thin opening in the high fence.

"*Are* my shorts too short?"

"Not to my way of thinking . . ." He cut his eyes at me. They were playful and mischievous. "I think you look just fine. Mrs. Givens, on the other hand, thinks anything an inch over the knee is too short. She was one of the high school teachers who used to give the girls around here a fit."

We stepped into a small crowd of people who ambled toward the bleachers on the right side of the field. Rob slipped his hand around mine as naturally as if he'd been doing so for years. It felt warm. And rough from his work.

And good.

I allowed my fingers to curl around his. When I did, he squeezed.

The night air grew thicker; my skin clammy under the weight of Nicole Miller body cream. I could smell the flowers and sandalwood, which blended nicely with Rob's aftershave wafting around us. The whole experience was intoxicating. Not just our scents mixing together like familiar lovers, but the animated cheers from young girls with pom-poms, the chatter and shouts of the crowd, the songs of the marching band—more drumbeat than medley.

"Do you mind sitting with the Deckers?" Rob asked with a jut of his chin, indicating he'd spotted them.

I smiled, hoping it looked sincere. "Not at all. I like Bobbie and Shelton." And I had a bone to pick with William.

"They're good people."

"Yes, they are."

Will Decker did a double take when he saw me. "Nice," he said, keeping his voice low as I sat to the right of him and on the seat cushion Rob opened for me.

"The outfit or the seat cushion?" I let my left brow rise, as though I dared him to answer the former over the latter.

He grinned at me with a shake of his head, leaned forward, rested his elbows on his knees and cracked his knuckles.

Just like Dad . . . and my grandfather.

From between her husband and her grandson, Bobbie Decker clapped her hands in time with the chant coming from the cheerleading squad. She looked at me. "Couldn't you just jump up and down right now? Oh, I wish I could still do what those girls are doing."

Shelton leaned over and winked at me. "She ain't the only one who's wishing it."

I laughed, looked over at Rob, and whispered, "Okay, so what happens next?" I glanced over the field, noting the white lines and the giant numbers—50-40-30 . . .

He offered a sheepish smile. "You really are a novice."

I looped my arm through his, giving him my full attention. "But I'm with a good teacher, right?"

"Yes ma'am." He looked to his right. "Okay, then. You see that tall U-shaped thing rising up on a pole down there?"

I nodded.

"Don't look now, but there's another one on the other end of the field."

I kept my eyes on the U-shaped thing rising from the right side of the field. "Okay . . ."

"They're called goalposts . . ."

17

When the game ended with victorious cheers from our side of the field—and groans from the other—Rob and I stood, and folded our chairs as though we'd been doing so in harmony all our lives.

"What'd you think of our boys?" Bobbie asked from the other side of her grandson, who'd spent the majority of the game either yelling at the players or looking quizzically at me.

"They're wonderful," I said. "And that Number 75 really was something spectacular to watch, wasn't he?"

"That's our Sean," Shelton said. "Boy's going places. And my old buddy Coach Meriwether will make the state High School Coach of the Year for sure."

I handed Rob my folded seat cushion. He gripped both in one hand and placed the other hand at the small of my back. "You ready for something better than popcorn and a Coke?"

I nodded and smiled. I was more than ready. I'd passed on the chili dog Rob had suggested and I was fairly starved. Rob looked at Will and his family. "You folks are welcome to join us."

My heart plummeted. Much as I liked the Deckers and as much as I could manage to tolerate their grandson, I didn't want them tagging along on the first real date I'd had in forever.

"Don't be silly," Bobbie said. "Besides, it's past our bedtime, near 'bout."

Shelton harrumphed.

We'd started down the bleachers with the rest of the crowd when Will asked Rob, "Where are y'all going?"

"Where do you think? The Sit-a-Spell."

"Is that a restaurant?" I asked Rob. Because, I had to admit, it sounded like a place to buy living room furniture.

"More like a hangout," Will answered for his friend. "Not really up your alley."

"Come on now, Will," Rob said. "You know better than that. Give the girl a break. Look how much fun she had at the game." His hand, once again, took mine in a protective hold.

We placed our feet on the well-worn grass path along the front row of bleachers and turned left toward the parking lot. "I did have fun," I said, to no one in particular, and more to myself. I'd shouted and cheered and clapped along with everyone, feeling a part of something so . . . communal. I couldn't wait to tell Gram about it. To let her know that *this* was what I'd wanted back in junior high. What I'd hoped for. For a few exhilarating hours I'd allowed the wall around my heart to fall ever-so-slightly and look what I'd gotten—an experience that was everything I'd always thought it could be.

She'd be thrilled to hear it. So would Leigh.

"So, what's it going to be?" Rob asked Will after we'd made it to the edge of the parking lot and said good-bye to the senior Deckers. "Coming with us?"

I eyed Will carefully, begging my eyes to dare him to intrude on my time with Rob. But he only smiled at Rob, giving me not so much as a glance. "Have I ever missed going to the Sit-a-Spell after a game?"

"Yeah, I know. But you know you can sit with us, right?"

He looked at me, eyes playfully narrowing. "If it's all right with Ashlynne, I'd love to join you."

And what was I to say? I could only mutter one polite thing, albeit insincere, and he knew it. "Of course, Mr. Decker. What could *possibly* be more fun?"

"The Sit-a-Spell is *the* place to go after a game," Rob told me on the way there, "providing, of course, we won the game."

"And if not?"

"Then we still go but only to lick our wounds."

I smiled. "Y'all really do take football seriously, don't you?"

His face turned slowly toward mine and he grinned.

"What?" I asked as he looked forward again.

"You just used the word 'y'all.' Now all you have to do is learn the difference between y'all and all y'all."

I crossed my arms and settled farther into my seat. "Did I really?" I asked, even though I knew I had indeed said it. "I guess I'm starting to get comfortable here then."

"Becoming a real Southern gal." He pulled into the parking lot of the Sit-a-Spell, which was loaded with a few cars, but mostly trucks.

"Wow, this really *is* the place to go."

Just as he had in the high school parking lot, Rob exited first, coming to my side of the car to open the door. While he walked around the back of the car, I stared out the windshield, taking everything in.

The Sit-a-Spell resembled a log cabin with a wide porch stretching across the front. Nearly every inch of it was occupied by picnic tables and benches, and most of them were filled with patrons. Massive picture windows spread across the front. Inside, people milled around or sat in red vinyl booths. Laughter and music—the same kind I heard in Will's truck every time we got in it—permeated the night air.

Rob opened my door. "Hope you're hungry. The Sit-a-Spell has some pretty good barbecue if you're up for that kind of thing."

Barbecue . . . "Like . . . what?"

We started toward the restaurant. "What do you mean?"

"Barbecue what?"

Rob seemed stunned by my question. "Say what?"

I stopped. "Don't laugh at me."

I saw his cheeks flush in the light coming from the porch. "I wasn't . . ."

"I know, but . . . I know *what* a barbecue is. It's one of those things you grill on. Or it's when friends get together *to* barbecue. But I don't know what you mean when you say they have *good* barbecue."

Understanding washed over him. "Oh . . . I getcha." He reached for my hand and walked me to the single step up the porch that wasn't really a step at all. When I stopped to stare at it, he said, "It's an old cut-down railroad tie."

"Oh." I put my foot on it and it moved enough to make me loop my arm with Rob's.

"You kind of have to put your foot down and then go up with your other one real fast. These things aren't known for being steady, but I guess it beats a cinder block."

"A what?"

He didn't answer. Instead, for the next several minutes we went from one outside table to the next, greeting friends of Rob's whom—I suppose—he'd known his whole life. While they talked—in general about the game—I pulled my hair out of its ponytail. After raking my fingers through my hair and relooping the scrunchie, I looked around for anyone I might know. Or even Will. But he apparently hadn't arrived yet.

From my left, a hand waved at me. I turned fully to see the arm was attached to Alma. "Girl, look at you," she said as she approached. "At the Sit-a-Spell after a game." She nudged me with her elbow. "I saw you sitting down there between Will Decker and your young buck," she said.

Thankfully, Rob had engaged in a conversation with a woman who looked to be of our parents' age, and hadn't heard her. I breathed a sigh of relief. "Alma . . ."

She laughed. "Aww, you know." She looked around. "I just came for a burger and some fries and then I'm back to the paper so I can write up my column. What a game. Did you like it?"

I nodded. "I did. A lot, actually." I leaned closer. "And, listen. About what you overheard today . . . the argument between Will and me. I didn't mean—"

Alma shook her head as though she were trying to loosen something. "You didn't mean diddly-squat. I know you better than that." She looked over her shoulder. "That Will Decker's got you all riled up, I'd say." She elbowed me again. "And I'm thinking I know why."

Alma wasn't one for office gossip—she'd made that clear—but I hoped she'd offer some wisdom to my situation. "Why?" I asked.

Alma crossed her arms. "I know opposites attract, that's what I know. You two got just enough in common and just enough *not* in common."

I raised a hand and opened my mouth to protest. To say, "No, no, nothing like *that.*" But before I could, a raspy voice came over the intercom. "Alma, your takeout is ready."

Alma's large chocolate eyes grew larger. "That's me."

"No, wait . . . ," I said, again hoping to correct her assumption, but as I did, Rob turned. "Oh, hey Alma."

"Hey yourself, Romeo." She winked.

My face grew hot. Rob blinked as though his eyes had caught dust. "Oh, go on . . . ," he said.

"Yes," I said. *Before I find myself so far over my head, I drown.* "See you Monday, Alma."

"Let's go in," Rob said. "See if we can't find a booth."

"You don't want to sit out here?"

"Well," Rob said, "not really. Most of the smoking and drinking goes on out here and the inside is a little more family-friendly."

My eyes swept across the porch. He was right. Nearly everyone sitting or standing outside held a beer bottle. A light veil of cigarette smoke hung in the air, but with the ceiling fans spinning overhead, I'd not noticed it so much before. "Okay."

We went inside where the music wasn't as loud but the laughter just as contagious, and were shown to a booth about halfway back. Rob stood aside, I slid along the bench facing the front of the restaurant, then he slid in beside me. Before we could get truly comfortable, a teenage girl bounced up and asked if we knew what we wanted to drink.

Something told me they didn't have Pellegrino. "Water and lemon," I said.

"Sweet tea." Rob shot a look at me, then back to the girl. "I can go ahead and order for us, if that's okay."

She stood poised and ready. "Go ahead, Mr. Rob."

"Two pulled-pork dinners." He looked at me. "You like coleslaw?"

I had no idea. I'd heard of it, of course, but had never eaten it. Still, I was willing to try, if doing so was part of the after-game ritual. "Sure," I said.

"With coleslaw and baked beans." He looked at me again. "You like baked beans, don't you?"

Gram made the best baked beans, using a recipe she said she'd had since she and my grandfather had first married. "I do."

"Corn bread or Grecian?"

Again, Rob looked at me. "Corn bread?"

Again . . . no idea, though, again, I'd heard of it. I smiled. "I'll try just about anything once." Just about. Even a football game couldn't make me eat too unhealthy.

Rob's brow furrowed, and for a moment I thought he would ask me if I was serious. Instead, he turned back to the girl and said, "Corn bread with your honey-pecan butter."

When the server had stepped away from the table, Rob turned back to me. "What are you grinning at?" he asked.

"The way you said pecan. Pe-cahn."

He shrugged. "What do you say? Pee-can?"

"Well . . . yeah."

The table rocked slightly as Will slid into the opposite side of the booth. "The age-old debate," he said, pulling his hat off and placing it on the seat beside him. "Does it really matter?"

I felt my lips pull tight. Well why didn't he just jump right into the conversation like he owned the place? Because he was William Decker, that's why. A man with no boundaries. No fear of what others might think or say or do.

No, no, no. Alma was wrong if she thought his antagonism had anything to do with a romantic inclination toward me. He'd made that clear at lunch the first day. *No more than any other girl,* he'd said, when speaking of Brianna. Will Decker was not the "looking for love" type.

No sooner had Brianna come to mind than, again, she appeared. Copper-colored hair whipping behind Will's shoulder caught my attention. "Brianna?" I called over the music—a song about some girl being everything the singer ever wanted. Everything he needs.

Brianna turned from a small group of people getting into the booth in front of ours. "Hey," she drawled, her eyes bright. "Hey, Rob. Will. What did y'all think of the game tonight?" She brought one knee up and rested it on the bench where Will sat.

"Good one," Will said.

"Where's that little girl of yours?" Rob asked.

Brianna's eyes momentarily looked toward the ceiling. "With her daddy. It's his weekend." She looked at me. "He brings her back on Sundays before church. So you'll still get to meet her on Sunday."

"Oh, good," I said.

"Heard she did real good over at the 4-H fair last weekend," Rob interjected.

The what?

"She did," Brianna said, her smile growing wider. "Her pig got first place."

"Her *what*?" The words blurted from my lips before I had a chance to catch them.

Brianna brought her attention back to me. "Her pig. She showed him at the 4-H fair last weekend." She sighed dramatically. "Truth is, it's her daddy's pig, but she loves that thing so much, Cliff lets Maris claim it."

Brianna looked over her shoulder at the booth where her friends ordered their drinks from our server. "I reckon I'd better be getting on back." She looked at Will and then at Rob. "Good to see you both again. Y'all come on by the drugstore sometime for lunch, all right?"

"See you soon, Brianna," Will said.

"See ya Sunday," Rob said.

I looked at him as Brianna waved good-bye to me and turned away. "You'll see her Sunday?"

"We go to the same church."

The server was back at our table. "Mr. Will? What can I bring you to drink?"

"Sweet tea." Then, across the table, he said, "Y'all done ordered?"

"Yeah. Pulled pork." Rob tipped his head toward me. "She's never had it before."

Will grinned. "Of course she hasn't." He looked up at the server. "I'll have the same."

"That's nice of Brianna's daughter's father to bring her little girl home before church," I said after the server had walked away, half in observation and half to get the discussion off of my never having had pulled pork.

Rob looked at me. "Couple of young-and-in-loves got caught up in something bigger 'n them, but I'll tell you one thing. They make sure they have Maris at church every Sunday. They walk in together. Sit together. Can't say I agree with their decision *not* to get married, but I applaud their dedication to parenthood."

Will leaned his forearms on the table. "Rob has always had a soft spot for kids."

As if he, apparently, didn't.

I nuzzled closer to my date. "Children are special," I said, as though I knew it firsthand.

Rob smiled.

A sudden thought washed over me. "Pulled pork . . . ," I said. "That's . . . *pig*, isn't it?"

Will laughed at my discomfort over the revelation. "One hundred and ten percent," he answered.

"But it's not Maris's pig," Rob said quickly.

Well, thank the good Lord.

18

Rob?" I asked on our way back to the cottage, elevating my voice just enough to be heard over a song on the radio about some girl whose boyfriend had cheated on her. A Louisville Slugger and four slashed tires. The tune was catchy and the message—I had to admit—made me grin.

Rob turned down the volume. "Yes, ma'am."

"How long has Will been back from Chicago?"

His head turned toward me long enough that I could see the shock in his eyes. "You know about that?" He looked back at the road before us.

"Only that he worked there, came back here, and he has a *Chicago Star* coffee mug on his desk." Ahead, the silhouette of trees filled both sides of the road. As we drove between them, the road grew darker still.

Rob remained quiet for a moment before answering, "About a year now, I guess."

"So, he worked at the *Star*?"

He nodded in answer.

"Working at the *Star* is a fairly high accomplishment."

"He thought so."

"What did he do there?" We turned a corner, the car coming out from between the trees. The moon—full and large—stared down on us, filling the car with pale yellow light.

Rob glanced at me again. "He was one of their top journalists. Didn't he tell you that?"

Surely he was joking. How had a boy from Testament, North Carolina, ended up as one of the "top journalists" at the *Star*? And, why would anyone with that kind of position give it up for *The Testament Tribune*? "Ah . . . no, he didn't tell me. But, you know . . ."

"He's never been one to talk much about himself."

Maybe not, but he was certainly full of himself. "Well, yeah." I crossed my legs and turned ever-so-slightly toward Rob. "So, he was successful?" I paused. "As a journalist for the *Star*?"

Again, he was silent, until, "He was one of their best."

An ad playing for Testament Tires and Radiators had managed not to sell me, but to get on my last nerve. I reached to turn off the radio. I had come too close to learning more about Will Decker and nothing but nothing was going to keep me from it.

"Then why did he come back to Testament?"

Rob made a sharp right into the Decker driveway. We bopped along in silence, the moonlight now flickering through the leafy boughs of the trees. I felt the elevation of the winding road and, when it became apparent Rob was not going to answer me, I faced forward. Everything that had become familiar to me—the shrubs, the tree line, the shimmer of water in the pool, the proud U-shaped house, which we now drove around—seemed to pass by in slow motion until Rob brought the car to a stop beside the cottage.

"You're home," he said, his voice quiet. Too quiet.

"I . . . ," I began, then faltered.

Without looking at me, Rob opened his door, "Let me come around and open the door for you."

"Thank you."

The door opened and closed with a click. Rob ambled around the back of the car, then opened my door just as I unbuckled my seat belt. I swung my legs out. When I scooched forward, his hand came out, palm up. I looked at his face. His eyes seemed sad, but his face bore a hint of a smile. "Help you out?"

I slipped my hand into his strong one. He pulled me up and out. When we were face-to-face, I said, "I didn't mean to hit a bad note in our date. I just"—I shrugged—"didn't know what it might have been to bring him back from such a fabulous place like Chicago and a position with a prestigious paper like the *Star*."

"Because you can't imagine anyone wanting to leave Chicago and the *Star* for a place like Testament and the *Tribune*?" He seemed genuinely wounded, though I couldn't understand why. After all, Rob Matthews hadn't left the *Star* for the local paper. William Decker had.

"It does seem to be a little strange by my way of thinking, if I may be honest."

"Let me walk you to your door," he said, turning.

"Rob?" I said from beside him. I tried to slip my hand into his, but he'd brought his arm around so that his hand rested somewhere between the small and the middle of my back.

"It's okay," he said. "I understand."

I stopped. Looked at him. "No, I don't think you do."

His eyes rested on mine. "Then explain it."

I looked around. The moon and the front porch light lit up the rock garden and the Adirondack chairs as though it were daytime. "Can we sit for a few minutes?"

He led me toward them, waited for me to sit, then chose the chair beside mine. "I'm listening."

I chose my words carefully. "I know Will is your friend," I said.

"More like a brother."

Of course. In Testament, friends were family. "But ever since I've arrived, he's been . . ." I searched for the right word.

Rob's eyes narrowed. "What?"

"Difficult. To say the least. It's been very evident, to me, that he hasn't wanted me here. Which I can't understand. I've tried, but I can't. He didn't know me—doesn't know me, really—and yet it's as if he's been set on making my time here as difficult on me as he possibly can."

Rob blinked several times before he smiled.

"What's so funny?"

"I'm sorry." Rob's eyes darted over my right shoulder and back to me.

"For smiling?"

"No. For Will. I could . . . I could tell you what I *think* is going on, but it wouldn't be right of me." Again, his eyes darted to the right, then back.

I glanced around. "What are you looking at?" I turned back to him.

"The lightning bugs."

"Lightning bugs?"

Rob took my hand as he stood. He guided me to the Adirondack settee, which faced the dark, expansive lawn sloping toward the highway. "Sit," he said.

We sat together and his arm slid around my shoulders. I settled in next to him, felt the warmth of his body against mine. Breathed in the scent of his cologne and the cooling night air. And then . . .

. . . nature put on her show.

I gasped. "Look at that," I whispered. Tiny dots of light flashed against a blue-black backdrop. One here. One there. Another one and then another. And still one more.

I felt Rob's eyes on my face. He said, "You've never seen lightning bugs before?"

I shook my head, unable to answer audibly. Afraid of breaking the magic of the moment. When several long minutes had passed, and dozens of bright pinpricks had broken the darkness, I said, "I've heard Gram talk about them. About being out in the country, watching them with my grandfather when they were dating and newly married. She said . . . she said there was nothing more romantic on earth . . ." I stopped speaking, not wanting Rob to get the wrong idea. At least not so soon. If ever.

His arm tightened, drawing me closer. "Now you know why so many call our corner of the world 'home.'"

I rose early on Saturday, the full-to-the-brim day ahead of me providing both goose bumps of anticipation and chest pains from the anxiety that said I couldn't possibly fit it all in. The previous night, after the lightning bugs and before I walked inside, content for the first time in a long time, Rob had said we'd head over to Chimney Rock for a morning of shopping. But I also had to work later in the day. With Will. The birthday party for Helen Baugh. Followed by another date with Rob.

I pressed the top of the Keurig to make my tea just as my phone rang.

Rob.

"Hey there," I answered with a smile.

"Ashlynne." From the tone of his voice, I knew something was wrong. "I'm so sorry. Something here on the property needs my attention. I have to cancel taking you to Bubba O'Leary's."

"Oh." Well, then . . .

"But, listen. Tonight we're still on, right?"

"Sure." Which made me happy, but not as happy as the day being bookended with him.

"Okay. Go on to Chimney Rock. The staff at Bubba O'Leary's can help you. I promise, you'll be fine."

Of course I would. I'd been shopping alone plenty of times. At least that part of it wasn't new. "Okay. See you later."

After my tea and a shower, I left the cottage in the rearview mirror of my Jag. With my GPS set for Chimney Rock, I turned left at the end of the driveway.

For the next half hour my car wove around deep bends lined by foliage and slabs of jutting rock. Trees stretched and arched. Breaks gave way to vibrant displays of land, lush grass meeting rolling hills in the distance. For a while the road narrowed. Tree branches hung low over the car and the world grew dim.

When it opened again, I passed through the community of Lake Lure, where Rob had promised to take me to dinner that evening. I dared to take my eyes from the curves of the road for a moment.

The lake's water shimmered between cliffs rolling and jutting northward, all brilliant in the early-morning sunlight.

Around another bend, Chimney Rock came into view. I craned my neck to see where the American flag flapped as though it hadn't quite woken. Already, a small group of people gathered on the landmark, while others on the ground moved to and fro in front of the western and Native American–themed storefronts.

I found Bubba O'Leary's, swung my Jag into a parking spot nearby, and exited the car. Outside, the air had already turned warm. I dreaded the eventual heat of the day, but right then it felt good on my skin.

Bubba O'Leary's wasn't like any store I'd ever been in. Highly polished, narrow plank floors greeted the same shoes I'd worn the night before. Old fruit crates, turned on their sides, displayed hats and throw pillows. Antique sideboards and highboys held silver-framed photographs from days gone by, nestled between scarves and backpacks. Clothes—nothing even remotely close to what I typically purchased—hung off peg boards bolted to "log cabin" walls or in clusters on racks. Bins and long tables were stacked with folded tees, jeans, cargo pants, and thick sweaters I couldn't imagine needing any time soon.

Dressed mannequins were positioned strategically around the long, narrow room that smelled a little like vanilla and a lot like leather. Near the wide front window, an old metal hat rack boasted a collection of hats, scarves, and purses. A suede purse drew me; I pulled my fingers through the bottom fringe. Then—curious—flipped the price tag to read it.

Remarkably affordable.

I pulled the purse from the hook and turned to find a salesclerk—young, slightly overweight, but pretty—approaching. "Hey there," she said. "Do you want me to start a dressing room for you?"

"I do." I handed her the purse. "Actually, if you could point me to what I might need for hiking, going to work every day around here, to dinner in Lake Lure at night . . ."

Her eyes brightened at the prospect of what my purchases would mean to her—I felt certain—commission-based pay. "I sure can," she said. "Here, let me put this in a room there in the back for you." She took two steps toward the rear of the store, turned, and said, "Give me two seconds, okay?"

"Not a problem," I said and flashed my best smile. Without thinking about it first.

And for "two seconds" I thought over the past twenty-four hours. The nail salon and the new relationships I'd formed there. I'd attended a football game, tried barbecue, and avoided a near disaster with a new friend. And fireflies.

I'd experienced fireflies . . . watching their nighttime play while leaning against the warmth of another human being who seemed to like me—me—for . . . *me*.

By ten-thirty the backseat of my car looked like Christmas, and Lorelei—my salesclerk and hiking boot expert—was practically financially set for college. She made certain to let me know that she worked three evenings a week—Monday, Tuesday, and Thursday—and always on Saturday mornings. "Should you ever need anything else that I can help you with."

"Thank you, Lorelei," I said. She and I stood outside the store, loading the Jag. "I'm sure I'll be back after the weather turns cooler."

"Until then, I think we have you good and covered should the first dip in temperature be sooner than later." Her eyes widened. "And you never know around here. It just might."

I thanked her again, got in the car, pulled out, and headed back to Testament. I had passed through Green Hill when my cell rang. I reached my hand into the purse sitting on the passenger's seat, dug around until my hand found it, and pulled it out, careful in my reading of the caller ID.

Will Decker.

"Hello?"

"Hey there," he said, his voice low and sleepy. "Wanted to touch base with you about the party this afternoon for Miss Helen." He cleared his throat as though to scare the frogs, as my grandfather used to say.

"All right."

"Uh . . . if you'd like, we can meet at the paper around one-thirty. I'm happy to drive us both out there since you don't know the way to the family's homestead."

I felt too good to argue, but threw an idea in for good measure. "How about we meet at the paper around one-thirty and *I'll* drive us out there."

"You don't want to do that."

"I don't? Why not?"

"Because the house is way out in the piney woods, that's why."

My mind conjured up some of the farms and shacks from *The Andy Griffith Show.* Deeply rutted dirt roads leading to unpainted wooden structures, with rickety steps and dark porches boasting unstable rockers and butter churns. "So what are you saying? My car won't make it down a dirt road?"

"Not these dirt roads."

"What if I said I was willing to take that chance?"

He cleared his throat again, but didn't answer.

"Did you just get up or something?" I asked.

He chuckled. "It's Saturday, remember? Don't tell me you're an early riser, even on Saturday . . ."

"Why wouldn't I be?" I glanced at the sky. A bright blue canvas dotted by cotton-balls of white seemed to be threatened by larger dark-gray monsters. Occasional trees in wide pastures shimmied in a growing breeze.

"Because then I'd have to change one of my opinions about you," he said.

"Which is?"

"That you languish in bed on Saturday mornings until the maid or some other house servant brings you your coffee."

He'd gotten part of that right. "I guess you don't know me as well as you thought. First of all, I prefer tea to coffee; secondly, I don't have a full-time maid; and thirdly, I'm already on my way *back* from Chimney Rock."

"What'd you do there?"

"I don't really see where that's any of your business, but if you must know, I went clothes shopping."

A loud sigh met my ear. I pulled the phone away as though I'd felt the warmth of it. "That must have been a short shopping spree," he said when I returned the phone. "We don't have Nordstrom's or Saks Fifth Avenue in Chimney Rock."

"I wasn't shopping at Saks or Nordstrom's. I went to Bubba O'Leary's, thank you very much."

Silence met my declaration.

"Hello."

"I reckon that's two things about you I'll have to mark off my opinion list."

"I *reckon* so."

"Back to the driving issue. Listen, I'm trying to be nice here—especially after the whole sixty-yard-line issue . . ." He paused long enough to add a low chuckle. "But if you insist on driving, I don't guess my backside will mind sitting on luxurious leather."

"Meet you at the paper at one-thirty then," I said.

"If you say so."

19

Clouds grew darker and the wind more threatening with every quarter mile I ventured down dirt roads so rutted, I thought my car would end up in pieces, drizzled between the main road and the site of Helen Baugh's party. I gripped the wheel. My knuckles grew white. My eyes darted between vine-wrapped shrubs lining the road and the hard-packed dirt in front of us. The ruts appeared like waves on the ocean. Some deeper and wider than others.

Beside me, Will Decker read the owner's manual he'd retrieved from the glove box as though he might need to know more than just how to adjust the passenger-side air-conditioning. The muscles in my shoulders pulled taut. I shot a glance toward him. If he'd tried any harder to swallow the smirk on his face, he would have choked and I would have been forced to perform CPR.

He should be so lucky.

Without so much as a look up, he said, "Told you the truck would have been better."

"Hush." I returned my concentration to the road. "That piece of junk wouldn't have made it this far, to my way of thinking."

"Hunk-a-junk."

"What?"

"We call them 'hunk-a-junk.' If you want to say it right, you say 'hunk-a-junk.' "

"How enlightening." My eyes burned from needing to blink, which I dared not do.

Will chuckled. "That hunk-a-junk has been down this road more times than I care to count, so I hate to disappoint you, but . . ."

I elected to say nothing in response.

"You'd best hope it doesn't rain." He leaned forward, pulling the seat belt with him, and looked out the windshield. The brim of his hat touched the glass. "Looks promising . . ."

My choice to ignore him only seemed to further stir his mirth at my expense.

"How much farther?" I finally asked.

Will leaned back. "Another few miles."

"Define 'few.' "

"Great-granny, girl. I dunno. Five. Six."

The bones in my neck cracked as I whipped my head to the right. "Are you serious? How far out did Miss Helen live?"

His lips pursed. "About fourteen, fifteen miles, I reckon. I've never really measured the distance."

"I have a question for you . . ."

"Another one?" He closed the manual and returned it to the glove box.

I bit my lip and counted to ten. "Yes, another one." I glanced at him. Surprise jolted me physically; his attention was solely on me. "Have you worn a cowboy hat your entire life or is this something new?"

His index finger rose to the brim and pushed against the felt, exposing more of his eyes. Mine locked on them, for the first time really seeing the chocolate and amber that, when mixed, built a fire of their own making. "I see you got some new duds."

I ever-so-briefly glanced at my lap. For the party, I'd chosen an outfit purchased at Bubba O'Leary's—a lightweight cotton scoop-neck top and a pair of slim-leg denim jeans. "I did. This morning."

"You look nice."

My head whipped toward him again just as the front wheels of my car hit a bump. The car pitched to the right, the back tires swung to the left. The steering wheel took on a mind of its own, spinning with such force, my hands flew back.

Will reached over. "Hold on, hold on," he said. His hands gripped the wheel and spun it to the right, the left, back to the right. "Ease into the brakes!"

I did as he ordered, my hands pressing against the leather at my thighs. His elbows jabbed my chest, pushing me farther into my seat. When the car slid to a stop, we faced the wrong direction. Heavy breathing filled the inside of the car, lessening until Will twisted the gearshift to park. "You hit a pothole."

I pressed a hand to my chest, felt the thudding of my heart. "A what?"

Will let out a deep breath through his nostrils. "Do you want me to drive the rest of the way?"

I shook my head. "I can do it. I'm not completely inept."

He pulled his hat from his head, raking his fingers through his hair, and replaced the hat. "Just when it comes to fishtailing."

Potholes and fishtailing. "To *what*?" Gram should have told me I'd need an English-to-Southern dictionary to survive six months in Testament.

"Nothing. Turn the car around. And for pity's sake, drive slowly."

"Slowly? I've barely been crawling. The last thing I want to do is beat *my* car to death."

The fire in his eyes met mine again. "I *told* you."

"I *know*!"

"Do you want *me* to drive?" he asked through clenched teeth.

I clenched mine in response. "I can do it," I ground out.

"Then *do* it!"

I growled at him, turned the selector to drive, and eased the car in the right direction.

"Your car," he said, with no lead-in, when we'd inched a few yards forward.

"What about it?"

"How much did it set you back?"

"Does it matter?"

"Just thought I'd ask. You being so protective of it."

"And I'm going to answer you so you can criticize my spending habits?"

"Doesn't matter what it cost you. It's extravagant. You going to deny that?"

"No. But I earn enough, and I don't have children to spend my money on . . ."

"What about other children? Children who are less fortunate? Ever think about what the money you spent on this one car could do for them?"

I took several deep breaths before answering. And, even though my breathing returned to normal, my heartbeat had not. Where had his anger come from, this intense emotion inside him? He'd made his unnecessary remarks before about my car, but now to blame me—practically—for the unmet needs of *children*?

In junior high I'd believed—albeit briefly—that my family's money, that living where we lived and how we lived and being who we were, would buy me into the hearts of little girls I'd wanted to be like. When that turned out not to be so—when it worked against me rather than for me—I learned to accept what I could afford for what it was. A means to whatever end I wanted. And I'd told myself that there was nothing wrong with having what I wanted. I was a nice person, after all. Deep down. Whether anyone recognized that, was not my responsibility.

Still, if I were to be honest with myself, even for a millimeter of a moment . . .

"I admit," I said finally, "that I've not really thought much about children who are less fortunate." I glanced at him. Disappointment registered on his face. "You're shocked?" I asked, the anger returning. "You think so little of me, and you're shocked?"

He drew his teeth over his bottom lip. "I don't think little of you."

"No?" I flexed my fingers and regripped the steering wheel.

"No."

"Then . . . what? Because you've done nothing but prejudge me since I got here. I have somehow managed to live through the longest week of my life, thanks in large part to you."

"Not very Christian of me, is it?"

His voice had filled with grief. I recognized it easily. This had been the sound Gram made, shortly after Papa's death, when she realized she'd live the remainder of her life without him. This had been the sound of grief I'd heard when Leigh's twin brother, Lawson, had died. When she called to tell me. When we sat huddled in a corner of her bedroom, with our knees drawn up to our chests, my arms wrapped awkwardly around her shoulders. Leigh had buried her mouth in the palm of her hand and wailed. In agony at the loss of her brother. In anger at the drug that had stolen him.

And this was the root of emotion that had come from my gut when the girls in seventh grade hadn't accepted me the way I thought they would. Had *expected* they would.

How odd the same sound of sadness should come from William Decker. Different, but the same.

I stopped the car.

"What are you doing?" he asked me.

"Stopping."

"Why?"

"Are you okay?"

His eyes narrowed. "I'm fine. Why?"

My mind ran over the words we'd spoken in the last five minutes. "It grieved you that you didn't—as you say—act very Christian."

His face jerked. "Yeah," he said between lips that barely parted.

"And?"

He looked to his lap, pulled the hat off again, and turned his face slowly toward mine. "It's not really you. Okay?"

"So Rob indicated." At least, sort of indicated.

Will's jaw flexed. "Oh, yeah? What *did* Rob tell you? Exactly."

The anger I'd felt earlier had left me and settled on him. To such extent it frightened me. Not that I thought Will might hit me, but more that it seemed to come from someplace so deep and so controlled, it would consume him.

"Nothing, really. He told me nothing." I kept my voice barely above a whisper. Something Mom had taught me. Keep the voice calm and the situation will remain calm as well. "Just that he understood why you've acted like you have, but that it wouldn't be right for him to talk to me about it."

He said nothing, just fingered the rim of the hat's brim. But his eyes remained narrowed and only short breaths came in and out of his nostrils.

I tried a new tactic. "Rob indicated it should come from you."

He chuckled then. "Nice try." And just like that, the anger dissipated.

I tried to smile, but confusion wouldn't allow for it. "Does that mean you aren't going to tell me why you're such a bully?"

"I'm not a bully." He returned the hat to his head.

"You're an enigma, that's what you are."

Will looked at me again. The glint in his eyes told me he liked hearing that. "In what way?"

"One minute you bark at me for coming in late when I didn't even know the starting time. The next minute you're doing something like removing the goo from the seat belt of your truck. You open doors for me—which is nearly unheard of these days—but don't introduce me to people in anything that remotely resembles a proper fashion. You brutally tell me what you think of me but won't allow me to tell you what I think of you. You work with children on your time off, and you go to church on Sunday."

"I do." He paused. His eyes searched mine as if they were trying to gaze into my soul, to see what I might truly be made of. As if to say that maybe he didn't know my "type" as well as he thought he did. "What else?"

"You love your grandparents enough to come back from Chicago—"

"Let's not talk about Chicago, shall we?" He looked forward. "Enough about me. Come on. Drive. We'll be later than we already are."

I returned my hands to the wheel. "And the moment is gone," I muttered.

Helen Baugh lived in a sprawling farmhouse at the end of a narrow dirt road with grass growing between the ruts. Vine-wrapped brambles grew on both sides, intermittently entwining with skinny trees whose leaves appeared lifeless. When I first saw the house, I blinked at the size of it, then frowned at how badly it needed a new coat of paint. "Tell me about Helen Baugh," I said to Will as I parked at the end of a mammoth row of cars and trucks, and one old school bus with "Testament Nursing Home" painted on the side. "Other than that she is the birthday girl."

"She's ninety years old."

"I *know* that part."

We both opened our doors and got out, me not willing to wait for him to come around. After all, I had been in the driver's seat.

From over the roof of the car, Will said, "Be nice."

I gawked at him. "I'm being nice."

"Then don't be smart-alecky."

I lifted my eyes to heaven. "Okay. Whatever you say. Tell me whatever you can about Helen Baugh, please, sir."

He shut his door with a grin. I grabbed my new suede purse and did the same, but without the smile.

Will came up beside me and we started to the front porch steps. "When Helen Baugh was fairly young," he started, keeping his voice low, "she married the man whose family had owned this farm. He was older than Miss Helen and—it was often rumored—into one thing or another. He'd already been married once before. For reasons no one *ever* talks about, the previous Mrs. Baugh had taken off for parts unknown."

I looked at Will and he shrugged. "I have no idea where she went," he said, answering my unspoken question.

"Did they have children?" I asked. "The first Mr. and Mrs. Baugh?"

"Three. They were all grown by then—early twenties—and older than Miss Helen."

I stopped. "You're kidding."

Will stopped too. "That's the way of some things, you know? Back then?" He looked down, his face shadowed by his hat.

"I reckon."

One side of his mouth turned up. "If you're going to fit in around here, you might as well say it right and not half right."

If I were going to fit in? I swelled at the statement—it meant that the one person I was trying hardest with and gotten the least far with, had opened a door. "What did I say?"

"I reckon."

"Wasn't that how I said it?"

"Yes, ma'am, you did. But you said it wrong." The lopsided smile grew larger. "Try: Shoot, I reckon."

"Shoot, I reckon."

Will shook his head. "More emphasis on the 'shoot.'"

I took a deep breath. "*Shoot,* I reckon."

His eyes widened, but his lips broke into a full smile. "Not *that* much emphasis. Try it again; this time give the 'shoot' a little more attitude but not so much emphasis."

I couldn't help but smile back. "But you said 'emphasis.'"

He pulled on the hat's brim. "Never mind what I said. Try it. Add some sass. You know how to do that much, right?" The right half of his lips came up again. "Right?"

I cocked my head as my eyes locked with his. "*Shoot*, I reckon."

Will clapped his hands together once. "There ya go!"

"Hey!" Rob's voice came from the front porch, causing us both to turn. He stood on the top step and waved his arm in greeting. "Glad to see you made it," he said, then trotted down the steps and over to where we stood.

I smiled, happy to see him, yet, strangely, felt put upon. I'd enjoyed talking with Will in those few moments between the car and where we now stood. Even though earlier he'd pushed every button inside me, I wanted to reach something inside him. If he'd let me. For a second—the tiniest of brief seconds—I thought perhaps I could get close enough. Clos*er*, perhaps. We'd had a moment back there on the road. Another one here. And I wanted it back. Long enough to see what lay on the other side if we pushed through.

"When did ya get here?" Will asked Rob as they shook hands.

"Half an hour ago." He looked at his watch. "And boy, you're late. Most folks have eaten, the cake has been cut, and your grandfather is frothing at the mouth." Kind eyes found me. "I'm glad you came, but . . . did you drive *your* car?" And then to Will, "I can't believe you let her drive that Jag out here."

"Believe me," Will said, "you don't want to go there."

"We'd better go in," I said, more to Will than Rob. "Before your grandfather fires me."

"Like that's going to happen."

The three of us continued forward. "Will was just telling me about Miss Helen," I said to Rob.

"About her marriage to Old Man Baugh," Will supplied.

"What a horrible thing to call someone," I said.

"You didn't know the man. Well, *I* didn't know the man. But my grandmother told me enough stories . . ."

"And most of them are probably true," Rob concurred.

We climbed the front porch steps. Laughter and conversation poured from inside. The aroma of fried chicken mixed with the sweet scent of a flowering vine wrapped around the porch posts. "Sounds like quite a crowd," I said.

"Oh there is. And let me go ahead and warn you—hot as blue blazes in there." Rob's hand found mine. "Hey," he whispered. "I know you're here to work . . ."

"You've got that right," Will said. I cut my eyes toward him and gave him my best "Don't you dare" look. The same look I'd given my father not so many days ago in Gram's office.

"Come on now, boy," Rob said. He pulled me along the left side of the wraparound porch. "I was just going to say that I have some people I want to introduce her to."

"I'd love to meet them."

Will chortled. "You don't even know who they are."

"If they're friends of Rob's . . ."

"More than friends," he said. "My mom and dad are here. My sister and her family . . ."

I looked up at Will, whose eyes held a mixture of "I told you so" and amusement.

I took a moment, just long enough to swallow apprehension. "Oh," I said. Nothing more. Just "oh."

20

We neared an old, decorative screen door. The rusty screen buckled. The gray paint was more off than on. But ferns spilling out of wicker planters placed between antiquated rockers gave a cheerful hello and the aroma of Southern food only enhanced the welcome. I made out silhouettes and shadows of the crowd inside. "Is the entire town here?"

"Near 'bout," Rob said. "Miss Helen is a bit of a legend."

Will opened the door. It squeaked in resistance.

"There you are," his grandfather boomed before we'd even crossed the threshold where warm, thick air met us. The house, old as it was, had never had air-conditioning added. This, plus the number of people inside and the cooking, made for instant heat.

"Hey, Big Guy. We had some . . . car—uh—problems."

"You're here now," Shelton said over conversation and the clatter from the kitchen. Then to me, "Come on in, girl. Come on in. The birthday girl is excited to meet you."

"Me?"

Rob beamed beside me. "She remembers your grandparents," he said.

I felt my smile travel all the way to my toes. "Really? She knew Gram and Papa?"

Bobbie came up beside her husband. "Come with me, dear."

Rob released my hand and I followed Bobbie out of what appeared to be a small den with outdated furniture into a larger family room. Certainly not a formal living room. The furniture was just as archaic, but not as old. None of it matched and none of it seemed to matter. The birthday "girl," who sat in an overstuffed recliner, commanded the room and stole the show.

Even sitting, Helen Baugh appeared short but ample. She wore a pink suit that looked new and stylish, and a pink feathery tiara atop her carefully coiffed silver-white hair. Large eyes met mine from behind oversized glasses. "Is this her?"

"Miss Helen," Bobbie Decker said, her voice rising a decibel, "this is Ashlynne Rothschild. She's Connie and Richard's granddaughter."

Helen Baugh shooed away a young man sitting on an ottoman in front of her. "Skedaddle," she said. "And go get me some more punch. I'm so hot in here I could die." She beat the ottoman with a walking cane that had been resting against her chair. "Come sit, girl."

I did as I was told.

"You look a lot like Connie," she said, bringing clammy hands to my face. "I can see it in your eyes."

"Thank you." I placed my hands over hers and brought them down to rest between us.

"She was a beautiful woman."

"She still is."

The young man who'd been sent to get punch returned. "Here, Granny."

"Set it on the table there," she told him with a wave of her hand. Then to me, "One of my grands."

"I'm one of your *great*-grands, Granny," he said with a shake of his head. Then, to me, "Can I get you anything, ma'am?"

"Punch would be nice," I said, relieved to have something cold coming my way.

"Hot, ain't it?" Miss Helen asked.

I nodded. "Yes, it is."

"Tryin' to figure out how in the world we ever lived like this, I 'spect."

This time I chuckled. "I admit, I am."

"Well, chile, when you didn't know no different, you just made do. Course in the earlier years of my marriage, we didn't have the kitchen as part of the main house."

"Really? How interesting . . ." And it was. "You'll have to tell me more for the piece we'll write about your party."

An older woman sitting nearby laughed heartily. "Mama will be more than happy to fill your ears with stories. She's got a million of them."

I glanced at the woman, smiled briefly, then turned back to Miss Helen.

"Never mind that now," she said. "How's Connie?" I couldn't help but notice that her eyes had not left my face.

"She's doing well. When I talk to her tonight, I'll be sure to tell her I met you."

"She'll remember me," she said with a nod of her head. "I was there, you know, the night the four of them"—she nodded toward Bobbie and Shelton, who'd joined us—"the night they all decided to start the magazine."

"Well, I guess Miss Bobbie told you I'm here to help start it back up."

The old woman patted my hand. "Good. That was a awful good magazine in its time and I bet it could be again."

"I hope so." I glanced at Bobbie. "I'm hoping that by the end of next week I'll have everything in motion to start."

Miss Helen grinned then; a few of her teeth were missing. "You could do a story on this old girl," she whispered. "And put my old mug on the cover."

"She means her picture," Will's voice spoke from over my shoulder.

I looked behind me. He stood, cowboy hat dangling from between his fingers. I mouthed, "Thank you," grateful my vision of Miss Helen's coffee mug gracing the cover of the magazine was in error.

"We went to a restaurant to celebrate," Miss Bobbie added. "Your grandparents and Shel and I."

"To celebrate?" I asked.

"The night we decided to join our talents and go into business together."

I couldn't help but think of what the four of them must have looked like. Young. Eager. Ready to take the world by storm.

"Celebrated at Harry's where I worked as a waitress," Helen said. "That was after Mr. Baugh had passed, and I needed the extra money to raise my young'uns."

"Harry's," Shelton said, as though he were in a world of his own. "Sure miss his fried catfish."

Miss Helen chortled as she looked at Mr. Shelton, who stood next to his grandson. "Them was good eats, weren't they?" She returned her attention to me. "You going to cover football?"

Will shifted behind me. "Miss Helen, football isn't exactly Ashlynne's forte."

"Gotta have football," Miss Helen said. "And gotta know something *about* it."

I heard snickering. And muttering. And I knew the voices, knew them too well. They had robbed me of any moments of joy—or at least they tried to—every day for the past week.

The girls from advertising.

Tension ran through my veins. Nothing I'd done had swayed their sarcasm, but that didn't keep me from trying. Nor did it keep me from turning and smiling at them now, but to no avail.

Rob entered the room with a cluster of people behind him. He carried a small pink paper plate with a large slice of cake and a clear plastic cup filled with punch. "I intercepted," he said, bringing them both to me.

"Oh." I swallowed frustration at the cattiness of the three women. Kicked myself for allowing them to get to me. Most of the people here who knew me, liked me. Why was I allowing myself to even *think* about the three who did not?

Ignore them, Gram would say. So I focused on the kind man who stood before me with punch and cake. "Thank you, Rob." I took the plate and punch and swung around to give Miss Helen my full attention again.

"Tell me something, young lady," she said. "How is it you live in the South and you don't know nothing about football?"

I took a much-needed sip of punch. The tartness tickled my tongue and quenched my growing thirst. "It's not that I don't know *anything* . . ." And Winter Park, Florida, is *hardly* "the South." Old Florida, yes. But you'd have to go north to get south of there.

"Well, then. Tell me what you do know," she ordered.

"Ah . . . well. Ah." I peered over my shoulder once more. The girls from advertising seemed to have grown all the more interested in my discomfort. I looked back to Miss Helen, my mind scrambling over everything I'd learned the night before, searching for some little tidbit beyond the goalposts and the yard lines that would help me appear somewhat knowledgeable. "Well, I know one thing for sure," I said, elevating my voice, "Number 75 is a running back heading straight for the Heisman trophy."

The rain started shortly before the party's intended end time, but fell like a deluge, creating enough noise to make conversation difficult. Water cascaded from the roof in narrow waterfalls, spilling to the ground where deep, muddy puddles formed among leaf-bare shrubs.

"We'd better get out of here while we can," Will mumbled in my ear. "Before everyone else tries to."

I stood at one of the floor-to-ceiling windows at the front of the house, looking out to the blur of automobiles, including mine, in the grass-sparse yard. I turned and crossed my arms. "Why?"

"Because if we go last, we'll get bogged down in the ruts left by the others. Not to mention that road's gonna be slick as an eel's belly."

Ew.

I uncrossed my arms. "Won't everyone make a beeline for their cars and just stir up the mud?"

"Most have decided to wait it out." His eyes traveled to the floor. Back up to me. "Besides, don't you need to get ready for your date tonight?"

I looked at my watch. Rob and his family had left more than a half hour before for that very reason. "Yeah, I guess so." I took a few steps. "I'll say good-bye to your grandparents and to Miss Helen."

"I'll meet you on the front porch."

I walked past him, then looked over my shoulder. "How are we going to get to the car without an umbrella?"

He gave a half-smile. "Run."

I said good-bye to the Deckers, then to Miss Helen. "I wish you didn't have to go," she said. "I've had a good time talking to you about the old days."

"I wish I didn't, too, Miss Helen," I said, and it was true. I had spent hours on the opposite side of normal, and yet had felt comfortable in my surroundings. At home. "But Will thinks it's best that we leave before the roads get . . . slick."

The old woman nodded. "I know that's right. But I'd appreciate it if you came to see me sometime at the nursing home. I have a lot of stories I could tell you," she said.

I kissed her dry and wrinkled cheek. It felt awkward doing so, but I wanted to nonetheless. "I'll do that," I said, fully intending to do so.

I said good-bye to a few others, including the girls from advertising, who had nothing to say back to me. I shrugged. "You know," I said to them in a low voice, "if you came to my hometown, I'd at least be nice to you."

When they still had nothing to say, I sighed and walked out of the room.

As he said he would be, Will stood a foot from the front porch steps. Several others had gathered there as well, but they stood against the wall in a futile effort to stay dry.

"You'd better let me drive," he said without looking at me. "And I'm as serious as a heart attack about it."

I knew he was. "All right," I said over the rhythm of the storm. I held the purse close to my chest. "My purse is going to be ruined."

"Tuck it under your shirt there."

"Will that help?"

"Probably not."

I did it anyway. Will's right arm slid around my shoulder while his left hand reached across and grabbed my left arm. Without so much as a "Go!" he started down the steps, taking me with him.

We were drenched within seconds. "Sopping wet"—or so Will said—when we made it inside the car.

I ran my hands down the exposed parts of my arms to draw off the excess water, then slung my hair from my face. Will pulled his hat from his head, popped it a few times with his hand, sending a spray of water to the dashboard.

"Careful," I said.

"Like it's going to matter," he shot back.

I looked at him. He returned the glare. Hard as I tried to keep my lips in a straight line, when his broke into a smile, mine did too.

"You look like a wet rat," he said.

I pulled the visor down and looked into the mirror. I burst out laughing. "Oh dear. I sure do."

Will flipped the visor back up before pushing the starter button.

"Have you ever driven a Jag?"

He turned the selector to reverse the car. "Would you believe me if I said I had?"

"I guess so. You haven't lied to me so far, I don't think."

We eased out of the yard and into the muddy road. Will kept the car steady as the wiper blades swiped back and forth, barely making a dent in clearing the water away. I had to remind myself to breathe. Every other second I had to keep myself from saying something stupid, such as, "Don't wreck my car." I knew if I did, I'd end up on the side of the road.

After twenty minutes, I said, "How far have we gone?"

"Not far enough."

I turned the air conditioner as far down as it would go and rubbed at the gooseflesh on my arms. Will caught the movement; his eyes glanced over as the car revved then spun and slid. My eyes widened and my mouth gaped as I watched his hands fight the wheel, but to no avail. When we finally stopped, my door on the passenger's side had pressed into a mucky embankment.

Will unbuckled his seat belt faster than I could gasp. "Are you all right?"

I turned my face slowly to his. "I'm—I'm fine." I looked out the window to where razor-wire branches pressed against the window and dark mud oozed upward on the glass. "*My car*!" The driver's door opened, taking my attention with it. "Where are you going?"

"To get us out of the mud before we're buried in it."

I unbuckled my seat belt and crawled over the console. "What does *that* mean?"

"Get behind the wheel," he said.

I already was. Once settled, I stuck my head out and watched him trudge through the rain and the mire to the back of the car. If his shirt hadn't been clinging to his frame enough, it surely was now.

"And close the door, but power down the window."

I blinked, forcing my mind back to the issue at hand and followed his instructions. "Do you know what you're doing?" I hollered.

"There's not a boy in these parts that hasn't gone boggin' at some point or another." He hunkered down behind the fender. "All right. Put it in neutral."

I did.

"Now give her a little gas . . ."

Mud covered Will Decker, but the car—banged up as it was—now rolled westward toward an asphalt heaven. Neither of us spoke. He was too filthy and I was too shaken.

Truth be told, if I'd said one word, I'd have burst out laughing. My $95,000 car was banged up on the passenger side, the interior now held a layer of mud and rainwater, and a sludge-covered man who growled with every other yard we traveled. All-in-all the entire scene was pretty amusing.

We were mere feet from the highway when Will said, "See that narrow driveway right there?"

"Where?"

"To the right. There." He pointed and his voice sounded agitated.

"Oh. Yeah."

"Turn there."

"Why?"

He growled again. "Just turn."

I did. As the rain continued—now more of a summer shower—I drove between leafy sycamores lined behind white split-rail fences. Then the paved road became a drive, winding its way around a grand two-story house with large white columns and sprawling wings. "What in the world . . ."

"Drive around to the back," Will said.

Behind the house stood a small guesthouse next to a pool. Behind the guesthouse, mist rose over a lake where a short arched bridge led to a white-latticed gazebo. "Where are we?" I asked.

"Be it ever so humble . . ."

I jerked the car to a stop and my head to look at the back of the mansion. "Excuse me?" He'd condemned me for being brought up in privilege and he lived *here*?

But Will pointed to the small 1940s guesthouse where a large dog sat on his haunches and barked. "No. There." He looked down at himself. "I need to change. If I stay like this any longer, I'm going to be permanently caked in mud."

I wasn't willing to let it go. "Do you mind telling me, then, who lives in *that* house?" I asked, pointing.

He opened his car door. "I don't mind at all. My parents." He hoisted himself from the passenger's seat.

My mouth fell open as the door closed. His parents? *His parents*? The missionaries?

I got out of the car and trudged to the front porch as Will stuck his key into the front door lock. The dog, who wagged his wet tail and seemed unimpressed with a stranger on the porch, looked anxiously up at his master. "Wait a second," I said. Droplets of rain pelted my already damp skin.

He looked at me as the door swung open. “What?” The dog ran inside.

“I hate to ask, but do you have a bathroom in there you’d feel comfortable with me using? I’m miserable wet and I’ve got to . . . you know.”

His brow furrowed under the brim of his hat. “Why wouldn’t I feel comfortable?”

No surprise that the one thing Rob was concerned about, Will didn’t bother to consider. “The two of us? In the house? Alone?”

“Ah.” He looked inside and back to me. “Tell you what. I’ll run up to the main house and shower and change. Feel free to use the guest bath, shower if you’d like, and I’ll meet you back here in about a half hour.” He eyed me. “I think my mother’s closet has something left in it that I can bring down to you.”

I stepped onto the porch and out of the rain. “That would be great.” I peered into the house. “What about your dog?”

“Rufus? He probably went straight to his bed in the laundry room to dry out. You don’t have to worry about him. He’s an old boy.” With that he darted off the porch, around the pool, and to a set of French doors he slipped another key into before stepping inside.

“Wow,” I said. “Wait till Leigh hears about this.”

21

I inched through the still house, taking in the décor and the furnishings a man like Will Decker chose for his home.

These were no ordinary pieces. Many were hand-carved and Will's attention to detail was everywhere—from the carefully chosen artwork to the throw pillows on the sofa and the thick, spice-scented candles clustered in the center of the dining room table. As at Bobbie and Shelton's, antique pieces shared the space with newer, giving the house a warm and homey feeling.

I searched for the bathroom. Not that it was so difficult to find. Its door stood open toward the back, on the right side of the house, exposing a retro room of black tile and white porcelain. There were two pedestal sinks with an antique bench between them. On the bench, a wicker basket filled with rolled towels and hand cloths. Over each sink hung a large oval mirror—antique and authentic to the period of the house. On both sides of the mirrors hung brass sconces; between them a brass towel hoop. Along the painted hardwood floor, thick oval rugs had been thrown for the comfort of cold feet on wintery mornings.

"Nice," I said.

After using the facilities, I washed my hands, dried them on a white hand towel embroidered with a scrolling black *D*, then refolded it and looped it through the hook. Only then did I peer toward the door as though the dog, Rufus, would saunter in and, upon seeing my misbehavior, would run to find Will and tell on me. When he didn't, I pulled the medicine cabinet door toward me, popping it open so expertly, no telltale sign followed.

What might lie behind it, I wondered. What secrets now-hidden but soon to be revealed might shed some light on the owner of this house?

The door was fully open and I frowned; nothing rested on its narrow shelves.

I left the room and searched for the kitchen, which I found at the back of the house. Long, narrow, and unadorned windows stretched across three walls. On any other day, the room—decorated like a farmhouse kitchen complete with antique wooden bowls filled with fresh fruit—would have been washed in sunlight. Today, the room was bathed in gray and blue.

A BrewStation coffeemaker stood to the left of the white porcelain sinks. Metal cabinets hung overhead. I opened both doors wide to find, for the most part, what I had been in search of. No tea, but plenty of coffee and mugs. I set about preparing a pot, then ambled back to the bathroom, fully intending to leave my exploration of Will Decker's charming home with the kitchen. But a small room between it and the bathroom—its door opened wide and inviting—stopped me.

I peered in. Stopped when I heard the dog's groan, as though he were settling down on old joints and bones. I waited. When the house returned to silent, I looked into the room again. An antique rolltop desk stood catty-corner against the far side of the room. A green, red, and blue plaid wingback chair, floor lamp, and a short stack of books dominated the other corner. And, on both sides of the narrow room, impressive floor-to-ceiling bookshelves took up most of the wall space.

"Well, would you look," I said aloud. And, in spite of knowing full well that snooping of this caliber was wickeder than merely peeking into medicine cabinets, I walked into the room. Held my breath. Allowed my eyes to adjust to the near-darkness because I didn't dare turn on a light.

I ran my fingertips—wrinkled as they were from being cold and wet—along the leather-bound classics. *Of Human Bondage. To Kill a Mockingbird. The Innocents Abroad. Pilgrim's Progress.* Even a collection of Dickens and Hardy—to more current titles. Some in hardback. Some in paperback. One shelf held nothing but theological academic titles. Others "Christian Living." An entire shelf had been dedicated to a collection of Bibles.

I came to the end of the bookcase—the one nearest the desk—and stopped short. A large diploma, beautifully framed, hung on the wall. I blinked, stunned by what it proclaimed.

William Alexander Decker had graduated from my alma mater. The same university where I'd graduated magna cum laude, he'd graduated five years earlier, summa cum laude.

"Un-be-lievable," I breathed. And wouldn't you just know it . . .

I turned to face the other wall, bypassing the desk. There, between the bookshelf and the chair, hung several framed newspaper articles, each from the *Chicago Star,* each with the byline: William A. Decker, Senior Reporter. Other frames held newspaper articles showing Will receiving awards or shaking hands with dignitaries. One in particular caught my eye. I leaned in to study the caption beneath a photo of William, flanked by a stout but distinguished man on one side, and a glamorous blonde on the other.

"Chicago's Golden Boy of Journalism, William A. Decker," I whispered as I read, "senior reporter for the *Chicago Star,* received the prestigious Conrad R. Moses Award of Excellence in Reporting on Monday evening . . ." My voice trailed until the last line. "Pictured with Mr. Decker are Conrad Moses and his daughter, Felicia Moses."

Felicia Moses. Her arm linked possessively through Will's. Her face glowing like a woman in love. Her spectacular white gown a Vera Wang original if I'd ever seen one. And the pearl clutch a Natasha Couture I recognized because, one, I owned one much like it and, two, I *adore* Natasha Couture . . .

One final detail answered every question I'd had since arriving in Testament, North Carolina.

"Well, no wonder," I said.

I didn't need to turn a light on to see the obvious; the blonde looked remarkably like me.

—∞—

"Thanks for the coffee."

William Decker and I stood outside of his modest home, staring at the back of the mansion he'd grown up in through only a mist of rain. He'd brought me a wraparound dress, which was a tad outdated, from his mother's closet. Not that I complained. It fit. It was dry. And besides, I was too busy trying to sort through my feelings about Felicia Moses. The fact that we looked so much alike. The mystery of who she'd been to him, him to her, and if the hidden story of their lives together held the key to his on-again/off-again treatment of me.

Had she broken his heart? Had he broken hers? I couldn't ask, of course. To ask meant confessing to Will my compulsion to snoop. My tendency to go where I didn't belong. Instead, I'd showered, wrapped myself in one of the fat, thirsty towels, and poured two cups of coffee.

Now, fully dressed and standing outside, I studied the man standing near steps that led to a rain-drenched lawn. We both clutched our mugs of steaming coffee as though they were life preservers. I brought mine to my lips and took a sip.

"So tell me," I said.

He looked at me. He'd dressed in a clean pair of jeans and a Tommy Hilfiger polo shirt, which he wore untucked. His hat had been tossed to the seat of an old metal glider and his boots were airing out near his bare feet. "Tell you what?"

I glanced to the house in answer.

"My mother's father," he said. "Big Guy has done well for himself, as you've seen, but my mother's father was the tycoon."

"In what?"

"Lumber." He leaned against one of the porch railings and looked out over the property. "My grandmother—Mom's mother—died shortly after I was born, so I don't really remember her."

I pressed my back against the doorframe and took another sip of coffee, waiting.

"My parents were living in the guesthouse at the time . . ." He cast a look to the front door. "They ended up moving in with my grandfather to help take care of things. After he died, we stayed in the big house and used the guesthouse for out-of-town family or guests of the newspaper."

"Were you close to him? Your grandfather?"

"Not like I am to Big Guy. My other grandfather—this grandfather—was first and foremost a businessman." He smiled. "Big Guy is too, but he's also a man who loves the land. Fishing. Hunting. Hiking in the woods."

Take long walks . . .

"I bought hiking boots today."

Will's eyes widened. "Did you now?"

"Rob is going to take me hiking on the trails in Chimney Rock." I spoke the words matter-of-factly, as though *of course he would.* But in my heart, I knew—I *knew*—what I wanted was for the man in front of me to volunteer to guide me along those trails. Or any trails. I wanted to know him.

Better.

Or at all.

What was *wrong* with me? This was not like me at all. I—who hardly dated, *ever*—had an adorable young man picking me up within a few hours for a date *he* had asked *me* out on, and I couldn't seem to get Will Decker from under my skin.

Will Decker, who took another sip of coffee as though he were not interested at all in my declaration of hiking with Rob. But his eyes studied me nonetheless. "Is that right?"

I nodded, then nervously drained the last of my coffee. I looked into the empty cup for lack of something else to do. "I'll take my mug back inside." I focused on his mug. "How about you? Want more while I'm in there?"

Will peered into his cup. "Nah, I'm good."

The screen door slammed behind me as I entered the house and walked straight to the kitchen. I washed the coffee mug, turned it upside down in the drainer, and walked back through the house toward the front door.

"Hey, Ashlynne?"

I stopped just inside the screen. Will was sitting on the glider, pulling his boots over thick socks. "Yes?"

"The lamp right there next to you . . ."

A traditional brass table lamp rested on a crocheted doily atop an antique occasional table.

"Would you turn it on for me before we go?"

I flipped the switch. Light spilled to the tabletop below. A book lay in front of the lamp as though it had been purposefully put on display. "Hey," I said, picking it up and holding it toward the screen. "I've been reading this book every morning."

Will straightened and stood. Shimmied one heel farther into the boot. "That right?"

"Yeah." I opened the door and walked out, still holding it. "I get up early, sit outside with my tea and Buddy and Sis, and read one section. It's good for—"

"—contemplation," he and I said together.

"Yeah," I whispered.

He stared up at me, saying nothing.

"Did you buy it around here?" I asked. "I'd love to send one to Leigh. And maybe one to Gram and one to Mom . . ."

He shook his head, but only slightly. "No." He took the book from my hand and ambled to the door, leaving behind a new trail of tension. "We'd best get going," he said, opening the screen. He placed the book on the table without fully entering the room, then pulled the front door shut. "The rain has let up and, if I'm not mistaken"—he turned and his eyes met mine—"you have a date."

And just like that, I was back to square one with the man who could make or break the future of my career.

While dinner at the lakefront restaurant was wonderful and my date very much a gentleman, I couldn't keep my mind from wandering. My eyes focused on Rob, on his lips and the way he folded his hands. My ears heard the words he spoke, but with so many thoughts of William Decker, I couldn't say I *listened.*

Why was he affecting me this way? Or at all? More than that, why did I allow him to have this kind of control? I told myself over and over—*A male/female relationship is not why you came here, Ashlynne. This is not the objective. Think* professional, *girl, not* personal.

I took a deep breath, refocused on Rob, and made a new determination to enjoy my evening with him and to leave any other thoughts of his best friend—my "boss"—behind.

Later, with dinner and small talk behind us, Rob opened the passenger door to his Prius for me. I noticed two boxes in the backseat I'd not seen before.

"What's in the boxes?" I asked after he'd started the car.

He glanced behind him. "Those? School supplies. Book bags, crayons, paper . . ."

I grinned at him. "Are you going back to preschool?"

He smiled in return. "Nah. Will, he's the one."

I felt my brow scrunch, frustrated that *he* had been thrust back into my thoughts. I struggled to keep my words apathetic. "*Will* is going back to preschool?"

Laughter rolled out of Rob. "No, no, no. He heads up a small organization that gathers school supplies for children whose parents can't afford it otherwise."

"Poor children?"

Rob shook his head. "Children aren't poor. Their parents may be strapped a little, but that doesn't mean they shouldn't have a fair shake at education."

"And Will heads it up?"

Rob's face illuminated in a flash of streetlamp light. "His brainchild. He gets several of us businesspeople to donate. Then we take the supplies out to the elementary school in a bus. You know, the old-fashioned kind?"

I nodded, but said nothing. The road twisted ahead of us, but the lights from Rob's car lit the way, exposing banks of jutting rock and packed soil. "Even at night," I said, "this place is beautiful."

"I can't imagine being anywhere else." After a few silent minutes, Rob added, "Name the date when you want to take a day and go hiking up in Chimney Rock."

"That would be nice," I said. "I'll check the schedule for this coming week and see when I have some time off."

"Sounds good." Rob kept his focus on the road, saying little until, "You have feelings for him, don't you?"

My head spun so fast it nearly broke off my neck. "Who?" I asked. But I knew who.

He blinked, his eyes shimmering with what I could almost swear were tears. "I can tell, you know."

"No," I exclaimed, probably a little too forcefully. "No," I said again, this time much closer to a choked whisper.

He chuckled then. Looked over at me. Back to the road. "I think you do."

"What—what—I mean—*what* makes you think so?"

Rob's chuckle became a laugh. "Well," he drawled, "for one thing . . . *that*."

"That *what*?"

"You know, just the way—the way you're always asking about him. Talking about him. Arguing with him." He swallowed. "And the way you look when you do all three."

I didn't speak for a moment. Rob Matthews had become a friend. One I felt I could trust. With my feelings, if I could only figure out what they were. And he was Will's friend, too. His best friend. I could talk to him.

I could.

"He's so . . . so . . . *frustrating*," I began. "Never in all my life has anyone treated me so . . . so . . . no, that's not true. Once in my life."

"Someone hurt you?"

I bit my bottom lip. "Yeah."

"Someone hurt him too. Once."

Could it be . . . the woman in the picture? But I didn't ask. Because I knew, if I did, Rob wouldn't tell me. He was loyal to his best friend, as he should be.

"So what happened?" Rob asked. "If you care to share."

I chewed on the inside of my mouth to keep from spewing tears. "I was rejected, you know? Because of who I am." I shook my head. "I had some crazy notion that I'd be accepted because of who my family is, but instead I was pushed . . . aside." I glanced out the window, to the shadowing trees and bushes. The house that told me we were one away from the Decker Ranch. "They didn't even have the decency to accept me for what it could get them. They didn't even try."

We reached the driveway. Rob turned in, but he didn't say anything. When he brought the car to a stop by the cottage, he put it in park, but didn't switch the ignition off. Instead, he turned to me and said, "Him, too."

Rob's eyes told me he wasn't kidding. And, after what I'd seen that afternoon, I knew the possibility was real. "Because of his family? Because he is a Decker?"

"No."

"But you said . . ."

"Will was rejected for being *what* he is."

I didn't understand. Not fully.

I looked beyond Rob's shoulder, through the car window and out to the darkened lawn sloping toward the highway. The lightning bugs had begun their ritual. I returned my attention to Rob and I found him studying me in much the same way as I had watched the animated insects. "And what—what is he?" I asked.

He smiled, albeit faintly. "A good man."

I clutched my hands together. Stared at them for long minutes, trying to understand. Something. *Anything* about William Decker. "I don't—I don't know what that means. How could he have been rejected for being a good man?"

He wasn't Jesus, after all . . .

And Rob wasn't answering. "I'll walk you to the door," he said.

He got out of the car, walked around, and opened my door. I placed my feet on the rocks and my hand into Rob's upturned palm. He pulled me to him, squeezed my hand, and brought his lips to my ear. "You'll have to wait for him to tell you the rest," he whispered, as though the night would carry his words back to the guesthouse behind the mansion.

I nodded.

This would have to do for now.

22

I attend a nondenominational "mega-church" in Central Florida. The building is new and expansive. There is a bookstore and a café. A stage and multimedia system to rival any Broadway theater. A praise and worship team who put on what some would call a choreographed show, but which ushers thousands into the presence of God six times over each and every weekend.

It also has a ladies' restroom near the sanctuary that airports should take note of. It was the *only* ladies' room I'd ever been in that could actually "house" every woman who could possibly need to use the restroom during the church service at the exact same moment. So vast, so well-furnished, you could just about hold church in *there*.

After an insistent invitation, on Sunday morning I rode with Bobbie and Shelton to Cabbot's Creek Baptist Church because, "You'll never find it on your own and we might get separated if you drive behind us."

The Deckers' church, according to what Shelton proudly told me on the way, had been built in the 1700s. "The building you'll see today isn't the one erected way back then," he told me. "That one was made of logs and it burned."

"And this one?" I studied his eyes in the rearview mirror and could see that Will had inherited his grandfather's eyes.

"The current building is actually the third for the church, but even it's old."

Bobbie turned in her seat to make it easier to see me. "The old church, the original one, was a meeting place for Patriots back when we were still citizens of Old England."

The original building of the church I attended in Central Florida had originally been a Taste-A-Burger Restaurant in the 1960s. I decided not to share that tidbit of trivia—it couldn't compare.

"After service, if you care to look at some of the old graves behind the place, you'll find some going all the way back to the Revolutionary War."

I brightened at the thought. "That sounds interesting."

"Oh, it is," she said. She turned to face forward again.

The inside of the church was what I'd expected. The stonework and arches gave the sanctuary a Gothic appearance. Short pews—hard and shiny with age—formed rows of moderate length. The end of each pew had been cut high and carved like rolled scrolls. A center aisle, carpeted in red, led to a prayer altar of dark wood. Beyond it, an ornate lectern, and beyond that a floor-to-ceiling stained-glass window. On both sides of the sanctuary, dimly lit by antique brass chandeliers, arched stained-glass windows. Some depicted saints such as John, Peter, Paul, Francis. Others shared stories our faith is established upon—Moses and the Hebrew children crossing the Red Sea, Ruth gathering wheat, David slaying Goliath, Jesus raising a child from the dead. Jesus himself, ascending into heaven.

I inhaled deeply. The scent of lit candles and polished wood rushed my senses. This was . . . *lovely*. Reverent and sacred.

Music from an old organ filled the room, nearly drowning out the chatter from clusters of those standing between the pews or in the aisle. A few older members had already sat, including Will, who seemed to sense our entrance. He turned from a pew near the front, smiled, stood, and walked toward us.

I nearly tripped over my feet. Will wore a dark blue suit and a tie that I'd wager a month's salary came from Armani's men's collection. His hair, so typically finger-brushed straight back and hidden beneath his hat, looked freshly washed, groomed, and combed.

When he reached us, he took his grandmother's elbow to guide her to their seats. But over his shoulder he said, "Good morning, Miss Rothschild." Then, of all things, he winked at me.

"Good morning, Mr. Decker," I said.

Beside me, Shelton Decker chuckled.

We sang old hymns—songs I had not sung in years. It didn't take many stanzas—two at most—before I felt them resonate within my spirit.

We followed the program printed on the bulletin. Recited ancient texts from prayer books tucked between hymnals in the "back of the pew in front" of us. Each word and phrase stirred things in me. Between the meditation texts from the book I'd found at the cottage and this, I could almost feel myself growing as a Christian. And as I looked straight ahead, book spread over my open palms, listening to the pastor, a growing sense of "home" settled over me. As though I'd been here for all of my life.

Or that I'd remain here for the rest of it.

And even though those thoughts disturbed me, I found myself unwilling to push them away. I liked this sense of being. Very much so. That and the sound of the voice next to me, strong and sure of the recitation. Of his shoulder so close to mine. For the craziest of moments, I realized what I'd been missing all of my adult life. Not just the sense of belonging, but of belonging *perfectly*.

At Bobbie's insistence, after service William took me for a walk through the sloping graveyard behind the church. We wove around old headstones and wildflowers, stopping along the way to read mold-encrusted epitaphs written on stone. I marveled at the dates. "Can you imagine . . . ," I said, more times than I care to admit.

"Do you think that," William said, "one day, a couple of hundred years from now, someone will stand over our graves, asking that same question?"

Unable to read the emotion in his eyes—they were shaded by dark sunglasses—I studied his face. To see if there might be a hint of humor, a slight curl of the lip. But there was none. Will Decker's question was both reflective and serious.

"I've never thought about it," I said. "We have a cemetery in Winter Park. Huge, really. Under live oaks, which means the markers—most of them quite ornate—are constantly shadowed." I swallowed. "Sometimes I like to go there. To mill around the precise, perfectly sectioned rows. I like reading the names, checking out the dates, seeing how people were related to each other." I tilted my head toward him. "Do you think that makes me weird?"

And then he grinned. "Not *that*." Before I could respond with anything more than a swat at his arm, he laughed and said, "Come look back here near the tree line. Something interesting to show you."

He ambled off. I followed behind, watching a little too intently as he slid his suit coat off his shoulders and down his arms with a "Gettin' warmer by the minute." Then he looked back at my feet. "Careful with those shoes."

By habit, I'd worn a pair of shoes from my "pre–Bubba O'Leary's" fashion, which of course had been all of the day before. I'd already figured out that I had to walk on the balls and toes of my feet to keep the heels from sinking into the rich earth. Manolo Blahnik divots were not my idea of "leaving a legacy."

Will stopped in front of the decorative tombstone of Noah Swann, who had been a captain in the Civil War. His wife, Emily Todd Swann, lay next to him. "They died thirty years apart," he said, "and if you note the date, it's not the war that took him."

"Do we know what did?"

"His death certificate—and yes, I've seen it—says pneumonia."

I nodded at the graves, as though giving the souls of the "dearly departed" some form of approval for having lived and died. "You said *something interesting*?"

"Ah," Will said, stepping farther toward the tree line. "Check these out."

Along the line, facing the trees, were small stones with carved first names such as "Sallie" and "Isaac" and "Big John." Some had only initials. Some held the years of death, others nothing more than the first name of the departed. "Are these . . . the graves of slaves?"

"They are. And they go all the way back to the Revolutionary War." He pointed to a tall tombstone, arched along its topside. "Now check this out."

MARGUERITE, it read, CONSORT OF NOAH SWANN.

Then along the bottom, in script: *Her children rise up and call her blessed.*

"Well, well . . . ," I said.

"Notice the date of her death?"

I did. Only a month previous to her lover's. "He must have loved her very much."

"In a day when such things were known but never discussed." He remained quiet for a moment. "I think," he then said with a light chuckle, "that Miss Emily over there lived so long out of revenge."

I had to chuckle with him. "The power of a scorned woman," I said. Then, hearing our names, I looked up. Miss Bobbie stood at the top of the hill, calling for us to "come on now or starve."

"That's our cue," Will said. "Ready?" He extended his hand in invitation to walk ahead of him.

I nodded, but not before looking back at the small nearly unmarked stones, wondering about the connection between them and the dead lying beneath Rob's property.

23

After returning to the cottage from lunch with the Deckers, I changed into comfy clothes and called Gram. "Good timing, my darling," she said. "I've just now returned home from Sunday dinner with your parents. Do call them as soon as you can."

I pictured her smile, making me feel both sadly nostalgic and happy at the same time. "How was service?"

"Good as always. And how about you? Did you enjoy yourself?"

"I did. I went to church with the Deckers at Cabbot's Creek Baptist."

"Lovely place. Your grandfather and I attended there, you know."

I found a seat on the sofa, all the while picturing my grandparents, young and sitting side by side on one of the pews. Near the front. As William and I had. "You did?"

"We certainly did."

"Gram?" I let her name hang in the air for a moment. "When did you know you loved Papa?"

"When he left for the service. We'd known each since we were children. When we were in school, you know, and he was the most frustrating young fella I'd ever known."

"In what way?"

"In *every* way. But there was something about him I suppose I was always drawn to. And then, the night before he went off to

Basic, I went to his going-away party. We sort of . . . we had a moment. And then, when he was gone, I knew. I wrote him a letter every day he was away, without fail."

I closed my eyes at the thought of my grandmother writing letters to her young "fella," of waiting for his return, of praying for him daily, and of marrying him.

"Ashlynne?"

My eyes opened. "Yes?"

"You think you're in love with him, don't you?"

"Who?" I feigned ignorance.

"Don't get smart with me, Ashlynne Paige Rothschild. You know who I'm talking about. William Decker. Every phone call we've had in the past week, you've complained more about him than you've talked about the young man who took you to the football game and bought you barbecue."

"Oh, Gram. Don't you think falling in love in one week is about the silliest thing you've ever heard? Not that I'm *falling* in love, mind you. That's so . . . so . . . *Harlequin.*"

"Well, my dear, at least you didn't insult me by denying it."

I stood, brushed imaginary lint from the front of my blouse, and walked into the kitchen. "I only admit that he is intriguing."

I opened the refrigerator and peered inside. "I'm scared, Gram," I said, pulling out a bottled water.

"Of what? Love?"

I screwed open the top. "I've never been in love before. I've never even been in *like.* Besides, it's only been a *week.*"

"Never be afraid of love, sweet one. Just hop on in and enjoy the ride."

I gulped the water. The cold slipped down my throat, bringing immediate relief to the knot forming there. We said our good-byes and ended the call.

"But it's not the objective," I whispered to the sweet kitchen. "That's not why I'm here."

24

I drove to Brianna's small but tidy home, located near the courthouse on one of the side streets downtown. She met me on the front porch as soon as I stepped out of the car. "What happened?" she asked, gaping at the side of my Jag.

I frowned. "Will and I went to battle with an embankment and the embankment won."

Her mouth remained open as she skipped down the steps. "Is it fixable?"

"Probably not around here," I said. "It's unattractive, but drivable." I reached into the backseat and brought out a small cosmetics bag, then closed the driver's door.

She shook her head at the other side of the car. Held up a finger. "No, you know what you should do? Call my daughter's daddy. He's good at stuff like fixing cars. He can buff that out in no time and you'd never know the difference."

Uh-huh. "I'd better wait until I can get it back to Orlando." I walked around the front of the car.

She frowned. "Maybe, but Cliff's real good."

I reached her, looked at the damage one more time, like I'd done a hundred times by now, thinking that if I stared at it long enough, it would fix itself.

"Mmhmm." Brianna pointed to the bag in my hand. "Whatcha got there?"

I lifted the cosmetics bag. "Some cosmetics . . . brands I like. I thought I'd show them to you."

A shy smile broke across her face. "I guess that's why you're here. Come on in, then," she said. "Maris is sleeping, but she should be up soon."

We entered through the front door into a nondescript living room, sparsely furnished—and mismatched. As though she'd hit every secondhand store in North Carolina until she came up with enough pieces that she could call the room a "room."

"It's not much," she said. "But it's home."

I forced a smile. "It's lovely. Warm and inviting." I raised the cosmetics bag again. "Where shall we have our makeup party?"

"There's a table in the kitchen back here," she said. "Lots of light."

"Sounds good."

I followed Brianna into her kitchen. As in William's kitchen, windows ran across three of the walls. But Brianna's had thin, ruffled curtains pulled to the sides. White linoleum countertops buckled at the seams but had otherwise been scrubbed clean. She also kept a glass cookie jar filled with Oreos pushed into one corner beneath painted-white overhead cabinets.

"Would you like some sweet iced tea?" she asked.

"Water will be fine," I said. "If you don't mind."

"Not at all . . ."

I sat at the table and opened the bag while Brianna pulled a bottle of water from the refrigerator. She placed it before me, sat in a nearby chair with one leg tucked under her backside, and leaned forward with her arms crossed and resting on the table. "Wow. You've got a lot of pretty things in there."

I smiled at her. "Do me a favor. Go wash your face." I handed her a half-filled bottle of my favorite cleansing milk.

Brianna took the bottle, left the room and, by the time she returned, I had bottles and tubes of my favorite cosmetics laid out on the kitchen table.

She touched her face with her fingertips. "That made my skin feel real nice."

"It does, doesn't it?"

"I really appreciate you teaching me some things, but I bet all this is way more expensive than what I could ever afford." She sat in the chair she'd left a minute earlier.

Well . . . it wasn't cheap. "Sometimes, buying less-expensive items means spending more because you have to replace them more often." I chose a bottle of facial serum. "Squirt a little on your fingertips and then massage it into your face."

She did, closing her eyes.

"Just dot around your eyes," I said. "Don't pull."

Her eyes opened.

"Like this," I showed her, using my own fingertips. A sense of satisfaction washed over me as I demonstrated the action. For the second time that day, I realized I'd found something I liked very much. This, showing someone who'd never had the opportunities I had, what I'd learned—just because I'd been born into the "right" family. Someone who seemed to *want* me to show her. Wanted to know what I know.

The experience was completely new to me and too long coming.

Brianna repeated my actions, dotting around her eyes. "Now what I have here," I said, picking up a small silver jar, "is a daily moisturizer. What you use at night and what you use during the day—two different things."

"Do you like Rob Matthews?" she blurted, her eyes locked with mine.

The question came from nowhere, or so it seemed. I placed the jar of moisturizer on the table and blinked. "I do."

"As a boyfriend?"

Shaking my head, I said, "No. But I do like him very much as a friend."

"*Just* . . . as a friend?"

I tilted my head. "My turn to ask questions—do *you* like Rob Matthews?"

Her cheeks grew rosy—and I knew it wasn't from the application of facial serum. She covered her face with her hands, then removed them as if we were playing peekaboo. "Are you sure you don't? 'Cause he seems like he likes you a lot."

I folded my hands. "I think," I said slowly, "that perhaps Rob hoped for more." I raised my brow.

She pulled a tube of mascara toward her and fingered the twist-top. After a moment of chewing on her bottom lip, she said, "I'm sure he thinks I'm just a kid."

I did the math. If Rob and Will were best friends, then Rob was probably thirty-six. Thirty-five at the youngest. That made Brianna eleven years his junior. Still, they were both adults and, based on the story of Miss Helen, this wouldn't be the biggest scandal to hit Testament in the "love and marriage" department. "Have you told him how you feel?"

"Oh, no," she said, handing the tube of mascara back to me. "Besides, I've got Maris and he probably wouldn't want someone with a kid."

"There's only one way to know for sure," I said.

She shrugged one shoulder.

"I could talk to him . . ."

She covered her face again and stifled a giggle. "This feels like we're in high school or something."

Worse. Junior high. But I didn't say it. "Well?"

Brianna dropped her hands and chewed on her lip again. "All right." Her eyes grew large. "But only if it should come up on its own."

I couldn't imagine it would. "Brianna," I said. "What goals . . . have you set . . . for yourself? Beyond working at the drugstore restaurant and cleaning other people's houses?"

She looked down. "To be honest, I've never really had a goal. Which is probably what got me in trouble in the first place." She smiled weakly. "No direction. I mean, I was popular in school and all. Homecoming queen. But truth is, I couldn't succeed long term, because I didn't know what I was doing next week much less after school."

I took a long swallow of water and allowed her words to sink in. With the exception of a few friends, I'd stayed to myself most of my life. Opting for solitude over popularity. But I had always had a goal. A goal was what had brought me to Testament and, no doubt, after this one had been achieved, I'd point my nose toward another.

"It's not too late," I said. "If you could be anything at all, what would it be?"

Brianna didn't hesitate. "A soccer mom."

My shoulders dropped. "A socc—" I shook my head. "That's it?"

"That's . . . *everything*. The way it stands now, I'll be working so hard, I'll never get to be there for Maris if she goes out for soccer or ballet . . . or anything. All I want is to marry a good man—a Christian man—and be able to stay home, so I can be a good wife and a hands-on mom. That's what I want."

Which was not what I would have imagined her answer to be. But every goal had to have steps toward it. "So what are you doing to meet . . . that goal?"

She grinned. "Letting you talk to Rob Matthews."

We laughed together. Which felt really good. But so much more was at stake, not that it was *any* of my business. "But, Brianna . . ." I busied myself, rearranging the bottles and jars and tubes between us. "Are you interested in Rob because he's a good catch or because you think you could actually feel something for him?"

She stood, walked to a cabinet, and pulled out a glass and then to the refrigerator, from which she pulled a large pitcher of tea. Pouring the tea, she said, "I think Rob Matthews is about the finest man around . . . even better than Will. He's godly, he's cute as a bug's ear, and he's kind."

A bug's ear? Well, all right then.

I picked up the moisturizer again. "Here, put a little of this on, applying it like so," I said, showing her how to sweep her fingers upward.

She placed the glass on the table. Took the top from the jar as she sat. "Smells pretty."

"Brianna . . . ," I began slowly. "Speaking of Will . . . do you know anything about his return from Chicago?"

She applied the cream, just as I'd shown her. "Nothing, really. He was gone for quite a while, though." She looked at her fingertips. "That good? The way I did it?"

"Perfect." I chose a light foundation and a clean cosmetic wedge. "Close your eyes," I said.

"Of course," Brianna spoke so that her lips hardly moved as I dabbed the sponge over her face. "I was a child when he left for college."

Of course . . . How silly of me not to realize. "So you really don't know anything about why he came back from Chicago." I closed the top to the foundation laid the wedge wet-side up, and picked up a compact. "This is a highlighting blush . . . because with your fresh face, you don't need anything more."

She smiled as I stroked a brush across the glittery surface. "No, I don't know anything."

"Make your cheeks into little apples," I said, showing her with my own. She did.

"But my mama said she'd heard he'd gotten into some kind of trouble up there."

I dropped my hand from her face. "What kind of trouble?"

Brianna blinked. "I can't remember what she called it. Mama heard Miss Bobbie talking to Mr. Shelton one time when she went by to drop off the church news to the paper, and I heard her telling my daddy about it."

"The church news?"

"Yeah. My mama gathers the church news once a month from all the county churches and then takes it down to the paper."

Church news? I didn't ask the obvious, but instead inquired as to why she didn't simply e-mail the information.

Brianna shook her head. "My mama doesn't believe in computers or the Internet. She says it's the devil's playground."

I nodded. "Do you remember anything else about what was said?" I returned to my work as I swept the blush brush across her cheek, hoping to appear nonchalant to the question.

"No. But it was something about . . . what was that word?"

I closed the compact, picked up my tweezers, ready to bring a little shape to Brianna's brow. "A word?"

"Something to do with journalists."

"Do you mind if I tweeze your brows a little? You've got great shape, but you need just a little framing to your eye."

She shook her head. I stood over her, tilted her head back and angled it toward the light. The only sound in the room for several moments was that of our breathing, until her eyes flew open and found mine.

"I remember the word."

My arms dropped. "Okay," I said, again trying to keep my face expressionless.

"Ethics. Mama said he broke the rules of ethics."

25

Ethics?

William Decker?

After visiting more with Brianna and meeting her adorable little girl—an exact replica of her mother—I drove back to the cottage as fast as my car and the speed limit allowed, anxious to go online in the privacy of my bedroom. But as soon as I pulled around the Deckers' home, I found Will and a young man standing in the middle of the driveway, blocking my path.

I slammed on the brakes. Powered down the window.

"There you are," William said. "Someone here I want you to meet."

I put the car in park and got out.

The young man—tall, slender, with a head full of dirty-blond hair—walked to the other side of my car, whistled, and said, "Yep. You did it all right."

I looked at Will as if to say, "Excuse me?"

"Ashlynne," he interjected quickly, "this is Cliff."

"Hello," I said.

"Ma'am." He placed his hands on his hips, splaying his fingers. "You got yourself a nice dent there, but it's fixable."

I pushed past William and joined . . . *Cliff*. "Maris's father . . ."

Pride washed his face. "Yes, ma'am. You know my little girl?"

I pointed toward the highway. "I just came from Brianna's."

"Oh, yes, ma'am. Well . . . just so you know, William called me a little while ago and asked me to come over and look at your Jag." He whistled again. "Nice car, by the way. What'd it set you back? Around a hundred?"

Yes, not that it was any of his business. "I appreciate your help, Cliff, but I think I'll just drive the car back to Orlando in a week or two and let someone from a specialty shop look at it."

"No one's better than Cliff at this kind of thing," William said. "You ought to at least—"

I clasped my hands together and held them in front of me. "I really do appreciate your help, Cliff, but I *seriously* don't think—"

"Oh, stop being so snooty and let the man at least look at it," William barked from the other side of the car.

My head grew fuzzy with anger. "I'm not . . . *snooty*!"

"You are too. You think that just because your car cost a lot of money, Cliff here doesn't know anything about getting rid of a few dents?"

My cheeks grew warm, even as I took deep breaths to control my emotion. The old hurt rising in me. "It's not that I don't think—"

"I can do it," Cliff said, so quietly I almost missed the words. "I'll have to contact Jaguar and see about the paint, of course. To match it."

"I'm sure you are very good with trucks and . . . four-wheel drives . . . and that kind of thing," I said, as kindly as I knew how.

"If you must know," William said, now clomping to where we stood, "Cliff is as good at cosmetics for cars as you are at cosmetics for chicks." He pretended to laugh at his sordid attempt at humor. When I didn't respond, he continued by clearing his throat and saying, "He can repaint your car and you'd think it was the original."

"I'm sure—"

"Tell you what," William interrupted. "You let Cliff take your car, take out the dents, repaint the door, and if you aren't one hundred percent pleased, I'll drive the car down to Orlando myself and I'll pay to have the whole thing redone at one of your"—he forked his fingers in the air—"specialty shops."

"You won't be any worse off," Cliff muttered beside me.

I shook my head, clearly outnumbered. "But what will I drive in the meantime?"

"I've already talked to Big Guy. You can drive one of their vehicles."

Backed into a corner. The proverbial rock and the hard place. I sighed. "Again, that's very kind . . . and I . . ."

William crossed his arms and sighed. "Just say yes, for crying out loud. Let the boy do what he does."

I threw my hands up in defeat. "Oh, all right. Yes." I looked at Cliff, who grinned broadly, no doubt anxious to get his hands on what he probably considered automotive artwork. "Should I just drive it to your shop in the morning? You *do* have a shop, don't you?"

"Yes, ma'am. Behind my daddy's house."

Of course it was.

"Less overhead," William added with a grin.

"But I promise you . . . I'll treat her like she's gold."

"She practically is. What about the paint job? Won't you need to have her, you know, somewhere special for that? Dust-free?"

"Oh, yes, ma'am. I've got a friend over in Asheville. He'll let me use his place. State-of-the-art." He took a loving look at the Jag. "But if you want, I can just take it now."

I looked at the lineup of cars and trucks behind the Deckers' home. I assumed the one I didn't recognize—a sports car—to be Cliff's. "What about your car?" I asked. "Will you leave it here?"

"I can drive your car to Cliff's," William said. "Cliff, you won't mind bringing me back for my car, will you?"

Cliff shook his head. "Not a bit."

I set my jaw and gave Will my most forced smile.

"Say 'Thank you,' " he said.

I walked past him to the driver's side to retrieve my purse. "Thank you . . ."

With my car somewhere between the Decker Ranch and Cliff's daddy's backyard, I climbed into the center of the upstairs bed, crossed my legs, and opened my laptop. While it came to life, I looked out the large window, through the trees with their spiraling leaves. From where I sat I could see the deep woods and, snaking through them, a packed red-mud path. I rose on my knees, allowing my eyes to follow until it disappeared into the thicket.

I settled back on the bed, ran my finger over the mouse, entered my password, and then typed WILLIAM ALEXANDER DECKER into the search engine.

The first link was to his Twitter account. I clicked on it, but the account had been closed.

The second was to his Facebook account. Like the Twitter account, it was no longer "available."

A short Wikipedia article informed me only of the numerous awards Will had won while living in Chicago and that his growing career in journalism ended abruptly.

There were several images of him, but none with his hat. I found that interesting. The blonde I'd seen in the framed newspaper article showed up in a few. And, in each of those, she looked completely starry-eyed.

After a half hour of research and nothing solid as to the information Brianna had spoken of, the proverbial lightbulb went off over my head. I grabbed my cell phone, which had been lying on the bed beside me, leaned back, and dialed my father's cell phone number.

After a few minutes of general chitchat, I asked the question. The reason for my call in the first place. "Hey, Dad? What's Courtney doing these days? I mean, with me not in the office."

"We keep her plenty busy, why?"

"She'll move right on up with me when I return, though, right?"

"Of course, honey. What, are you suddenly worried about her future?"

I frowned. To be honest, I'd not once thought about what would happen to Courtney, not with me gone and not even when I returned. I knew Gram well enough to know she'd find something for her—some position—but I'd not, well, worried. "No, I just wondered . . . if I were to call the office, say in the morning, would I still find her working there?"

Dad paused. "Why don't you just call her cell phone and ask *her*?"

I stared at the ceiling, not wanting my father to know that my inability to be a "people person" had developed to the point where my assistant's cell phone number—or any of her numbers for that matter—was not something I had possession of. "Uh . . ."

"You don't have it, do you?"

I fell back onto the pillows. "No. I suppose I should, but . . . I . . . don't."

My father remained silent for the longest possible string of minutes. "You can still find her at her desk outside your office."

"Dad . . . ," I said, closing my eyes. "I want you to know that . . . I've only been here a week, but I'm already . . . seeing . . . what you wanted me to . . . see. To learn." When he didn't respond, I concluded, "I'm almost anxious to see what changes will come after another twenty-five weeks." More or less.

"I'm glad to hear it, Ashlynne," he said, his voice as serious as I'd ever heard it. All business. Right then, at that moment, I wasn't his daughter, I was the woman being primed to take over his position at the magazine.

Minutes later I called my office at *Parks & Avenues* and left a message on Courtney's voice mail. I asked, kindly, for three things: (1) to see what she could find on *any* battle fought near Testament, North Carolina, from the Revolutionary War forward; (2) anything she could find on the professional life of William Alexander Decker while he worked for the *Chicago Star*; and (3) to keep my call between the two of us. "You know how much I enjoy research," I told her in conclusion, "but let's face it, you're the queen. I bow to your expertise." And then I smiled, hoping she could "hear" it across the miles.

I ended the call with a "Hope you are doing well," scrambled off the bed, and changed into my new hiking clothes. Minutes later, I flew out the front door, stuffing the house key into a pocket of my new cargo shorts. I turned left and hurried over low-lying shrubs and brambles until I found the path I'd seen from my bedroom window.

The road was rocky. Broken. Wide in some places. Narrow in others. Light flickered between the branches of the black-and-white oaks, the pines, and the maples. At times, the path grew dark, overcome by shadows. My fingers reached for my cell phone in one of the pockets of my cargo shorts. Feeling it, a sense of safety washed over me.

The snapping of limbs brought me to a stop. I whirled around, but saw nothing. Shook off any notion of forest ghosts. Turned and continued forward until I came to an oblong clearing, high above a ravine. I observed below the straight, flatness of the land. Placing my hands on my hips and bracing my feet about a foot apart, I leaned over ever-so-slightly. Trees, ancient and gnarled, though some straight as soldiers, affirmed what I'd suspected.

"It's part of the Revolutionary War road," a voice from behind said.

I gasped, lost my footing, and tumbled headfirst down the slope. Buried rocks—their tips jutting out of the earth—jabbed at my muscles. Thorny bushes tore at the exposed parts of my flesh. As I tumbled, I focused on keeping myself tucked in. An instinctual motion of survival, which I only partially managed. I wrapped my head with my arms, felt my body bump and flop until it came to rest with a thud on the road below.

"*Ashlynne!*"

I lay sprawled on my back, my hair tangled about my face, my arms flopped outward. I groaned, and my name was called again. Footsteps half ran, half clomped into the ravine. I opened my eyes to see the trunk of a tree rising over me—a pine, whose branches didn't bother to start until they'd nearly touched the blue of the cloudless sky.

"Are you . . ."

I jerked my eyes to the left. Will Decker, his face covered by panic and glistening sweat, came to an abrupt halt. No cowboy hat rested on his head. "Owww . . ."

"Don't move," he said, squatting next to me.

I blinked. "I think I'm okay."

"Let me see. Don't move, you hear?"

I didn't answer. I couldn't. His fingers worked like tiny massage therapists, first down one leg, then the other. I kept my eyes on his, seeing the concern. The fear.

"Any pain?"

"Not really." Just embarrassment. Did that count?

Warm fingers and hands worked up my right arm. Down my left. Across my shoulders to my neck. "Anything at all?"

"Just sore already." And my chest hurt. Though I knew it wasn't from falling. William Decker's fingers running up and down my body, even in a platonic fashion, made it difficult to breathe.

"I don't think anything is broken, but roll over on your side. Don't try to sit straight up."

I did as I was told until I could push myself up and onto my knees. Will's arms came around my waist. He lifted me as though I weighed nothing more than a pillow.

"Can you put weight on your feet?"

My left foot went down without issue, but my right refused to accept any pressure. "My right foot," I said. "I think it's the ankle."

William helped me to lean against the tree, squatted before me, and took my foot into his cupped hands. I looked first to him, then up the hill I'd rolled down, and over my left shoulder to where the old road stretched and bent. I hissed between my teeth as he pressed against the bone of my ankle.

"Nice shoes," he said.

"Hiking *boots*," I retorted, gazing down on him.

His grin was lopsided and his right eye squinted. "I know. Just wanted to see if you still had any spunk in you." He stood. Brown eyes met mine. "I guess you'll live."

"Of course I'll live," I said. "The question is, how will I get out of here?"

William rested his hands on his hips. He looked behind him. To the right. To the left. Back to me. "Only one way I know of," he said. And, before I had a chance to protest, his right shoulder caught my middle, doubled me over, and hoisted me up. Strong arms came around the back of my legs at the bend of my knees.

"*What*?" I screamed. "Put me down, William Decker." The dull pain in my ankle became a throb.

"Stop wiggling. You'll end up hurting you and me both," he said, already ambling to the left. "There's a slight incline just down the road a piece. Won't be so difficult to tote you." His breath came in ragged spurts. "Hold on."

I grabbed hold of the belt looped in his jeans. "Don't you dare drop me."

"Just be still."

"I am being still," I said, gritting my teeth. I watched the road below me and attempted to keep focus on the path, the packed mud, the patches of grass, the embedded rock. My head grew fuzzy from every ounce of my blood rushing to my brain, so I craned my neck as far back as it would go. The trees lining the Revolutionary War road bobbed and blurred. I closed my eyes, painfully aware of the intimacy of being carried by a man . . . *this* man . . . in such a way. I wanted to die.

I wanted to dance.

"Can I ask a question?" I ventured.

"Can I stop you?"

I couldn't help myself. I smiled. "What were you doing? Following me?"

"No." He took several deep breaths before continuing. "I brought you the keys to my grandfather's truck, so you'd have it in the morning."

I pictured the dilapidated vehicle parked behind the Deckers' home. "The *truck*?"

"Don't look a gift horse—"

"You did that on purpose," I said, squirming. "You knew good and well the last thing I'd want to do is drive his *truck*."

"Would you *please* be still before I drop you on your backside and put a real hurt on you?"

I dug my elbows into his back, harder than necessary, and rested my chin on my fists.

"Thanks," he said, then remained quiet until, "Right up here. We've made it, no thanks to you." He took a deep breath. "All right. I'm going to try hauling you up the incline, so please work with me."

"*Hauling* me?" I jerked.

His grip grew tight. "Be *still*, for crying out loud."

"I *am* being still. But what do you mean by *hauling me*. What do you think I am? A load of lumber?"

"A load of lumber," he said, taking angled steps upward, "would be a whole lot easier to tote." He grunted under my weight.

"And how do you see that?" The pain in my foot intensified. The pressure in my chest deepened.

"Lumber doesn't talk back."

I started to slip and Will's hold tightened. "Hold on," he repeated. I clutched his belt again until my knuckles turned white.

"Just watch where you put your hands."

He guffawed. "Lady, please . . . *hush*."

We reached the top of the incline. William's hands relaxed. "I'm going to set you down right here on this boulder." I slid backward, up and over his shoulder. "Easy now. Don't put any weight on that foot."

"Don't worry."

I came to rest on my left foot. My hands clutched shoulders that flexed beneath them, my forehead pressed down against the left. "Easy now," he repeated, less bossy. More coaxing. I hopped slightly on the left, pressing myself against him for balance. His arms slipped around my waist. Held me in place. I took in a deep breath, smelled the sweat of his labor mixed with the morning cologne he'd chosen. Marc Eckō "Okay?" he whispered.

I nodded, unable to speak.

"Ready?"

I nodded again, my lips pressed together, almost afraid to let go. To do so would mean more than just releasing the strength I felt from him. Stepping away meant allowing him to see my face.

And, perhaps, my vulnerability.

26

I rested on the boulder, keeping my right leg extended, while Will returned to the cottage to get the truck.

His or his grandfather's, he didn't say.

How could it be, I pondered in the interim, that in one week William Decker had done this to me? Made me so angry I wanted to slug him one minute, so crazy I wanted to kiss him the next.

Or have him kiss me.

I buried my face in my hands. "Falling for William Decker is *not* the objective," I groaned into them, just as the engine of the old Dodge rambled toward me. I frowned. The whole thing was kept together by rust and good wishes. A hillbilly hotrod. I could hardly believe he expected me to drive it . . . not that I'd be able to anyway. Not now. Not with this foot.

Will brought the truck to a stop but didn't kill the engine. He opened the driver's-side door. It creaked and moaned in protest.

"I'm surprised it doesn't just fall off," I hollered.

"It has a time or two," he said back.

That figured. He stood over me, smiling, daring me to say something in return. He wore sunglasses, probably in an effort to block the still-bright light of the sun in the western sky. I couldn't read his eyes, but I took the dare. "And you wanted *me* to drive it?"

"Thought you might be able to handle it."

"Oh, I could handle it."

He squatted. Pulled his sunglasses to the tip of his nose and peered at me over the lenses. "Could ya now?"

I switched my attention down the length of my right leg. "Looks like I won't be driving anything. For a while."

His gaze followed mine. Back up again. Slowly. As though he enjoyed the view.

"Are you going to help me to the truck, or are we going to sit here the rest of the night?"

He shifted. "Keep up the sass, and you *will* sit here all night. *I* can walk and *I* can drive."

My mouth gaped open, but he only chuckled.

"Don't get your dander up, girl. Put your arms around my neck."

"Why?"

His eyes narrowed. "Just do it . . ."

I didn't want to.

Who was I kidding? Oh, yes I did. I complied, feeling his muscles flex again as one arm slid under my knees and the other wrapped itself around my back. He lifted me, puffing as he stood. I kept my right leg straight and my chin tilted over my right shoulder, watching the truck as we neared it.

Then again, I would have looked at anything to keep my eyes from the five o'clock shadow along the angular jaw of his face. From the cleft in the middle of his chin. From the amber flecks I knew were hidden behind those sunglass lenses.

"I'm going to bring you down, rest your back against the cab," he told me, bringing me back to the moment.

And he did. Then he opened the door.

"Hold on to my arm and try to hop over."

Even through the throbbing pain, we managed to get my backside near the old vinyl seat, which was stained in places. Torn in others. The smell of dirt and age met me fully. "I'm going to have to pull myself in," I told him, my eyes searching for something to hold on to.

His hands splayed across both sides of my waist and he lifted me onto the seat, doubling me over, forcing me against him.

I gasped in pain. Stars formed behind my eyelids.

"You all right?"

"I will be," I said, struggling through the agony.

"I'm sorry." He gently drew my knees up and slid my legs forward. "Easy does it."

He found the stained seat belt and brought it around me, buckling it into place before I had a chance to tell him that my arms and hands weren't harmed in the fall. Our faces came a breath apart and we both inhaled quickly. Me through my mouth. Him through his nostrils.

"You ready?" he asked, stepping back. He stumbled. Caught himself.

"Be careful," I said too quickly. "We can't have both of us hurt."

He didn't respond. He closed my door, walked around the front of the truck and got in. "I'm taking you to the hospital," he said, his breath ragged.

He gripped the steering wheel with one hand, forced the gearshift into reverse with the other.

"The hospital?"

"Gram and Big Guy went out tonight. Of all nights. I'm sure she'd insist I take you. So I am." He shifted to drive and turned the wheel forcefully to the left. The truck bounced along the rugged terrain. Pain shot up my leg. I wrapped my hands around my knee and squeezed. He caught the movement. "Sorry," he said, and slowed the truck.

"I'm sure some ice and a little Aleve will make it all better," I said. "I probably don't need to go to the hospital. You can just take me back to the cottage."

"Don't argue with me. I'm not in the mood."

"*You're* not in the mood?"

"Just sit tight," he said. "And Great-granny, girl, quit arguing with me."

Several hours later my ankle had been poked, pulled, and x-rayed, then wrapped so tightly I worried it might fall off. Sometime after eleven o'clock, Will drove his grandfather's old relic through a sleeping downtown. Between us, a pair of crutches rattled from the relentless rumbling of the truck.

"I've been thinking," I said, breaking the silence of voices.

"About?"

"The Revolutionary War road."

Outside of the city limits, darkness wrapped itself around the old truck as it sputtered toward Decker Ranch.

"What about it?"

"Where you left me . . . the level from where I fell . . . is that part of the Confederate road?"

"Yeah."

"The graves on Rob's property, they're closer to the Confederate road than the Revolutionary."

"Right."

"It seems to me that it's more likely the graves are from that era than the earlier one."

William nodded, his movement nearly imperceptible in the pale moonlight. "I got a call from the historical society."

"What? When?"

"Late Friday."

"And you didn't tell me?"

"Calm down . . . they left a voice message and I just didn't get it until this afternoon."

I bit the inside of my cheek as I pulled my hair up in a makeshift ponytail and then let it fall. "Sorry. All right. And? What did they say?"

He glanced at me with a grimace. "Sorry, kiddo. They have nothing on those graves."

I sighed. "Are we *sure* people are buried there?"

"No. But the graves are eight feet in length, so I'm assuming."

I looked out the dirt-cluttered window at the familiar landscape, then through the windshield where the mountains made a dark, jagged impression against a paler sky. "Here's what I was thinking—

the Civil War was a hundred and fifty years ago and no one here is old enough to remember it."

He chuckled. "Not even Miss Helen."

"But," I said, bringing my finger up to make a point. "Miss Helen may actually remember stories."

He looked my way again. "Say what?"

"Think about it, Will, and keep your eyes on the road." He looked forward. "She's ninety and she's sharp as a tack."

He grinned. "She is that."

"There's not that big of a stretch between the 1860s and the 1920s when Miss Helen was born. What if she remembers hearing stories? You and Rob had stories about *her.*"

"Okay. It's possible."

"Possible? Will, in the days before radio, television, computers, and texting, people communicated with each other by talking face-to-face. They told stories."

"So what are you thinking?" he asked, turning the truck into the Decker Ranch driveway. "Hold on. This could get rough."

"I know." The truck rocked back and forth. I lifted my foot as though it might help. "I'm thinking," I said through gritted teeth, "that perhaps if I go talk to Miss Helen, she may remember a story or two. Oww. Maybe something that connects to the graves."

The truck's engine revved as we moved up the driveway. Will didn't comment. He seemed focused on getting around the house and to the cottage. I remained silent as well, waiting for the outline of the cottage to greet me from the top of the hill. I'd left only a single light on in the living room. Remarkably, it seemed to smile in spite of the night's shadows, happy to know I had returned home.

"I find myself coming to like this place very much," I said.

"The cottage or Testament?"

I smiled slowly in answer.

Will brought the truck to a stop. "I think your idea about Miss Helen is a good one."

I nearly gasped. "You do?"

He turned the key in the ignition to OFF, and shifted toward me. "You find that so impossible to believe?"

"I admit. I do." I wrapped my left hand around the metal of the crutches.

"I've given you a hard time so far, haven't I." It wasn't a question.

I dared to bring my eyes to his. "You have."

"I'm sorry."

"You're forgiven." Just that easy.

His eyes bore into mine. The air in the truck's cab turned thick. Warm. Outside, lightning bugs glowed in their ritual evening dance. I watched them only briefly, then returned my gaze to Will. To his face. His eyes.

"How did your visit with Brianna go today?" he asked, as though seeking a change of subject.

"Good."

"Did you doll her up?" he asked with a grin.

"A little. She's a natural, she doesn't need much." I pulled the crutches closer to me. "I—uh—I ordered her some things when I returned home. Had them overnighted, so she *should* get them tomorrow afternoon."

His eyes narrowed as though he were trying to figure out my reasoning. I waited for him to say something—anything—but he only nodded.

Then: "I should help you inside."

I pulled the door handle. It groaned. "Amazing it doesn't just come off in my hand," I mumbled. I looked over my shoulder to see if Will had heard me. He had. He couldn't keep himself from grinning.

"It has a couple of times."

I laughed as I slid my good foot to the ground, bringing the crutches with me.

The driver's door opened and the cab shifted under the movement. "Let me help you."

"I've got it." I pulled the door key from my pocket.

"Let me . . . ," he said, then his voice faded until he came face-to-face with me. "Here." He extended his arms as though he wanted to do something but didn't know what.

"Take my key," I said, handing it him.

He took it. "Is there anything? Anything else? Something you need now?"

I shook my head. "Seriously, unless you're going to move in with me—which you clearly are not—I think you'd best let me handle the rest." I swung forward. The crutches caught on the river rock and I stumbled, then caught myself. "I need to keep to the stepping-stones," I muttered.

"I can carry you if necessary," he said.

"No. Enough of that humiliation for one day."

"Stubborn woman. At least let me get the door for you." He strode beside me, half jogging the last few steps. He swung the storm door open, inserted the key, entered the code to the house, and pushed the main door open for me. "Here you go. Home again, home again."

I swung up to the front stoop. "Jiggidy-jig."

I made my way into the living room.

"I'll call you in the morning. Make sure you're okay."

"I'll be fine," I said, turning. "But there is something you can do for me . . ."

"What's that?"

"Bring me as many copies of *Partying Grounds* as you can. I'm going to use these next few days to get started on that."

Will snickered. "Think you'll ever learn the name of the magazine?"

My ankle throbbed, stealing any rebuke I might have.

"Question," he said.

"Another one?"

He glanced toward the stairs. "How are you going to make it upstairs?"

I looked at them. Sighed. I could sleep in the downstairs bedroom, but everything I needed for bed was upstairs. Nothing downstairs. Not a single thing. "Well, sir," I said, "I imagine one step at a time."

The following morning I somehow managed to hobble my way back down the stairs without falling and breaking my neck. I made tea, got my morning devotional, and eased my way outside. After I'd lowered myself into my favorite seat, and after Buddy and Sis had come to commiserate with me over my upset, I opened the book to the first page and reread *Take Long Walks.* As I propped my foot on one of the wooden footrests, a funny notion occurred to me.

The first time I'd read the words, I'd thought to ask Will where I might do such a thing and had joked with myself that I hoped he didn't suggest a high cliff. "Careful what you ask for," I told Buddy. "Or think about," I said to Sis.

I flipped a few of the pages until I came to that morning's devotion. *Grow,* it said. The picture showed three daisies, their petals stretching left, right, up, and down. The Scripture verses read: *You plant them, and they take root; they flourish and bear fruit.*—Jeremiah 12:2; and *It's the smallest of all seeds. But when it's grown, it's the largest of all vegetable plants. It becomes a tree so that the birds in the sky come and nest in its branches.*—Matthew 13:32.

At the bottom of the right-hand page, the words: GROW IN CHRIST.

Growing in Christ had been something I'd aspired to my whole life. How well I had done was yet to be seen. But, that morning, as I reflected, I knew my growth during week one had been along the lines of what Gram and Dad had hoped for. And, perhaps, the Lord.

I read the second verse again, the one about the birds, then looked up into the trees where leafy branches had become the home to so many songbirds I couldn't keep count. Not only of their number, but also of their melodies. In one week I'd done more with *people* who couldn't have been more unlike me than I'd ever imagined I would. I had . . . *grown.* By the time I returned to Winter Park, when I returned to the magazine and my new position, I would have grown even more. Just like I'd told Dad the previous afternoon.

"Yoo-hoo!"

Bobbie Decker's hoot from down the drive caused the dogs to rise from where they'd lain at my feet.

"Hey, Miss Bobbie," I called back.

I spied her coming from behind the red-tipped bushes. "I just talked to William," she shouted.

I didn't say anything in return. I simply watched her march upward.

". . . and he said you didn't get back to the cottage until well after eleven o'clock."

"Yes, ma'am."

She passed through the red-tips and into the rock garden. "My goodness, look at that foot all bandaged up."

"It doesn't feel as bad as it looks," I lied.

"Enjoying the book?" she asked, pointing toward my lap.

"Very much so."

Bobbie sat in one of the chairs. Her elbows went to her knees and she leaned forward. "So, tell me. What did the doctor say?"

"I sprained it. He said to rest today and tomorrow, but by Wednesday I should be able to do a few things. I can't *drive,* but if I can get to the newspaper, I can still work."

Bobbie waved as though driving away an insect. "Between Shel, William, and me, we'll get you to work." A frown clouded her face. "Oh no. You won't be able to dance Friday night."

Oh no was right. "No," I said. "I'm afraid not."

"But," she said, brightening. "Thursday is the Movie in the Park. You can still do that, I 'spect."

"The what?"

"The Movie . . . hasn't William told you about it?"

I sighed with a smile. "Your grandson has a way of telling me things about ten minutes before they happen."

Bobbie slid back in the chair. "I need to talk to that boy."

I held up a hand. "No. We're fine. Tell me more about the movie."

"Every quarter we hold a 'Movie in the Park.' Always family-friendly. Townspeople come out, bring their blankets, something to snack on, and then we kick back and show a movie on the side of one of the local stores that butts up against the park."

"I haven't seen a park . . ."

"Oh it's lovely. Near the courthouse. Sort of around it and down a ways. Anyway, it's a lot of fun for everyone and, of course, the newspaper covers it."

"I look forward to it," I said. And I did.

Bobbie clapped her hands together. "I spoke with your grandmother yesterday. Did she tell you?"

"No . . ."

"I told her you were getting along just fine and she had nothing to worry about. 'Course that was before William sent you tumbling down the ditch."

I tried not to laugh, but failed. "He didn't exactly *push* me. He just startled me."

Bobbie pushed herself out of the chair. "He should have been more careful. At least that's what I told Shelton." She looked down the hill to her house. "Gracious goodness, I have a lot to do today so I'll leave you to it." She took a few steps before looking down at her dogs. "I see you have found new loyalty," she said to them. "I guess I should be annoyed, but I'm not." Then, to me, "William says he'll see you later. Says he'll bring the magazines when he heads out to get lunch. Mondays are busy days, you know."

"So I've heard."

I watched the older woman until she stepped into her house using a back door visible to the cottage. "She's something else, isn't she?" I asked the dogs.

Buddy panted in response and Sis sighed.

I turned the pages of the book open to where I'd been reading when Bobbie had called out to me.

Grow, it said.

Contentment slipped over me like a warm blanket. *I am growing,* I thought.

I am.

27

Later that morning, and well before lunch, I received a call from Courtney, who said she'd gotten my message and that she was "on it." There wasn't a lot of excitement in her voice. Or interest. But my grandmother didn't pay her to be either excited *or* interested. She paid her to be a good assistant and *that* she had always been.

Not that I'd told her often. So I said it before I hung up.

"Wow," she said. "And after only one week."

I laughed lightly as I ended the call.

Before the day was over I'd received calls from my parents and Gram, who clucked a little but then said I was made of solid stock so I should be fine.

William stopped by around 1:00 with a stack of musty magazines. "I'd read these outside," he said, "or your allergies will flare up."

"I don't have allergies," I told him.

He adjusted the hat on his head by pulling at the brim in front. "You will," he said with a slow smile.

And then he left.

That night, shortly after dinner and while I lay on the sofa watching—much to my chagrin—a television game show, I received a call from Brianna. She gushed properly over the gifts she'd received in the mail, followed by reminding me she could never afford to replace them after "the little jars were empty."

"Not that I don't appreciate it," she said. "I do. I felt like a princess opening those boxes."

"Tell you what," I said, reaching for the remote so I could lower the TV volume, "set aside, each month, what you might have spent on your drugstore brand and see if, six months from now, you don't have enough to repurchase these name brands."

"Six months? These will last six months?"

"Not if you overuse them, but you don't seem like that kind of girl."

"So I should be able to save enough to buy them?"

"I think so, yes. But if you don't, I'll buy the second round and I will never bother you about it again."

"Oh no! It's not a bother, Ashlynne, I promise."

"Good enough," I said. "I'll see you tomorrow, right? You're still coming to help with the cottage?"

"Yeah," she drawled. "You'll be there?"

"Well, yeah." I looked at my wrapped foot, propped on several throw pillows at the end of the sofa. "I can't believe you didn't hear what happened to me yesterday."

"You mean Will Decker pushing you down some hill?"

I burst out laughing. "Yeah, that. But he didn't *push*. I fell."

"Not what I heard, but small-town gossip can get the best of itself at times."

In other words, people were talking about Will and me. I wasn't sure if that was *good* news or *bad* news.

My phone rang as soon as we ended our call—Rob.

"Hey there," I said, truly happy to hear his voice.

"Ashlynne? Are you okay?"

"You've heard too?"

"Yeah, from Will . . ."

"And what did Will have to say?" I asked.

"That he'd pushed you down the ravine to the old Revolutionary road."

"*Will* said that?" Well, now I knew where the gossip started.

But Rob chuckled and said, "Nah. He said he called your name and you fell. But I heard it at The Dripolator."

"The what?"

"Great little coffee shop. You should try it sometime. They also have a selection of teas and some fairly yummy desserts."

"Mmmm . . . Hey," I said, ready to change the subject. "I went to Brianna's yesterday."

"Oh, yeah. How'd that go?"

"Really well. She's . . . she's such a nice girl and she's . . . a wonderful mother to Maris."

"She is that."

I reached to my foot and scratched the bandage, wishing I could get beneath it where the real itch lay. But the doctor had told me not to remove the bandage for a few days. "I know we have little in common," I added, "but I find her to be a lot more mature than what I'd expect of most girls her age."

"Well," he said, as though pondering, "she'd have to be considering all she's been through."

"She's pretty, too."

"Very much so. Very pretty girl."

"I'd hardly call her a girl."

"That's the Old South for you, Ash. Those of the fairer sex are always girls, even when they're on up to Miss Helen's age."

"And are those of the *other* sex 'boys'?"

"Hardly."

"I see." I needed to refocus to Brianna. "So, Brianna . . . does she date? Much?"

Long pause. If I knew human nature, the pondering had really set in. "I don't think she dates at all."

"How could that *possibly* be? I mean, she's a good . . . girl . . . she's pretty, she's a great mother . . ."

"I—I—uh—I dunno, Ashlynne. I guess I haven't thought about it. Before."

I smirked. "Maybe you should," I said, as though I knew all.

After we hung up, I looked at my phone and said, "Now, Rob Matthews, if you don't 'get it,' you are, as Gram always puts it, 'dumber than a rock.' "

The next day, as soon as I heard Brianna's car arrive at the cottage, I jumped up from my seat on the sofa to greet her. Well, not jump exactly. I flung aside the old magazines and legal pad sprawled across on my lap, grabbed my crutches, and hobbled to the door. When I opened it, she stood on the other side of the storm door, and I gasped.

Tears poured down her cheeks. Her chest heaved. I could see the resolve to "be strong" on her face, but every other part of her refused the order and she broke down.

"What?" I asked while throwing the storm door open. "What's wrong?" I hobbled backward to keep the doorway open. "Come in . . . sit right here in the chair. Let me get you something to drink."

"No. No . . . I . . . I should be waiting on you." In spite of her words, she plopped right down. Brianna reached for the box of tissues by the wingback chair, pulled one, then two, and blew her nose.

"Coffee? Tea?" I asked, pointing to the Keurig and not knowing what else to do but offer something to drink.

"Do you have water?"

"Sure." I opened the refrigerator door and pulled out two bottles, then somehow managed to get them to the living area.

After handing Brianna hers, I eased myself onto the sofa. "Tell me . . . what's wrong? Does this have something to do with Rob?" Had I totally messed up the night before?

Brianna shook her head. "No. Not Rob." She placed the unopened water bottle between her leg and the chair's arm.

I leaned forward, propped my foot on an ottoman, which I'd dragged over earlier, and said, "Then what?"

Fresh tears found their way down her cheeks. "I don't know if I can . . ." She pulled another tissue. Blew her nose again. Buried her face in her hands. "This is bad. Really, really bad . . ."

"Maris? Is it Maris?"

She shook her head.

I knew so little about Brianna, I didn't know where else to go with my questions. She cleaned houses and she worked in a café. Oh . . . "Did you lose your job at the drugstore?"

Again, she shook her head.

What else did I know? She had a child with Cliff, who had my car . . .

"*My car!* Did something happen to my car?"

Brianna looked up. "I don't know," she wailed. "Why would I know about your car?"

"Cliff has my car and . . ."

"Really? You trusted him?"

"Yes, Brianna. I trusted him. I *trust* him, in fact. So, trust me. Tell me what's wrong."

She opened her water bottle, took a long swallow, then recapped it and set it on the floor at her feet, next to a discount-store purse. "I clean the Flannerys' on Monday mornings . . ."

"Jean and Darrin Flannery?"

She hiccuped lightly. "But Miss Jean called on Sunday and asked me if we could switch her cleaning day from Monday to Tuesday. Something about she'd now be home on Mondays and she wanted to give me the run of the house."

Was that last little tidbit of information important? "Okay."

"So I went out there early as I could. None of them was home . . . and . . . I was cleaning Sean's room and . . ." The tears resumed.

Sean. The golden boy of Testament's high school football team. "And?"

"I don't snoop, Ashlynne. I don't. That's my number two rule. Number one is don't steal. Number two is don't snoop."

"I believe you." My water bottle grew sweaty in my hand. I placed it at my feet as Brianna had done, then rubbed my hands together. All the while, the thought that *I* had no trouble snooping through medicine cabinets and home offices fluttered across my mind. Briefly.

"But Sean . . . his bottom drawer—the drawer of his highboy—was half open. I tried to close it so I could run the polish rag over it, but it was stuck." She buried her face in her hands again and groaned.

"So, what did you do?"

She looked up. "I jerked it. You know, like this?" Brianna demonstrated. "And when I did, the whole thing came out and . . ."

"You think you broke the furniture?"

She shook her head. Reached for her purse, opened it, and pulled out a small vial along with a packaged hypodermic needle. Brianna extended them toward me.

I didn't have to ask. I knew. I'd been down this road before. With Leigh. But I took them. Stared at the bottle, pretending to read it.

I looked at Brianna. "He's on steroids." The same drug that had taken Lawson's life. My stomach clenched.

She nodded. "Do you understand what this means?"

"I do. He's the best guy on the team because he's bulking up illegally."

"My little sister, the one who's still in high school, she says that sometimes Sean is real nice and sometimes he's real mean. I think"— she hiccuped again—"the drugs are why."

I leaned back. "You're right about that. Mood swings are one of the side effects."

"What am I going to do, Ashlynne?" she whispered. "I can't *not* say something. What if . . . what if he died or something worse?"

Something worse. I supposed there *could be* worse, though I couldn't imagine what. Not after holding Leigh in her grief. Not after seeing her parents ripped into a million pieces over their son's death. More so, that they'd not known what he was doing. Did Jean and Darrin?

"Was this all there was? The whole stash?"

Brianna shook her head. "No."

"I wonder where he's getting it." I studied the bottle. No doctor's name. No pharmacy. "The coach?"

"I would find that hard to believe. Coach is one of the best Christian men I know. He has children. He wouldn't. I don't think."

I stared at the vial and the syringe awhile longer, as if doing so would somehow make all the answers rise to the surface. "Let me talk to Will," I said, rolling the vial in my palm. "It's the only thing to do."

"Do you think I'm going to get into trouble?"

"For what?"

"Snooping? I mean, if this gets out, no one will want me to clean for them. And, not only that, the whole town is going to be angry. You have to understand the South and—"

"—football," I said with her.

But it wasn't only football we were talking about. The déjà vu made me want to get in my car and leave. Leave rather than walking this path again. I looked at my foot, propped near the book I'd been reading. *Grow.* I was surely growing, and like it or not, I wasn't going anywhere.

28

Brianna managed to dry her eyes enough to clean the cottage, providing me with a new stack of freshly washed, dried, and folded fluffy towels. After she left, I sent a text message to William, asking him if we could talk. He texted back:

> *Can't today. Busy w/only me here. See you 2morrow tho, right?*
>
> I returned with: *I have appt in am to c doc. Ur G-ma taking me. Not sure I WILL b n ltr. Or if I will use the afternoon 2 go c Miss Helen.*
>
> I waited nearly five minutes before he texted back: *Ok. Let's just plan 2 Tlk Thursday nite @ movie/park?*

I'd nearly forgotten about the movie. The only question was whether or not I could wait that long. *Sure. Pick me up?*

Another five minutes went by before I received: *Yep.*

I quickly sent back: *Time?*

I watched the face of my phone until he returned with: *Movie begins at 9. 8:30?*

I sent an "OK."

Then I texted Brianna: *Do nothing until you hear from me. All will b ok. I Promise,* I wrote, completely unsure as to the validity of my words.

Within a minute, her text came in: K. I TRUST U.

I took a deep breath, blinking at the words, fearful of what they meant if we didn't move fast enough. If we didn't move at all. I thought to text back a note of thanks, but as I did, my phone rang.

I recognized the number. "Courtney?"

"Yeah. Hi. Just wanted you to know that I've gotten somewhere on the first part, but getting all the information you need is going to take some more time."

"Not a problem. I understand, believe me. But what about the second part? Did you find out anything?" Because, in all honesty, if Courtney couldn't find specifics, no one could.

"It's a little vague, to be honest with you."

I pulled the legal pad onto my lap and poised a pen. "I'm listening to whatever you have to offer."

"Here's the deal: I have a friend who has a friend who has a connection at the *Chicago Star*. From what he gathered—my friend, from his friend and the connection—William Alexander Decker was something of a hotshot journalist-slash-celebrity in Chicago during his time at the *Star*. He was also the boyfriend—and everyone assumed, the eventual husband—of Felicia Moses, daughter of Conrad Moses."

That much I more or less knew. "Who *is* Conrad Moses exactly?"

"He's one incredibly successful businessman, according to the contact—who wants to remain completely nameless in all this—with a lot of political and . . . *other* . . . ties in Chicago. Now, I'm not sure why you're asking, but I looked up Felicia and, *holy Moses*—if you'll take the pun in which I just offered it—she looks just like you."

I knew that, too. What I didn't know was what unethical thing William had done that landed him back in Testament. "What I really need to know, Courtney, is what caused Mr. Decker to leave Chicago."

"My source says that Mr. Moses had ties with one of the city's commissioners."

"Does he know which committee?"

"Trade, Commerce, and Tourism."

I jotted the notes on the legal pad. "Okay."

"The commissioner had a rather interesting life story, which Mr. Decker wanted to write about, in conjunction with the positive work he and Mr. Moses had done for the less-fortunate communities and the city at large."

"Does the commissioner have a name?"

"Eric Boscano."

I scribbled the name. "All right."

"So, Mr. Boscano had Decker shadow him. Somehow, and my source doesn't know how, Mr. Decker overheard something that put Boscano in a gray light—from the way he remembers it—something Boscano was doing."

"Illegally?"

"Yes."

"And he told?"

"That's where the details get shadowy. Ethically, Decker couldn't say anything because, according to my source, he was in a political closed-door meeting, but not in an official capacity. The story was *his*, not something the *Star* had asked for. So, ethically he couldn't say anything, but morally . . ."

"Gotcha." I finished my notes. "Anything else?"

"My source's connection says that, not only did Decker get out of town fast, there was such a cover-up that finding particulars about it—anything at all—on the Internet or in newspapers, simply won't happen. The only reason I was able to get this much, Ashlynne, is because I knew the right person who knew the right person who knew . . ."

"The right person. Got it."

We ended the call. I spent the next several minutes staring at the information I'd learned about William Decker. I bit my lip as I read the notes over and over again. Then I asked myself why knowing any of it was so important.

"Because," I said to the room, "you've always been curious to a fault."

Leigh once said it was my natural curiosity that drew me to journalism, not the family business. And that it was that same nosiness that led me to peek behind closed medicine cabinet doors.

"And into rooms where I have no business," I said.

I looked at the scrawled information again. So now I knew . . . a little more than that I looked like someone Will used to date, which might or might not explain his hot/cold responses to me.

"This is not why you're here," I reminded myself. "Do your job and, in six months, leave. *That's* the objective."

But I couldn't help what I was feeling. Nor could I help how those feelings—and this man I felt compelled to know more about—affected me.

Perhaps, I thought honestly, if I found out enough, and soon enough, I could put William Decker where he belonged. Out of the forefront of my mind. That way, leaving in December would be easier.

On Wednesday morning, after a "You're doing well" from the doctor and Miss Bobbie had brought me back to the cottage, I called Alma and asked if she could pick me up and drive me to the nursing home that afternoon.

"Is Will busy?"

"I'm assuming. Besides, I'm hoping for time to get to know you better." Which was true.

"One o'clock work for ya?"

"One is perfect," I said.

I called the nursing home and asked to speak to the charge nurse, who secured time with me to talk with Miss Helen. "She'll be delighted to see you," the nurse said.

As soon as Alma drove up, I hobbled out.

"Girl, please," she said, scooting around the front of the parked but still-running SUV. She opened the passenger door for me. "Let someone help you."

"You're driving me, aren't you?" I said with a chuckle. I dropped my purse—one of my new ones—onto the floorboard where it joined a squished McDonald's bag, an empty Yoo-hoo bottle (something I'd never actually seen until that moment, but had heard about in a song playing on Will's truck radio), and a pair of scuffed black high heels.

"So *that's* a Yoo-hoo," I said.

She picked up the shoes. "Mmhmm. And *these* are my church shoes," she said. "I come out of these things as soon as my rear end is back in my car." She tossed them into the back.

I nodded in understanding. Wearing even pricey shoes came with consequences, I knew. Although before moving to Testament I never would've admitted it. "What I find amazing, is that here it is Wednesday, and you haven't yet taken them out of your car. Unlike me, the girl who keeps her shoes in shoeboxes when they aren't being worn."

She scooped the bottle and the bag into her hands, ready to throw them in the back where the shoes had been deposited. "Sounds about like something you'd do."

"Should I guess how old the Yoo-hoo is?"

"Prob'ly not. They're my weakness. Well, that and Doritos and fast food and Snickers. Pretty much anything I shouldn't eat." She took the crutches while I settled in, closed the door, and laid the crutches along the backseat.

Alma drove around the cottage. "I bet you never eat bad stuff."

"Rarely," I said, thinking of the pork I'd had the Friday before. "My mother is a stickler for healthy living and I guess, to some degree, I am too. Although"—I pointed to my foot—"my recent 'take long walks' plan fell short." I cut my eyes at her. "And I use the word 'fell' on purpose."

"So what *did* happen? Because all I've heard is that you and Will were walking together, you tripped on a tree root, and fell into a ditch."

I opened my mouth. Closed it. Opened it again. "We were *not* walking together. I was walking alone, he was walking behind me—unbeknownst to me—I stood too close to a ditch, Will scared me, and I fell.".

"Lawd, Lawd. And it must have been a big ditch."

"The one to the old Revolutionary War road."

"Lawd, Lawd." She turned the car onto the highway. "How in land's sake did he get you out?"

I felt heat rush to my face. "He carried me."

She looked at me—only momentarily, but long enough to say, "Uh-hunh."

"What?"

"I know that look. Girl, you've got it bad for Will Decker."

"Nooooo . . ."

"Then stop gushing."

"I'm not," I protested around a laugh. "All right. I am. But if you say anything . . ."

"And what happened to Rob Matthews? Y'all were pretty cute out there the other night."

"He's a sweetheart but . . . he's just a friend." I paused. "Hey, Alma? What do you think about—say—someone Rob's age and someone—say—Brianna's age?"

"Brianna Fletcher?"

"Yes." A last name I knew only because I wrote it on a check the day before. Another switch for me. Another "something new."

I realized it then . . . that something else had changed. I no longer thought of people by their last names, as I did most of the staff at *Parks & Avenues,* but by their first. I wasn't even sure of Alma's last name. Or Garrison's.

"Well," Alma drawled, "my mother and father are about twelve years apart in age. I have an aunt and uncle who are twenty years apart."

"Does your family have some sort of May-December fetish?"

Alma laughed. "Not one bit. Now, of course, you know that Miss Helen and her husband had a big-ole gap in age."

"I've heard."

"You writing a story about that?" She turned the car into the nursing home parking lot.

"No. I'm still trying to unearth—if you'll pardon the pun—those graves out on Rob's property."

"What graves?"

"You know about the graves, right?"

She parked the SUV. "Can't say as I do."

I unbuckled my seat belt. "Come on in with me then," I said. "Maybe you can help."

The nursing home was typical, I suppose, as nursing homes go. I'd never been in anything but private assisted-care facilities, which have more of a home feel. This one—Testament Nursing Home—felt more like a hospital. And it smelled like one, too. Antiseptic and . . . what *was* that?

"Hate that smell, don't you?" Alma said from beside me. "Always smells like urine when you first walk in. They can't help it none, and that's okay, but it just kind of gets you at first."

"Is that what that is?" I swung along beside her, heading toward the front office.

"Haven't you ever been in a nursing home before?"

"No."

"Mmmm-mmm-mmm."

After we signed in, the receptionist led us to the nurses' station of the wing where Miss Helen resided. I was introduced to an aide whom Alma already knew, and who led us down a hall with polished linoleum floors, ecru walls with handrails, and scuff marks made by wayward wheelchairs.

We stopped at an open door. "Miss Helen, you got visitors," the aide said.

I swung into a bright room with two beds and bedside tables, both laden with clutter. Miss Helen sat in a gold vinyl recliner beside a neatly made hospital bed. She wore a pair of polyester slacks and a classic cotton camp shirt—pink with white polka dots and large pink and white daisies. "Well, lookie-here," she said. "Chile, you came to see an old woman."

Alma walked in behind me as Miss Helen added, "What in land's sake happened to ya?"

"Just a little fall," I said. "I'll be fine soon enough."

"Hey there, Miss Helen," Alma said. She pulled two padded chairs to Miss Helen's chair. "Here ya go, Ashlynne."

I eased into the chair and handed the crutches to Alma, who rested them against the made, but unoccupied, bed on the other side of the room, nearest the door. "Miss Helen," Alma said, raising her voice a little, "where's Miss Sophie today?" Then to me, "Miss Sophie is her roommate."

"Been roomies for two years now," Miss Helen told me. Then to Alma, "She's gone to the knitting and crocheting class." She chuckled. "That woman loves to knit and crochet. All kinds of handiwork." She pointed to an embroidered pillow at the head of her bed. "Made that for me without so much as a pattern."

"I'm impressed," I said. To Alma, "How is it you know who Miss Helen's roommate is?"

"Alma comes out here a couple of times a month and volunteers," Helen answered.

"Like one of the Bingo Angels?"

"Not *like* . . . I *am* a Bingo Angel."

I tried crossing my legs, but the throbbing in my ankle insisted I change positions. "Alma," I said, "can I have another chair to prop my foot on?"

I hardly got the full question out of my mouth and Alma was out the door and back in, carrying an armchair. After she helped me get comfortable, I said, "Miss Helen, I wanted to ask you something . . . about a piece of property with some unmarked graves. I'm hoping maybe you know something."

"Because I'm as old as Methuselah?" Miss Helen chuckled. "Well, who knows? I've managed to keep my ear to the ground over the years. What property are we talking about?"

"The Robert Matthews property . . ."

"Out on the highway heading toward Lake Lure and Chimney Rock," Alma supplied. "About a quarter mile before Candy Creek Road."

"Unmarked, you say?"

Excitement rushed through me. The way she said the words . . . "Yes, ma'am."

"How many?"

"Close to a hundred. Maybe more."

Miss Helen leaned back in her chair, turned her face toward the lone window, which overlooked a small garden of flowers and statues of children playing. I remained silent, feeling Alma's eyes on me. I looked at her, widened my eyes, and smiled. But Alma remained stoic.

"Now then," Miss Helen said, leaning in, "if they're unmarked, how do you know they're graves?"

We were so close, I could practically count every wrinkle on her pretty face. "Well," I said, "they are marked by stones, but no names are on the stones. And the graves themselves are sinking. It's obvious they're graves. Human graves. And I've been thinking, maybe they're slave graves."

Miss Helen and Alma exchanged knowing glances.

"You're right," Alma said.

I shifted to look at her. "I am."

"Right as rain," Miss Helen said. "Them's slave graves."

29

I had a feeling," I whispered, remembering when I'd offered the same idea to Will. He'd become sullen, nearly unresponsive. "What I don't understand," I said to Alma, "is why Rob or Will wouldn't have thought this first."

"Well . . ." Alma shifted in her seat. "From what I know about Will, he doesn't like to talk about that part of our history. Not a bit. Says it's a blight on our history and he'd just as soon not remember it."

"But we have to. We need to remember. Not remembering makes it too easy to repeat," I said. "Like the Holocaust. Or 9/11. If we forget it, we'll allow it to be repeated." I took a breath. "We *have* to remember. We *have* to know. *Knowledge is power—*"

"—I remember . . ." Miss Helen interrupted my soapbox sermon.

Alma and I stopped talking to each other and focused on the older woman. At first she said nothing more, until, "I remember my husband talking one time." She looked at Alma. "Now don't think I'm like he was, but he hated the coloreds."

"Yes, ma'am," Alma said. "We all know about your husband."

Helen's eyes bored into mine. "He was *not* a good man. Said and did cruel things. He was twenty-eight years older'n me, did you know that?"

A gasp escaped my lungs. "*Twenty-eight*?" Hearing "he was older" was one thing. This was . . .

"I was fourteen," she said, interrupting my thoughts. "He was forty-two."

"When you got *married*?"

Helen leaned back. "That's right."

I looked at Alma. "There should be a law . . ."

"Well, there wasn't. Not back then, at least."

Helen chuckled, but not happily. "My daddy and Eb—Ebenezer Aaron Baugh was my husband's name—they were friends. Eb needed a woman in the house—all three of his kids were married already, even the sixteen-year-old, Nettie, had managed to escape home—and my daddy needed to get shed of one of his twelve young'uns."

I shook my head. "I don't understand that . . ."

"We were poor as dirt, girl. Nineteen hundred and thirty-five was a bad year for my daddy. Eb's farm was doing fairly well as farms were doing in those days. Marrying me meant Daddy could come to the farm and pick vegetables. Eb also gave Daddy some chickens. A sow."

My stomach turned. And I thought Brianna's story of young motherhood was tough.

"You all right, Ashlynne?" Alma asked. "You're whiter than . . . well . . . normal."

"I just . . . ," I said when I'd caught my breath, "I can't imagine being married to someone so my father could have vegetables."

Miss Helen chuckled again. "Not just my daddy, hon. My whole family could eat on what Eb provided. Marrying Eb meant feeding my little brothers and sisters."

I swallowed. "So, then . . . what does this have to do with the graves?"

Helen nodded. "Eb was born in 1893."

"Not terribly long after the Civil War," Alma said.

Miss Helen waved a hand. "The War of Northern Aggression, Eb called it. Said his daddy's farm—the one we lived on . . . the one you all came out to for my party—thrived when the coloreds were there. Then, he said, they had to pay them wages, and it made life more difficult."

Uneasiness rushed through me. "For whom?"

"Mmhmm," Alma added.

Out in the hall, a disheveled older woman passed the door in her wheelchair, using her feet to shuffle along. She mumbled to no one about needing to get to the school to find her children.

"I remember," Miss Helen said, again bringing my thoughts back to the conversation, "Eb talking about his daddy and some men . . . they wanted to stop the coloreds from becoming too independent, from having their clandestine meetings out in the woods past Thicket's Holler."

I made a mental note of the place, steeled myself, and asked, "And did they?"

Helen looked first to Alma, then to me. "One way or ta-other." She sighed so deeply I feared she'd run completely out of oxygen. "Tell you what you do. Go look up who owned that land back in the day. If I'm right, it's old Levi Jefferson's place. Married into the Iris Clinton family. That land had belonged to her family, but then Levi and Iris married and he moved in rather than her moving out. Pretty soon, it was the Levi Jefferson place. He and Iris had one son, and after he grew up and married, he and his wife—what was her name?" Miss Helen paused, thinking. "Winnie Dickson, that's what it was. The younger Levi and Winnie's babies all died early on, so when the older Levi and Iris got on up in age a little, they thought to sell the land. That's when the Matthews bought it, if I remember right."

"What happened to the house?" I asked.

"Your young man's mama and daddy live in it."

"My young man?"

Alma shifted in her chair. "The *Matthews* property is quite expansive. Rob bought about a quarter of it from his parents a few years ago. That's where you were. Where the graves are."

Miss Helen waved her hand again. "Y'all go on and look that up. See if you don't learn that several of the former slaves and their families from around here went missing after 1870."

"Why 1870?" I asked.

"Because," Alma said, "that's the year the names of former slaves were recorded on the census."

"You'll find them in 1870, but not in 1880, you mark my words," Helen said. "My husband, Eb, had too much to drink one night—many nights, but this one in particular—and he told me."

"Then why . . ." I stopped, wanting to choose my words carefully. This news—this story—was beyond anything I could fathom. I didn't want to offend Miss Helen, but I felt like we were talking about something out of another country.

"Why what, hon?"

"Why . . . and don't be offended when I ask, but . . . why, if your husband gave you some indication that murders had taken place . . . why didn't you tell somebody?"

Without blinking, Helen Baugh answered, "I never reckoned it had anything to do with me." Her eyes bored into mine as I tried to catch my breath. "You go back and look, now. The Jeffersons and the Clintons and my husband's daddy." She nodded. "They were behind it."

"I know I need to get to the football field," Alma said, once I'd hobbled back to the car with her, "but what you're doing is far more interesting than Sean Flannery."

I jerked at the sound of Sean's name. But Sean's drug usage would have to wait. At least for a while. "I'm not sure where to begin."

"County records. We've got a little place out on 221 where all the records are kept for our county plus those bordering us." She started the car and drove out of the parking lot.

"Alma," I said, after a few minutes of reflection and of trying to calm my stomach, "what does all this mean?"

"It means," she said, "that if I were a betting woman—and I'm not—but, if I were, I'd be laying bets that Rob Matthews' property is the final resting place for a lot of folks. And their people, their descendants, just might want to know about it." She shook her head. "Girl, you may end up being a hero."

"A hero?"

"Yeah," she said with enthusiasm. "Can you imagine? For those folks who get into ancestry, which is just about everybody I've been talking to lately. I'll tell you one thing. As soon as I get home, I'm calling my grandmother. See what she might know. Stories like that, they tend to get buried. You know, so the *storyteller* doesn't."

"Mmhmm . . ." I only half heard her. My mind remained on her previous comment. I wasn't sure I wanted to be a hero. Here I was, finally in a position to be liked by *everyone,* and I wasn't sure I *wanted* to know all of what I'd just learned. About the Jeffersons. The Clintons. The Baughs. I especially didn't like the images of a fourteen-year-old Miss Helen, being bartered for food and chickens and a sow. "Helen Baugh basically lost her childhood," I said. "Do you realize that?"

"Helen Baugh probably didn't have much of one to speak of anyway, girlfriend. Those days were bad. Everyone worked. Even the children. People were hungry. No jobs. No food. No hope."

"But to be fourteen and pretty much forced to marry a forty-two-year-old." I quivered.

"Someone step on your grave?" Alma asked.

"What?" I looked out the window. We were nowhere I'd been yet.

She laughed. "Old saying. When you get the willies like that, we always say someone has stepped on your grave."

"I'll remember that."

Several miles and a few strip malls and convenience stores later, we turned down a long stretch of road that seemed to go nowhere. Finally a small, white-brick flat-faced building came into focus on the left side of the road. Alma turned in and parked next to the sole car that reminded me more of a boat than an automobile. "We're here," she said.

We entered a room in which shelves lined the side walls, tables crammed in the middle, and small white boxes ran in rows toward an area in the rear. The smell of old cigars permeated the air. A small-framed older woman sat at a desk near the back, which Alma walked and I swung toward. The desk was strewn with papers and opened books and a brown paper sack, which I suspected held the remnants of lunch and perhaps an afternoon snack. The woman looked up, removed her reading glasses, and said, "May I help you?"

"We're from *The Testament Tribune*," Alma said. "We'd like to do some research, if you can point us to where to start."

The woman placed her hands flat on the desk and pushed herself up. "There's not a whole lot around here that I can't put my finger on," she said. "Where would you like to start?"

"Land records," I said. I hobbled in an effort to balance myself between the cramped furniture.

"Take a seat," the woman said, "and give me some names and dates."

Alma supplied the information. She joined me at the table and, less than a minute later, we had several books lying open in front of us. "Here ya go." The older woman pointed to one of the pages. "Look here and you'll see which microfiche box corresponds to what you're looking for." She stood straight. "Over there," she said, indicating the rows of boxes, "is the microfiche. And right over here," she said, turning to reveal two viewers, "is where you'll load it." Her eyes shifted between the two of us. "Do either of you know how to use the viewer?"

"Yes," I said. "And thank you so much."

"I'll be right over here if you need me," she said, then left us to our task.

I pulled my notebook and a pen from my purse. "We'll start with the land grants," I said. "Then the census records." My foot throbbed. I chose to ignore it.

"Sounds like a plan."

We found the names Miss Helen had mentioned and the corresponding microfiche boxes. After several tries at winding the machine, the records worker walked over and asked if she could help. Alma and I both laughed, said, "Yes, we could use some help."

"It's temperamental," she said. She wound the film, slid it between two narrow pieces of glass, then spun it to the next reel. "There you go. Now, don't go too fast or you'll miss what you're looking for. There's an awful lot on these films."

I peered up at her. "How will we know where, exactly, to stop?"

"Everything's in alphabetical order."

"Oh," I said, surprised. "Wonderful."

Alma and I began our search. Spinning first one way, then rolling the film back slowly in the other direction. When we were done, I turned to Alma and said, "Miss Helen was right. The land belonged to all the people she said."

"Next is the census records."

I placed my hand on Alma's arm and her chocolate eyes focused on mine. "Oh, Alma. Do we really want to uncover this information?"

"Shame on us if we don't," she said.

Hours passed before we managed to form a complete list of freed slaves who were listed in 1870 but not in 1880. Only the total wasn't a hundred, it was many, many more.

"Take into consideration," the records office employee said after we'd shared with her a bit about our task, "that some of those freed slaves would have left the area on their own and some would have died."

"But if they moved," Alma said, "they wouldn't have gone far, do you think?"

"You may find some in neighboring counties. We have those records here, too."

"This could take days," I said to them both. "To look up death certificates. Land grants. Record everything."

Alma glanced at my crutches leaning against the desk next to me. "Fortunately, time is something you've got, my friend."

Alma picked me up early the next morning.

"Sleep well?" she asked.

"Not really," I said. I pointed to my temple. "Too much going on in my head."

"I know what you mean," she said. "Finding out the truth about the past can be disturbing."

I thought of Will. Of what little bit I knew about him and his time in Chicago. "It sure can," I muttered.

We changed the subject to mindless topics as we continued on to the records office, where she dropped me off with a promise to return around lunch. I'd brought my laptop, opened up a spreadsheet, and set about recording names. I also found myself indebted to Miss Leila, the records employee I'd met the day before.

"There's a method to tracing former slaves," she told me. "What you need to know is that, often, the slaves took on the surnames of their former owners."

I sat at the same table Alma and I had been at the day before and propped my foot on a chair from the other side of the table. I looked up at the older woman. "But the race will be recorded with a 'B,' right?"

"That's right." She looked past the microfiche viewers to her desk. "I'm right over there if you need me."

A little after noon I received a text message from Alma that she was in the parking lot. "May I leave my things here while I go out for lunch?" I asked Miss Leila.

"Honey, absolutely."

I hobbled to the parking lot and Alma's awaiting car. As soon as I got in, she grinned at me and said, "Girl, I've got something to tell you."

"What's that?"

"I was talking with my mama today about the graves and all. And, guess what?" She backed out of the parking lot, swung the SUV around, and headed toward Testament.

I grinned. "*What*?"

"She says there's some connection between what you're looking for and her mama's family. She said Nana has some old family Bibles with a lot of the information you're looking for. She said that Nana also knows something—and I quote—'about the stuff we dared not talk about years ago'"—she turned onto the highway—"'and now, when we can, we've managed to forget.'"

"To forget? How can you forget something like this?" I shook my head. "See, this is *exactly* what I was talking about the other day. If we don't remember, we forget."

Alma shook her head. "But we've made progress, you know? Think about the differences in 1865 and 1965."

"Civil rights."

"In 1965 Malcolm X died. Bloody Sunday in Selma."

"I remember studying that in school." But I knew so little. "I don't see how that makes 1965 any better than 1865, but maybe I'm just being cynical right now."

"Well, then just think about it—in 1965 Congress passed the Voting Rights Act."

I smiled. "That's positive."

Alma smiled too. "And, not too many years later, look where we are. Even South Carolina has an African American elected to Congress." She turned the car into a strip mall. "Great little café in here," she said.

"Good, because I'm starved."

"I'm sure they have a healthy salad or two that you'd like. Me," she said, parking the car, "I want a juicy steak sandwich, open-faced, smothered in gravy."

I frowned. "You really should think about your health, Alma. Good food doesn't have to taste bad, you know."

She crossed her eyes at me, then laughed with me. "Back to what we were talking about, 'cause I think this is important. *Very* important."

"Okay . . ."

"Look at me, Ashlynne. I'm a sports reporter. Me. Not for a major newspaper or anything, but a reporter nonetheless. I own my own home. I go where I want, when I want. I think what my nana was trying to say is that, once you find a calm spot in the water, you don't rock the boat."

"But what if stories like the one we now know about need to be told? Do you just stay silent because you're enjoying the good things in life now?"

"Sometimes. I think mostly what Nana is saying is that you can be afraid you'll lose the good stuff if you keep bringing up the bad. Does that make sense?"

"Perfectly." I opened the door. "So, does that mean we shouldn't dig any further?"

"Oh no." She opened her door, got out and walked around to my side of the car, where she opened the back door to retrieve my crutches. She handed them to me. As I hobbled up, she said, "There's a big difference in *you* finding information like this on some old graves and my nana making some grand announcement from her living room with old family Bibles spread open around her."

I closed my door. "I understand."

"Good." She took a step forward and I followed. "I'll arrange for the two of you to meet."

"Hummmph," I said as a thought played with my mind.

"What's that?"

"I'm just thinking how I spent Sunday afternoon teaching Brianna about cosmetics and now you're teaching me about . . ."

Alma stopped. I did too. "About?"

"Something just dawned on me."

"Wanna share?"

Hadn't I done the same thing as Alma's ancestors? As the people whose names could be found in her nana's Bible? After seventh grade I'd closed a door, unwilling to discuss what had happened to me in public school. To talk about it meant to reveal the truth and to possibly shatter the wall I'd built. To talk about it meant . . .

. . . to *remember.*

30

William arrived at the cottage on Thursday evening between 8:15 and 8:30, driving a Cadillac Escalade.

"Where's your truck?" I asked as I swung toward it. Fading sunlight illuminated the sapphire-blue metallic paint. Overhead, birds chirped like the songbirds in a Disney fairy tale. I glanced upward. *Stop it,* I ordered telepathically. *I am* not *Cinderella and he is* not *Prince Charming.* Although the pumpkin-to-carriage comparison didn't escape me.

"I thought you'd be more comfortable in my dad's car." Will opened the passenger's-side door and reached for my crutches.

Recognizing the car to be a newer model, I said, "I thought your mom and dad had been away for a while." I hobbled over, hoisted myself in as efficiently and as gracefully as possible. After situating myself on the plush seat, I eased my feet toward the pristine, carpeted floorboard.

"You mean because this is a newer-model car?" He closed the door on the question.

When he'd gotten behind the wheel, I said, "Yes."

"Dad and Mom came home a year or so ago so Dad could have some medical testing done. Nothing serious." He started the car. "And while they were here, they bought the Caddy because . . ."

Will drove the car around the cottage without bothering to finish his explanation.

"Because?"

Will shook his head as though he were amused. "Dad found a great deal." He glanced at me. "My father *loves* a great deal."

"But *why*? He can't drive it if he doesn't live here and he apparently wasn't thinking in terms of taking it wherever he is. Where *are* they, by the way?"

"England."

"*England?*" I chuckled in spite of a half-determined resolve not to be amused at anything Will Decker said during our time out. But, I had naturally pictured his parents serving in a third-world country and living in an adobe hut.

"Don't snicker," he said, laughing with me. By then we were on the highway, heading toward town. "You have no idea of the need for Christian missionary work in England."

"I guess not."

"You like research so much, you should read up on it sometime."

I didn't answer. I only stared at him for a long moment and tried to steady my thoughts. William Alexander Decker. Accused of unethical journalistic practices. I couldn't fathom it. Difficult to work with at times, yes, but *unethical*? To the point where he had lost his position as the star reporter—the golden boy—at the *Chicago Star*?

The golden boy.

Sean Flannery was another golden boy. And tonight I had resolved to tell Will what I knew. I had to convince him of the importance of bringing Sean's drug usage to light. It wouldn't be easy, not with everyone in town putting all their hopes for football glory on the young man. But it had to be done.

Will turned his attention to me. Night had nearly fallen. Only the faint light from streetlamps exposed the grin forming in the shadow of his hat's brim. "What are you looking at, Miss Rothschild?" he asked.

I blinked, feeling heat rush to my face, and turned to look out the windshield. "Nothing."

I heard faint chuckling, which I refused to acknowledge. *Not the objective, not the objective . . .*

We ventured past the courthouse. Will turned the SUV first to the right, then left into a makeshift parking lot beside an auto repair business that looked to have been around since the Model A. When he caught me studying it—the old Coca-Cola signs, the antiquated gas pump off to the right from more modern-day pumps, the closed bay windows—he said, "Our very first service station here in Testament."

"A *service* station?"

"Many, many years ago, when someone brought their car to get gas or whatever, they received complete service. Thus, they were called service stations." He parked. Turned off the car. "See that old pump? It still reads forty-seven cents to the gallon."

My eyes widened. "You're kidding."

"Guy who owns it—Jesse—he decided to keep it for old time's sake. Jesse is a grease monkey—as he puts it. So was his daddy and Jesse's two sons are too." He tipped his hat back a fraction of an inch. "By the way, I heard from Cliff today. Your car will be ready soon."

"Really?"

"He says it looks good as new. I've already filed with my insurance on it, so you don't have to worry about the cost."

The insurance. I hadn't even thought about that. If I'd been in Winter Park when the accident occurred, my father would have handled everything for me. "Yours? Why not mine?"

He brought the rim back to its starting place. "My fault. My responsibility." He opened the car door. "Let me help you down. Hold on."

A few minutes later, Will and I ambled toward the silhouettes of a fairly large group of people gathering on a grassy mound. Some—mostly older—sat in lawn chairs along the crowd's edges, but most rested on blankets. Everywhere, candles flickered. "Citronella," Will told me when I commented on it. "To keep the skeeters away."

"Do you have one for us?" I pointed to the wicker basket Will carried.

"Yes'm. Along with something for us to sit on and some snacks for the movie."

"Well, then you've thought of everything," I replied.

He smiled at me. "This ain't my first rodeo, you know."

We found a vacant spot near the back of the crowd. I propped myself on my crutches while Will spread an old, somewhat ratty, blue-and-white quilt. He dug farther into the basket and brought out two boxes of Gobstoppers and two more of Boston Baked Beans candy. "My favorites," he said, looking up at me. "Can't watch a movie without them. But I'm not done so don't worry."

"Uh-huh." I scanned the crowd, some sitting, some milling about, all ready for entertainment. A lone figure moved toward us.

Rob.

I braced myself for the disappointment I feared he'd carry on his face at seeing William and me together but, instead, received a look of concern.

"Hey there," he said. "Doctor know you are out and about?"

"He says I'm healing well. And I try to keep it elevated."

Rob crossed his arms. "Have you heard the latest?"

Whatever smile I might have had on my face fell. "The latest?" Was he talking about Sean?

Rob chuckled. "According to the last rumor I heard, Will was chasing you with a snake when you toppled down the ravine."

Will shook his head as he rested on his haunches and removed his hat, tossing it on the old quilt. "I hope you cleared things up."

"Why bother?" Rob asked.

From over his shoulder I spied Brianna, sitting alone on a blanket. She waved to me and I waved back. "Hmmm," I said. "I wonder where Maris is tonight?"

Rob glanced in the direction of my gaze. "With her daddy and his family," he said. "Maris and Bri were sitting not too far from me. A few minutes ago, Cliff came and got Maris. He asked if Brianna wanted to join them, but . . ."

"And she said she didn't?"

He shrugged. "Yeah," he said, as though he were amazed by Brianna's answer. "She said maybe she would later, but not right then. She seemed all right with Maris going, though." He shrugged again.

Good girl. "Hey, Rob," I said, using my sweetest voice, "I really hate to see her sitting alone. Don't you?"

He looked over his shoulder again, then to me. "It is kinda sad. Like you said the other night, it's amazing she doesn't have every young buck in town knocking on her door."

From the corner of my eye I saw Will shake his head, but I chose to ignore him. "Well . . . ," I drawled, "why don't—you know—you?"

Rob's brow shot up so fast I was surprised it didn't get lost in his hairline. "Me?" He pointed to his chest.

"Why not?" I asked, hobbling a little to steady myself. "She's a pretty girl. A sweet girl. You're a good-looking guy who couldn't be any nicer. You have a *lot* in common . . ."

Rob blushed as he stared at his shoes. "Um, don't you think, Ashlynne, that she might be just a tad too young for me?"

Will feigned a cough. I raised my left crutch and jabbed his shoulder. "Hush," I said. Then to Rob, "I'm not asking you to marry her, Rob. I'm only asking that you sit with her for one movie."

Will broke in, "And it's not like you're Old Man Baugh and Miss Helen."

I jabbed him one more time. He rubbed his shoulder as if I'd really injured him. "Do that again and you'll *walk* home."

I shook my head. "Sure I will." Then to Rob, "So? Go . . ."

Again he blushed. "Well, all right. Sure. I can do that."

I grinned and my heart soared. *Score one for Ashlynne.*

"Go on, then, Romeo," Will told him. He glanced skyward. "It's getting pretty dark. Movie ought to start soon."

Rob walked away, and I grinned at Brianna, who waved one more time. She looked up as Rob walked toward her. The way her smile illuminated the night, the movie may never start.

I eased myself to the quilt and I felt Will's hand on the small of my back, guiding me. I wished he wouldn't. More than anything, I wished I didn't need him to. The foreign felt familiar. The thing I found objectionable, I liked.

Once settled, he brought his lips to my ear and said, "Smooth."

"What?" I feigned ignorance as I shook off the raised gooseflesh.

"I can see what you're doing there with Rob and Bri."

I smiled. "She likes him. Did you know that?"

William had placed a citronella candle between us, pulled a lighter from his Western-wear shirt pocket, and lit it. "Yes," he said. "As a matter-of-fact I *did* know that."

"How?"

"I've suspected for some time."

"Does Rob know? Or suspect?" I didn't want my new young friend to be embarrassed.

"Clueless." He eyed me. "Don't you think she's a tad young for Rob?"

"After what I learned in the past couple of days, no."

His brow furrowed. "What does that mean?" He reached into the basket and brought out a bottle of Coke and a bottle opener.

"I'll tell you later."

He opened the soft drink and handed it to me. "Got a little surprise for you," he said, winking. Shivers skipped down my arms in the warm night air. *Good heavens, wouldn't Gram be amused?* And Leigh. Leigh would roll on the floor when—if—I told her.

"It's a cola," I said, trying to regain my composure. Reminding myself of the objective. That this man may very well have been guilty of unethical journalism.

And that I was leaving in about twenty-four weeks. Or was it twenty-three and change?

He reached into the basket again "Not quite," he said pulling out a packet of peanuts. "Remember?" He tore the top corner from the packet.

"The first day in your truck," I said so quietly I wasn't sure he heard me.

"Yep." He picked up my Coke.

I narrowed my eyes. "Are you really going to . . ." He fashioned his left hand like funnel and poured nuts into the drink. "Oh my."

"It's good." He repeated the action with his own drink.

I peered into the narrow opening of the bottle. The peanuts floated near the top.

"The secret is in the glass bottle," Will said. "Not plastic and for heaven's sake not a can." He tilted his bottle toward mine in a mock toast. "And roasted, salted nuts. Never raw, boiled, or unsalted."

Our bottles clinked together.

"Take a swig," Will said, "get a nut and be sure to chew on it."

I did, following his lead.

"Salty *and* sweet," I said. "Not bad."

The building in front of us flickered to life with color. Voices died down, people who stood, sat. Those who sat, settled. And I leaned back on my hands and extended both legs. I had chosen a simple pair of denim jeans and a North Face tie-dyed tee, one multi-colored Ked and one thick sock. "What are we watching?" I leaned over and whispered.

"*The Bachelor and the Bobby-Soxer.*"

I sat a tad straighter. "Cary Grant and Shirley Temple?" Talk about your "young girl crush on an older man" story.

Will grinned back at me. "Cary Grant fan?"

"Yes, you?"

"He was the best at what he did. But truth is, I'm crazy about Myrna Loy."

"So you have a thing for redheads?"

He made a face. "No, I have a thing for actresses who began as silent-film stars. Now shhh . . ."

"Bet I can guess your favorite scene," William said on the way home. His hat rested on the console between us.

"Oh?" I asked, as though I couldn't care less. I glanced out my window and peered up at the inky sky. To the stars that glinted like diamonds.

"Yoogie-doogie," he repeated the Cary Grant line.

I looked at him. Watched his slow smile. His silly words and sweet smile disconcerted me so, I turned my attention to the navigation system built into the faux-woodgrain panel, and focused on the "car" displayed on its screen.

"You remind me of a man," I said, mimicking the movie's memorable line, spoken by Cary Grant in an effort to one-up Myrna Loy.

"What man?" Will asked, playing along.

"The man with the power."

"What power?"

"The power of hoodoo."

"Hoodoo?"

"You do."

"Do what?"

"Remind me of a man."

"What man?" he asked. His laughter filled the car. Mine joined with it. This was fun. It felt good to let loose. To not think about Chicago or Winter Park, the *Star* or *Parks & Avenues.*

"What I really appreciate," I said, swallowing the amusement, "is how she uses the same words to tell him she loves him at the end of the movie. Class-A writing, I think."

Will turned the car into the Decker Ranch drive. "You're nearly home, Miss Ashlynne," he said, drawling his words as if he were a fine gentleman and we were in the mid-1800s.

My breath caught. "Speaking of which, there's something I need to discuss with you."

"About?"

"I've been doing a little research while recuperating."

"On?"

The car rocked back and forth, more gently than any other vehicle I'd traversed this road in since arriving in Testament.

"The graves on Rob's property."

His eyes jerked to me, then back to the driveway shrouded in shadows. "Really? You didn't tell me."

"Uh-huh. Surprised?"

"A little."

"What'd you think I was doing with myself all day since you chased me with a snake and threw me down the hill?"

"It wasn't a snake," he said. "It was a . . . a . . ." He looked at me. "I can't come up with anything worse than a snake."

I could think of a few things. We could have been walking along the wooded trail, hand in hand. We could have stopped to look down the ravine, to scope out the Revolutionary road. He could have turned to me, and then, taking me by my shoulder, eased me to face him. He could have drawn me close . . . closer . . . he could have kissed me . . . my knees could have buckled and . . . the next day the word would be all over Testament that Will Decker—catch of the county—and the stranger from Winter Park were making out in the woods when God pushed her down the cliff to prevent sullying Prince Charming's reputation.

No . . . no . . . no!

When I didn't respond, he said, "I thought you were working on the magazine."

"A little." I linked my arms as he brought the car to a stop. "But, I've also been at the county records office, scanning books, taking notes, and looking at microfiche until my eyes have nearly crossed. Permanently, I might add."

He unbuckled his seat belt and leaned toward me, slipping his hat from the console to the back floorboard, and leaning his elbows onto the console. The light from the outside lamp I'd left on shone onto his features, angular and handsome. I inhaled slowly through my nose.

"Let me see those eyes," he said. "In case you need a doctor, or something."

I chuckled, crossed my eyes, and inched my face closer to his. His became shadowy, but I could see his thick lashes as he blinked and drew back. His hands came up as though they had a mind of their own, rested tenderly on both sides of my face. The thumb pads caressed my cheeks and my eyes fluttered shut, even as *not the objective* became nothing more than a pitiful whimper.

The kiss was warm—his lips soft—and over too soon. When the gentle pressure from his fingertips released, he kissed the tip of my nose, and sat back. We stared at each other for a long moment before he said, "Hi."

"Hi," I managed around the knot in my throat.

"You all right with that?"

I could hardly speak. No. I wasn't "all right with that." But I couldn't let him know that. Not now. Not ever. I had a job to do here so I could have a job in Winter Park. Kissing William Decker less than two weeks after arriving in Testament could easily usurp years of hard work toward my father's office at *Parks & Avenues*. Then again, it was just a kiss. A simple kiss on the lips.

And the tip of my nose.

Oh how adorable was *that*?

I raised my chin a fraction of an inch. "Sure. I'm all right. Why wouldn't I be? We're adults, after all."

He didn't answer with words. His eyes traveled over my face until he cleared his throat and said, "Yeah, well, I'd best walk you to the door."

I didn't want to walk to the door. I wanted to stay inside the car, to breathe in the scent of his cologne I knew lingered on my face, and to simply *be* with him. I wanted to throw my original objective for being there into the ravine I'd fallen down a few days earlier and to dare it—*dare it*—to try to crawl its way out. I wanted to keep talking. To bring him up to speed on what I knew so we would be on the same page. So I said, "Don't you want to know about the graves? Who they belong to?"

I waited while he appeared to ponder my question. "Not tonight. Not right now."

"When, then? Tomorrow?"

"Sure." His voice remained whisper-soft.

"Can you pick me up in the morning? The doctor said I'm okay to work, just not to drive."

He nodded. "Sure." He opened the car door, came around to my side while I unbuckled the seat belt tethering me to my seat. He opened the back door, pulled out my crutches, then opened mine. "Your walking apparatus, m'dear."

I sighed as I slid toward them and guided my good foot to the ground. "Got it." I pulled one of my new purses from where it had rested on the seat beside me and onto my shoulder.

William closed the doors.

"There's something else I need to talk to you about," I said as we made our way to the front of the cottage, with me using the large stepping-stones that curved to the stoop. "And I really shouldn't wait any longer."

His hand rested, once again, on the small of my back. Protective. Guiding. "What's that?"

"I have to show you . . ." I hobbled onto the narrow pine boards, rested my back against the storm door and the crutches against the wall. Opening my purse, I said, "Brianna came over the other day, hysterical. She'd been out at the Flannerys' and"—I extended the vial—"she found this in Sean's bedroom when she was cleaning the day before." I extended the vial.

He took it, studied it, then brought his eyes to mine. "Am I looking at what I think I'm looking at?"

"Steroids. Yes."

"And you've been walking around with this since . . . ?"

"Tuesday."

Fire blazed in the amber of his brown eyes. He took a step back, tightened his fist around the tiny vial of death. The air stretched thin between us. "What are you?" he asked. "Crazy?"

Crazy. Yeah, I must have been. Crazy to have trusted him. Crazy to have thought we could be friends. Friendly—or some faraway day, more.

Crazy to have thought another journalist, even one with an ethically shadowed past, might be interested enough in the vial of steroids from a local high school star athlete's room to be concerned. Not just about the name of his supplier.

But about Sean Flannery's *life*.

I'd misjudged people before. I'd let hopes and expectations soar so high that when I fell, I fell hard. But never, in all my life, had I ever been as wrong about someone as I was about Will Decker.

31

What is *wrong* with you?" I reached for my crutches, in need of support. "Do you *not* understand the implications here?"

He extended the vial toward me. "What I understand is that Brianna *stole* from the Flannery home."

"Technically, yes . . ." *Technically.* Wasn't that my father's word?

William's boots clomped against the pine boards as he paced. "And you don't see a problem with that?"

I looked into the darkness down the hill, to the U-shaped brick house below, the single light shining on the back patio and the dim illumination from a small window. "Sean Flannery—*your* golden boy—has been using steroids, for pity's sake. Aren't you more interested in *that* than how I came about the evidence?"

"No." He pointed a finger at me, leaving the rest of his fingers wrapped around the vial. "And you should know better. You're not new to journalism, Ashlynne. You studied ethics." *Ethics.* There it was. The word suspended between us, whether he realized it or not. And he was using it against me.

Against *me.*

He returned his hand to a fist. "Not to mention—"

I waited for the rest of what he had to say, studying his face in the interim. His jaw had set. A slight quiver of his head, almost imperceptible in the dark. But in the illumination of the porch light,

I could see. I could tell. So I pressed on, speaking between clenched teeth. "Not to mention what?"

He flung the vial toward a nearby tree, the one I sat under peacefully every morning, reading the devotional book I'd come to cherish. The vial struck it, hit the ground, and rolled no more than an inch. Will raked his fingers through his hair. "I cannot believe this." He continued to pace. "No worries. No crises. No scandals."

And there it was. I no longer had to wonder. Now I knew. Will Decker was no longer speaking about Sean Flannery, but about whatever had happened in Chicago. Whatever it had been that caused him to return to North Carolina. To Testament. And to a tiny newspaper that wouldn't garner him any claim to fame, but where he'd be safe from disgrace.

Safe. I understood that. I'd done it, too, but as a seventh grader. Running home . . .

"Does . . ." My voice caught in my throat. "Does this have something to do with Chicago?" I needed to hear the answer. From his lips. Right now.

The fire in his eyes returned in full measure. He spun and took a wide step toward me. "What do you know about Chicago?"

I pressed back against the glass, but I met his anger with doggedness. Tears of fury threatened my eyes, causing them to burn. "I know you left because of controversy. And something to do with a man named Eric Boscano."

He scoffed. Slammed his hand against the glass of the storm door, but not hard enough to break it. "You couldn't stand it, could you? Last week? When I was a bit of a horse's butt."

"A *bit*? I couldn't even inhale without you criticizing the amount of oxygen I took into my lungs. As if your precious Testament couldn't *stand* to share the tiniest molecule of air with a stranger from Winter Park."

His eyes bored into mine, but his voice quieted as he said, "Forgo the hyperbole, if you don't mind." He walked off the landing to the grouping of Adirondack furniture.

My shoulders relaxed. I pressed against the hand grips of the crutches. Looked at the vial lying on the ground. "Yeah," I said, lowering my voice as well. "I'll forgo the hyperbole when you forgo the drama."

Will walked to the vial, picked it up, and stuffed it into the pocket of his jeans.

I hobbled forward. "What are you going to do with that?"

"Never you mind."

I swung toward him. "Give it back to me."

"For what?"

"Because . . . you—you have to—at least give Bri a chance to return it."

His nose came dangerously close to mine. "Bri should have never taken it."

The image of Brianna's face—wet and swollen from crying—came to view. "You have no idea how this pained her," I said. I leaned into my right crutch and pointed to my chest. "And you have no idea what it means to me."

"Means to you? What do you think? That you're going to get some big *story* out of it?" He glanced over his shoulder toward his grandparents' home, then lowered his voice as though we might be overheard. "You're going to bring some high school kid to ruin so you can pat yourself on the back, run back to Daddy, and say, 'Lookie what I accomplished? Let me have that corner office now, if you please?' "

Had I been able, I would have slapped him. Hard. Instead, I asked the insufferable age-old declaration of damsels who have been verbally wronged: "How *dare* you." I hobbled closer to him, released the right-hand grip, and poked him in the chest with my index finger. "You thought you were something, didn't you? Telling me what you thought I was all about—my 'type'—that day in front of the school. Well, you don't know me at all, William Alexander Decker."

He threw his head back and barked a laugh. "So you know my full name. Want my social? Or do you have that, too?"

"I don't want *anything* from you."

He came within a breath of me again. I gripped both crutches and hobbled one step back. "Good," he said. "Because you aren't going to get it. Nothing from me." He turned and strode a few feet to his father's car, turned and stomped back. "You almost had me, you know that? Almost made me forget. Well, I haven't forgotten. I remember it all very well." He walked away and, again, returned. "Stay out of the affairs of Testament, North Carolina, Ashlynne *Paige* Rothschild."

I gasped.

"Yeah," he said. "Two can play that game."

I cried most of the night. Not only for the sole kiss I'd experienced—one of the few of my lifetime that had come from somewhere sweet and tender—but for Brianna. For her disappointment in me when I had to tell her that, not only had Will not promised to help us, but that he'd taken the vial. Then I cried for Leigh. For Lawson. For the entire cemetery-flanking group of mourners who'd laid him to rest on a humid, misty day when even heaven seemed sad at our loss. Finally, I cried for Gram. For her trust in my ability to come to Testament, to work well with people I had little in common with, and return to Winter Park a better person for it.

Morning had nearly broken when I realized that, unlike the crying jag after my failed attempt at being normal in junior high, not once had I shed a single tear for myself.

And so, I did.

A little after 7:00, with about forty-five minutes of a solid nap behind me, I got up, showered, changed into the same jeans I'd worn the night before and a clean top. I climbed onto the bed to wrap my foot and realized how much better it felt than even the day before. The swelling had gone down enough that I could wear both hiking boots.

Mom always said I healed fast.

Maybe, like my ankle, my heart would too.

I picked up my cell phone to call her, then changed my mind. Instead, I hobbled down the stairs, made a cup of hot tea, got my book, and went outside. I waited a minute or two for Buddy and Kelsey to amble up the hill and, when they didn't, I opened the book and attempted to read past fresh tears.

Maybe they'd heard the argument the night before, I thought.

Maybe they didn't like me anymore. Either.

I looked into the cloudless, blue sky to blink the tears away, then returned to my book.

GIVE LOVE, the tile read. Two hands throwing three hearts into the sky demonstrated the action. The text read: *Hate stirs up conflict, but love covers all offenses.* —Proverbs 10:12; and *Conduct yourselves with all humility, gentleness, and patience. Accept each other with love.* —Ephesians 4:2.

At the bottom of the page were three simple words: LOVE ONE ANOTHER.

"I'm trying, Lord," I said aloud. "I promise you, I'm trying. But . . . what did I do that was so wrong? I don't get it. Help me to understand. Help me to love more. Better." I smiled. "More better."

I closed the book, sipped on my tea until the mug was empty, and went back inside in time to hear my phone ringing.

Brianna. Before she had left my home on Tuesday I had given her my number, and she'd called me several times since. Always asking if I'd told Will. Before, I could say, "no." Now I'd have to tell her the truth. My heart grew heavy as I answered.

"Hey, Bri."

"Oh, Ashlynne," she said, nearly breathless. "Last night was fabulous. Thank you. Thank you so much."

I forced a smile. "I take it things went well."

"I think so. I told Cliff he could take Maris home with him if he wanted. Of course, he did. And then Rob and I stood outside my car and we talked and talked until the *bugs* nearly took us away."

"I'm so glad."

"What about for you and William? You looked pretty cozy," she said, singing the last two words.

I swallowed my angst. "Bri, I need to tell you . . . I showed William the vial."

"And?"

I walked slowly to the nearby wingback chair and sat. My ankle throbbed so I propped my foot on the ottoman. "He's a little upset. I'm—I'm not sure why . . . exactly. I mean, I think there is more to it than what he is saying—"

"What is he saying?"

I scooted to the back of the chair and laid my head back. "Not much, really." I rubbed my temple with my left hand, then drew my hair back and over one shoulder. "He—he doesn't want us to do anything about this, but—"

"—but, Ashlynne. We *have* to. If someone is giving him drugs, he could die or something."

My tongue darted across my lips, moistening the dryness. "I know. Believe me. I know."

She didn't respond initially. I waited. I knew she needed the time to digest my unexpected news. "So what *are* we going to do?"

Now it was my turn to pause. To ponder. To wonder what the right move to make would be.

When you don't know what to do, Gram always said, do the next right thing.

Was the next right thing to see another young boy die? To watch another family grieve? I couldn't do that. Even if it made me the outcast in this town, I couldn't. "Bri? When do you go back to the Flannerys'?"

"Tuesday, why?"

"All right. We'll go—you and me together—and we'll see what else we can find. See if there is something connecting Sean Flannery's usage of steroids to the person who supplies him."

"You'll do that?"

"Yes." I closed my eyes against the thought of what this meant. All of it.

"But, Ashlynne . . . I don't . . . I mean, my rule is . . ."

"I know. No snooping." I opened my eyes. "Fortunately for you, I'm sort of a pro."

An hour later, the crunching of tires over gravel caused me to look up from my laptop, which I'd placed on the kitchen bar, and where I typed my notes from the last few days. I leaned over to gaze out the window. My Jag was now parked just beyond the tree that had, the night before, taken the tiny brunt of William's wrath.

Sliding off the stool, I hobbled to the door where my crutches had been propped. I grabbed them for support and then stepped outside in time to see Will coming around the back of the Jag.

"Oh," I said.

He stopped. His eyes, shadowed by the brim of his hat, were downcast. Nearly colorless. He looked as if he'd cried as much as I had the night before, if that were possible. "Hey," he said. The key fob dangled from between his fingers. "Brought your car back to you."

"So I see."

He took another step. Stopped. "Can we—can we talk?"

I wasn't sure we could. Or, to be more exact, I wasn't sure *I* could. There were no words left to say. My heart had been stripped bare and beaten. Left bruised. I'd opened a door. A infinitesimal door. Just enough to let someone come in and—possibly, maybe—form a friendship. An alliance that would grow a newspaper. Resurrect a magazine. And—possibly, maybe—end with my "corner office" as Will had so indelicately put it the night before.

Regardless of my hesitancy, I nodded. "I don't see why not."

32

I pivoted toward the rock garden's sitting area. "Out here fine?"

"Of course."

The crunching beneath his boots followed me and, when I leaned the crutches against the arm of the settee, William bridged the gap between us with wide strides. His hand extended in an offer to help me sit and I took it. After I settled, he sat next to me, removed his hat and hung it on the armrest.

He looked at my feet. "You're in shoes."

"I'm in hiking boots."

"But you're still using the crutches."

I blinked. "Do you want to talk to me about my shoes? Or something else?"

He "humphed." Extended the key fob. "Here."

I held out my hand and he dropped the fob into the palm.

I focused on the car. "Thank you."

He raked his fingers through his hair then tossed the ends between them as if he were freeing himself from something. "I need to apologize to you."

As I'd done before, I knew I could say, "Apology accepted," but the easiness of the words didn't seem appropriate. This time, there had to be more. "For?"

He rested his elbows on his knees, dropped his head between his shoulders, and turned his face to mine. A hint of a grin broke across his face. "You're not going to make this painless, are you?"

I extended my left leg. Folded my hands together as though in prayer, and rested them in my lap. "I have twenty-three weeks left here. I've barely gotten through the first two. If I'm going to survive this . . . plan . . . of my grandmother's and my father's, then, I've decided, it's important . . ." I swallowed. My ankle hurt and fatigue wrapped around me from my lack of sleep the night before. "No. I *know* that if we are going to move forward . . . as *coworkers* . . . we have to be completely honest with each other. Last night . . ." I stared at my hands. Clenched them. Released. "Last night you scared me."

He leaned back. Crossed one ankle over a knee. "You didn't seem scared."

"Well, I was."

"All right." He swallowed and his Adam's apple moved slowly up and down his throat. "You want us to be honest?"

"Yes." I felt the rise and fall of my chest with every shallow breath.

William stared toward the sloping of lawn leading to the highway. "When I went off to college, Big Guy thought I was going to come back here, be the best reporter *The Testament Tribune* has ever seen, bring the paper to new heights." He chuckled, but his eyes didn't register happiness. "He'd retire on my hard work—not to mention his own. But I had no such aspirations. I didn't want to be a big fish in a little pond. I wanted to be a *big* fish in a *big* pond." He grinned sheepishly at me.

I didn't smile back. I couldn't. My grandmother's words were too loud in my head. What had she said to me a mere two weeks ago as she told me about my upcoming move to Testament?

You need some time away from all that Winter Park has afforded you. You are a recognized fish in the Winter Park pond. But I—and your father—feel it's time you know what it's like to be, as the old saying goes, "a little fish in a little pond."

Well now I knew. And so had William. And he had wanted more. Like me.

"Go—go on."

"So. During my senior year, with me about to graduate summa cum laude, one of my advisors suggested she contact someone she knew at the *Chicago Star*. I couldn't believe my luck. Even though I knew I'd be walking into a lion's den, what with Chicago's reputation for scandal"—he shook his head—"I didn't care. I wanted that job." Will glanced at his grandparents' home. "I *needed* that job."

I understood that, too. Wanting a job so desperately I was willing to do anything.

Go anywhere.

"Big Guy and Gram . . . they were hurt. Gram cried. Big Guy stomped around a lot." He winked at me. "You know Big Guy."

I couldn't help but smile, but I swallowed it quickly. "Yeah."

"But I promised," he said, raising a fist, "to make them both proud." His voice strained against the words. What he'd done—hurting his grandparents—had hurt *him*. Deeply. Because, in the end—as I'd already learned—he had not.

But I asked the question anyway. Half out of hurt over the night before. Half because I wanted to hear the rest of his story and I feared he'd stop at this point. "And did you?"

"No." He shrugged. "Maybe at first. At first I shot straight to the top. I was like Midas." He lifted his hands, palms up to the world. "Everything I touched turned to gold. Then I met Felicia Moses, daughter of Conrad Moses, one of the most successful, most powerful businessmen in the entire state of Illinois."

"The woman who looks like me?"

The question startled him. "How'd you—oh." He leaned back in the chair and opened his mouth as though to laugh, but nothing came out. His head lolled toward me. "That day in my house. You went snooping, didn't you?"

"Not on purpose."

His brow furrowed, quizzically. "How do you *not* go snooping on purpose?"

I squared my shoulders. "I don't know. Somehow, I just . . . do." I pointed at him. "This isn't about me."

William chuckled. "Okay, okay. And yes. Yes, you look like Felicia. The first time I saw you—in town—for the first brief second, I thought you were her. But you were . . ."

"Me."

His smile broadened. "I was going to say, 'not.' But, I guess that's accurate. You were you. You *are* you. But you also stirred up a lot of bad memories that I've worked a year to get over." He leaned over again. Cracked his knuckles. I opened my mouth to fuss at him, but caught myself.

"So, what happened?"

"Chicago's Trade, Commerce, and Tourism was headed up by a man of honor and principles."

"Boscano."

Will nodded. "I happened to be at a social function with Felicia and her father one evening when I overheard someone talking about Eric's background. Where he'd come from. How he'd pulled himself up by his bootstraps . . . self-made man . . . all that." William clasped his hands together. "He'd been homeless during the entirety of his high school years and still managed to graduate with a 4.0. Went to college on a number of scholarships . . . Well, the list goes on." He pushed at the air, as though he were throwing something away. "That night, I couldn't sleep. Kept tossing and turning. And at some point I realized the notion to write Eric's life story was nipping at my brain." He paused. Wiped his mouth with his fingertips. "I went to Conrad—Felicia's father—and asked if he could make an introduction, which he gladly did."

"And how did Mr. Boscano feel about having his story told?"

William smiled broadly. "Pretty jazzed. I spent hours with him. Interviewing. Looking through old family photo albums. When I could, I shadowed him at work." He hung his head again. "One afternoon, he asked if I wanted to come into this meeting. To sit and observe." Brown eyes met mine. "It wasn't an important meeting or anything. Just a meeting." He swallowed. "When it was over and everyone who'd been sitting around the conference table shuffled out, I slipped into Eric's inner office. And I—I left the door cracked. Not open. Cracked."

"Okay."

"I heard two men walk in. I didn't know who, but I heard two distinct voices along with Eric's. They were making him the proverbial offer he couldn't refuse." He cocked his head. "Only, he *did* refuse. One of the men told him not to be an idiot. To think of the kickbacks."

I hadn't counted on this. None of it. I'd believed the worst about William—just as the girls in seventh grade had believed the worst about me—before knowing everything there was to know. I leaned over the arm of my chair, reached across what felt like a chasm between us, and touched his arm. "That could have been so dangerous for you," I whispered.

"I guess, in the end, it was. But to answer your question, I pressed myself against the built-in bookcase and prayed neither of them got an itch to go into Eric's office."

I pulled back my hand. "And then? Did they leave?"

He squinted, his eyes focused on the hand that had touched him, then left. "Mmhmm. Eric came into his office. By then, I'd slipped into his private bathroom and walked out like I'd heard nothing."

"Why? Why not just tell him you were proud of him or something?"

"I don't know, Ashlynne. I just didn't want to rock the good-fortune boat I was in with any kind of scandal." He shifted. "But, months later an article came out in the *Star* that insinuated that Eric had, in fact, gone to *them* with the offer. I couldn't figure it out. Why would the paper print such nonsense? I went to Conrad, told him what I knew and that we had to retract the article."

"Of course."

William shook his head. "No. That's when I realized what was going on. Conrad Moses owned a large amount of stock in the paper. Enough that when he said jump . . ."

The enormity of what Will said dropped over me like a quilt made of metal. "The paper asked how high."

"Yeah. Turns out he was behind the men coming in that night."

"He told you that?"

"Mmm. Said things that I thought I'd only hear in the movies. You know, like, 'Boy, you keep your nose clean here and you'll keep moving on up.'" Will's voice changed to match that of Conrad Moses. "'Run your mouth and I'll have you bumped down to a G.A. so fast your head will spin and with the salary to match.' Then he kind of leaned back, rested his hands on his chest and said, 'And I don't think my daughter will take to marrying a lowly general assignment editor.'"

"And?"

He sighed. "I said some things I shouldn't have said, stormed out. Went back to my apartment, called Big Guy and told him I needed to come home for the weekend. Needed somewhere to clear my brain."

I looked toward the house again.

"I got here to discover that my grandfather was overworked, overtired, and the newspaper falling apart. Still, nothing felt better than sliding into a pair of jeans, some boots, and riding around in that old truck you fell down the hill to keep from driving."

His smile was infectious and I laughed. "Yeah. That's why I did it. That and the rattlesnake you were chasing me with."

Will chewed on his bottom lip, which made me mildly uncomfortable. "I told Big Guy about what happened. I told him I wanted to come home. To make things right at the paper. And, like an idiot, I told him I wanted to bring Felicia back here. To marry her. Because she was a good person and I knew that, when she heard my reasons, she'd come back with me."

"And yet, no Felicia Moses Decker lives here in Testament."

"No."

I wasn't sure if I should ask why not. I wasn't sure I even wanted to know.

"I flew up to Chicago, put in my resignation, drove immediately to Felicia's apartment, and asked her to marry me. Presented her with the two-month-salary ring and everything." His head quivered. "She threw herself into my arms, squealed like a schoolgirl, then bounced all around the room, holding the ring up to one light and then another and finally to the light coming in from the window." His breath came like the air from a balloon. "And then I told her the rest of my plan."

"And she shot you down."

He blinked. "She never loved me." He pulled at his nose. "She couldn't have possibly. She said, 'I wouldn't be caught dead in some redneck town in North Carolina, William. You should know that about me.'" He smiled sheepishly. "She'd never even been here. And she said 'North Carolina' like a cussword." He sighed. "And," he drawled, "I guess I *didn't* know that about her."

"And then you did."

"Yep."

"So you came home without her."

"Yep."

"But did you do anything to help Eric?"

He cracked his knuckles again. "I didn't have to. I went to him, told him everything, and he said, 'Don't worry about it, Will. These things have a way of working themselves out, but I appreciate it.' So, I'd more or less put it all on the line for something he wasn't even worried about. But in the end, I knew myself better, I knew the woman I *thought* I wanted to marry better—and certainly her father—and I'd managed to keep my ethics."

Ethics. There was that word again.

33

So, *that's* why you were so angry when you met me. You thought I was like Felicia." Which, of course, I'd already figured out. But it wasn't the *looking* like her he had reacted to, but the *being* like her, on the inside, that riled his dander. "You thought I was going to ridicule Testament."

"Yes, ma'am." This time, his smile reached his eyes. "You have to admit, walking into the office every day that first week, wearing all those name-brand clothes. And shoes that are *only* going to give you back problems one day. Purses that, I bet, cost the same amount most families around here spend on their monthly mortgage payments."

"I thought . . ."

He shifted so as to bring his back to the settee's arm and his knee up to the seat between us. "What? What did you think?"

"That maybe *somebody* here would think I looked nice." I shook my head. "Presentable. Professional. That if I looked the part, people would respect me."

"No offense, but you just looked hoity-toity. And when it comes to earning respect? Around here? That's done with a hard day's work. An *honest* hard day's work."

Honest. My mind flittered to Sean. To the *dis*honesty of using steroids while playing sports. How would the people of Testament feel about him when they learned the truth? Worse yet, how would they feel about *me?*

"What are you thinking?" Will asked.

I sighed deeply. "That I want to tell you *my* story now. If you'll listen."

His jaw flexed. "Have I ever not listened?"

"Well," I said, drawing the word out. "You did prejudge me. 'Your type' and all." I repeated the words he'd used to chew me out in front of the school.

His eyes met mine as he remembered the moment, bringing a new level of regret. "I'm sorry about that." He nodded briefly. "Too."

I didn't say, "I accept your apology." I didn't need to. Sharing with him my worst moment was a gift beyond any acceptance, and showed I was willing to take the chance—once more—for either approval or rejection.

I always expected rejection. But, maybe this time . . . "When I was in the sixth grade, more than anything in the world, I wanted to be what I called a 'normal kid.' I wanted to go to public school. I wanted to have scads of giggling girlfriends around me." I looked up to the sky. "I had been reading Baby-Sitters Club books and The Saddle Club books and had gotten some ideas as to how 'normal' girls lived."

Will narrowed his eyes. "I guess I missed out on those books."

"They were and are wonderful books. And they're about normal girls doing normal girl things."

"Like?"

"Like babysitting and horseback riding."

"Well there you have it. I had more or less pictured you with some equestrian training behind you," he said with a grin.

I frowned. "Well, yes. I *do* have equestrian training. But no adventures."

"Like the Saddle Club girls."

"Right."

"I see."

"May I continue?"

"Please."

"My best friend was—and still is—Leigh. And she was the greatest, but . . . I wanted more. I tried so hard to explain it to her . . ."

"Did she get it?"

"No. No matter how hard I tried, she couldn't even begin to fathom what I saw, first, in the books and, second, in the whole 'normal' experience I wanted to have."

"And you were willing to go it alone?"

"If that's what it took. I'd never been afraid of a challenge, but this was truly the first one that took me out of my comfort zone."

"I guess coming to Testament was your last."

My last. And my second. How could I explain the wall I'd built? The one I cautiously lived behind?

"Well, anyway, between sixth and seventh grades—that summer—I pitched one grand campaign to get my parents to let me go to public school. At first they were fervently against it." I felt heat pinch my cheeks, remembering some of my antics. "Eventually, though, they relinquished." An insect played about my face and I shooed it away.

"I take it you went?"

"I did. I walked into that school thinking all these fresh-faced girls were going to be my friends." I tugged my hair behind one ear. "That they'd practically fall all over themselves to see who could be my . . . what do the kids call it today?"

Will shook his head; he didn't know.

"A . . . um . . . a bestie! All those girls would want to be my 'bestie.' Only, they wanted nothing to do with me. They let me know without so much as a 'who-ha' that I was the outsider."

Will chuckled. "A *who-ha*?"

I shrugged. "I heard that in one of your songs on the radio."

"A who-ha," he repeated. "All right. Keep going."

I swallowed past the more painful memories of my short stint in public school. Felt tears sting the backs of my eyes, threatening. Not that I'd give them the satisfaction. I'd cried enough the night before. I didn't need to add to the waterworks. "In two weeks' time I returned to my old school, scarred but much wiser than the girl who'd left in May." I raised my bum foot, hoping for some of the throbbing to ease. "To this day, I'm sensitive to those who I believe are prejudging me. And, in some ways, I don't let anyone in. Not too far, anyway. Only my grandmother. My parents. And Leigh."

He ran his thumb across my cheek and caught a tear, brushing it away. "And, maybe now . . . me?"

I drew back just enough to wipe my cheek with my own fingertips. I couldn't have him touching me. Not yet. Even with his attempt at humor. "The truth is—and I figured this out last night after you left—that awful year, I went into public school thinking all these girls would want to be my friend because of who *I* am. I never realized that—like Gram tried to tell me before I came here—to *have* a friend I must first—"

"—*be* a friend," we said together.

"Yeah," Will said. "My grandmother has said that more times than I can count."

"I suppose that's why I got along so well with Brianna and Alma right away. I offered Brianna something she needed and, quite frankly, who couldn't get along with Alma?"

"For sure."

"When we first met, that day in your grandparents' kitchen, I got that old sensation of not being good enough. *Right* enough to be a part of this world. *Your* world. Not for six months, for sure. Maybe not even for six minutes."

Will tilted his head. "Let me ask you a question. And be honest."

"Okay."

"How do you feel about your new clothes? Really *feel* about them? About wearing them and being seen in them?"

"Honestly?"

"One hundred percent honesty required."

I ran my palms down the legs of my jeans and lifted my shoulders. "Will, these are the most comfortable clothes I've had since . . . since I don't know when." I laughed. "But I can't say I would want to give up some of the things I brought here with me. Because they are *also* me. Who I am."

"Who says you have to give them up?"

I cocked my head. "Didn't you?"

"Not really." He extended one foot, showing off the right cowboy boot. "I guarantee you these cost more than, say, those Ferragamos you had on your first day. And I probably didn't fool you, on Sunday. Did I?"

I guffawed. "So you *were* wearing Armani."

Will laughed with me. Then he sobered. "It's not giving up, Ashlynne. It's expanding your horizons. Finding out that you're more than you thought you were. Or, in my case, that being who you were had always been just fine."

I understood. When I'd gone to Chimney Rock to Bubba O'Leary's, I'd not left feeling as though I were giving anything up. The closet in the upstairs bedroom of the cottage still held the name-brand clothes and shoes I'd always known. Now, they also held clothes and shoes that had taken nothing away from me or my life, but rather added to it.

Will clapped his hands together. "Are we done with this? Because the air around here is starting to get real thick . . ."

I could only nod in response. Nothing had been settled. Not really. But we—William and I—were at least back to an even playing field.

"All right then. Tell me what you found out about the graves."

I held his eyes with mine. "And then can we talk about Sean Flannery?"

"Do you really want to go there again?"

"Yes. And I have my reasons."

"I'm sure you do."

After a momentary standoff, I sighed and said, "The graves are for the bodies of freed slaves who didn't suit with the white landowners' ideas about what they should and shouldn't be doing. Even though their comings and goings should have no longer been dictated by former owners." I looked Will directly in the eye. "I don't think I had any idea how bad it was back then. How much risk was taken or how big a price they were willing to pay."

"The Thirteenth Amendment didn't come easy. Even a war—a lost war for us—couldn't change the minds of men who'd grown up in a certain way of life." He returned his hat to his head. Rested his elbows on his knees. “Generations have to die out to make those kinds of changes. Not just one. Many.” He cracked his knuckles. “What kind of information have you gathered?”

“I’ve made a list of names of people who appear on the 1870 census but do not appear on the 1880 census. Some of those are crossed out because I found them in nearby counties. I guess people moved in those days, they just didn’t move far. But, Will. Every one of the missing I’ve been able to account for so far had been adults. Some of the children who are under their names in 1870 seem to correspond to names I find living with other families ten years later.”

“So, they would have been taken in by loved ones. Friends, family, or neighbors.”

“Alma says her grandmother has some information in an old family Bible.” I paused. “I’m meeting with her later today.”

“Really?”

Nodding, I answered, “Alma’s coming to get me soon.”

Will looked to the highway as if her car would appear.

“I also want to go back to some of the old newspaper reports from those days to see if there is anything about a group of freed slaves who simply vanished,” I added. “I can’t, for the life of me, wrap my mind around nearly a hundred people being killed off and no one blinks. No one says anything.”

The faraway look returned. The same look I’d seen when I first mentioned the possibility of slaves being buried in the graves. Then he blinked, turned his face to mine and said, “Do you have any idea who may have been behind their deaths?”

“Their murders, you mean? Yes, I do. I went to see Miss Helen—”

“When did you do that?”

“Alma took me the other day. Miss Helen told me what she remembered from some of her husband’s stories. Stories he told when he was drunk, which she said could be quite often.”

“He wasn’t a nice person. Or so I’ve always been told.”

“Miss Helen claimed her husband’s father and a Mr. Jefferson, along with a Mr. Clinton, were behind it.”

Will’s brow shot up. “I know those names. They were icons in our town’s history. Some of their people still live here.”

"And are *they* highly respected?"

"Yes, ma'am. They are."

"Well, being an icon in one generation and highly respected in another doesn't mean they didn't do it."

Will thought for a moment. "What are you planning to do with all this information?"

I straightened my spine. "A story like this will raise a few brows . . . stir some nasty stuff in the pot."

He looked at me sideways. "I know."

"Are you okay with it? Even if it means things aren't peaceful and calm? Even if it raises a scandal?"

Will cracked his knuckles again. Hung his head low between his shoulders. Then turned his head to face me. "It's hard. After Chicago. But I'll work on it." After a slight nod he added, "I'll work on being okay with it."

I touched his hand with my own as though I were touching the dead for the first time. Tentative. Afraid, but curious. "Will, we still have to talk about Sean."

"One pot-stirring at a time, okay?"

I shook my head. "I can't leave this alone, Will."

"You can." His face turned shadowy. "Football is *serious business,* Ashlynne. Remember?"

I remembered. Faith. Family. Football. Still . . . I chose to keep my voice calm as I said, "And the murder of ex-slaves isn't?"

His jaw flexed once more and this time his teeth clenched as he said, "You know what I mean."

"Yes I do. But, Will? What if I'm right?"

"Then the rest of the year will be miserable. Slave graves is one thing. But you're in a no-win position here, Ashlynne." He retrieved my crutches, handed them to me, and stood. "Besides, you're leaving in about five and a half months. News like what you're proposing to report will hang in the town for much longer than that."

I hobbled up. Positioned the crutches under my arms. For a moment, I stared at the rocks around my foot. Pressed my lips together. "All right," I said without looking up. "If you insist. I'll leave this subject for another time."

As if . . .

"Hey," he said, tilting my chin upward so I was forced to meet his eyes. They were now tender. Filled with concern. "I'm putting my foot down for bigger reasons than a desire to stay scandal-free. Ashlynne, a few months back the biggest outrage to rock this town was when the waste management folks wanted to change the order of trash days. People here, they don't get riled up in a bad way about much. But challenge them on anything to do with football and you've got yourself—as my grandmother often says—a pupu platter full of problems."

I forced myself not to laugh. But I did smile.

"Sean is their hometown hero. *Our* hometown hero. With the graves, you'll upset a few folks and sully the names of some dead folk. But with this . . . you won't win, no matter if you're right or wrong. You'll get hurt and"—he shook his head and sighed—"I care too much for you to allow that."

"Do you?"

"Of course."

I nodded, removing my chin from his fingertips. He was right. I was in a no-win situation. But it was also a no-win situation for Sean. Maybe more than the boy realized.

But I knew. And Leigh knew. And so did Lawson.

Still, for now, I'd go along with Will's demands.

Or at least pretend to.

34

Alma's grandmother lived not too far from Brianna. Their houses appeared to have been built around the same time—both postwar "crackerbox"—and both had been refurbished with white aluminum siding.

Alma's grandmother had added French-blue shutters to the front windows, however, which gave the home a more welcoming feel.

As soon as Alma opened the front door and called "Nana," an older woman replied, "Come on in and have a seat."

Unlike Brianna's home, Alma's grandmother's home was elegantly furnished in antiques. Miniature tea sets graced end tables and the fireplace mantel. The fireplace itself had a rose-carved brass screen over it.

"Have a seat," Alma said, pointing to a high-back sofa.

I touched the wood running along the top. "This is lovely."

"It's a Duncan Phyfe," she said, her voice kept low. "Nana bought it back in the early fifties. She only lets certain people sit on it, so consider yourself blessed."

Something told me, even before we'd arrived, that Alma's grandmother was a proper lady. I had changed into a simple skirt and top purchased at Bubba O'Leary's along with a pair of flats and was now glad for it. Although my ankle throbbed and I knew I'd have to pack it in ice later.

Alma stuck her head around a wide opening leading to the dining room, also elegantly decorated and papered in a pattern of large chintz roses. "Nana, do you need help?"

"Thank you, Alma. I could use a hand."

Minutes later, "Nana" shuffled in from the kitchen using a walker, dressed in what I thought might be church clothes, pillbox hat included. Alma stayed about two steps behind her, carrying a large silver tray topped with a serving set.

"Don't know how in the lands I thought I was going to carry that tray and walk with this walker," she said. Then she cackled. "You must be Ashlynne."

I stood, extended a hand. "I am. Nice to meet you, Mrs.—"

"Robinson. And it's so nice to meet you too, but you must promise to call me 'Nana.'"

Alma placed the tray on the coffee table. "I hope you like tea," she said. "My grandmother doesn't think four o'clock should come unless tea is served."

I felt my smile pull at my lips. "I prefer tea, actually."

"Really?" Alma asked, straightening. "Did you ever tell me that?"

"It doesn't matter." I returned to my seat and patted the cushion beside me. "I hope you'll sit next to me," I said to Mrs. Robinson . . . Nana.

We enjoyed our tea over the next half hour, which we filled with talk about the weather, the differences in Winter Park and Testament, and my family.

"I remember your grandmother and grandfather," she told me.

"You do?" I felt myself brighten.

"Mmm. Good people, good people . . ."

"They are. Well, Papa was . . ."

"Your grandfather passed, did he?"

"Yes." The air-conditioning came on, and billowed the sheers hanging at the front window.

"So many die," she said. "Me, I'm hanging on at ninety-one."

"Ninety-one?" I said, looking to Alma.

"Which is why she's so good for you to talk to." Alma leaned from the occasional chair where she sat toward her grandmother. "Nana, where's your family Bible?"

"Back there next to my chair in my sitting area." She pointed to a small door I'd not noticed before.

"Be right back," Alma said. True to her word, she returned within a minute. "Here you go," she said, handing the Bible to her grandmother.

Nana opened the book to the very back. The few pages of text I saw were onionskin thin. Yellowed on the edges from its owner's fingerprints. "Right here," she said, pointing to a family tree chart. "See if there is anything here that might interest you."

I reached for my purse, which I'd placed next to me. "Do you mind if I write some things down? If I see anything?"

Nana looked at Alma, then to me. "I suppose not. Alma says it's important that this be told, and I reckon at ninety-one I don't have much time left on this earth for secret-keeping."

I could only blink at her, wondering how that might feel—knowing your time was so short. I pulled my reporter's pad and a pen from my purse and got to work.

Within a few short minutes I learned that Alma's grandmother, Louise, had been thirty-six when she gave birth to Alma's mother, Valeria, and that Alma herself would be thirty-six on her next birthday—October 6.

Louise's father, Louis Rucker, had been born in 1900, in Testament. His mother, Katherine, had also been born in Testament twenty-eight years earlier, in 1872.

"Not even a decade after the war ended," I said.

"That's right," Nana said. "And her daddy," she added, pointing to the page of varying script, "was born a slave."

I looked at the date of birth for a baby boy named Abraham. January 22, 1862.

My vision traveled to the name of Abraham's mother and I gasped.

"Marguerite," I said.

"Now there's a story," Nana said.

My mouth remained gaped. I turned to the old woman, her hair silvery-white, fine, and perfectly styled. Thin lines etched her face, but not so much as to betray her age. Her eyes, I noticed then, were gray-blue. Shimmering. And her skin, unlike Alma's, was the color of warm caramel. "Are you—a descendant of Marguerite? The consort of Noah Swann?"

"Yes'm, I am."

"You know about that?" Alma asked.

"Will showed me . . . the graves." I placed my hands, palms down, over the names scrawled on the pages. "Does he know about this?"

"I don't think so. Can't imagine why he would. Most folks around here don't talk about Noah Swann and my four-times great-grandmother."

"The Swann family never wanted it talked about," Nana supplied. "Course, you know, Alma told me all about the graves you found buried on the young man's land. And, so you know, Marguerite died along with the others."

I tried to take that in. Somewhere between 1870 and 1880, nearly a hundred people had seemingly disappeared from Testament. All of them ex-slaves. None of them had been given so much as a proper burial. None except Marguerite. She lay beneath a fine-cut stone. Her name and position in the world recorded as though there had been no shame. Her children had called her . . . *blessed.*

"Back in those days," Nana said, "a woman wanted by a white man had no choice. But, from the stories we have—and the letters we've kept hidden all these years that went between Marguerite and Mr. Swann—we know they were very much in love." She patted my hand. I brought both of mine up to clasp hers.

"Story goes that when the men who killed those gathering in the field for a political meeting realized Marguerite—Noah Swann's lover—was among the dead, they panicked. Left all the bodies there for their kin to find. When they did, one of Cap'n Swann's old slaves ran and got him. They say he fled his home in the dead of night, got to her, and cradled her body like that of a small child. Said over and over, 'Why did you have to be a part of this? Didn't I give you everything?'" Nana's eyes filled with tears and they spilled over. "Much as he loved her, he couldn't really understand what it was like, being a slave. Not wanting to 'know your place' all the time, but wanting something more. Wanting the same thing afforded all Americans."

I understood. Oh how I understood. I'd never been a slave, of course. But I knew what it meant to "know your place." I shook my head at my self-centered thoughts. "This is like Thomas Jefferson and Sally Hemings." I looked at Alma. "What a *story* . . ."

"Nana?" Alma said, raising her voice. "You think it's time to tell all this?"

Nana nodded as she squeezed my hand. "I think it's time." Her gray-blue eyes found mine. "Maybe Testament can handle the truth now," she said. "And there's no telling what white people we're all related to, now is there?"

She chuckled and I along with her. But Alma only shook her head. "Lawd, Lawd," she said. "We're cooking with gas, now."

Alma drove me home at five-thirty, practically speeding through town as though she were late for something. Meanwhile, my own thoughts raced. Thinking about the Jefferson/Hemings controversy. Those who swore by DNA that there had been an affair. Offspring and descendants. Others who claimed the rumors were only that—rumors. Once we released this information, would the same thing happen in Testament? Had I gone on a hunt, flipped a rock to find a rare diamond, only to realize a python held it in its mouth?

At a traffic light, while waiting for the red light to turn green, I looked at the Walgreens marquee and saw "Homecoming 2014! Go Gamecocks!"

Homecoming! The dance. I'd forgotten.

"Looks like I'll be home alone tonight," I told her as the light changed. I patted my purse where the reporter's pad, full of notes, rested. "But I've got a lot of research to do."

Alma looked at me as though I'd lost my mind. "You'd give up the football game and the homecoming dance for a secret over a hundred years old?"

"Alma, *this* is history. *This* is far more important . . ."

Alma chuckled. "If you say so."

William's truck was parked behind his grandparents' home when Alma drove past. I expected he'd be inside, probably eating dinner with them or, at the very least, getting ready to go out before the game. Instead, we found him standing at my door, but looking over his shoulder at the sound of Alma's car.

He met me at the passenger's door. "There you are," he said after opening it and extending a hand to help me out.

"My crutches are in the back," I said. I looked at Alma, "Hurry up so you aren't late. And thank you again." I patted my purse once more.

"See ya later, Will," Alma said. "And you, too, Ashlynne. Think about coming on down to the game and leaving that other for later."

But I shook my head. "Not this time. I feel like Woodward and Bernstein."

After Alma drove off, Will escorted me to my door. "Gram sent me up to see if you'd like to join us for dinner before we leave. And maybe go to the game?"

I couldn't help but smile. Not quite two weeks ago I'd had "Sunday dinner" (a phrase I'd learned since being in Testament) with the Deckers, much to Will's chagrin. But now, here we were, technically only a few days later, and he had *asked* me to join them.

I pointed to the front door with my thumb. "I was just going to have a sandwich," I said. "Sit down with my notes from Alma's grandmother."

Will leaned against the opposite side of the doorframe. "What'd you find out?"

I crossed my arms. "I'd rather work a little more before I share, if you don't mind."

His brow furrowed and he cocked his chin to the left. "Keeping things from your boss?"

I nodded but grinned to lessen the effect. "For now."

He stared, long and hard, then a smile came to his eyes. "Well, you can at least join us for dinner. Gram's made my favorite."

I pointed to my chin as though I were pondering my options. "Which is?"

"Ham. Mashed potatoes. Sweet peas and corn bread."

Grimacing, I said, "Doesn't sound healthy."

"But it sounds good, doesn't it?" He shrugged. "And then maybe I can talk you into coming to the game *and* the dance. You don't have to cut a rug, you know. Just go . . . with me."

I shook my head. "As enticing as that sounds, my ankle is starting to throb big-time and I really, *really* want to work right now. Please tell your grandmother 'Thank you' and, if I can have a rain check for next week, that would be wonderful."

"Well," he said, putting his hands on his hips and looking around the landscape, "I can't say as I blame you. Personally, I don't like going to these things as much as I used to."

"The game or the dance?"

"Oh no. The dance. I'll always love the game."

I punched in the key code. "Spoken like a true . . . what's that thing y'all are called?"

Will shrugged.

"I heard it in one of the songs on your radio. The one with the line that I also heard the cheerleaders chanting in one of their cheers." I snapped my fingers. "Something about chewing tobacco . . ."

Will laughed as remembrance swept over him. "A redneck?"

"Yes." I snapped my fingers again, proud of myself for remembering, much less knowing the word. "Spoken like a true redneck."

He chuckled. "Well, all right. Go do what you do." He started to step away, turned again and said, "Can I call you when I get home?"

I looked at my feet, then back up to the warmth of his eyes. "If it's not too late. I'm pretty whipped."

He leaned over and kissed me on the cheek. "Get some rest. I'll call you in the morning."

He walked away, leaving me alone with a sigh and my thoughts.

William Decker would be aghast at what I knew. Not because of the details—Marguerite and Noah Swann—but because the story would cause scandal in his small town.

And William Decker didn't like scandal. Especially not the kind I knew was about to hit town.

There was more, of course. That "one other thing" that hounded me constantly.

I pushed the door open and entered the cool sanctuary of my home.

I had one more call to make. And if I thought Will would be upset about Noah Swann's "other" descendants, this would really set him off.

35

Once inside, I placed some ice in a ziplock bag, sat on one end of the sofa, and propped my foot on pillows at the other end.

Then I called Brianna. "Here's the way it goes," I told her. "You and I are going to have to do this alone."

"I thought we were going to do this *together*."

"What I mean is, I have tried more than once to talk to Will about this and it's been a no-go every time."

"Got it. Um . . . I want to know more, but Rob will be here soon." I could almost hear the wide grin. "We're going to the game together."

What a difference a week makes.

"I won't keep you, then. But . . . Bri . . . promise you won't say anything to anyone until we know more about all this. Until I've had time to gather more . . . facts."

"Oh don't you worry none. I'm not saying a word."

"Not even to Rob."

"Especially not Rob. I don't want him to think I'm the kind of girl who snoops in other people's stuff."

I squeezed my eyes until the burning behind them eased. "Yeah. I know what you mean." My cell phone beeped. I looked at the caller ID, then brought the phone back to my ear. "Bri," I said quickly,

"Will is on the other line. I'm going with you on Tuesday to the Flannerys'. We'll take care of all this then."

"Okay."

"Have fun tonight . . ." I clicked to the other line. "Will?"

"Hey. Just a thought. Tomorrow morning I'm taking school supplies to some less-fortunate kids. It's a thing I do—"

"Yes, I know. I—um—Rob told me about it."

"Ah. Well. Would you like to go along? Afterward we'll catch lunch and maybe by then you'll want to share more about what you know."

"About?" I asked, hoping to avoid the topic altogether.

"The graves."

I thought so. And I doubted I'd want to share. Yet. But, if nothing else, I could see the work Will did as a good story for the magazine. "Sounds great. What time?"

"I'll pick you up at nine."

"See you then." I started to hang up but heard Will's voice. "I'm sorry. What?"

"I said," he said with a chuckle, "dress casual."

Cute.

I took a hot shower, ate a sandwich, and then sat on the sofa with my computer linked to Ancestry.com. My plan had been to work on the story for only an hour. But more than three hours later, I forced myself to click off of the website and carefully climb the stairs for bed.

I'd already fallen asleep when Will sent a text: *2 lte 2 call. I'm dog tired. C u in the a.m.*

I looked at the time stamp above the text—it was after midnight. I returned with: *ditto that.*

The next morning, shortly after nine, Will and I arrived at the parking lot of the elementary school—the same one where he'd verbally assaulted me. The bed of his pickup had been stocked with shopping bags full of school supplies. In the center of the parking lot stood an old school bus bearing a long banner with "Testament School Supply Center" printed in large primary colors.

I clapped my hands. "This is great," I said. I looked at Will, who smiled at me. "You're wonderful to do this."

"Just giving back to a community that's always been good to me."

"Is that why you do the work at the museum, too?"

"Yes, ma'am. Knowledge is everything."

The line caused my brow to rise. "I always say 'Knowledge is power.' "

"Then we're practically switched at birth." He winked, then continued, "I want the children of Testament to get that if nothing else. Feed their natural desire to learn and you'll plant seeds they'll glean from for years to come."

I pretended to take notes in the palm of my hand. "May I quote you, Mr. Decker?"

He squared his shoulders playfully. "Please do, Miss Rothschild."

"Because I'm thinking this will be a great story for *Guns & Teacups*." If the magazine ever went to print. Deep down, I knew, once I revealed what I'd discovered about the graves, there might not be a magazine. My job might be shadowing Will Decker for the remainder of the twenty-three weeks and six days.

"I think you're right," Will said as he parked the truck near the bus. He chuckled. "*Guns and Teacups.* Great-granny, girl."

When the engine shut off, a man I thought I recognized—broad-shouldered and stocky—stepped from the inside of the bus. "Who is that?"

"Coach Meriwether. You saw him at the game—he's the football coach. And he's instrumental in all this. Kids love him. He plays games with them in the parking lot while their mothers and fathers come inside the bus, redeem their vouchers, and 'buy' what they otherwise couldn't afford."

"That was your idea, wasn't it? Having the coach play with the kids."

He shut the engine off. "Actually, Big Guy's. He and Coach go way back, but I totally agreed to it. As important as their minds are, so are their bodies. We have way too many kids with weight issues. Kids shouldn't have weight issues."

"Too much *or* too little."

He opened his door. "What do you mean?"

I opened mine.

"Wait up," he said. "I'll be right there."

I waved at the coach as Will let down the tailgate, calling out, "Got a lot to unload," to Coach Meriwether. The coach nodded, waved back to me, and then half jogged to us.

My door swung open. "I still say you should have brought your crutches."

"As long as I keep my ankle supported with these hiking boots, and try not to overdo, I think I'll be fine." He closed my door after I'd hobbled ever so slightly on the pavement. "And what I meant was, when I was in high school, there was a tendency for girls to try too hard to stay skinny."

"Ah. Think you can carry a sack or two to the bus?" He pulled two plastic sacks from the bed.

I held out my hands. "Ashlynne Rothschild, reporting for duty, sir."

Five trips later, we'd filled the bus seats with merchandise, had orange cones set in the parking lot for activities, and Coach Meriwether and I had been formally introduced.

"This is a good thing you're doing," I said to him as Will made a final trip to the truck.

"Mostly Will there," he answered, adjusting the waistband of his sport shorts. "He's a good man."

I smiled, watching Will as he sauntered back, carrying a small wicker basket. "He is that."

Will raised the basket. "For the vouchers," he said, answering the question my eyes must have held. He looked at his watch. "Fifteen minutes to spare. Rob should be here soon."

"Rob?" I wondered if Brianna would be with him. And, if she were, if we could possibly not look at one another with any telltale signs in our eyes.

"Yeah. He volunteers. A few others. When the parents or guardians come in, we're there to answer any questions they might have. Then, they come up to the front of the bus and pay the bus driver."

"Who is the bus driver?"

Will grinned. "That'd be me."

Coach Meriwether looked past us. "Here comes someone." He clapped his hands as coaches do.

"Rob," Will said. We stood waiting for the Prius to park next to the truck, then Will smiled at me. "And look who he has with him."

I tried to smile, though my heart quickened.

Brianna.

When the bus had been "bought out" and all the children, their parents, and the volunteers had left—with the exception of Rob, Brianna, Will, and me—Brianna and I started for where Will and Rob had moved their cars out of the way.

"You aren't working today?" I asked.

"No. Sometimes I figure in a day off while Maris is with her daddy. Lets me get some things done I need to do or that I'd like to do." She smiled at Rob.

"You haven't said anything, have you?" I whispered. "To Rob?"

"Uh-uh. I said I wouldn't and I haven't."

"Good," I said. "We'll talk more about it later."

We arrived at the truck. "'Kay," Brianna said, her voice remaining low.

When we were in route back to the cottage, I said to Will, "Isn't it funny how things work out?"

"In what way?"

"Well, if Rob hadn't found the graves, you and I wouldn't have gone out there. And, if we hadn't, Rob and I wouldn't have talked. Wouldn't have become friends. And, if you and I hadn't gone to the café that day, I wouldn't have met Bri, I wouldn't have told her I'd show her the ropes about makeup and facial care—"

"She looks pretty, by the way."

"She always did. She just needed good advice on how to apply the products. And better skin care."

A low chuckle rumbled in his chest.

"Anyway," I drawled, "if not for Brianna and me talking about her feelings, about Rob, and me sort of encouraging them along . . ."

A sly grin spread from his lips. "Is that what you call it?"

"I do."

"Whatever you say." Mirth glinted in his eyes.

I watched the landscape outside the passenger window. The town had come into view, its square-faced buildings, the window displays, and the planters and benches I'd come to appreciate seeing. "By the way," I said. "I'm going to take off Tuesday morning."

"Oh? Nails again?"

I looked at my hands, to the still perfectly groomed fingertips. "No. Just something I need to do."

Will parked the truck in a parking space across the street from the drugstore. "Care to elaborate?" He turned the key.

"Are we eating here?"

"Yep."

"Yum. I'm starved."

"Does this mean you aren't going to tell me what you're doing Tuesday?"

"Yep," I said, mocking him.

"Does it have anything to do with the graves?"

"Nope."

"Are we going to talk more about that?"

"Not today." Because I couldn't trust him. That he'd support me. My feelings about the descendants and . . . Sean. "Today, let's just . . . eat."

On Sunday, after church, I returned to the graves at the foot of the hill and against the tree line. With Will standing beside me, I stared at Marguerite's headstone. Reading over and over the words carved there. Thinking of how Noah Swann had printed the line from Proverbs 31: *Her children rise and call her blessed.*

Her children. *His* children.

"What's the attraction?" Will asked, crossing his arms.

"I'm thinking—and let's not even get into the sin factor here because, yes, I know this kind of thing was done all the time—but, I'm thinking about the snub to society that it took to put this headstone up."

"What I'm thinking," he added, "is how Miss Emily over there didn't have it knocked down after her husband's death."

"She couldn't," I said, looking at him.

"What do you mean?"

"It was in his will. She couldn't tamper with it or do anything against their offspring, otherwise she'd lose her inheritance, which was quite impressive."

His brow furrowed. I imagined that, behind the dark shades, his eyes narrowed. "How do you know that?"

I had said too much. I shrugged in an attempt to appear nonchalant. "I got carried away at Ancestry.com the other night. No biggie." I walked away from the headstones. Will followed.

"When will you be ready to show me what you've found?"

My stomach dropped, as did my heart. Even without Will's help, I'd already figured out what I needed to do.

First, finish my notes on the slave graves.

Second, get into the Flannery home and see if I could find out who had given Sean the steroids. After that . . . after that . . .

I felt my home calling. The apartment in Orlando. My too-small office tucked behind Courtney's desk. Dad would be disappointed. Gram heartbroken. But in the end, I now knew "my place." I knew who I was in the grand scheme of *Parks & Avenues.*

An investigative reporter. If I could find the right kinds of ideas—story lines—well, surely Old Florida was chock-full of ancient stories to tell.

"When will I be ready?" I asked around the knot in my throat. The corner of the old church shimmered into view, blurred by the tears I forced back.

"I asked you first," Will teased.

"Cute." I dug into my purse—one I'd brought from Winter Park, purchased at Nordstrom—found my Dior sunglasses, and slid them on as camouflage.

"Well?"

"Um . . . how about Wednesday?" I tried to make my voice sound as normal as possible.

"What's wrong with tomorrow? Or this afternoon?"

I shook my head. "No. Wednesday. For sure."

Not that it would make any difference in the end. After all, by Tuesday night, William Decker would vow never to speak to me again.

No doubt.

Which was, of course, the hardest pill of all to swallow.

36

I worked from home on Monday, but promised Will I'd make it to the newspaper office in time for, as Alma put it, "story time."

"This information you're collecting," he said from the other end of the line, "is it going to make me happy or will I be upset for a month of Sundays?"

The answer lay in the latter of the two choices, but I managed to laugh despite my worry and say, "I hope you'll be happy." I flipped my thumb through a small stack of old magazine copies. "I've also nearly finished my proposal for getting the magazine up and running again. I'm figuring the first issue will release in October for the November/December issue."

"Do you know the *name* of said magazine, by chance?" The lilt in his voice was unmistakable.

"Of course I do," I said. "It's *Swamps and Dining Out.*"

"Woman, you won't do."

We ended the call and I went back to work, forming two piles on my countertop, one with information about the slaves and their descendants, the other about Sean Flannery's steroid use. Around 3:00, I took a shower, dressed in simple Topshort skinny trousers, an even simpler Camuto tie-front blouse, and a pair of the flats I'd bought in Chimney Rock.

Chimney Rock. The mountain I'd never gotten to climb.

But maybe one day. Years from now? Soon? Just. Not. Now.

Will noticed my attire, of course. He hadn't mastered all the name brands, but he managed to mutter, "Reverting, Miss Rothschild?" just before the afternoon meeting started.

I smiled as sweetly as I knew how. "No. Just being true to myself."

During the meeting, I couldn't help but think how the fight had gone out of us. The spark that kept us feisty. Yet my feelings for him as a man—new and as unfamiliar as they were—hadn't waned. We'd spent the majority of Sunday together. Eating with his grandparents. Laughing over an old movie watched in their family room. Later, dining on tomato sandwiches—a first for me. He'd kissed me good night at the cottage door. Tenderly, leaving me to lie awake and stare at the ceiling all night.

At least the better part of it.

So, *that* spark remained. It would die out soon enough, I knew. Or at least I hoped. Just like the girls from the public junior high had forgotten about me soon enough, so would William Decker.

Whether I'd forget *him* was another issue. I'd not forgotten Margo. Or Trudy. Or that really awful girl, Jennifer.

With the meeting behind us, I expected Will to ask me to dinner, but instead he told me he had a city board meeting to attend. "A reporter's work is never done," he added with a roll of his eyes.

"Let's just hope they don't try to change trash day," I teased.

He walked me to my car. Kissed the tip of my nose. Said he'd call me later. "I'm probably going to turn in early," I said. "So text me before you call."

His text, which came shortly after 10:00, found me sitting in the semidarkness of the cottage, staring at a rerun of *That Girl*. I didn't respond to it. I'd also not responded to the calls from my parents, Gram, and Leigh. I couldn't. I only wanted to drink in the country ambience of the room. The cottage. Decker Ranch.

So I didn't respond. My mind was too weary and my heart too heavy. If this was the last message I'd get from Will, I wanted to keep it exactly the way it was, full of friendly possibilities and hope. I hadn't meant to, but in two short weeks I'd latched on to him. When he inevitably pulled away, I'd need something to remind me that for a moment, for a small, tender group of days, I'd let myself dabble in love.

By the time the sun started its early-morning climb on Tuesday, nausea had gripped my stomach—and I didn't think it would let go. Fear blanketed me, drenching me in sweat. Complicating matters was the knowledge that Will's reasoning—that this was a no-win situation—could not have been more accurate. I played each and every scenario in my mind. Time and again. None of them came out with me as the winner.

Yet, when my alarm rang, I thought of Lawson and I knew I wouldn't turn back from what I had to do. Another young man could possibly be making the biggest mistake of his life. Maybe I was, too. But that was okay. Exposing Sean, exposing his drug usage, and exposing the person or persons supplying him with poison, equaled giving him back his potential. What he could be, without them. Even if "what he could be" *wasn't* "the golden boy."

But at least he'd be alive.

I'd made it only a little more than two weeks in Testament, which was longer than I'd made it at Bear Gully Middle School. Just as in seventh grade, I'd grown in the fourteen-plus days. Or, at least I'd changed.

Brianna shoved the key into the back door of the Flannerys' home.

"And you're sure no one is here," I said, resting most of my weight on my left foot. I'd brought my crutches, just in case, and left them in the car. Thankfully, every day my ankle had gotten stronger, and the hiking boots kept me from falling flat on my face.

"No one is *ever* here. Well, sometimes she was here on Mondays, but the whole point of changing my cleaning day to Tuesday was so that I could have the house to myself."

"Okay. When we get in, show me where you found the vial and the needle. Then go about doing whatever it is you do when you're here."

Bri reached for my hand. Squeezed. "I'm so nervous."

"I know."

"But why? I haven't done anything wrong."

I drew in a deep breath. "I know," I repeated. "Let's get this done."

She pushed the door open and we walked onto the herringbone rug that ran the length of a small mudroom. On the right side, just past a large antique butter churn, stood four cubbies fashioned from white, wide-slat pine boards. Inside each were brass pegs and deep bases, perfect for shoe storage. "Nice," I whispered.

"I hang my purse here," she said, hooking it in the first cubby.

"I'll hook mine in the next cubby then." I grinned at her, in hopes of lessening the tension.

Brianna stepped to a tall utility pantry, opened it, and brought out a caddy with several cleaning items. "Tools of my trade," she said.

"So I see."

"Come this way," she said, taking me by the hand again. We walked through the kitchen, the dining room, and the living room where I'd first met Sarah Flannery. Memories of that morning swept over me. William Decker's cold shoulder. His lecture about being on time. His telling me to take notes when he, in fact, recorded the interview. His glare when I mentioned that the people of Senegal speak French. But, just as quickly, I recalled the night we'd gone to Movie in the Park, the laughter on the way home, the kiss in the cab of his truck. The feel of his lips against the tip of my nose. Soft. Warm. And just a tad moist.

I sighed. *And you, Scarecrow, I will miss most of all.*

"This way," Brianna said, releasing my hand. We started down a short staircase into a shadowy cluster of rooms. I clutched the handrails for support.

"It's so dark . . ."

"Not a lot of natural light. And I think Sean likes it that way, to be honest with you."

"I didn't realize this house was split-level."

"A lot of houses around here are. You just can't tell from the road." She flipped on a hall light. "There's only three rooms down here. A game room right here." She pointed to the door in front of us. "The bathroom is right here." She reached into the doorway and flipped on another light, revealing an untidy bath, strewn with dropped towels and dirty clothes. Hair, toothpaste globs, and spit had dried into the sink.

"Yuck," I said, for lack of anything else to say.

Brianna crossed her arms. "I always do this down here first. I get the worst over with, you know what I mean?"

I shook my head. "I can honestly say I've never seen anything quite like this. Even in college."

"My mama says some men are pigs when it comes to the bathroom." Her head bobbed and she added, "Actually, what she says is that *most* men are pigs when it comes to the bathroom, but I don't like to prejudge *most* men."

I thought of the tidiness of Will's guest bath. And walking through his office. Of the framed articles. The one of Conrad Moses and Will and Felicia . . .

I drew in my breath.

"What is it?" Brianna asked.

Shaking my head, I said, "Nothing. Just something I thought of. "

"About Sean?"

"No." I looked over my shoulder to the only other doorway. "Is this his room?"

"Come on," she said, stepping inside the darkness, flipping on the light.

If I'd thought Sean's bathroom to be in disarray, I had no words to describe the bedroom. My mouth gaped open. "This must take you all morning."

She shook her head. "Not really. I just strip the bottom sheet, scoop up the clothes and throw them in the laundry. Add a clean fitted sheet, throw his comforter over—that's apparently all he sleeps with—dust, vac, and I'm done. I don't spend a lot of time in here." She frowned. "Who'd want to?"

I pointed to the highboy. "Is that where you found the vial?"

She nodded. "Bottom drawer."

All the drawers were pushed tight into the bulky piece of antique furniture. I took Brianna's hands in mine, looked her in the eye, and said, "Here's what I want you to do. Go across the hall. Start working in there."

"What are you going to do?"

"Don't worry about it." I turned her toward the door. "Just go."

She left the room with a final look over her shoulder. Tears formed in her eyes. *God love her,* I thought. I pulled my iPhone from my pocket, took a photo of the highboy. I walked across the room, stopping every step to throw discarded clothes into one pile as I made my way to the highboy. I knelt before it, slid the bottom drawer toward me, noting exactly how items were placed—an unnecessary step. Everything was chaos. Using a pencil I found next to one of the highboy's claw-foot legs, I shifted things around.

There they were—four additional vials. A handful of syringes, still in protective packaging. And all of it in a collection of football programs, school papers, and magazines—the latter I could bet his mother didn't know about.

I snapped another shot with my iPhone. Then another with the vials resting in my palm—label side up.

I pushed the drawer shut. As I did, a simple flip-style phone slid from under one of the magazines. I reached in carefully, picked it up as though it were dirty underwear, and pulled the cover open. Powerless, the screen came up black. On instinct I pushed the Send button and waited a second until the phone came to life. When it did, I pushed the Contacts button. There were none.

I gave the Send button a tap. Several calls were outgoing and incoming, all to and from the same number. I entered it into my phone and saved it. I then pushed Menu, followed by Media Center. There were no pictures. No videos.

I clicked up one level to the Messages center, clicked on Inbox, scrolled to the bottom of the stored texts, then read each one to the top. They were all from the same person. The same number as the sole contact. But nothing indicated *who.*

"Ashlynne?" Brianna spoke from the door and I jumped. "I'm sorry. I'm done with the bathroom. I'll run a dust cloth over the game room and I'll be ready to come in here."

"Okay."

"Did you find anything?"

"Yeah. I'm just not sure what. I'm going to need to take photographs of some messages I found on the phone, which could take awhile."

"You could always go upstairs. Sit in the living room. I'm sure it's more comfortable."

"Sounds good."

I closed the drawer, rose slowly, gained my balance, left the room and went up the stairs to the kitchen. I pulled a chair from the breakfast nook table, sat, and worked on snapping shots of several of the texts, making certain I recorded the date and time of each one.

Clicking out of Inbox, I went to Sent Messages. There were, according to the recorded data, twenty-three sent versus twenty-seven that had come in. I began photographing those, once again starting at the bottom, working my way to the top, snapping as I went along. I came to the fourth outgoing text. I raised my camera to capture the image, then stopped.

From outside, a car door slammed.

"Oh Great-granny," I whispered.

37

I jumped, scooping up the phone. Without returning the chair, I darted into the mudroom, opened the pantry door, and folded myself inside up against the hanging mop and broom. I pulled the double doors to, holding my breath as the back door opened.

"*Brianna*?" Jean Flannery's voice echoed. Footsteps clicked through the room, past the pantry in which I hid, and into the kitchen. "That boy," she said. "If he ever puts his chair back I'll faint and fall over dead." After a pause, "*Brianna! I forgot something so I'm up here!*"

I cracked one door so as to hear better and spied my purse hanging in the cubby. I bit my lip as I listened to Jean's footsteps continuing through the house. "*Brianna?*"

I stepped from the closet, grabbed my purse, and returned to my hiding place.

"*Mrs. Flannery?*"

I had to remind myself to breathe.

"I forgot . . . I'll need to . . . how much have you . . ."

"I just finished the downstairs except . . . I was about to . . ."

I inhaled. Exhaled slowly. Unable to hear their entire conversation put me at a disadvantage.

No. Actually . . . hiding in the broom closet of a house I had *technically* illegally snooped through put me at a disadvantage.

"I'll leave again . . . not until after . . ."

"Oh," Brianna said, her voice close, as though she were in the kitchen. "Okay."

I could picture her, looking wildly around, wondering where I might be. I slid down to a squat with my knees around my chin. My phone, Sean's, and my purse were still clutched in my hands. My ankle throbbed. In the darkness, I opened Sean's cell phone, checked the time, and then powered off. I turned the volume of mine to Silent.

Any thoughts I may have entertained of Jean leaving shortly after her arrival became slim as the minutes passed without hearing her footsteps coming back through the mudroom and out the back door. Apparently, my crime had sentenced me to period of undetermined time in a tiny prison.

To pass time I sent a text to Leigh, telling her what I'd managed to get myself into: *On an investigative lead. Almost caught. Hiding n a tiny broom closet.*

She returned with an *OMG,* followed by *LOL.*

Yeah. She could laugh.

Nearly two hours went by, most of it occupied by the two of us texting—about Will, Sean, Lawson, the importance of what I was doing, and what I'd learned not two seconds before his mother arrived home. Somewhere in the middle of the texts, Will sent one that read: *Pick you up at 1. Need u this afternoon.*

I didn't have the heart—or the nerve—to ask if he would mind picking me up from the Flannerys' broom closet. Will Decker would hardly see the humor in this moment. I hardly did, although Leigh continued to get a kick out of it.

After an eternity and an uncountable number of texts, I heard footsteps enter the mudroom.

I turned wild eyes to the pantry doors as they opened, then relaxed when I saw Brianna's peering back at me.

"There you are," she whispered.

"Where is Jean?"

"Upstairs." She slid the caddy onto the shelf over my head. "We have to get you out of here."

"Don't you need to sweep something? Mop?" I jerked my head to the cleaning instruments hanging behind me.

"Not with those." She helped me up and out before pulling keys from her purse. "Hurry. Go get in the car and keep your head down. I don't think she's leaving until after I'm done."

My ankle nearly refused to cooperate, forcing me to hobble to the back door. I opened it just enough to squeeze out, and miraculously, managed to get into the backseat of Brianna's two-door car without a major upset. A half hour later, the car door opened. Brianna got in without saying a word, started the engine, and backed up. "Don't move until we are well out of the driveway," she instructed.

"Don't worry," I said. I wiped the sweat from my face. "If you don't mind, turn your air conditioner as high as it will go. I'm melting back here."

The air's intensity increased. Then, "Okay. You can sit up now."

I did. "That was close," I said. I looked at myself in the rearview mirror. My cheeks glowed red.

"Too close. I'm probably going to be shaking for a good long time."

I reached between the bucket seats and extended my hand.

"What's that?"

"Sean Flannery's phone."

"Oh. My. Mercy me."

"Don't worry. There's a lot of incriminating evidence here." Okay, so I could be found guilty of stealing. ("Your Honor, my intent was to take the photographs and then use what I knew to incriminate the supplier. I promise you I had no idea I'd end up in a broom closet with the phone.")

Brianna jerked her head toward me long enough for me to see the fear in her eyes. "And you *don't* want me to worry? What are we going to do with it, Ashlynne? I mean, I was thinking about this while I was finishing up in there. How are we going to show that Sean is using drugs unless we admit the truth?"

I laid a hand on her shoulder. "Bri, did you do anything wrong?"

Her breath was shaky. "No. Unless you count taking the vial. And letting you come into a house where you don't belong. I mean, other than *that*. No."

"Then don't worry about it. The Flannerys are going to have far more to worry about than you and me."

Brianna rolled her car to a stop at a red light. "Are you sure?"

"Trust me," I said, giving her shoulder a pat, although I could hardly be sure. Sometimes, I knew, all people needed was a common enemy to deflect them from the real problem.

For sure, I was about to have a target on my front *and* my back.

William picked me up at the cottage a little after one.

"Before we go to the office, we have an assignment we need to hit first," he said. "Traffic accident."

"Can you please tell me," I said as we walked to his truck parked next to the cottage, "how it is that a traffic accident is an *assignment*?"

"Easy. One of the vehicles is a city truck."

"I see," I said, though I really didn't.

After we'd gotten to the highway, Will asked, "Did you get everything done this morning you'd hoped to accomplish?"

Heat built in my cheeks. "And then some."

"So . . . ," he drawled, "what were you doing exactly?" He took a deep curve in the road and his camera case slid from the middle of the floorboard to my feet.

"Magazine stuff."

"Oh?"

"Yeah. You know. *Forests and Fairy Tales* . . ."

He turned his face toward me and back to the highway. "I've decided you're doing that on purpose. Making fun of our magazine . . ."

"Now *why* would I do that?" I pushed the camera back to the center of the floorboard. "Seriously, I *do* have a question for you, if you don't mind."

"I'm listening." He turned the truck down a road new to me. Within seconds we traveled between thick foliage running on both sides of a narrow asphalt road.

"Since you already know that I went into your home office . . ."

"Mmhmm . . ."

"Can you tell me *why* you have a framed photo of you, Conrad Moses, and Felicia? Are you sure being in Testament, where a city truck in an accident is big news, versus being in Chicago is what you want? That you aren't still a little hung up on Felicia Moses?"

"Oh-ho." He laughed. "Do I spy the green-eyed monster over there?"

"No," I said, keeping my voice steady. "But what I'm wondering is if you really don't miss the *Chicago Star* more than you might realize. Or, at least, *that kind of* reporting." I shrugged. "Maybe you *thought* you wanted one thing—a scandal-less career—only to discover what you wanted was something else?"

We drove several yards before he said, "Sometimes I miss it. Yeah. But then I remember everything and . . . which is why I keep the picture. It's my way of staying humble. Focused on what is really important to me now." He slowed the truck and I looked ahead. A city truck and a Toyota, both mangled, rested on the right-hand shoulder. Two police cars and one ambulance, lights blazing, stood at odd angles, blocking both sides of the road.

Not that any traffic other than us was affected. "I hope no one was hurt," I said.

"They weren't."

I raised a brow in question.

"I heard it on the police scanner."

"Then why the ambulance?"

He grinned as he brought the truck to a stop. "Something to do, I guess." He turned the key and unbuckled his seat belt. "I thought about something last night. Something I want to share with you." He reached for the camera.

"What?"

"I realized I've not forgiven Felicia for rejecting me. For making me think she loved me. That she would marry me for who I am versus what I do for a living." He pulled the door handle, but didn't push the door open. "I have to do that."

"When?"

"Well . . . I *did* do that. At least between God and me. But . . ." He pressed his lips together. "I have to call her, I think. I have to tell her I've forgiven her."

"She wasn't a believer, was she?"

He pushed the door open. "She went to church. What's between her and God, I don't know. I thought I did, but . . . Stay put. I'm coming around to get you. Us being parked on the shoulder, you'll fall right out."

The very idea made me laugh. But when Will had come to my side and opened the door, I placed my hands on his shoulders and said, "You *should* call her." *And maybe*, I thought, *you could renew your relationship. Forget about me.*

His brown eyes sparked, sending flutters through my stomach. "Thank you." He looked to the scene of the accident. "Come on. Work awaits."

I called Dad that evening, using his business cell phone rather than the home phone.

"Hey, Princess."

"Hey. Where's Mom?"

"Shopping with Heidi Vandewinter." He chuckled. "Did you try to call her cell and she didn't answer?"

"No." I stretched out on the small sofa in the cottage's living room and rested my ankle on one of the accent pillows. "I wanted to talk to you privately, but didn't have time before now."

Dad cleared his throat. "Sounds serious."

"It is."

"Talk to me."

I adjusted a legal pad full of notes on my lap. "I met a young woman up here named Brianna. She cleans houses for a living. Well, that, and she works at a café."

"Okay . . ."

"I hired her to clean the cottage—you know, every other week—and she came last Tuesday."

"Okay . . ."

"When she got here it was after she'd cleaned the Flannerys' house. The Flannerys have a son named Sean. He's a real football hero around here. Folks have him set as the next big thing to hit college football and then, I'm sure, the pros. And Shelton Decker said something the other night, at the scrimmage game, about how the coach would get some Coach of the Year award."

Dad chuckled. "I cannot believe my little girl is using words like 'football game' and 'scrimmage.'"

"Dad."

"Sorry. I'm just relishing the moment." He paused. "Okay. Please continue."

"So, *anyway* . . . when Bri got here, she was crying. Like, sobbing. She told me, through the tears and hiccups, that she'd found vials of steroids in Sean's bedroom—by accident—and she even brought one vial and one syringe to me. To show me."

I waited for the severity to click. When it did, he said, "I see."

"I, uh, I tried to talk to William about it, but he adamantly refused to address the issue."

"Did you tell him about Lawson?"

"No. He's never really given me a chance. But . . . today . . . I, uh, I went into the Flannery home with Brianna."

"For what purpose?"

I closed my eyes and prepared myself for what I knew my father's response would be to the answer. "To see if I could find out who is supplying him with the drugs."

"Ashlynne Paige. You know better—"

"—I know, Dad. I know." Ethics and all . . . "But this is actually where it gets worse, so before you start your lecture, hear me out."

"I'm listening."

I pictured my father's face, pinched with anger and concern. "I also found a cell phone, which I more-or-less accidentally ended up bringing back home with me."

"More-or-less accidentally?"

"Dad."

"This just keeps getting better and better."

"I know. But Dad, listen. I went through all the messages, photographing each one with my phone while I was hiding in a broom closet and in between texts to Leigh."

"Excuse me?"

"Seriously, not important. The supplier is his coach, Dad. Coach Meriwether. Who, by the way, happens to be a dear friend of Shelton Decker, so before you tell me to turn this over to Shelton, I'm not so sure that's a good idea."

Dad remained quiet until he said, "The police?"

"I've thought of that. But then I have to admit I went into the house and . . ."

"Broke the law. *And* your code of ethics."

I sighed, felt tears moisten my eyes. "I don't know what to do, Dad."

"I'll have to think on this." Again, he paused. "There's something else, though, isn't there?"

"There is. I don't want to hurt anyone here. Especially not—to be honest here—Will Decker. He doesn't deserve that."

"Will Decker? I thought he was giving you a hard time."

"He was. But not anymore. Dad, he's been emotionally wounded in the past. By someone who looks a lot like me and I don't want to bring additional pain."

"With this information and how you got it?"

Yeah. Something like that. That and so much more. "Dad, I need . . ." The tears that had threatened spilled over. "I'm going to need to end this six-month period early. Very early. Before good people get really, really wounded." I gasped as I fought the torrential downpour of anguish. "I'm sorry. And I'm happy to keep the job I have now. At the magazine. To expand on it actually."

I lost the fight entirely. I bent until my nose nearly touched my knees as the angst won. I hurt. But I was about to hurt others more.

For the first time, I realized that's what hurt me the most. Knowing I was going to hurt others—Will, the Sheltons, Alma, the Flannerys, a community of people I'd grown to love. I knew the truth needed to come out, about Sean's steroids and the graves. But I couldn't stay to watch the fallout. I just couldn't.

"What I'm saying is . . . I want to come home, Dad. Okay? I want to come home."

38

If you want to come home," Dad said quietly, "then come home."

I heard the disappointment in his voice. I felt it across the miles. "The good news," I said, as though what little tidbit I'd found was worth mentioning, "is that I now know what I want to do."

"And that is?"

"Be an investigative reporter. I'm good at it, Dad. You should see some of the stuff I have over here on the kitchen bar."

"Well," he said slowly. "We'll talk about all that when you return. When do you think that will be?"

"Tomorrow?"

He didn't reply at first. Then, "I'll let your grandmother and mother know."

I swiped at the tears running down my face. "Thanks, Daddy."

All for the best, I told myself. And I'd tried, hadn't I? Tried harder this time, to make a go of it?

Maybe so. Maybe not. I didn't know anymore.

The next morning I sent Will a text as early as I dared, telling him I would work from home again. His return text came within seconds: *Thought we were talking today.*

I texted back, asking him to come by the cottage:

About 1:00? I'll have all the info together by then.

My breath caught in my throat and fresh tears burned my eyes as I pressed Send. In an effort to keep from completely falling apart—yet again—I decided to read the last entry in the devotional book.

With my mug of tea and the book, I stepped outside to the rock garden I'd come to cherish. Wagging-tailed dogs met me, as though they'd anticipated my early-morning entrance to their domain. "Hello," I said. "Let's have our last read together, shall we?" I waved the book in the air.

The last entry—KNOW LOVE—showed a wooden tile with a lopsided red heart. Inside the heart a dark curlicue had been engraved, as though stirring the heart to action. The complementing verses came from Deuteronomy 7:9 and an excerpt from 1 Corinthians 13:

> Know now then that the Lord your God is the only true God! He is the faithful God, who keeps the covenant and proves loyal to everyone who loves him and keeps his commands—even to the thousandth generation!
>
> If I speak in tongues of human beings and of angels but I don't have love . . . If I . . . know all the mysteries and . . . if I have such complete faith that I can move mountains but I don't have love, I'm nothing. If I give away everything that I have and hand over my own body to feel good about what I've done but I don't have love, I receive no benefit whatsoever.
>
> Love is patient, love is kind, it isn't jealous, it doesn't brag, it isn't arrogant, it isn't rude, it doesn't seek its own advantage, it isn't irritable, it doesn't keep a record of complaints, it isn't happy with injustice, but it is happy with the truth. Love puts up with all things, trusts in all things, hopes for all things, endures all things.

> Love never fails . . . Now we see a reflection in a mirror; then we will see face-to-face. Now I know partially, but then I will know completely in the same way that I have been completely known.
>
> Now faith, hope, and love remain—these three things—and the greatest of these is love.

The last page gave the author's final comment: HE IN ME, I IN HIM. WE LOVE YOU.

I closed the book with a determination not to cry. Not again. Not anymore. I sipped on my tea, took in everything around me and engraved the surroundings on my heart, allowing them to stir me like the curlicue. I drank in the sloping of the land. The mountains etched along the sky in the distance. The green grasses, the tall trees.

I closed my eyes. Listened to the songs of the morning birds. The cry of insects in the woods behind me and below, reaching all the way to the roads of a long-ago era, where people had traveled and, just up the road, a massacre had occurred. And I knew that, one nearly forgotten day, scarred but proud people had discovered their dead, had buried them quietly and placed stones to mark their final place of rest. Then said nothing.

Nothing.

The irony struck hard. Some had chosen to remain silent and, many of them, to continue living here as though nothing had happened. I had chosen to reveal a crime. And leave.

With that thought, I stood. Patted the dogs and told them I'd see them around.

They seemed content with that.

I went inside, sat at the bar dividing the kitchen from the living room, and worked like a college student cramming for finals. Hours later, done with my task, I climbed the stairs and searched my briefcase for a couple of flash drives. I tenderly made my way back down, inserted the first one, and uploaded a file titled FREED SLAVES' GRAVES. In the report I wrote the words: "Alma's Nana has written verification in an old family Bible. Please talk to her about this."

I loaded the second flash drive with transferred photos I'd taken of Sean's phone's screen, along with a detailed description of how I'd gleaned the information.

"Above everything," I wrote in the last paragraph of the report to Shelton Decker, "Brianna is innocent in all this. She's just a kid trying to make a living. Please protect her. As for me, I'll await my fate in Winter Park and will return if necessary. I have spoken with my father and I prayed for most of the night, and I believe that you will do the right thing. Perhaps not the easiest thing, but the one that is right."

I removed the flash drive and shut down the computer.

Then I arranged a stack of handwritten notes, slid them into a manila envelope, took a Sharpie and wrote across the center: *Hunting Grounds & Garden Parties.*

Everything they needed to revive the magazine could be found within the pages. The only additional thing they'd need was someone to run it. For certain, it would not be me.

I closed the storm door behind me but left the main door open. I stuck a Post-it with "Come Inside" on the glass, hoping William would see it, walk in, and find the envelope.

A minute later, I drove down the driveway a final time, car packed solid, and stopped at the back of the Decker home. I eased out of my car, walked slowly to the door, and opened it. "Miss Bobbie?" I called.

"Ashlynne?" she yelled from the other side of the house. "Come on in!" Her footsteps echoed, growing louder as she came nearer. I stepped into the kitchen and waited. When she'd arrived at the door leading to the far side of the house, she stopped. "Land's sake. Look at you. No crutches."

I extended my arms in a "look at me" pose and said, "My foot is still a little tender, but much, much better."

Bobbie finished her trek into the kitchen. "I'm so happy to hear that. Are you heading to the office?" She looked at her watch. "Although it's nearly time for lunch."

"No," I said. "I'm—ah—I have to do some running around." I held up the two flash drives and said, "Bobbie, will you do me a favor? Will you give both of these to Shelton when he comes in?" I pulled Sean's phone from my purse. "And this?"

Her expression raised all the questions I'd expected it would. Bobbie Decker was, by no means, a stupid woman. "Why don't you just give them to him yourself?"

"I'm . . ." I sighed. "I'm returning to Winter Park, Bobbie. And I want you to know how much I've appreciated your hospitality, but I *must* return . . . home." I placed the drives and phone on the nearby counter. "These hold some work I wanted to finish before leaving. And the phone . . . well, he'll know. It's . . . imperative that Mr. Shelton get them."

Bobbie's confusion meshed with shock. Her hands went to her face. "Oh dear. Did we do something to cause this? Say something?" Her hands dropped. "Is it William? Has he done anything inappropriate?"

I hugged her quickly. "Oh goodness no. You didn't say or do anything. And William is a fine grandson. You have *every* reason to be proud."

She placed her fingertips on both sides of my face, drawing my eyes to hers. "You promise me this is what you *need* to do?"

I nodded, unable to speak.

"Ah. I remember asking the same question of your grandmother all those years ago." She released me with a kiss to both cheeks. "Well, darlin', you have to do what you have to do, I suppose. I'll tell Shelton, but he's going to be quite upset you didn't go by the newspaper."

"I can't," I said around the "rubber band" that twisted and pulled in my throat.

"Afraid you'll see William there?"

I nodded. Pressed my own fingertips to my lips to stop the quivering, and said, "Please, Miss Bobbie. Tell everyone I said good-bye."

I turned and walked out the door to the Jag. I started it up, gasping to keep from crying, then drove it down to the end of the driveway, where I stopped to call Rob.

"Hey, there. Where are you?" I asked.

"Just pulled up in the driveway, why?"

I turned my car in the direction of his house. "Could you stand some company for about five minutes?"

"Well, I don't know." He chuckled. "Whose company would it be? Yours or St. Valentine's?"

I choked on my laughter. "I confess, but come on. She . . . never mind. I'm pulling up behind you. Bye."

I parked the car. Rob walked toward me as I got out.

"Hey, there," he said. He looked darling and tousled as always.

"Hey," I said.

He peered into my car and said, "You look a little loaded down there. Going somewhere?"

"Home."

His brow rose. "William know about this?"

I shook my head. "And I'd appreciate you not telling him." I shrugged. "I just wanted to say good-bye. That I really, really enjoyed getting to know you and—yes—I played Cupid. But you have to admit, Brianna is a special young woman."

He crossed his arms and shifted until he'd braced his feet about six inches apart. "Funny how I never thought of her like that—I mean, other than as just being a girl—until the night of the movie." He squinted a little. "You know . . . afterward, we talked a lot. Really got to know each other. We want the same things in life, you know what I mean?"

I did. In many ways, William and I did, too. With one difference. We'd both returned "home," when our aspirations backed us between the proverbial rock and hard place, but his "home" was here. In Testament. Mine was in Winter Park. His was a paid-for guesthouse out in the middle of nowhere. Mine was a condo with a view of the city and a too-high mortgage.

We wanted the same, different thing.

"Yes, I know what you mean," I finally answered. "And I think that's wonderful." I extended my hand for a shake. He took it, and pulled me to himself for a hug.

"You take care now," he said.

"Send me a wedding invitation?" I opened my car door and eased in. When I looked back to him, a bright blush continued to stain his cheeks. I laughed easily this time.

"Let's just take it one step at a time," he said.

"I'm sure you will." I waggled my fingers at him. I took a deep breath, tried to be strong. But when I said, "Bye . . . ," my voice broke.

I found Brianna at home. Maris, who played in the front yard with a couple of her little friends, told "Miss Ashlynne" that her mommy was inside unloading groceries and "to just go on in."

I opened the door as I'd done at Bobbie's and called to my young friend. Her eyes brightened when she saw me at the door. "Heeeey," she said. "What are you doing here?"

"I heard you're unloading groceries so I thought I'd come help."

"What?" She tilted her head. From outside, the laughter of Maris and her friends reached us. "Oh. Maris." Brianna giggled like a schoolgirl. "Come on back. If you're volunteering, I'm accepting. It's been a long day."

We went into the same kitchen where I'd recently shown Brianna about skin care and how to better apply her makeup. This time, the table was loaded down with plastic sacks spilling over with Bri's recent purchases.

"Can I get you something to drink?" she asked me. "Water?"

"No." I pulled a few items from the sacks and placed them on the countertop. "Actually, I'm here to say good-bye."

Brianna stood with a five-pound bag of sugar in one hand and a bottle of ketchup in the other. "What?" she asked, her smile fading to a distinct frown.

I reached for more of the food.

"No," she said, placing the sugar and ketchup back on the table. "Is it because of me? Because of what I showed you?"

I clutched the back of one of the chairs. "No. Not because of you. But, yes, because of what you showed me. Partly. I've—ah—I've written a full report of what I found in Sean's phone and left it with Mr. Shelton."

Brianna pulled out a chair and sat. "I can't believe you'd just leave like this."

I pulled out the chair in front of me and said, "Believe me, Bri, it's for the best. If Mr. Shelton needs me to come back, you know, to testify or . . ." *To go to jail.* But I couldn't say that. Couldn't tell Brianna what I knew she had never suspected—that my entering the Flannery home and opening Sean's bureau drawer had been both unethical and illegal. Even if it meant that I, in the end, saved his life. "But I made sure he knows that you are innocent in everything."

Brianna laid her hands flat on the table. "I don't care about that. I like you, Ashlynne. I don't want you to leave. I like having you as my friend."

My heart skipped. "You do?"

"Yeah." She looked toward the kitchen window. Tears formed in her eyes. "Not because of you coming over and doing all that skin-care stuff and not because of all those nice things you sent me." She looked at me again. "I just like . . . *you*."

I pressed my hand against my chest. "Thank you," I whispered. "I like you, too."

"So then don't go."

I shook my head. "I have to, Bri. But I have your number and you have mine. We'll stay in touch. After all"—I felt a smile wobble upward—"you have to keep me posted on how things are going with you and Rob." I stood. Pressed my hand against the flat of my stomach. "I have a long trip. I'd best be going."

Brianna stood with me. Brushed tears from her cheeks. "I reckon."

We started through the house. "Hey," I said. "Do you mind if I use your bathroom before I leave?"

"Not at all." She extended her left arm. "It's just right in there." She chuckled. "You can't really get lost in this house."

I went into a bathroom decorated with a Disney Princess shower curtain, purple and pink towels, and a large purple throw rug. A classic white over-the-toilet étagère had Disney Princess stickers in the four corners of its glass doors. I reached for the stainless-steel knobs to open them. To peer inside as I'd always done. Then stopped myself. My snooping had caused enough chaos in Testament.

I did what I'd come into the room to do—I washed my hands, then started for the door. Stopped. Turned to the étagère and took three steps backward. "Oh who am I kidding?" I asked myself. With a deep breath, I pulled the doors open.

Inside, I found a "Princess" toothbrush, cup, toothpaste, and additional towels and washcloths, along with three rolls of toilet paper. On the top shelf, a short stack of magazines took up the left-hand side. I reached for the top magazine. When I did, a small book I'd not seen slid toward me.

The devotional.

The same book from the cottage. The same one I'd seen at Will's. Without caring that I'd have to admit I'd been snooping, I picked it up, walked out of the bathroom, and called for Brianna.

"I'm back in the kitchen."

I walked in, holding the book up. "Please don't ask how I came across it, but where did you get this book?"

She hardly seemed nonplussed. "William."

"Decker?"

"Mmhmm." She pulled a few more groceries from a bag and placed them in the opened refrigerator. "He gave them to several people for Christmas gifts last year."

I stared at the book.

"Why are you so curious?" She walked to where I stood.

"I've read this every morning—or nearly—since I've been here. I love this book. It's ministered to me in the most amazing way." I paused at a memory. "Come to think of it, when I saw it at Will's, when I asked him where I could get one, he didn't really answer." I looked at her. "Now why wouldn't he just tell me where I could buy it?"

Brianna grinned. "Because it's *not* for sale anywhere. It's just his."

"I'm sorry? What?"

"He wrote it. You know that mirror in the downstairs bath at the cottage?"

"Yeah . . ."

"He took photos of the tiles, then compiled the Scriptures to go along with each one. I'd let you take mine, but he signed it special to me."

I opened the book to the inside page. Sure enough, Will had written: *Live life to the fullest, Bri. Merry Christmas, William A. Decker.*

"Did he—did he also make the mirror?"

She nodded. "He's very talented." She clasped her hands together as though she were in prayer. "I can't believe you're leaving Testament *and* Will Decker. Most girls around here would think you're totally crazy."

"Maybe I am," I said. I gripped the book firmly in both hands and handed it to her. "I heard a song one time . . . in William's truck. It says something about not telling everyone I'm crazy . . . after losing the someone your heart, you know . . . fell for."

"I know it. Jason Aldean."

"Well . . . don't tell anyone, okay? That I'm crazy?" I tried to laugh, but instead, more tears fell. I brushed them aside. Hugged her with a quick squeeze and stepped away. "Good-bye, Brianna."

39

After a hurried good-bye to Maris and her friends, I got back into my car. I looked at my watch. Time had slipped by quickly. William would have found the envelope by now. Perhaps talked to his grandmother. He'd suspect I'd visit Brianna, and he'd be right behind me.

I had to hurry.

I turned the selector to reverse and prepared to ease out of the driveway. A blur of black shot across my rearview mirror and forcing me to slam on my brakes. I jerked my head around to see Will's old truck blocking my exit. I turned the selector back to park and waited.

The truck's driver's-side door flung open. Will hopped out, almost exactly as he'd done when I first saw him on Main Street, two and a half weeks earlier. "Do you care to explain—"

I lowered my window. "Will, don't . . ."

He squatted so that we were nearly nose-to-nose. Aware we had a young audience, I looked to the right, ducking enough that I could see out of the windshield. Maris and her friends scampered up the front porch steps. Brianna stood at the opened front door, both hands covering her mouth.

"Where do you think you're going?" Will asked, bringing my attention back to him.

"Home," I said, crossing my arms. "To Winter Park."

He pulled the cowboy hat from his head and wiped a trickle of sweat from his brow with his forearm. "So that's it, huh? Just like back in middle school." He replaced the hat. "When things got tough in middle school, what did you do?"

I looked straight ahead, unable to answer him.

"You went back to private school."

I faced him again. "So? Didn't you do the same thing?"

He stood. "Get out of the car."

"Absolutely not."

"Please. So I can talk to you."

"No, Will." I started to cry. "There's nothing to say."

He squatted again. The look in his eyes—hurt, bewildered. I couldn't stand it, so I looked forward. "Look. I went through your notes on the magazine—apparently you *do* know the name of it—and . . . you've . . . we've got something here. We can do something really great. With our knowledge about publishing and your journalistic nose . . ."

My heart skipped. I looked at him. "Did you see your grandmother?"

"I did." A long sigh escaped through his nostrils. "And I saw the flash drives."

I hadn't wanted him to catch me. I'd wanted to be gone by now so I wouldn't have to see him. To see his anguish and disappointment . . . over the coach. Even to see his respect over my work with the slave graves.

I just wanted to go home . . .

"Then you know. Everything."

He nodded. "Nearly. I didn't have time, really, to read the whole thing." He paused. "And I know about Lawson. I'm sorry."

We stared at each other for long moments as our eyes searched the other's, looking for the next right thing to say. Our hearts seeking the next right thing to do.

"Hey," Will whispered. "Don't leave. Come back to the office and we'll sit down with Big Guy. Talk this out. We'll figure out what to do about Sean's phone. The *best* thing."

I shook my head. "I can't. I—"

"Come on, now . . ."

But again, I shook my head. "Please let me go," I half whispered, half cried.

He waited. I suppose hoping I'd change my mind. But when nothing came but silent tears, he stood again. Patted the top of the car. "Well," he said, his voice deep and low. "If you're that determined, I can't stop you."

I glanced up. His face, shadowed by the hat, seemed like steel. Then it went soft. Tender. "But I'll miss you. We all will."

I reached for something light to say, something to ease the pain. For him. For both of us. "I bet the girls in advertising won't feel that way."

He grimaced. "Well, maybe not *all* . . ."

He leaned in. Brought his lips to mine. Gently. "Call me and let me know you got home all right."

I nodded, keeping my face straight ahead. *Just go . . . just go . . . just walk away and go.*

And then he did.

Somehow, through the tears and hiccups, I made it through town and to the highway leading to Charlotte.

According to my GPS, I was eight hours and twenty-six minutes from home.

You're only six minutes from home.

The voice, almost audible, seemed to fill the space—what little bit was left—in my car.

I shook my head. "No. No. No."

I pictured myself driving into Winter Park. If I didn't stop, except maybe for a few stretch breaks and calls from Mother Nature, I'd be home before midnight. Who would be on night duty at the guard station?

Probably Erik. Erik worked a lot of nights.

I liked Erik. He had always been nice to me.

If not Erik . . . maybe Ann. Sometimes Ann worked nights. Ann had always been nice, too.

I'd call Gram in the morning. Ask her if we could have lunch together. Then I'd go to Windsong. See my mother. Ask her to hold me. For a long, long time . . .

I tried to picture it, but instead of my mother's arms around me, I saw William's. Felt the strength of him as he'd lifted me and carried me out of the ravine. Smelled his cologne as he'd worn it on that first day.

Boss.

"No." I had to be strong. *Can't turn back* . . . I just wanted to go home.

Even as I conjured the images—Winter Park, Park Avenue, the office, my condo in Orlando—visions of Testament rose to the surface. Main Street and ice-cream cones, dusty roads leading to Miss Helen's, a long drive winding through Decker Ranch, the front of the cottage with its wide windows that always seemed to welcome me home.

Home.

The tree-lined drive leading to William's home. The dog on the front porch. The scent of rain and spice-scented candles.

I turned on the radio, hoping to distract myself, but was met with nothing but static.

I pressed Scan. Music immediately filled my car. William's kind of music. And Rob's. And Bri's . . .

The song about the redneck . . .

"Great-granny, girl," I said out loud.

Then I laughed. And turned the car around.

Magically—almost—if I believed in such things—my car found the right street, then the dirt road that stretched to William's parents' home. Beyond it, the guesthouse.

I slowed the car, partly wanting to savor the moment, and partly hoping I was wrong. Hoping that same voice would come through the radio and tell me to turn around. That I was mistaken. *Testament* was not my home. *Winter Park* was.

There was safety in Winter Park—a place where it was okay to be Ashlynne Rothschild. Here . . . here there was no safety. None at all. Here I would live at risk. Of the fallout from some light-skinned people, who might not like knowing they were related to people with darker complexion. Or those who felt we should all turn a blind eye, when their beloved coach should be fired at the very least, and at the very best, prosecuted. Or any who believed it unfair that their golden boy's veneer was tarnished.

Most of all, I'd live at risk of falling so head over hills in love, I could never go back home.

But . . . I was home. With every yard I drove, I knew it. Felt it in my bones. In my spirit. *Home* in Testament. Even thinking it felt . . . wonderful.

Natural. Like that first day in the church. As though I'd been here forever.

Or would be here for the rest of my life.

I drove around to the back of the house and parked my car in the same place as before. Will stepped out on the porch, his dog behind him. He reached down, gave Rufus a good pat, then leaned against the railing.

I got out of the car.

For long moments, we stared at each other. He looked tired. Beat. Unsure of what life held tomorrow.

I felt certain I didn't look much different, but I hoped he'd see past that. See something—someone—he wanted. If nothing else, as a business partner.

"How'd you know where to find me?" he finally asked.

I shrugged. "A hunch."

"Did you forget something?"

"Myself."

"Meaning?"

I took a step. "I want to . . . I don't want to . . ." I took another step. "I want to make a go of it. Here. With the magazine. And . . ."

"And?"

I took another step and stared risk in the face, keeping my eyes on his—without the hat, unshaded. "You?"

Rufus dropped onto the planking of the porch, rested his head on his front paws as though he'd seen this scene before, in about a hundred movies.

I smiled. Will smiled back. He moved down to the top step. "You've stirred up a hornet's nest. You know that, right?"

"Did you read it all? Everything in the flash drives?"

"I did."

I clasped my hands in front of me. "And what would you do? If you were me?"

He raised his chin. Looked to the right, to the gazebo and the lake. "I think," he said, returning his attention to me, "that I'd try sticking around this time. To see how it all turned out."

"What about you and Felicia?"

His brow furrowed. "What about us?"

"Did you call her?"

"Not yet."

"When you do . . . do you think you'd . . . like to . . . I mean . . ."

"Start over with her?"

"Yeah."

"No."

Heavenly relief bloomed from somewhere deep inside me. I looked at my shoes. The hiking boots. Back up to Will. "Promise to take me to Chimney Rock?"

Mischief played in his eyes. "The air can get pretty thin up there." He came down another step.

"Do you know CPR?"

He grinned. "Yes, ma'am."

I took in a deep breath—inhaled the faint scent of his cologne. *Bond. No. 9. Wall Street.* The curlicue stirred.

"You know, I didn't come back just for you."

Will threw back his head and laughed.

"Because—once I get out of the mess I've made for myself—I've got some big plans for *Hunting Grounds & Garden Parties*."

One brow shot up.

"Stories I want to write," I said past a giggle. "You know . . . the museum, the school bus ministry you have going . . . and Harvest Day. I wouldn't want to miss the parade."

"I'm sure you wouldn't."

I exhaled, fighting for the next best thing to say. But nothing came to mind until I took another step and said, "Yoogie-Doogie."

William chuckled. "That's my line."

I stepped closer. Challenged him. "Then say it."

He closed the gap between us. Our hands found each other's; our fingers wove together like a tapestry. "Yoogie-Doogie," he whispered. Close enough that I could smell the coffee on his breath.

"You remind me of a man." I tilted my chin up, my eyes found his. Found the warmth. The safety.

"What man?"

"The man with the power . . ."

His lips came to the tip of my nose. "What power?"

"The power of hoodoo."

"Who do?"

I laid my forehead against his chest. Felt the rhythm of his heartbeat. "You do."

His lips tickled my ear. "Do what?"

I allowed my head to fall back in an invitation for him to kiss me. At least one time. Before I got back in the car and returned to the cottage. Returned . . . home. And to the work waiting there for me and the music to face. "Remind me of a man . . ."

He took my invitation. "What man?" he asked against my lips.

I wrapped my arms around his shoulders again and, with a giggle, I whispered, "The man with the power . . ."

"Oh yeah?" he teased.

"Shoot, I reckon."

Discussion Questions

1. In the opening chapter of *The Road to Testament*, Ashlynne is challenged by her grandmother and father to do something out of her comfort zone. Have you ever been challenged to do something like this? How did it turn out for you?
2. Going to Testament and working in the newspaper business is uncomfortable for Ashlynne but not because she thinks she is better than everyone there. Did you understand fully why Ashlynne had such difficulty with "normal" people, as she called them?
3. What do you think was the cause behind Ashlynne's need to look into people's medicine cabinets?
4. William had preconceived feelings about Ashlynne that resulted in vacillating treatment between "mean" and "nice." Why do you think William could not consistently stick with one treatment?
5. Do you believe Ashlynne really knew the name of the magazine or was she being flippant about its title on purpose?
6. Ashlynne and Alma—two people from two totally different worlds—become fast friends as do Ashlynne and Brianna. Why was Ashlynne able to make such a connection with these two women so easily when such connections had eluded her before?
7. What was it about William that tugged at Ashlynne's heartstrings when someone as fine as Rob only managed to make it to the "good friend" level?
8. Do you see any significance in the periods of time seen on the roads (the Revolutionary War road, the Civil War road the road to Testament)?
9. In the process of doing one thing (shadowing William and working on the magazine), Ashlynne discovers her true talent for "digging up information" and research. This puts her, once again, possibly at odds with the "normal" people

of Testament. Why do you think she was willing to risk her career and possibly her freedom to reveal the truth about Sean and the dead buried on Rob's property?

10. Both William and Ashlynne have misjudged each other based on past histories. Have you ever done that to someone else or had it done to you?

Bonus Question: What do you think happened to Ashlynne after the end of the book? Do you foresee a relationship between her and William?

Want to learn more about author
Eva Marie Everson and check out other great
fiction from Abingdon Press?

Sign up for our fiction newsletter at
www.AbingdonPress.com
to read interviews with your favorite authors, find tips
for starting a reading group, and stay posted on what
new titles are on the horizon. It's a place to connect
with other fiction readers or post a
comment about this book.

Be sure to visit Eva online!

http://www.evamarieeversonauthor.com/